What
the River Knows

by

Katherine Pritchett

What the River Knows

Cover Art by *Kim Mendoza*

The Wild Rose Press, Inc.
PO Box 708
Adams Basin, NY 14410-0708
Visit us at www.thewildrosepress.com

Publishing History
First Mainstream Mystery Edition, 2015
Print ISBN 978-1-5092-0376-5
Digital ISBN 978-1-5092-0377-2

Published in the United States of America

He slowed his pace

within twenty feet of a gray and twisted tree trunk that must have once supported a massive cottonwood, but now instead provided a windbreak that allowed sand to settle in its lee and let shrubs gain a foothold. He looked down the sloping bank of the dike toward the river, noting the lazy flow as it rippled barely a foot deep in half a dozen shallow braided channels within the banks. A gray heron took off from a sand bar, long legs dangling behind him.

He stopped and squatted to view the path from a different angle. Just this side of the tree trunk, he saw indistinct grooves in the sand of the path that could have been made by a body being dragged. Big bluestem waved behind the tree trunk, and a sand plum thicket guarded the north side of the approach. Buffalo grass carpeted the ground from the path to the tree, obscuring any sign from this angle. He stood up again.

Now it looked like there were faint marks in the grass, here and there, that could be drag marks. He continued on the other side of the path, careful not to disturb the sign. At last he was even with the northern edge of the sand plum thicket. Again, he went down to see what he could observe from this angle. He spotted some broken branches and a few tufts of buff fur, where the dog had bounded in to make his discovery and dragged the man in his wake. He followed the path of fur and branches with his eyes, and finally saw something large and too pale a pink to belong in that environment. Reminding himself to stay detached and professional, he stepped up on the tree trunk to get a better view.

Kudos for Katherine Pritchett

Third Place won in the
Wichita Area Romance Authors
2013 Practice Your Right Hook Contest

Dedication

This book is dedicated to justice
for the victim who inspired it,
as well as the many others for whom justice
has yet to be realized.
And to the tireless officers
who never stop thinking about those cold cases,
always alert for that missing link.

Chapter 1

Something jarred his sleep. The phone. The phone had done it. It rang again, insistent. Scott Aylward grabbed the back of the couch to raise himself, and the newspaper he had been reading slid from his chest to the floor. The phone jangled once more. "All right, I'm coming," he growled as he stood. Where was the damn thing anyway? He slipped on the papers he was supposed to be sorting through. Rica would have his ass if he didn't get this stuff put away or pitched by the time she got home. He had promised and, he eyed the clock by the front door, he had two hours until four. Finally, he found the phone beneath the lid of the pizza box. More stuff to take care of. "Yeah?"

"Aylward?" The voice of Sergeant Mullens punched into his ear. "Get down here, pronto!"

All drowsiness snapped out of Scott Aylward; something had tightened the cadence of Mullens' usual slow drawl. "What's up?" He glanced at the scanner on his desk. Damn, he'd forgotten to turn it on. After all, Rica kept telling him that days off should be days off.

"Just get your ass in. We'll brief you when everybody gets here."

"Everybody?"

"Everybody."

"I'll be there in five minutes." It must be big, to call in all personnel. He took a few seconds to gather all the papers into a box. Crossing the kitchen toward the bedroom with the box in his arms, he remembered the chicken in the refrigerator. He'd at least completed that task today. The breast filets were spiced and in the dish, ready to pop in the oven the minute Rica arrived. He had done that first, hoping a good meal and a clean house would ease some tension. Now it sounded like there would be no supper tonight. He sighed and dropped the box to the floor on his side of the bed. Rica knew what he was when she married him.

He picked up his gun from the nightstand and snapped the holster on his belt over his right hip. Taking a minute to make the bed, sort of, he palmed his ID and badge from the dresser into his pocket.

Pausing by the door, he surveyed the living room. Damn, he'd left his soda can on the coffee table without a coaster. At least whatever it was would delay the argument for a while.

He clattered down the stairs and jumped into his pickup. He debated for a moment while the oil began to circulate through the motor of his fifteen-year-old Ford Ranger pickup before he elected not to flip on the red lights. In just under four minutes, he swung into the parking lot of the Law Enforcement Center, searching for a spot to park, finally pulling onto the lawn at the back. He didn't want to be late.

He trotted into the conference room in time to grab a cup of overcooked coffee and the last of the Krispy Kreme donuts from the table at the back of the room. He slid into a folding chair just as Mullens stepped to the podium in front of the whiteboard.

"Afternoon, ladies and gentlemen." Mullens cleared his throat and opened the manila folder he carried. "We'll run through this quick, so you can get out there on the street." He pushed the remote on the projector connected to the laptop on the table beside him. The face of a pretty blonde, apparently a driver's license photo, popped up on the whiteboard, next to what appeared to be a snapshot of her at a picnic. The face in the license photo looked tired, stressed, but the picnic shot showed a woman full of life. "Missing person, Delia Enfield, 29, 5-4, 130, blonde, blue," Mullens intoned. "Left work at Moran Construction Company at 3:15 yesterday afternoon, with a company bank deposit to make. Never showed up for work this morning, but the office wasn't too concerned. Ex-husband called her in missing at noon, said they were supposed to meet for lunch."

He clicked the remote again to show a worn compact car in a parking lot. "Car spotted in the parking lot of the Casa Taco a couple hours ago. Purse on the seat, beside the bank bag with the deposit receipt. Cell phone in the purse. Car unlocked, no signs of struggle." He faced the officers, the strain of too many briefings like this, with too many tragic endings, etched on his face. "We're starting to interview all the office staff, Casa Taco employees, bank personnel, the ex-husband, neighbors, acquaintances, family, and so forth." He sighed. "We need extra eyes and ears on the street and extra personnel to get the interviews done in a timely manner. You all know how important the first hours after a disappearance are." Clicking the screen to return the woman's photos to the wall, he consulted the clipboard on the podium before him. "Anderson and Jeffries, you take beat four…"

Scott tuned out the voice, instead staring at the face

from the picnic. She looked familiar, as if he'd seen her somewhere in the past, not just a passing glance, but had interacted with her somewhere. He studied it, memorizing it so he would know her if he stumbled across her on patrol.

"Aylward—" Hearing his name, he jerked to attention. "You head to Moran. They have twenty people to interview, and I only have Bates out there now."

"On the way, Sarge." He drained the coffee in the bottom of his cup and dumped the dry half of the donut that was left in the trash with the cup. He hopped in his pickup, as there were no spare unmarked cars to take to the construction company at the edge of town. He flipped open his cell to leave a message for Rica on her cell. Just in case she didn't check her phone when she got off work at the hospital, he left a message on the home phone as well. "Called in to work, not sure when I'll be off. I'll call later."

He flipped it shut and hoped the explanation was enough for her. Lately, she didn't seem to be so understanding about his dedication to his job, although she never turned down an extra shift in surgery when it was offered. He sighed. He'd just have to deal with however she reacted when he made it home again. He pulled into the gravel parking lot at Moran and parked in the only area left, the "No Parking" zone at the entrance.

Chapter 2

Scott flashed his gold detective's badge at the receptionist and requested Bates. Young and thin, she looked like she was close to tears, and her fingers trembled as she paged the room where Detective Bates was interviewing her co-workers.

She looked up at him. "He said come on down." She stood and pointed down a hallway. "Turn right. It's three doors down." She sat back down and began to fiddle with her pen, staring at the phone console as if it had answers.

"Thanks," Scott said. He would ask if Bates had interviewed her yet. His gut said she wasn't a likely suspect, but she was certainly shaken.

He trotted down the hall to the conference room. In every tiny office along the hall, curious faces watched him pass. The narrow rectangular window in the conference room door showed Del Bates on the side of the conference table that faced the door, making notes in his pad while a middle-aged woman, with red hair that looked fairly close to what must have been her original color, sat with her back to the door, shoulders shaking as if she were sobbing. Bates looked up when Scott's face appeared in the window, and held up his index finger. Scott waited, observing the woman. Bates nodded at something she said, and she stopped to bring a tissue to her face. Bates glanced back at Scott. His coffee looked cold and his face weary. Finally, Bates rose from his chair as the woman stood. She turned to go, her face haggard, and she met Scott's eyes. He opened the door for her. She brushed past him, still sniffling.

Bates met him just inside the door. "Glad to see you, Aylward." He took a sip of the cup from the table, made a face, and tossed it in the trash. "Even with help, this will take a while."

Scott nodded toward the notepad. "What have you got so far?"

Bates turned to pick up the pad, consulting his notes with the thoroughness that had earned him Chief Detective, even though he probably had every detail stored neatly in his mind. "Not much. She left work with the bank deposit before 3:30, just as usual." He glanced up. "She has an office to herself, but the door is usually open with three other ladies just outside. Several of them mentioned that she had gone through a divorce about a year ago, but after the initial emotional trauma, that had seemed to settle down to be a fairly amicable one." He laughed. "As if there is such a thing."

Scott nodded. Many of his fellow officers had first-hand knowledge of the bitterness of divorce. It was an occupational hazard. "What do you want me to do?"

Bates pulled a sheet of paper from his notebook. "I've got fifteen left to interview." He wrote some names quickly on another sheet and tore it from the notepad. "Would you take seven and I'll take eight?" He handed the sheet to Scott. "Check with the receptionist for a room to use and to get them in there."

Scott glanced at the list. "Are they all as upset as

the last one?"

Bates nodded. "At least the women have been. The last one was here when she was hired."

Scott headed back down the corridor. Again, curious faces watched him.

He was just interviewing his last witness, Sandy the receptionist, when Bates' face appeared in the window of the smaller conference room Scott had been assigned. Scott motioned Bates in. His bulk filled the doorway as he edged inside. Sandy glanced up at him. Though her eyes were rimmed with tears, and she had stopped to master herself often, she hadn't cried during the interview. "Sandy, would you please tell Detective Bates what you just told me."

"Sure, Detective Aylward." She turned to face Bates, who stood at the end of the table, another cup in his hand. "Delia had a direct line, so not many of her calls went through the switchboard, unless she didn't answer, then they would roll to me." She glanced back at Scott. "I've been here about a year and a half, so I was here when she went through her divorce. I know her husband's voice, and he's been calling her a lot the last two or three months. Or maybe she's not taking his calls and that's why they've been rolling to me." She glanced down at her hands. "I haven't asked her." She took a deep, shuddering breath. "Maybe I should have."

Scott put down his pen. "Thanks, Sandy, you've been helpful."

"I hope so," she said, standing. "I hope you find her soon." She turned toward the door, glancing at Bates briefly. "And safe."

Scott sighed and closed his notebook. "How did your interviews go?"

Bates dropped into the chair Sandy had just left. "Hard." He gulped the coffee in the cup, stared at it, and tossed the cup. "Everyone seems to like her, though she kept to herself somewhat. No indication that she may have just taken off. From what they say, she was pretty content with her life, things were smoothing out between her and the ex; they were doing fairly well in sharing custody of their three-year-old daughter. He had the baby this week, or the sitter might have raised an alarm if she wasn't picked up."

"Have we talked to the ex-husband?"

Bates nodded. "When he called her in missing, and again when we found the car." He laid his notebook on the table. "Guy seemed pretty shook up." He looked up at the clock in the room. "Shit, we'd better get these interviews typed up."

Scott glanced at his watch. Five-thirty. This office must be ready to close; he'd seen several people heading past the door as he interviewed people. And his phone hadn't vibrated, no call from Rica, even though she must have been home at least an hour by now. She was likely very pissed at him. "I'll just grab some fast food and head back to the station."

Bates chuckled. "Can't get used to typing them up on the laptop in the car?"

"All the cars were out, so I drove my own truck."

Bates stood. "I'm gonna run home for dinner, hug the wife and kids, then I'll catch you at the station. Maybe we can have a meeting with the other investigators there, see if anyone's turned up anything."

"Roger." Scott stretched, not accustomed to sitting for such long periods. He followed Bates out of the room, and they bumped into a tall man in a good gray

8

suit.

"Did you get any leads?" the man asked Bates, with a glance at Scott.

Bates shrugged. "We'll see if anything goes anywhere."

The man followed them to the door and pulled keys from his pocket. "I'll let you out."

"Howard Moran, company president," Bates remarked, after they stepped from the cool office to the convection oven of Kansas in July.

"How's his reaction?"

"He's concerned. Small company, he knows all of the employees. But he's also got a tough bottom line to keep him occupied."

Scott turned toward his pickup. "Yeah, gotta keep an eye on that bottom line." He unlocked and rolled down the windows, to let the hot air escape, though it was so hot outside that there was very little change until he started the motor and kicked the air to high. It was the beginning of their third straight week of triple-digit heat. Even with the air on high, he was nearly to Thirtieth Street and the Arby's he had in mind before the cab of the truck was cool enough to dry the sweat on his face.

He pulled out his cell phone to double check for messages. Nothing. He knew he should call Rica, or stop by the apartment to share the dinner he had prepared, but he also knew she would be mad, likely to start throwing things, and he had too much to do on this case to deal with her now. It sounded from the radio traffic squawking out of the walkie-talkie at his belt like a typically busy summer evening—speeding, stalled cars, several fender-benders. All the street officers were working their asses off in this blast furnace, making Scott glad he'd made detective last year, even though it meant more irregular hours, and, perhaps, put even more strain on his marriage.

He pulled into the drive-through lane at Arby's, trying to decide if he'd go for one of the new sandwiches he'd seen on TV or stick with his standard regular roast beef, while he waited on the two cars ahead of him. The cab had cooled off, so he had to turn down the temperature as well as the fan on the air. That was the beauty of having a regular cab mini-pickup—it didn't take long to heat up or cool down. It was the only advantage.

The radio at his left side crackled. "Any available unit." He grabbed for it.

"Seventy-three here," he gave his radio number.

"Have a call that a walker has found a body on the dike by the river, just west of the Big D."

"Ten-four." He swung his little truck out of line. "I'm on my way."

Chapter 3

It took Scott eight minutes with his under-hood flashing lights to work his way through traffic to the south end of town. He crossed through the intersection of Highways Fifty and Sixty-one and turned west on the frontage road past a long-closed truck stop, now storage for highway construction material, that all the natives still referred to as the "Big D." Near the end of the road, where a locked access gate shut off traffic except for official maintenance vehicles, a middle-aged man with a yellow Labrador retriever sat on the gatepost. The dog panted in the heat, and the man looked up as Scott's vehicle approached.

Scott was pulling out his badge as he threw the truck in park and scrambled to the sandy roadway. "Detective Aylward, PD."

"Thank God, you're here." The man moved toward him, the dog at his side wagging his tail in greeting. Scott noted that he seemed pale under his sweat. "Ed Thorson," he said. As Scott drew abreast of him, he turned away, waving his arm to the south. "She's over there. Beau found her." He patted the dog beside him. "It was awful. I pulled him back as quick as I figured out what he found." His hands were shaking and scratched. "I didn't want to destroy any evidence."

"You're sure she was dead?"

The man merely nodded, his face growing even

11

paler.

Scott stepped over the access gate arm. "To the south?" It had to be south; to the north the path led under the highway, totally exposed to traffic. He knew the north end of the trail well; he ran it every day he could. The south end wasn't officially trail; just a footpath along the top of the dike that a few people like the dog-walker used. Even the dirt bikes and ATV's kept to the riverbed north of the bridge.

The man nodded, leaning over the gate, but making no move to cross it. "Almost to the big cottonwood." He indicated a huge gnarled tree about a hundred yards from the gate. "Maybe twenty feet from the pathway, by an old tree trunk, through a sand plum thicket."

"Wait here. I'll need to take a formal statement." Scott glanced back at him. "But you might wait in the shade over there." He pointed to a grove of scrubby autumn olive trees throwing a lengthening shadow along the ditch at the edge of the road.

He scrambled up the steep face of the dike, trying to maintain his professional demeanor and keep the sand out of his shoes as he waded through the deep pocket of sand deposited at the base of the dike. In years past, the dikes had protected the flat city from the waters of the raging Arkansas River when it flooded. In Scott's memory, the dikes had seemed pointless, as the once-mighty Ark now barely murmured as it flowed past the city, tamed by John Martin Reservoir in Colorado and increased pumping from the Ogallala Aquifer beneath it. He studied the ground at the top of the dike. The dry sand of the hardened path told few stories, as the relentless wind swept it daily. He saw shallow depressions that perhaps indicated the footsteps of the man and the dog, but they were indistinct. He pulled out the radio.

"Seventy-three to dispatch."

"Go ahead, seventy-three."

"Have the reporting party waiting at my truck at the end of the dike road. Might get another unit en route to help secure the scene if needed."

"Ten-four. Will send the next available unit." That meant that other officers were still busy. He would be on his own, even if he needed backup.

"Twenty-one to seventy-three." He heard Bates's tired voice crackle at him.

"Go ahead, twenty-one."

"I can be there in ten minutes."

"Ten-four. Thanks." He slipped the radio back in its case and started cautiously south along the top of the dike. Step by step, he walked as lightly as he could, scanning all around the pathway for anything not native to the site. Halfway to the cottonwood, the hairs on the back of his neck stood up, and he unsnapped his holster. He slowed his pace within twenty feet of a gray and twisted tree trunk that must have once supported a massive cottonwood, but now instead provided a windbreak that allowed sand to settle in its lee and let shrubs gain a foothold. He looked down the sloping bank of the dike toward the river, noting the lazy flow as it rippled barely a foot deep in half a dozen shallow braided channels within the banks. A gray heron took off from a sand bar, long legs dangling behind him.

He stopped and squatted to view the path from a different angle. Just this side of the tree trunk, he saw indistinct grooves in the sand of the path that could have been made by a body being dragged. Big bluestem waved behind the tree trunk, and a sand plum thicket guarded the north side of the approach. Buffalo grass carpeted the ground from the path to the tree, obscuring any sign from this angle. He stood up again.

Now it looked like there were faint marks in the grass, here and there, that could be drag marks. He continued on the other side of the path, careful not to disturb the sign. At last he was even with the northern edge of the sand plum thicket. Again, he went down to see what he could observe from this angle. He spotted some broken branches and a few tufts of buff fur, where the dog had bounded in to make his discovery and dragged the man in his wake. He followed the path of fur and branches with his eyes, and finally saw something large and too pale a pink to belong in that environment. Reminding himself to stay detached and professional, he stepped up on the tree trunk to get a better view.

She lay naked, legs spread as if inviting, one arm flung over her abdomen, the other at her side. Blood matted the once golden hair that splayed around her head, her throat black and gaping in a grotesque smile. Flies buzzed about the wound. Her eyes, wide open and as blue as the sky around him, seemed to seek his and hold them. He had seen death before, but his stomach clenched despite his resolve, and he hopped down from the tree trunk to grab the radio.

Hands shaking, he took a deep breath to steady his voice and coughed to quiet his stomach before he keyed the mike. "Seventy-three to twenty-one."

"Twenty-one. I'm almost to the gate. Got your reporting party in sight."

"Twenty-one, I found the forty." He paused,

gulping for air. "It's the one we were looking for."

The radio stayed silent a full two seconds. "Secure the scene, then, till we get the crew here."

Scott stood, the radio in his hand, eyes scanning the scene. The cottonwood swayed in the wind above him, leaves twinkling as if death did not surround it. What had the tree seen, not just Delia's death, but the other life and death struggles it must have witnessed in its half-century or so of clinging to the bank of the life-giving river? And the river. How many deaths had it seen, even caused, in the eons it had cut through the prairie? What secrets had it swept away in its deceptive currents?

He forced himself back to cold logic to keep from seeing her eyes. She had obviously been dead at least several hours, although he knew that the stages of decay after death accelerated rapidly in the kind of heat they'd had the past two weeks. And he hadn't seen any pool of blood around her wound, which probably meant she had been killed elsewhere and the body dumped.

The hot wind blew over and around him, drying the sweat from his face and body, carrying the scent of death away from him. He heard radio traffic, as the officers who doubled as the forensics team gathered near the gate. The dead end road would soon be very busy.

But for right now, he was alone out here on the dike. Alone with Delia. He looked toward where her body lay, still shaken by the sensation that she had looked directly at him, beyond him even, maybe into his very soul. And something familiar about her haunted him. They had some sort of connection, of that he was sure. He just didn't know what connection it could be.

"Twenty-one to seventy-three."

"Go ahead," he answered, glad of the steady voice of Bates.

"Team's on our way to you to work the scene."

"Ten-four." He wouldn't be alone with her much longer.

Chapter 4

Mags was gone. The best friend she'd known since third grade would no longer step in to rescue her from her own frailties. Now no one knew her better than she knew herself. No more late night calls or chick flicks or bonding over shopping and double mocha lattes.

Charlotte Daniels faced herself in the mirror and brushed on her blush. Her hand shook, and she put down the brush. For the moment, she was safe. Devlyn wouldn't be home until after she began her shift at the Thirsty Dragon. She laid her head down on the vanity and let the tears come until the well was dry.

She stood up, wiped away the last tears, and blew her nose. She went into the bathroom to wash her face and begin the painting over again. Her tips depended on the most flawless look she could achieve, on how short the skirt, how low the blouse.

Though she'd only had the job six months, just a part-time job on Fridays and Saturdays to earn vacation money, the monetary value placed on her looks validated her. It usually boosted her esteem, made her feel sexy and feminine by the time she came home to Devlyn.

Tonight, though, she wouldn't want sex when she got home. Tonight she would need to simply be held, comforted. Somehow, she knew that would never again come from Devlyn. She had seen what Devlyn was

17

capable of. She struggled again to hold back the tears. She finally lost the battle.

Chapter 5

It was nearly midnight when he let himself into the apartment as quietly as he could. Rica had left no lights on for him, so he flipped open his cell phone to give him enough illumination to pick his way through the living room. They had too much furniture for this tiny apartment, he decided. Maybe soon he could convince Rica they had saved enough money to buy a house. He glanced toward the kitchen. No plate sitting on the table waiting for him. She must have expected him to be gone for dinner. Or just didn't care.

He stopped in the bathroom, shutting the door to hold the light in as he brushed his teeth. He stared at himself in the mirror, face red from his hours in the sun and wind this evening, and wondered if he could see Delia's face in his eyes. As the District Attorney arrived on the scene to assure no evidence was compromised, he had been one of the officers forming a human grid to scour the path and its surroundings for evidence while the coroner and forensic officers snapped photo after photo. He had watched as the forensic officers bagged Delia's hands to preserve possible DNA of her killer and heard the DA make a careful statement to the media kept at bay on the dead end road. He splashed water on his face. He had to stop using Delia's name, and just think of her as "the victim."

Finally, shutting off the light before he opened the

door, he crept into the bedroom, where the street light illuminated the room despite the closed blinds. He unclipped his holster, badge, and radio from his belt, and left them on the dresser where he could grab them at a moment's notice. He pulled off his shoes while standing, then stripped off his clothes as quietly as he could before he slipped into bed, hoping not to wake Rica.

"So you're finally home." Her voice, muffled by the pillow, sounded flat.

"Yeah." He rolled toward her, placing a tentative hand on her waist, where he felt cotton beneath his fingers. She was wearing a T-shirt, not sleeping nude as she normally did. She must be really angry. "We had a missing woman, that we finally found, dead, and had to work the crime scene and write reports."

She rolled toward him, her eyes searching his face. "Was she murdered?"

He nodded, running one hand along her side to her shoulders. "I found her."

Her eyes widened. "You found her? Yourself?"

He blinked, trying to hold back the memory. "Yeah."

"Oh, *mijo*." She used the Spanish term of endearment she had learned from her Mexican mother and put her arms around him, bringing his head down to cradle it on her shoulder. He stretched out alongside her, holding her close, feeling her breathe, trying not to think how Delia must have breathed just like this not two nights ago. "That must have been terrible."

He nodded, his face buried in her neck, inhaling the sweet freesia scent of her shampoo, nuzzling her thick soft hair. He had always loved how she smelled, flowery and sweet, just a little bit spicy. So different from the smells he encountered in his work. Now she ran her hands across his shoulders and down his back, trying to comfort him with her touch. Any anger she carried for him had fled, replaced by her need to nurture him. He ran his hand from her waist to her breast, savoring the fullness of it. "I love you, Rica." He kissed her chin, and she pulled him closer to her. He slipped his hand down to the hem of her shirt and worked his way under it, caressing the smooth skin of her back. She curved against him, and he felt himself responding to her. She ran her leg along his.

The thought of the position he'd found Delia in flashed into his mind, and he shut his eyes against the sight, as Rica wrapped both legs around him. Without conscious thought, he moved against her. He pushed her shirt up, and she pulled it off in one smooth move, then stripped off her panties with the next. He gave himself up to loving her, hoping that if he let the head between his legs do the thinking, it would silence the head between his ears. He looked down into her face, at the tenderness there, remembering the first time he had seen her, in the night literature class at the college. He thought her even more beautiful now, love expressed in her shining eyes.

Eyes. Delia's eyes staring into his. He shut his eyes, trying to force Delia into that locked cellar in his mind. But as he opened the door to shove her memory in, others crowded into view, trying to escape. Aaron, the five-year-old his parents had covered in cigarette burns as they flew on the meth they made in the kitchen next to his room. He doubted that any amount of medical and psychological therapy would ever

21

overcome the damage they had done to the boy. Andrea, the woman who had gutted her boyfriend because he gave a ride to another woman. The man whose name he never knew, burned alive when his car rolled on a sharp curve in the county. They had become a multitude, a seething mass that pounded on the door when he least expected it, threatening to escape despite the new and stronger locks he kept fixing on the door.

Rica's hands played down his back, and his ghosts went silent for a while, as nature's forces won out over psychological wars. At last he lay spent beside her, holding her close, and Delia's eyes appeared before him again. And suddenly, he knew her!

"Margaret Stillman!" He sat up, shaking.

Rica sat up beside him. "Should I be mad at you for screaming another woman's name after you make love to me?" Her hands on his shoulders expressed concern.

He turned to her. "The dead girl looked familiar to me." He ran his hands over his face. "I just remembered where I know her from."

"Should I be worried about that?" She rubbed his arm.

"No." He focused on her for a moment. Did she think he had a mistress that kept him away from her? The only mistress he had time or energy for was his job. "They called her Delia Enfield at the briefing." He brought his knees up to wrap his arms around them. "But I knew her as Margaret Stillman."

He jumped from the bed, rummaging in the bookcase against the wall for the high school yearbook he thought was still there. At last he found it and hopped back in the bed, switching on the light on his nightstand. Flipping through the pages to the freshman class, in the S's he found her, a plain, shy girl with brown hair and enormous blue eyes behind owlish glasses. "Margaret Delia Stillman." He looked at Rica who was studying him with a half-smile on her lips and a serious look in her eyes. "She's—she had—changed a lot."

"Scott." Something in Rica's voice made him look at her. "I have a surgery with Dr. Ambrose at seven in the morning. Both of us need some sleep." She took the book from him, laid it on the nightstand, and turned off the light. She kissed him gently. "We should both be relaxed enough to sleep now." She tugged him down beside her. "Let it rest, Scott. All of the clues will still be there in the morning."

He hugged her close, inhaling the now salty sweetness of her. She was right. He knew that. Still, as she breathed softly beside him, he lay awake in the darkness, listening to those memories that might lead him to Delia's—Margaret's—killer.

****

He lay quietly and listened to Rica sleep. He had dozed for a while, even slipping into a deep sleep, but it wouldn't last. He rolled away from her, to stare at the alarm clock on his side of the bed. Three seventeen a.m. She had to be up in less than three hours. If he stayed in the bed, tossing and turning, it would disturb her sleep. Then she would not only be grumpy with him, she might make a mistake assisting in surgery and cost someone's life. That burden he didn't want to bear. Plus she wanted to impress this Dr. Ambrose—something about a promotion. He put his hand on the yearbook. Glancing back over his shoulder at Rica, he crept quietly out of bed. He pulled on his boxers and grabbed the book.

He headed for the kitchen. He could turn on the light over the table without it glaring into the bedroom. He set the book on the table and opened the fridge. Rica hadn't even cooked the chicken last night. A pang of guilt lanced his heart as he suspected she hadn't eaten at all. Then he remembered he hadn't either. Still, after what he had seen as they worked the scene, food didn't beckon him at all. He studied his options.

Beer sounded good, but didn't seem like a wise choice. At last, he pulled the bottle of L'Orval Merlot from the bottom shelf. He had bought it for Rica for their fourth anniversary last February. They'd had a drink from it occasionally, but there was still quite a bit left. He grabbed a glass and poured a small serving. It might help him sleep, though he would have preferred the taste of the beer.

With the glass before him, he took a sip and opened the yearbook. He barely remembered Margaret—Delia. In fact, he wouldn't have remembered her at all except for an incident during cheerleader tryouts after football practice. He wasn't a star player—he was too light for that—but he could play any position, remember any play, and he could turn on the speed when bigger players bore down on him, so the coach put him in often, and started him his senior year. A guy, Kyle—he couldn't remember his last name—tried out for the cheerleading squad that year, a boy that the others laughed at and teased. But his trying out angered the captain of the defensive team.

When the burly football player tackled Kyle as the tryouts got underway, Delia had stepped forward, unflinching, and hauled the bigger boy up by his ear. He came up swinging at first, until he saw that Kyle's protector was a girl. He backed off, but swore to get even. Kyle got several beatings that year. There would have been more had Delia not been around to stop some of them.

He took another sip of wine. It was unlikely that someone would carry a grudge for the fifteen years it had been since they graduated, but such things had happened before. He reached for the grocery list and pen magnetized to the fridge. Rica was so organized. He smiled. More proof that opposites attract.

Sipping on the wine, he went through the yearbook, writing down names of the students that he could remember had either backed Delia and Kyle or Dean, the football captain. He would take the book to work tomorrow, and they could begin winnowing out the leads.

He tossed back the last swallow of wine and rose from the table. Then he thought better of his actions and rinsed the glass before putting it in the dishwasher. No sense in pissing Rica off with something so little. Turning out the light, he waited for his eyes to adjust to the darkness before he crept back into bed and under the covers. He didn't touch Rica, wanting instead to just let her sleep, and finally, he drifted off himself.

Chapter 6

"Good work, Aylward." Chief Taylor closed the yearbook. He tapped his finger on the list Scott had stuck to the cover. "See how many of these people you can find contact information for." He glanced at Bates. "We may need to interview them if our interrogation with the husband doesn't give us a confession."

"When are you interviewing him?"

Bates brought up his arm to check his watch. "About ten minutes, I'd say." He turned to leave the chief's office. "Jeffries and Anderson should be bringing him in any minute."

"Why don't you sit in on the interview, Aylward?" Taylor looked toward Scott. "It would be good experience for you."

Scott scrambled to his feet. "Sure thing, Chief." He followed Bates down the hallway to the interrogation room. "Have we got the results of the autopsy yet?"

Bates nodded. "Got preliminary results this morning. Time of death between midnight and three a.m. the day you found her."

"So she was with the killer maybe twelve hours then?"

Bates stopped to open the door to the interrogation room. "Yup. Probably the longest twelve hours of her life."

Scott suppressed a shiver. He didn't want to

imagine what those hours had been like. "Any wounds besides the throat slash?"

Bates laid some files on the table. "Some minor cuts on her neck, like the killer hesitated before killing her. No defensive wounds."

"Any indication she was tied up?"

Bates shook his head. "They're doing more tests, but it looks like he maybe suffocated her to the point of unconsciousness before doing the slash." He pushed a file toward Scott. "She was also sexually assaulted."

Scott paused before he opened the file. "She was raped, then."

Bates picked up his Styrofoam cup of coffee. "No semen, what little DNA there was is not on file."

Scott shot a glance at him. "Bastard used a condom?"

Bates nodded. "Probably. Or a foreign object. They're looking for more DNA. It's in the file."

Scott looked down at the single-spaced text. He slid the photos under the paper, trying not to look at them, at least not until he could psych himself to be dispassionate and clinical about them. He wasn't there yet. He scanned the report. It appeared that Delia—the victim—had been penetrated, but there was no semen, no evidence of human contact. Perhaps a foreign object. That was odd. Men generally wanted to have sex with a woman for one of two reasons—either they found her desirable or they wanted to assert power over her. Whoever killed this victim had asserted the ultimate power; he had taken her life, but had refrained from actually having sex with her. Unless… Scott lifted the paper and started to slide the photos out when the door opened, and Ellery Enfield stepped past the uniformed officer who had opened the door.

"Have you found anything yet, Detective Bates?" Wearing a rumpled T-shirt that looked as if he had slept in it and stained jeans he must have worn to work at the motorcycle shop, Enfield stood as uncertain as a first-grader sent to the principal's office the first time. He glanced at Scott before returning his gaze to Bates.

"Not yet, Mr. Enfield." Bates waved at the chair across the table from him. "Why don't you have a seat?"

"Okay." Enfield shuffled toward the chair. Studying him full in the face, Scott thought he seemed dazed, his eyes red-rimmed, face unshaved for at least twenty-four hours, if not more. It appeared as if he had crawled out of bed and just run his fingers through his shaggy dark blonde hair. "My mom got here last night." He stared into the corner of the room. "She's stayin' with Gloria." Tears gathered in his eyes, and his lower lip quivered. "Baby doesn't understand." He looked down at his rough, grease-stained hands. "Keeps askin' me when momma's gonna pick her up." His shoulders heaved, and he put his hand across his eyes. He took a deep breath and then, blinking several times, faced Bates. "What do you need from me?"

Bates held his face taut. Scott glanced at him, hoping he could maintain his demeanor in the presence of Enfield's palpable grief. "We just need to know where you've been between three-thirty Tuesday and five o'clock Wednesday."

Enfield gazed toward the ceiling, as if remembering a sequence of events. "Well, I was at work till six on Tuesday, then I drove across town to pick up Glo from the sitter." He looked down at his hands. "Then we stopped at McDonald's for a bite and so she could play in their play world." He glanced up at Bates. "There's not much shade in my yard, so I figured she could burn off some energy in the cool before we got home."

Bates had made some notes on his pad. "And then what did you do, Ellery?"

"You can call me El, everybody does." Enfield smiled with his mouth, though his eyes didn't echo the move. "Or Joker. To match the tattoo." He pointed to his left arm and the artwork partially visible under the sleeve. He looked down at his hands again, and his shoulders moved. "Though I don't feel much like jokin' now." He drew another deep breath, and met Bates' gaze. "Glo and I played in the house for a while, then I gave her a bath, put her jammies on, and we read *One Fish, Two Fish* three times before she finally fell asleep." He gave a real smile then. "You know how a three-year-old is when they like a book. It's 'Read it again, Daddy' over and over." His face gentled beneath the tough biker exterior. "But I don't mind readin' to her. She's so much like her momma. She's got Delia's eyes—" His shoulders convulsed, and he buried his face in his hands.

Without comment, Scott set a box of tissues in front of the big man. He grabbed several. He sobbed for several minutes, then finally blew his nose before he could face them again. "You think I killed Delia, don't you?"

Scott's gut told him it was real pain he saw in the watery gray eyes. Bates spoke. "We're just covering all the bases, Mr. Enfield."

Enfield sighed. "I guess you have to." He faced

Bates and then Scott. "But I could never have hurt Delia. I loved her, still do." He looked down at his hands again, at the tissues crumpled there. "I just wasn't enough class for her, too stupid about books and such." He stared into the corner. "Don't know why she ever fell for me in the first place, but I thank God she did, else we'd never have had Gloria." He sighed.

"Okay, after Glo-baby went to sleep, I looked at the newspaper, watched TV, and went to bed. Got up at 5:30, got Glo up at 6:30 and took her to Sharon's, and then went to work."

"And you called Delia's office in the afternoon to talk to her."

"Yeah." Enfield looked serious. "We were gonna have lunch, talk about Gloria goin' to pre-school in the fall, but I waited and waited and she never showed. I called her office when I got back to work, and they said she never came in." He looked at Bates. "That's when I called 911, 'cause Delia took her work serious. She would never just not show up without callin' in."

"The office didn't seem too worried about it."

"Yeah, well, I don't think the chick at the front desk likes guys like me very much."

"What do you mean by 'guys like you?'" Bates focused on him.

"Rough guys. Bikers, laborers, uneducated guys."

"What makes you think that?"

"Well, when I'd call, she'd always sound real nice and perky, but when she heard my voice, hers would change." He met Bates' eyes. "Like you sound when you're scrapin' shit off your shoes, know what I mean?"

Bates nodded. "Okay, I get your drift. What TV

show did you watch?"

Enfield stared at the table. "Whatever was on the channel Glo had been watchin' before her bath. PBS channel. I think I stayed on that through a commercial or two, then flipped to Monster Trucks. Then I watched the news and a few minutes of Conan. I was pretty tired by then. You know our shop's not air-conditioned very much, and it takes it outta ya. Took a shower and went to bed."

"Do you know if Delia was seeing anyone?"

A frown crossed Enfield's face. "She'd been out to bars a few times with some of her friends from work, but I never heard nothin' about her goin' on any dates."

"How about you? Are you seeing anyone?"

Enfield ducked his head. "There's a gal comes in for work at the shop sometimes. We go out for a couple beers." He stopped.

Bates raised his eyebrows. "Just friends?"

Enfield glanced from Bates to Scott and back. "Well, if Glo's with Delia, we go to her place sometimes."

The room was silent except for the scratching of Bates' pen as he made some notes. Enfield sniffled a couple of times. "Anything else you want to tell us, Mr. Enfield."

"Naw, Mr. Bates." Enfield leaned back in his chair and rubbed his palms on his thighs. "I been thinkin' and thinkin' since Delia didn't show up for lunch. At first, I thought maybe she met somebody and run off, but that wasn't like her. I think I knew from the first that somethin' bad had happened to her." He leaned forward to place his elbows on the table. A Harley tattoo covered most of his right bicep. "Somebody took my

31

little girl's momma away from us. And now I'm all she has left." He sniffled. "I wish they'd killed me instead; Delia's a much better parent than me."

"What about Delia's family?" Scott couldn't remember much about them.

"Her mom's bad off, went to live with Delia's brother. I think she's in a nursing home now."

"How did you and Delia meet, Mr. Enfield?" Scott couldn't imagine a circumstance that would have crossed their paths.

"Delia was volunteerin' with a literacy program as a tutor." Enfield gazed off toward the upper right corner of the room. "I had decided I had to get my GED no matter how much it hurt my head to do it, or I was never gonna be nothin'." His face relaxed as if the memory was pleasant. "Delia was the tutor that was available when my turn came up. She was so good, so gentle, never made fun of how stupid I was." He faced Bates. "Took me three months to work up the guts to ask her out for coffee. I 'bout couldn't talk when she said yes." He looked down at the crumpled tissues in his huge hands. "Delia was like an angel come to earth to save me." His shoulders heaved. "I guess she's back in heaven where she belongs now." He brought the tissues to his face as the sobs overcame him.

Bates glanced at Scott. They gave Enfield a few minutes, until the sobs slowed. He sighed. "Thank you, Mr. Enfield." He stood and Scott scrambled to his feet. Enfield rose more slowly. "The officers will take you back home."

"Thanks, Mr. Bates." Enfield offered his huge hand. "Please, catch the bastard that did this to my Delia." With that, he turned and shuffled from the room.

Scott took a deep breath as the door closed. "What do you think, Del?"

Bates picked up his Styrofoam cup and glanced at the coffee before bringing it to his lips. He rose and tossed the cup in the trash. "On paper, he's the most likely suspect. He was paying some hefty child support, and he was still in love with his ex-wife." He stared at the cup in the can. "He's certainly big enough and strong enough to cut a woman's throat." He sat back down.

"But—" Scott began. "Your gut says he didn't do it."

"He might strangle a woman by accident or in sudden anger, but slash the throat of someone he cares about?" Bates shook his head. "From what I hear, he's a genius at tuning Harleys, but pretty challenged when it comes to the rest of life."

"I wonder what Delia ever saw in him."

Bates leaned back in the chair. "What was she like in school?"

Scott shook his head. "Not very memorable, except for that one incident I told you about. Bookish, pretty much hung out with the quiet girls, except for a couple of wild girls who transferred in from the city to foster at her house and didn't fit in with any other group." He slid out the photos from the file, concentrating on the one of her at the picnic, avoiding the clinical shots. "She certainly never looked so pretty then as she did here."

Bates glanced at the photo and nodded. "Late bloomer, maybe."

Scott shrugged. "Could be."

"I need more coffee." Bates stood. "Let's get this report done up, then start doing more in-depth with the co-workers she went out with, see if there was anyone she met up with at the bar."

Chapter 7

Scott's cell phone vibrated when he was within two strides of the Moran Construction Company's front door. Bates was already stepping inside. "Aylward." He stopped outside.

"Scott." Rica's voice carried excitement. "Come home as soon as you get off shift."

"Why? What's up?" Ordinarily she just accepted whatever time he got home and went on with her own plans.

"We're invited to a cookout at Dr. Ambrose's tonight at six!" She sounded like she was announcing that they had just won the Publisher's Clearing House sweepstakes. "You'll need to shower and change—wear your new khakis and your sport coat." She paused for breath.

"Okay, I'll be home as soon as possible, but you know things can come up."

Her voice stiffened. "I hope not tonight, Scott." She paused, evidently waiting for him to assure her that it would not. "This dinner is important for my career, Scott." He hated it when she pleaded with him over the phone; a wife shouldn't have to beg her husband to be there for her. He gave himself a silent tongue-lashing. "Dr. Ambrose can recommend who will be the next chief surgical nurse."

"I'm sorry, Rica. I know it's important." He

sighed. "I'll make sure I leave here on time."

"Thank you, Scott." He almost felt the kiss blown through the phone. "I'll see you at home."

The receptionist flashed a smile as soon as he walked through the door. She glanced at Bates and then swept Scott with a more assessing gaze. Scott rested his left hand, with its very visible wedding ring, on the counter in front of her. Her gaze dropped to the ring. "What can I do for you today, detectives?"

Bates opened his notebook, removing the pen. "We have a few more questions for some of your co-workers."

"Sure, Detective. Who would you like to talk to?" Once again, she smiled at Scott. She recovered from the loss of Delia rather quickly. Yesterday, he worried that she would suffer a breakdown at the thought that Delia was simply missing. Now that she was found murdered, gruesome details spread across the headlines despite the District Attorney's careful statements, the girl acted like it bothered her no more than a parcel lost in shipping. He stepped back from the counter.

"Let's start with the office manager." Bates consulted his notes, but Sandy offered the name before he said it. Bates probably had the names memorized.

"Pat Green." She picked up her phone and punched in the extension. "Pat, the detectives would like to talk to you again."

Ms. Green met them at the reception desk and then led them to her office. Glancing at the curious faces of her co-workers, she shut the door and then seated herself behind the desk. "It must have been horrible for poor Delia." She removed her glasses and rubbed the bridge of her nose. Taking a deep breath, she put her glasses back on. "What can I do to help?"

Bates flipped to a fresh page in his notebook. "Any idea who Delia hung out with outside of work?"

Ms. Green leaned back in her chair. "She didn't go out much, as far as I know. She had lunch with Trish O'Reilly and Shawna Turner once in a while. They could tell you if she ever spent time with them other than that." She looked down at her hands. "About once a month, a group of about a half dozen girls would go to a bar for a drink after work." Her lips tightened. "From what I hear, they usually ended up having dinner there and staying until the place closed. She might have joined them."

Bates glanced at Scott. "Do you know the name of the bar?"

She shook her head. "Sandy knows. I'm not sure it was always the same place."

"You didn't go with them?" Scott almost called her Mrs. Brady, after his childhood Sunday school teacher. They both made the same disapproving scowl.

Ms. Green shot him a look that made him want to sit in the corner facing the wall. "I would never go to one of those places."

"We'll ask Sandy which one it was." A twitch of his mustache the only indication of the grin Scott knew it hid, Bates glanced at Scott. "Could you let us talk to Ms. O'Reilly and Ms. Turner?"

"Of course." She consulted a sheaf of pink "while you were out" notes. "But Shawna called in sick today." She rubbed her temple. "I think she was the most upset by poor Delia's...death."

Scott and Bates exchanged a look. "We'll talk to Ms. O'Reilly then. And we'll need Ms. Turner's home number and address."

"Certainly." She consulted an address book in a drawer and wrote briefly on a company notepad. "Here it is."

****

"Poor Delia." Trish O'Reilly dabbed at her nose with a crumpled tissue. "She was so sweet, just getting her life back together." She dropped her left hand, still holding the tissue, in her lap. She propped her right elbow on the conference table, gathered a strand of her caramel hair, and began to twist it in her fingers. Trish paid a lot of money for her hair to look like it was naturally that color. Rica's caustic comments about women taught him that.

"How do you mean, 'getting it back together.'" Scott, sitting directly across from her, leaned forward.

Trish glanced first at Bates, then back to Scott. "Oh, I mean after the divorce and all." She smiled at Scott, then dropped her gaze. Deliberately, he laid his left hand across the top of the notebook as he jotted a note. Her gaze flicked to his wedding ring, but then she met his eyes and smiled again. "It's hard to get back into circulation after a breakup, but she was making the effort."

"Was she seeing anyone?" Scott kept his eyes on the notepad, although he could feel her looking at him. He'd let Bates read the body language; he needed to cool the way she reacted to him, or they'd not get the information they needed.

"Um." She brought the tissue to her nose again. "No one steady."

"Do you have the names of anyone she went out with?"

"Oh, she didn't really go out with them." Trish now focused on Bates, so Scott tried to observe her with his head lowered. "She just met them at a restaurant or bar, like a blind date." She smiled. "We had a lot of laughs about how dismal they were." Then her lips started to tremble, and her shoulders heaved. "Poor Delia."

Scott glanced at Bates. Getting information from Trish was going to be a slow process. They waited a few minutes until her sobs slowed. "Can you write down everything you know about anyone she went out with? When they went out, where, times, that sort of thing."

She nodded. "I can write down what she told me, but there usually wasn't much." She glanced toward the door of the room. "And then there was—" Someone walked past the door, and she stopped.

"There was what?" Scott asked the question he knew was also on Bates' mind.

"Oh, nothing." Trish's fingers tangled in her hair again. "She just…stopped going out for a little while."

"Bad experience?"

Trish shrugged. "She didn't say much, just didn't want to join us when we went out."

Bates sighed. "Can you have the list of guys she went out with for us later today?"

"Sure." She brought the tissue to her nose again.

"What about the place some of you went once in a while."

"Oh, that." Trish suppressed a smile. "It started out with some of us going out to the Thirsty Dragon to celebrate Shawna's divorce, then it kind of morphed into a payday evening thing."

"Must have been a bad marriage if she celebrated the divorce," Bates muttered.

Trish focused on him. "Oh, it was horrible." She did smile then. "But Shawna had the last laugh; she got the house, the car, and most of the bank account."

"What did he get?"

Trish flashed a brighter smile. "Free."

Chapter 8

"Nice house." They pulled up before a stone-veneer split level with an oversized two-car garage on a cul-de-sac in a neighborhood announcing its status with an imposing brick entrance.

"Must have been a pretty lousy marriage for him to be happy just getting out." Bates looked over the house. An unobtrusive sign in the velvety lawn advertised the name of the lawn care service.

"I guess freedom is worth different things to different people."

Bates merely grunted as they stepped onto the flagstone porch. Scott rang the doorbell. He lifted his hand to ring the bell again when the door opened. A tall brunette yawned as she opened the door as far as the chain would allow.

"Scott Aylward, PD." Scott held out his badge, and Bates did the same. "Are you Shawna Turner?" She nodded. "We'd like to ask you a few questions about Delia Enfield."

She rubbed a hand over her face as if to wake up. "Sure." She closed the door to remove the chain, then swung it wide for them to enter. The flagstone of the porch repeated itself in the large foyer. Shawna closed the door behind them, then slipped around them. Her shapely legs showed under the short, silken robe she wore as she led the way down into a family room. A flat-screen TV at least four feet across dominated the wall nearest the street. Tiny, but high-dollar, speakers sat in all corners of the room. Shawna crossed the room to settle herself on a sectional sofa of tan suede. She motioned to the matching sofa on the other wall for Scott and Bates. She drew her legs under her and waited.

Scott glanced at Bates, who looked down at his ever-present notebook. "We understand that you and Delia sometimes went out together."

Shawna nodded. "We were all single, about the same age, and none of us wanted to go out alone." She shivered. "I guess what happened to Delia proves it isn't safe to go out alone."

Bates nodded. "It always pays to be careful." Bates watched Shawna, though his head appeared bent over the notebook. "Can you think of anyone she might have met with alone?" He looked up. "Or anyone who might have wanted to meet with her, that she didn't want to see?"

Shawna met Bates' gaze. "She met a few guys for dates, never let them pick her up, always met them at a restaurant or club, being careful." She glanced at Scott. "There were never any she wanted to meet for a second date."

Scott nodded. "Any of them take the rejection hard?"

Shawna shrugged. "From what she said, and from the few of them we saw her with, they really didn't seem too into her, either."

"Trish mentioned that she stopped going out with you for a while."

She nodded. "Couple of months ago, she quit going

out for three or four weeks." She looked down at her hands. "She said she just didn't feel like going out, but…"

"You didn't believe her?" Bates' voice was gentle, sympathetic.

She looked up at him. "Well, there were rumors…"

"Rumors about what?" Bates still sounded like a best friend, rather than an interrogator. Scott could see how he had made Chief of Detectives.

"Rumors that she was seeing—" She glanced from Bates to Scott and back. "Look, I have to work there, you know." She looked down at her hands. "Now that Delia's gone, I'll have to make the damned bank deposits."

"I understand you're in a tough spot." He waited.

"Mr. Moran and his wife have…" She paused, looked at the ceiling, and heaved a ragged sigh. "An arrangement." She shivered slightly. "Neither one cares what the other one does, as long as the public face stays clean and happy." She clasped her hands. "As long as both of them are smiling and act lovey dovey at business affairs, they don't care what other affairs happen."

"So you think Delia was one of those affairs?"

"She would never say, but Howard—Mr. Moran— seems to pay a lot of attention to his employees when they go through divorces."

Bates glanced at Scott. "Did he 'pay attention' to you when you got your divorce?"

Shawna met Bates' gaze. "Oh, he started to." She looked away. "He bought me a potted plant and took me to lunch once, but I didn't want to get into that." She uncrossed her legs. "One of the women who got into it with him lost her job when it was over."

"How did he react when you turned him down?"

"He got real quiet when I told him I'd slap him with a sexual harassment lawsuit if he caused me any problems."

Bates let a smile tweak his mouth. "You play hardball."

"I do when I have to."

"Would Delia have played hardball if she wanted to end it?" Scott spoke up.

She turned her attention to him. "I don't think so." She clasped her hands around her knees. Her nicely manicured nails made him think of Rica. Because she worked surgery and wore rubber gloves, she kept her nails short, though he knew she loved to have manicures. He'd have to encourage her to have one soon. Shawna went on. "Delia was kinda quiet, not so much a fighter, unless it involved her daughter."

"Did she and her ex fight about the baby much?"

She sat in silence for a moment, thinking. "No, not really. They fought about money some, but he always seemed to want whatever Delia thought was best for the baby."

"Why did they divorce if they got along so well?" Bates turned a page in his notebook.

"I think they wanted different things out of life." She looked from one man to the other. "Delia was a sweet gal, much too smart for the job she had or for her husband. I think she just finally realized that his idea of the good life—beer and a motorcycle—was far different than hers, more like museums and fine cuisine."

"Marriages have fallen apart on far less."

"Did Mr. Moran approach Trish?" Scott's gut kept him pursuing this line.

Shawna stared at him, deciding, he assumed, if she should betray a confidence. "You should ask her that," she said finally, with her chin thrust out. Scott thought this formidable group would resemble a pack of she-wolves on the hunt. He suppressed a shiver.

"Could you give us a list of names of men that Delia went out with?"

"I don't know all of them, but I'll give you what I know. When do you need it?"

"Could you have it done by tomorrow morning?"

She nodded. "Of course. I should be at work tomorrow."

Bates stood, closed his notebook, and offered his hand to Shawna. "Thank you, Ms. Turner." She shook it without enthusiasm. "We'll contact you if we have any further questions."

Scott shook hands with her as well. Despite her bravado, there seemed to be a hint of fear in her eyes. She rose to let them out the door.

"That gave us some food for thought." Bates followed Scott down the flagstones to their car.

"Yeah." Scott opened the driver's side door. "So shall we go back and interview Moran?"

"That and get the list of dates from Trish." Bates slipped into the passenger seat. "Then we'll need to follow up on that list, too." He tapped his fingers on his notebook. "Should be easy enough to find out if Moran stayed in the office the day she disappeared."

Chapter 9

Sandy looked up as they came back through the door. "Hey, guys." Apparently, nothing bothered Sandy for long. "Who do you want to see now?"

"How about Mr. Moran?"

Sandy shook her head. "No can do. He's at the Oklahoma plant until Friday."

"Well, then, we'd like to talk to Trish again, if she's available." Scott waited by her counter, Bates silent at his side.

"I'll buzz her." Sandy pushed buttons on the phone console, spoke briefly and then looked up at him. "She's free. You want the small conference room again?"

"That would be fine." Bates started toward the room. "Thanks." Scott followed him.

Trish arrived at the room just as they did. Bates opened the door for her. She handed him the piece of paper she carried. "Here's the list of all the guys that Delia talked about going out with."

Scott looked over Bates' shoulder at it. Four names and another couple of sentences about men without names.

She shrugged. "I couldn't remember the names of all of them she talked about. Maybe Shawna would."

Bates nodded. "We'll ask her." She gazed at them expectantly, awaiting another question. Bates took a deep breath. "How long ago was your divorce, Trish?"

A frown creased her brow. "Not quite a year and a half ago."

"Just a few months before Delia's, right?"

She nodded. "That's why we went to lunch so often, because we were going through the same things."

"It must be tough." Bates' own marriage of twenty-plus years was rock solid. "What kind of things did you talk about going through?"

Trish waved her hands in the air. "Oh, dealing with exes. The paperwork. I don't have kids, so we didn't have that in common." She clasped her hands and looked down at them. "Trying to find a decent guy to date."

"Having trouble finding any?"

"Guys, no. Decent ones, yes."

Bates gave her a friendly grin. "What, are you saying there aren't many of us that are worth dating?"

"You'd be surprised what's out there."

"Like what?" Scott was genuinely serious.

"Like men with no rings who act like they are single." She frowned. "And you find out they're married when the wife calls you."

Bates smiled. "Sticky situation." He glanced down at the list she had given them. "Any of those guys date Delia?"

"He called her, but I had already warned her."

"Did he take it badly when she said no?"

"She said he acted like it didn't even bother him."

Bates glanced at Scott. "What about Mr. Moran?"

Trish sat up straight, her shoulders tight with tension, as she looked from Bates to Scott. "What about Mr. Moran?"

"Is he one of those guys who acts like he's unmarried when he isn't?"

She glanced between them again. "Did Shawna say anything?"

Bates stayed silent, waiting.

She fiddled with the rings on her hands for a few moments. "He—" She paused to look at the door.

"Would you be more comfortable discussing this if we went downtown to the station?"

She nodded. "Could we do it after five?" Her gaze flicked to the door's window again. "I'd prefer that no one here know what we talk about there."

Bates nodded. "Just come to the front desk and ask for me." He stood and offered his hand. "We'll see you this evening then?"

She did not meet his eyes as she took his hand.

Chapter 10

Scott headed for his desk as soon as they hit the station. "Gonna write up my report and track down those pictures in the yearbook while we wait on Trish."

"Good luck." Bates stopped at the coffee pot.

Scott checked his watch. He should be able to get some current addresses and phone numbers before he had to head home for Rica's party. He pulled the yearbook toward him and clicked into the white pages on his computer.

Bates tapped on his desk. "Trish is here."

"What?" He looked at his watch again. "Oh, shit." He hit the keys to shut down his computer, slammed the yearbook closed, and kicked back his chair. "I'm in hot water now."

Bates paused on his way to the front desk to retrieve Trish. "What do you mean?"

"I was supposed to be headed home ASAP at end of shift, which was—" He nodded toward the clock on the wall. "Over forty minutes ago."

"Orders from the boss?" Bates frowned.

Scott was almost to the back door. "Dinner with her boss."

"Get your ass in gear, then, boy." Bates continued to the front. "I'll interview Trish."

Scott barely heard him before the door slammed. He ran to his truck, and was halfway across the parking lot before he had the seatbelt fastened. He paused at stop signs and slid askew into his parking space. He dashed up the stairs; Rica opened the door as he reached for it.

The look she gave him said it all. He'd heard it often enough, she didn't need to say it. "Sorry." He brushed past her, stripping off his shirt and kicking off his shoes as he trotted to the shower. He heard the door open just as the water hit the right temperature.

"What was it this time?"

"Got sidetracked looking up leads while we waited on a witness to come into the station." No way he could come up with a lie that would sound any better—or worse.

"Don't you have an alarm on your cell phone you could have set?" Before he could answer—it really was a good idea—she spoke. "I have your clothes laid out on the bed. If you hurry, we can be just fashionably late." She let out a big sigh, as if she had more to say, then the door closed. He shut off the water.

****

"Rica!" Dr. Ambrose held open the door for them, a big smile creasing his mocha latte face. "And you must be Scott." He offered his hand. "I've heard so much about you."

Complaints, I'll bet. Scott returned the handshake. As expected for a surgeon, Ambrose had a long, slender hand with fingers to match. Ambrose and Rica introduced him around, though he had trouble remembering the names they tossed toward him. He just knew that they were all doctors and their spouses, except for an anesthesiologist and his receptionist.

"Would you like a drink, Scott?" Ambrose asked.

Maybe a drink would let him relax and be more social. "Maybe one."

Ambrose led the way to a bar off the patio. "What'll you have?"

"Beer?"

"Heineken or Bud Light?"

"Let's go with the Bud."

"Bud it is." Ambrose set the cold bottle on the bar. "Rica tells me you're working on the murder case."

Scott took a long swallow. The beer felt good going down. "Yeah."

"Any leads?" Ambrose smiled when Scott shrugged. "Or nothing you can talk about?"

Scott shook his head. "Just nothing concrete yet." He took another hit on the beer. "It doesn't work like on TV."

"Neither does surgery." Ambrose came out from behind the bar, carrying his own glass of wine and one for Rica, who was talking to a woman in the family room.

Scott raised his bottle to the doctor. It seemed they had some common ground, after all. Scott followed as Ambrose took the wine to Rica.

"Rica here is my best nurse." Dr. Ambrose threw an arm around Rica. Scott knew he needed to stifle the surge of jealousy. Ambrose looked down at Rica, and she gazed up at him with admiration in her eyes. He tossed back another slug of beer. She used to look at him that way.

"You make it easy, Bryce." Rica made no move to get away from Ambrose, and when they started toward the patio, his arm stayed around her shoulders. Ambrose only let go of her when he had to tend the steaks.

Scott had drained the beer, working on peeling off the label, when he realized Ambrose was standing in front of him, speaking. "Scott, how do you want your steak?" Many sets of eyes watched; Ambrose must have had to ask him more than once.

"Medium, please." He searched the crowd for Rica and saw her beside the grill, still nursing the original glass of wine, her brows forming a storm cloud above her eyes.

"There's more beer in the cooler by the pool," Ambrose turned back to his cooking. "Help yourself."

"I guess I'll do that," Scott muttered, so low he could barely hear himself. He wandered over to the cooler, and stood between the anesthesiologist and the wife of one of the doctors, but their conversation was about people he didn't know. Though he listened for ten minutes, he could find no way to jump in. He tried another group, gathered around the patio table, but their discussion involved surgical research. He found it interesting, but had nothing to contribute. He finished his beer and turned to see if Ambrose had a trash can or recycling bin for it. The receptionist took the empty bottle from his hand and pressed another into it.

By the time Ambrose announced the steaks were ready, she had removed that one from his hand, as well. He grabbed a bottle of water to have with dinner, but when he looked up from his salad, another beer stood beside it. He tried to ignore the beer, but when the water bottle ran dry, he reached for the beer.

Finally, the wife of the doctor sitting nearest him asked, "I understand you're working on that murder case."

He nodded. "Yes, we're on a murder case."

"The one where the woman was raped and tortured?" Her wide eyes and rapid breathing told him she wanted the sordid details.

"The Delia Enfield case." He wasn't about to offer information, sordid or not.

"I heard she was raped multiple times."

"Rumors run rampant on most cases."

"So that's just a rumor?"

"I can't discuss the case now." His refusal to offer information shut down conversation with him. After dinner, people drifted into small groups, and he found himself conversing with a ficus tree. He saluted it with the beer that had replaced the dinner one.

"So," he addressed the silent tree. "Do you just hang out on the patio all day?" The beer went down easy, and his companion asked no questions.

****

The icy silence in the car almost made the air conditioner irrelevant. Scott leaned his head against the window, hoping the ninety-plus degrees outside the car would thaw the way Rica felt about him right now. He felt her gaze upon him. "Rica—" he began.

"Don't even start, Scott." She cleared her throat waiting for the light to change. "Not until you sober up."

"But, Rica, I only had—"

"I don't care how much you had to drink, Scott." She punched the gas to pull away from the stoplight and the acceleration pushed him back against the seat. And his stomach into his throat. "The fact is that you had enough to be drunk and stupid." His head hit the window when she turned the corner onto their street.

"Enough to cost me my chance at chief surgical nurse."

"Rica, I'm sorry." He wanted to say more, but the words wouldn't form themselves into any order that made sense.

She swerved into her parking space, hit the brakes, hopped out of the car, and slammed her door. Scott opened his door. She stood at the front passenger corner of the car. "Get your ass in the house within the next two minutes or you'll be sleeping in the car," she hissed. She spun on her heel and marched toward the stairs.

Scott couldn't seem to get disentangled from the seatbelt. It wasn't fastened any more, but it wouldn't let him go, either. Finally, he more or less fell from the seatbelt and the car. Closing the door, he worked his way toward the stairs. He had to grab the rail to make it to the top. It swayed like a rope bridge instead of the solid staircase he knew it to be. Rica was right; he was drunk.

He got through the door to the apartment, though it took him several seconds to get it locked once he was inside. Rica hadn't left any lights on, so he fumbled his way to the bathroom. Brushing his teeth proved a challenge, but he completed the task. He turned toward the bedroom only to realize that the door was shut. He stared at the closed door, blinking, for several minutes before making his way to the couch.

Chapter 11

The front door slammed, then the sunlight through the east living room window slapped him in the face. Grasping the top of his head with his hands, he opened his eyes to slits. Sunlight meant it was morning. Morning meant the slamming door must have been Rica leaving for work. Rica leaving for work meant that he still had time for a shower before he had to be at the office. A shower—after coffee and aspirin. Now that the top of his skull seemed to have reattached itself to the rest of his head, he rolled from the couch to the floor, easing to his knees. When the floor stopped spinning, he rose slowly to his feet. That made the floor stand still and his head spin. Soon, though, he made his way into the kitchen. Safe now from the direct sunlight, he stood blinking before the cabinet that held the drinking glasses. Finally, nothing was spinning. He grabbed a glass, then opened the next cabinet to get the aspirin bottle. Shaking two out into his hand, he turned on the tap. He cringed at the sound as the jet of water hit the stainless steel, but he filled the glass, tossed the aspirin down his throat, and chugged the water. Because he knew that too much alcohol led to dehydration, he chugged a second glass. Then he headed for the shower and let the hot steam pull the rest of the toxin from his system.

****

Bates looked up from his desk as Scott walked past him. "You look like shit." He rose with coffee cup in hand and followed Scott to his desk. "Good party?"

Scott glared at him. "Do I look like it was a good party?"

Bates perched on Scott's desk. "Not really." Scott hit the power switch for the computer and took a sip of the coffee he'd grabbed at the McDonald's drive through. "I had too much to drink, and my behavior pissed Rica off." He signed on. "She thinks I blew her chance to be chief surgical nurse."

Bates patted his shoulder. "You'd better stop for flowers on your way home."

Scott stared at the screen as the system came up. "I think this is more than flowers can fix."

"Give it time," Bates advised. "Time and lots of groveling."

Not inclined to discuss it further, Scott changed the subject. "What did Trish have to say?"

Bates rose from the desk and crooked his finger. "Let's go to the conference room."

Scott hopped up to follow him. Before the door closed completely, his question popped out. "So did she have an affair with Moran?"

Bates sat and sipped at his coffee. "Took a while to get her to admit it, but yes." He drank again, made a face, and set the cup down. "She said he acted all sympathetic to her after the divorce, took her to lunch, and then within a couple weeks, they'd meet after work and sometimes at noon at his 'fishing cabin.'" He tried the coffee again, with the same result. "It didn't end until he went on a three-week trip. When he came back, Delia's divorce was final, and he started working on her. From the way Trish acted, she was kind of glad, though she liked the nice gifts he gave her."

Scott raised his eyebrows. "So we have two people with motive." He traced an invisible pattern in the conference table. "Trish if she was really jealous the affair ended and Moran if Delia didn't cooperate."

Bates nodded. "Though I don't think Trish was jealous of Delia. She said that she tried to warn her without giving her details, but Delia either didn't understand or didn't believe her."

"Do you know if Delia went through with it?"

He shook his head. "Trish wasn't sure. She never figured how to bring the subject up." He grinned. "She's not as direct as Shawna."

"Not many are." Scott sipped his coffee; his was evidently much warmer than Bates'. "So when can we interview Moran?"

"Three more days. Sandy said he would be back Saturday." He picked up his cup and headed for the door. "I left word for him to call us."

Scott, too, rose from the table. "I guess I'll try to follow up on the leads from home."

Bates paused. "Good luck. You know as well as I do that if we don't have a suspect soon, we'll have something else to work on, and this will go unsolved."

Not if he could help it; Scott owed it to Delia. And working on this case, even if he had to do it on his own time, would keep him from thinking about how long it would be before Rica cooled down this time. He pulled out the numbers he'd looked up the day after he discovered Delia's body. He started with Dean Gordon, the football captain who had tackled Kyle. He dialed the number.

"Hello?" A woman's soft voice answered.

"Scott Aylward here. I went to school with Dean. Is he there?"

"Yes, just a minute."

In seconds, a rough voice came on the line. "Dean here. Who is this?"

"Scott Aylward. From high school."

"Oh, yeah." The voice sounded tired. "You played defensive end."

"Yeah. Now I'm working for the PD."

"Oh." A year older than Scott, Dean had not befriended the lower-classmen on the team.

"What are you up to these days?" As Scott remembered, Dean left school with a football scholarship to K-State.

"Working my ass off for the tractor plant. Just got off shift a half-hour ago."

No wonder the voice sounded tired. "They keeping you busy?"

"Yeah, since the plant at Greensburg got wiped out by the tornado, we've been running three shifts."

"That sounds tough." Scott thought Dean had planned to major in biology.

"Yeah, they keep rotating shifts, so it cuts down on the time you have with the family."

"Kids?"

"Three. Twelve, nine and seven. Two boys and a girl."

Scott paused. If Rica would have agreed, they would have had kids by now. "That must keep you busier than work."

"It does. Little league, scouts, gymnastics. Me and the wife spend all our time on the road, seems like."

"Who'd you marry?"

"Janice, my best girl all through school." Scott recalled them as pretty well joined at the hip in school.

"You remember Margaret Stillman?"

There was a silence. "Not really. Was she a cheerleader?"

"No, salutatorian. Egghead-type."

"Sorry, I still don't remember her."

"Remember the boy who tried out for cheerleader?"

"That I remember. Damn fag."

"Well, Margaret was his friend. The one who stopped the fight."

Another silence. "Now I remember her." The voice sounded like it had a smile in it. "Feisty little broad."

"I have some bad news about Margaret. She's dead."

"Oh, I'm sorry to hear that." The regret sounded genuine. "What happened?"

"She was murdered three days ago. Going by the name Delia Enfield now."

"Really? That was her?" A pause. "Wow, I never knew someone that was murdered before. Kinda makes it seem a little too real."

"Definitely. Anyway, we're trying to piece together who she knew, now and from the past." He took a deep breath. "Since you didn't remember her, I doubt you've kept in touch with her or anyone else she hung with."

"No, not really. We moved away from here for about five years, going to school. By the time we moved back, most everyone was gone. But I'll ask Jan." It sounded as if he tried to cover the receiver, but Scott could still hear the gruff bellow. "Honey, you remember Margaret Stillman, used to hang out with that fag?" Scott could tell there was an answer, but he couldn't make it out. "She was the gal that got killed this week." Another pause. "Yes, really. You know where any of her friends are anymore?" The voice boomed in Scott's ear, as if Dean forgot he wasn't yelling for his wife any more. "Jan doesn't remember any of the kids Margaret hung out with, but I don't think they are still in town."

"I remember how we couldn't wait to blow that place."

"Yep." The voice softened. "But it's a nice place to come back to, especially with kids to raise."

"Will you give me a call if you remember any one who might know what path she might have taken after high school?"

"Sure. But you might call the school. Maybe one of the teachers stayed in touch with her."

"Good idea, Dean." Scott paused. "What shift were you working Tuesday?"

"Days. Next week I go to graveyard."

"Thanks, Dean. I'll try to get back home for the next reunion."

"No need to wait for reunion, boy. Any weekend will do. The beer's always cold at the tavern on Fridays."

"Maybe I'll do that soon." He hung up. The trip down memory lane had dug up more ghosts than he expected. And what he learned meant that Dean had a potential motive, but no opportunity.

Chapter 12

Scott took Dean's advice and called the school. He cringed when they referred him to Ms. Frank, the algebra and calculus teacher whose class time so many of the jocks had made a three-ring circus. On one occasion, when she had been summoned to the office for a phone call, she returned to a classroom devoid of desks, with every student sitting in his or her place, books neatly stacked before them. The desks had been handed through the windows and lined up outside. The whole class got detention for that one. She seemed to have forgotten the incident when she answered his call to her home.

"Yes, Mr. Aylward. How have you been?"

"I've been fine, Ms. Frank." He hesitated, the old habit of thinking of teachers as furniture and de-personalized nearly overcoming him. "And you?"

"Still teaching, Mr. Aylward." He heard a faint chuckle. "Though the desks stay in the classroom more these days."

He couldn't resist a grin. "They must have sealed the windows or nailed the desks to the floor."

"No, they got me an assistant, so the classroom is never unsupervised anymore."

"That was probably a wise decision."

"Mr. Aylward, I'm sure, from remembering your lack of enthusiasm for the finer points of algebra, that you didn't call just to chat."

He did recall her as being very direct. "No, Ms. Frank, I do have a reason for calling." He paused. "Do you remember Margaret Stillman?"

"Of course, I do. Margaret was one of my finest students. I wrote letters of recommendation for her for a number of scholarships. As I recall, she got several."

"Do you know where she went to college?"

"She started out at KU, but the last time I heard from her, she was considering a transfer to Wichita or Hays, or even laying out a semester."

"Did she say why?"

"Not in so many words. May I ask why you are so interested, Mr. Aylward?"

He felt like the same inept boy he had been in her class. "I'm sorry, Ms. Frank. I'm afraid I'm asking in an official capacity." He cleared his throat. "I'm with the City Police Department, and we're investigating Margaret's murder."

"Murder?" she gasped. "Margaret's dead?"

He should have tried to soften it a little. "Yes. She was using her middle name and married name of Delia Enfield—"

"The woman found a few days ago with her throat slashed?" Before he could respond, she went on. "Poor, poor Margaret. I was afraid that she was in with a bad crowd."

His pulse sped up. "Can you fill me in, Ms. Frank?"

"I guess I wouldn't be betraying a confidence, since the person who could be embarrassed is now dead." He heard her pause, and her voice sounded distant, as if she were talking to herself. "It's so hard to believe." Then her voice resumed its professional briskness. "She did quite well at KU the first three semesters, but then in her fourth, she fell in with some students and teachers who believed they could learn more and open up the mind if they enhanced its performance with chemicals."

"She got into the drug scene?" It didn't jive with the Margaret he remembered.

"Not the sleazy kind you see on TV. Or in your work." She stopped, then plunged ahead. "These were serious scientists, or so they seemed to think, trying to further work on the human mind and its capabilities. Then one of the professors took an interest in Margaret. She thought he was grooming her as a protégé, but I think he had ambitions that were more carnal for Margaret. She—" Ms. Frank stopped as if trying to gather her thoughts.

"Do you know the names of any of these people?"

"Margaret wrote me some letters that might have some of the names in them, but… It's been nearly ten years, Mr. Aylward. I receive a lot of correspondence from former students."

He bet all the letters were neatly filed according to a very orderly system. "I'm sure you do, Ms. Frank. Is there any chance you could find some of those letters from Margaret?"

"If I had a few days, I'm sure I could."

"Why don't I plan on coming to Homedale on Friday? Would that give you enough time?"

"I should think it would." He could almost hear her mind finger through the files. "Do you want to just come by my house?"

"I can do that. About ten?"

63

"That would be fine." She hesitated. "I really hope that some of this information will help you catch the brute that murdered her." Another pause. "Such a waste. See you Friday at ten, Mr. Aylward."

He hung up and tapped his pencil on the desk. With two people to interview and some promising leads, he could definitely justify a trip to Homedale. "Hey, Del, want to see where I grew up on Friday? It's like traveling through a time warp, and we can spend a week or two there in an afternoon."

"Friday?" Bates swiveled in his chair. "I can't Friday. I have to go to Wichita for a checkup with the dermatologist." Bates had had a small skin cancer removed two years ago; he never missed the precautionary checkup. "Sounds like I'll be missing a hell of a trip."

"If I can get enough leads on this trip, I may never have to go back."

"Don't you still have family there, boy?"

Scott shook his head. "No, my brothers never came back home after college. Dad died while I was still in high school, and mom has moved in with my oldest brother." He shrugged. "No need to go home. 'Home is where the heart is.' At least that's what they say."

"They do, do they?" Bates glanced at his watch. "I think home is where your dinner waits, and mine is waiting there now." He rose from his chair. "See you after lunch, rookie."

"Sure." Lunch didn't sound good to Scott yet. He wandered into the break room to grab some peanut butter crackers from the vending machine, but a couple of the clerks had heated up something that left a foul odor wafting throughout the room, so he headed outside for some air. It wasn't really fresh air, though. Humidity had moved in from an approaching storm front, forming an inversion layer that trapped the city's exhaust fumes near the ground. Between the smog, the smell of the fresh asphalt being poured on the parking lot across the street, and the stench of the soybean meal being processed into food additives at a manufacturing plant upwind of the Law Enforcement Center, Scott almost lost his coffee.

Food of some sort might be the best solution for him. He headed for his truck. Spicy Thai food should either kill him or cure him. He checked his cell phone as he walked across the parking lot. No calls or texts from Rica. She was genuinely pissed this time. He thought about sending an "I love you" text, but on second thought, no news was good news. No sense interrupting a cool down. He unlocked his truck and turned on the air full-blast. Yes, food was the best idea at the moment.

Chapter 13

Though Scott got home on time Thursday night, a note from Rica told him she was at a movie with another nurse. She said good night and shut the bedroom door when the movie ended, so he spent another night on the couch.

Now, as Scott rolled into Homedale at 9:30 Friday morning after an hour's drive, old elms, with the occasional cottonwood or maple, made a cool tunnel of the town's main street. The day promised to be a real July scorcher, but he rolled down the window of the unmarked Taurus anyway, only to be hit in the face by a ninety-degree blast. Determined to soak up the ambiance that he swore he didn't miss, he left the window down, but turned the air up high. He adjusted the vents to pour cool on his face.

There was the old Vencel place, once the fanciest house in town, now a fading apartment building, missing a couple of iron picket panels along one side of the yard, with a motorcycle parked on the expansive porch. Then came the "hacienda," a Spanish-style home that didn't fit the Midwest-gothic of the town's beginnings when it went up in the Forties. Restored to near-new splendor, the house didn't look so out of place now, with sprawling ranch-style houses tucked in among the two-story homes. He slowed as he came to Delia's house, more a story and a half than a full-fledged two-story home. If he recalled correctly from high school, and he hadn't paid her much attention then, it was neat, white-painted with beds of colorful flowers. Now, though it was still white, it needed a coat of paint, and no flowers grew in the yard.

The trees gave way to big brick buildings as he entered the two blocks of the business district. Attempts to refurbish the downtown led to small trees surrounded by brick footings planted in the sidewalks. At least a fourth of the buildings stared at him with empty windows, and there was a gap where two buildings had burned down the year he graduated. A gazebo and some flowers anchored that space, as if to say it was planned. On the corner of Main and Elm, the drugstore/mercantile appeared to be in operation, though a sign in the door stated "Closed." He turned right on Elm, heading north toward the "suburbs" where Ms. Frank lived. The door to the newspaper office next to the mercantile stood open. He stared at it a minute; the last he remembered, an eight-county conglomerate printed the local paper two counties away, adding local school sports and club information with the regional ads and obituaries. Maybe someone was turning the paper office into a trendy restaurant or antique store.

Two blocks before he hit the new section of town, he slowed again past his old home. He purposely kept his heart still as a rock in his chest as he surveyed the lines of the house. It had a two-story center section, holding the living and dining room on the first floor and two bedrooms on the second. An addition to the south housed the kitchen, while a smaller one to the north joined the house with a partially enclosed carport and held what used to be a utility room of sorts. His mother's favorite rose bush near the mailbox showed a few faded blooms. By the garage, the tree where he had built himself a swing and a fort still stood. The yard needed mowing, and he suppressed a surge of defiance as his memory heard his oldest brother berating him for needing a reminder of his duty to mow it. He pressed the accelerator and the peninsula of a plowed wheat field interceded between his memories and his mission. A couple of acres of farm ground, and he entered the "suburbs," a few blocks of homes built at various times during the past forty years.

He turned left on Rosewood and, five houses down, pulled into the driveway of a tidy rambler. A tangle of cottonwoods behind the houses indicated that a stream meandered where an alley might have been and was the reason for the cul-de-sac another half-block down. The front door opened as he stepped from the car. He didn't have time for the stretch his muscles wanted; he grabbed his notebook and strolled up the curving, edged sidewalk to the porch.

"Good morning, Mr. Aylward," Ms. Frank greeted him.

"Good morning, Ms. Frank." He paused to click the lock on the city car, though he knew it would be safe here. "Looks like it's gonna be a hot one."

"Yes, it does." She closed the door behind him. "Would you like a glass of iced tea?"

"That would be nice," he soaked up the dark cool of the house. "Ms. Frank, you haven't aged much since I graduated." Though her auburn hair showed more gray now that she had cut it shorter, otherwise, she looked like he remembered.

She laughed, something he never recalled hearing in school. "There wasn't much to make me age after your class graduated, Mr. Aylward."

He hunched his shoulders. "I guess we were pretty rowdy."

She laughed again as he followed her to a dining table set before an expanse of windows that looked out over the lush yard rolling out to the undergrowth next to the stream. She poured iced tea from a pitcher on the table into glasses that were already waiting there. She handed him a glass and then sat in the chair facing the kitchen. "You really weren't that bad, Mr. Aylward." She looked out over the yard. "Actually, the newer classes make me think every year of retiring."

"I can understand that." The juvenile officers told him horror stories more often than he wanted to hear them. "Did you find the letters from Margaret?"

She picked up a stack of papers beside the pitcher. "Right here, Mr. Aylward." She handed them to him. "They thinned out a bit after the first few months." She looked down at her hands. "Most of them do."

He glanced at her, for the first time considering how it would feel to get attached to a group of students only to lose contact with them every four years. Teaching must be harder than he thought in a lot of ways. "I can imagine." He skimmed the first letter, a chatty note about classes and dorms.

"I also included my responses to her," Ms. Frank offered. "I compose the letters on my computer, so I don't tell them the same things over and over." She looked out the window again. "Each year there are a half-dozen or so that stay in touch for a semester or two."

He ruffled quickly through the letters until they started to take on a darker tone. "This is the one where she started in with the bad crowd?"

Slipping on a pair of reading glasses from the table, she glanced at the letter. "Yes, and then she stopped in to see me when she came home for spring break that year." She fingered the letter gently. "She was quite disillusioned by the time the semester ended, even talked about going to cosmetology school instead of psychology."

He skimmed through this letter and the next. He looked up at Ms. Frank. "She doesn't mention any names."

Ms. Frank shook her head. "And she didn't when she talked to me, either." She reached for a notepad on the kitchen counter behind her. "But because I know people there, I put two and two together, and came up with some names."

"Always comes back to math, doesn't it?" He grinned as she handed him a sheet from the notepad.

"Always, Mr. Aylward." She pointed out the names with a pencil. "Dr. Athens was the head of the psychology department when she was there, but he retired five or six years ago, and moved to Montana." She went on down the list. "Mr. Denton graduated two years after Delia dropped out—I have no idea where he went after that, but I'm sure the school would." She paused, tapping the last name with her pencil. "But I think it was the graduate teaching assistant who got her in deepest." She leaned back. "His name was Robert Vanderwort. I couldn't track him down."

"May I have the list?" She had certainly given him more than he expected.

She nodded. "The letters, too. I made copies for myself."

He glanced down at the list. "Do you know what happened to the kids she hung out with?"

"The girls in the group home all either moved back with their families or moved on in the system. She never mentioned staying in touch with them, though I guess it's possible."

"What about Kyle?"

"Kyle was her best friend from elementary school on, but his family moved away the summer before his senior year." She shook her head. "That poor boy had an uphill battle ahead of him."

"How so?"

"He was gay, or at least appeared to be, and that didn't sit well with most of the folks around here. I think that's why his family moved."

"Did she stay in touch with him?"

"I'm sure she did, but she never mentioned him much."

"Do you know where he moved to?"

"No, I'm afraid I don't. He didn't take much math, mostly music and art classes."

"Thank you, Ms. Frank." He stood to leave. "You have given me a lot to go on. I'm very grateful."

"Just find her killer, Mr. Aylward." She rose to see him to the door. "That will be repayment enough for me."

Chapter 14

The car he'd heard roll into Ms. Frank's driveway belonged to a man who was applying some chemical to the shrubbery surrounding the house. Scott assumed it was a handyman or lawn service, but Ms. Frank walked to the man and gave him a quick kiss on the lips. "Welcome back, honey."

Shocked at this further evidence of humanity from someone he had assumed was celibate, Scott checked his watch while walking to the car from Ms. Frank's front door. Eleven-thirty. It would be at least three hours before he could talk to Dean. His stomach rumbled; the only thing he grabbed on the way out of town was the department car and some bad coffee. He could catch some lunch and read through all the letters more carefully, make some notes, maybe find someone else who knew what turns Delia's life had taken since Homedale.

He backed the car out of Ms. Frank's driveway, reviewing his lunch options. The grain elevator/gas station/convenience store near the highway would be fast, probably tasteless, and crowded with more people than he cared to have looking over his shoulder while he read. It was too hot to grab food and eat in the park, which only consisted of a single city block, a shelter house, and a tennis court.

There was Buddy's at the north end of the two-block main street, a burger and beer joint, with the emphasis on the beer, a cavernous dark room with plywood floors and walls, where covering the bathroom walls with corrugated tin constituted a major upgrade. The burgers were good, but better than the company.

The third option hadn't existed when he grew up there. Debbie's Diner sported blue checked curtains and a neatly painted doorway across the street from the mercantile. He decided to risk the unknown.

The ceiling fans washed cool air over him the instant he stepped inside. His nagging hunger moved up a notch to raging as he smelled fried chicken, with a hint of apple pie wafting around the room. The only waitress in the place, a dark blonde who could have been anywhere from 28 to 48, nodded at him. "Sit anywhere you like." She smiled as she followed him to a table in the corner away from the door, but next to a window. "You beat the crowd."

He opened the menu as she placed a big glass of ice water on the table for him. "Do you have a really big lunch crowd?"

"Comes in waves." She shrugged. "Farmers whose wives work come in early for coffee and breakfast, then the retirees show up and stay till about ten." She waited while he studied the menu. "Lunch bunch starts trickling in about now and may run till two. Then the after-school crowd hits, and suppertime starts about five-thirty. We close at eight."

"You work every shift?" He wavered between the meatloaf and the fried chicken. Though the chicken fried steak sounded good, too.

"Some days." She looked up when another customer entered the restaurant. "My sisters and I own and run this place. Be right back."

She approached the customer, no one he recognized, but then the town and its inhabitants had changed as much as he had since he left. "Hey, Al." She poured another glass of water. "What'll ya have today?"

"What's the special, Debbie?" He headed toward a table near Scott, but a row away from the windows.

"Same as it is every Friday, Al. Meatloaf."

"Better give me the chicken fry, then. No one else can make meatloaf like Sarah could."

She touched his shoulder as she set his water on the table. "I know, Al." She turned back toward Scott. "Have you decided what you want yet?"

"What do you recommend?" Scott tried to ignore Al watching him, even though he reflexively noted a description: six foot, two-thirty, blue, gray and balding, fifty-five to sixty.

"Special's always good."

"Never had a bad meal in here," Al offered. "Just go for whatever you're hungriest for."

Scott hadn't asked for the recommendation, but he should have expected it in a town as small as Homedale. He closed his menu. "I'll try the fried chicken, then."

Debbie picked up his menu. "Coming right up. What would you like to drink?"

"How about iced tea?"

"In just a jiffy." When she returned with his tea, she set a cup of coffee on Al's table, without him ordering it.

"You passin' through?" Al offered, sipping his coffee.

"Not really." Scott laid the letters on the table, hoping the view of him working would discourage Al. "Had some business here."

"Good, we need some business."

Scott was reading the letters, when Al interrupted again. "Gonna be a record-breaking hot day today."

"Looks like." Scott bent over the papers once more.

"Hey, Mac." Al spoke, this time addressing a man wearing blue jeans and a seed company baseball cap. Scott looked up, recognizing Ed McNeal, President and General Manager of the local co-op, though grayer and heavier than Scott remembered.

"Hey, Al." He pulled out the chair opposite Al and sat. "You gettin' that old press operating again?"

"I don't know." Debbie placed a large cola in front of Ed. "It may be too inefficient to deal with. I might keep it as a museum piece and invest in a nice computer printer."

Mac shrugged. "Whatever. It's just good to have another business in town." He gulped his soda, no straw for him, and swiveled his head around the room. His gaze landed on Scott. "Aren't you one of the Aylward boys?"

Scott was deep into the second letter. "What?"

Mac turned his chair toward Scott. "Aren't you one of the Aylward boys?" He tilted his head. "I mean, you bear a lot of resemblance to Dan Aylward."

Scott swallowed hard. "Dan was my dad."

Mac stood and thrust out his hand. "Fine man he was." Scott stood and let Mac envelop his hand in a huge paw. "You must be the baby."

Great, thirty-two years old, and they still think I'm

a baby. "Yeah," he nodded. "I'm Scott."

"How's your mom gettin' along now?"

"She's living with my oldest brother Dennis in Ohio." He cleared his throat. "She's doing fine now that her hip has healed."

"Good." Mac stepped back to the table with Al as Debbie placed the meatloaf special in front of him. "That house and ground was just too much for her to handle alone." He resumed his seat. "Al, this boy was once one of our fastest running backs here. His oldest brother was a basketball letterman and his middle brother was a track star." He cut off a bite of the meatloaf. "You know, Scott, Al here is from New York City."

Scott pulled out the department laptop and plugged in the air card, hoping the conversation would end. He wanted to get busy researching the names Ms. Frank had given him.

Mac kept talking. "Yep, Al married a gal from here, and finally brought her home."

"Home to die." Al's comment was so quiet that probably only Scott heard him. Scott looked toward him, but Al had his head bent over his plate, moving the green beans around with his fork.

"What're you doing with your life now, Scott?"

"I'm a detective with City PD."

"You workin' today?"

"Doing some follow-up to an investigation."

"Nothing happens here, so we don't need a detective. Sheriff's office is our PD. Makes us one safe community. In fact, it's part of our sales pitch on TV: so safe we don't need a police department. Brings us a few new folks." Mac went rolling on, giving a complete rundown of the changes since Scott's mother sold her house and moved away. All Mac required of Scott was the occasional nod or "Uh-huh."

Debbie brought his meal, and Scott concentrated on eating the excellent fried chicken and even better home-made rolls. When Debbie came back to refill his tea, he requested another roll, though he knew he'd have to run an extra half-mile to mitigate this meal. It tasted surprisingly similar to the meals he'd eaten as a boy, even though he didn't want to admit that he had missed such food.

Finally, Mac stood and Debbie brought him another cola in a to-go cup. He left a ten on the table. "See ya later, Debbie, Al. Good to see you again, Scott."

He left the restaurant, shaking hands and greeting people as he went. Scott shook his head. "He should run for office."

"Oh, he did." Debbie took his plate. "He's mayor now." She picked up Al's plate, barely touched. "Sorry, Al."

He patted her hand. "It's okay, Debbie." He sighed and looked out the window. "It gets easier all the time, but I'm not over it yet, either."

"You never will be, Al, but it'll get to be something you can live with."

Debbie walked away, and Al sat with his coffee, looking at something far beyond the window he stared through. Scott tried to concentrate on his Google searches, but something about Al got to him. He looked up, and his movement intercepted Al's gaze.

"New York City, eh?"

Al focused on him and smiled. "Not originally,

started in Connecticut and worked my way to the *Times*."

"*New York Times*, I assume, not the *Homedale Times*."

Al nodded. "Reporter, then editing, then management."

"And somewhere along the way you met a girl from Kansas."

Al picked up his coffee cup and moved to Scott's table. "She came to New York to dance and act, but she needed a part-time job." He leaned back, deep in his memories. "Those were the days before computers, so she wound up in our typing pool. I eventually assigned everyone else's stories to other gals, so she typed only mine." He sighed. "Then I made it legal and permanent." He ran his fingers around the rim of the cup. "We had two boys, both in college now, and life was good."

"Then she got sick?" Scott spoke softly.

Al nodded. "We came back most summers and holidays for visits, and I talked about retiring here and starting my own paper, but the timing was never right. Then when they discovered the cancer, time seemed too short." Debbie brought a pot to refill Al's cup, and Scott turned over the cup that sat at his plate. She filled his, too. "It was too short. She fought for two years, but lost her battle a year ago. Year ago next Thursday."

"That's hard."

"Yeah." Al looked up to meet his gaze. "You said you were with PD, following up on an investigation?"

"Murder of Delia Enfield." Scott's instinctive wariness around the press rose up.

"How is that connected to Homedale?" Al's

practiced nose for news made him ask.

"She grew up here."

"I didn't know that. It didn't say it in any of the newspaper articles." Al shook his head. "Reporters not doing their jobs thoroughly enough."

"Well, we didn't put out any info the family hadn't already given them. She wasn't born here."

"So you are tracking the hometown girl's roots within your own?"

"Not really, just following up on people who may have known her and where she went after high school." He didn't want to reveal anything. "Did I hear Mac say you were working with old presses?"

"Yeah, I bought the old *Monitor* building, including all the equipment. I plan to put out a small free paper, plus print some small jobs for folks around town. Something to keep me busy." Al leaned back in his chair. "You got some time before your next appointment?"

Scott hesitated. Al knew enough about investigation to know that he would have left the restaurant after lunch unless he had a reason to stay around. Yet, everyone seemed to like Al; maybe he could be a source of information. "Yeah, I've got an hour or so." He would meet Dean after his shift ended at the factory.

"Why don't we go over to my office then?"

"Okay." He could follow up the computer search later. Al might provide further information.

Debbie brought their lunch checks. They both paid her with ten-dollar bills, telling her, "No change."

"Debbie's nice," Scott said as the door closed on the restaurant.

"Yeah." Al led the way diagonally across the street. "Her sister married the oldest Ronson boy a couple of years ago, and within a year, the other two sisters moved here and opened the restaurant." He paused at the curb. "No one in Homedale crosses at the crosswalks." He walked into the empty street. "Cause there ain't none." They reached the other side without encountering a car. "Listen to me; I sound like a native."

"Not quite. I can still hear the east coast in your vowels."

"When we first moved here, we tried walking for Sarah's health." His voice shook a little over her name. "Took forever to get three blocks, because people kept stopping us to ask if we needed a ride, and then hung out to chat for a few minutes."

"That's Homedale." There were advantages to living somewhere that news traveled by osmosis, and everyone knew intimate details of each other's lives. And there were disadvantages.

Al took a few seconds to unlock the door of the old newspaper office. He pushed the heavy door inward to reveal a dark interior, with the original oak railings separating the customer service area from the massive presses. "I thought I wanted to get the old presses rolling again, maybe do some artsy printing." He opened the "gate" in the railing to stand before the first of the machines. "But after tinkering some, I don't think I have the skills." He perched on a stool beside it. "Nor do I want to work that hard."

Scott stepped forward, touching the iron side of the beast. "What's wrong with it?" When his dad still farmed the family's original homestead, Scott had assisted with keeping their ancient equipment running.

Al glanced at him. "It won't go. Sounds like it's jammed up somewhere." He pressed the switch. The machine groaned, started to cycle, and then stopped to groan some more.

Scott listened and looked over the press from several angles. "I think this cylinder is in backwards." He pointed to the part he meant.

Al shrugged. "Could be. They didn't come with instructions."

"Shut it off and I'll see if I can switch it." Thirty minutes later, his hands black with oil and ink, Scott hit the switch again, and the press clattered continuously, but didn't groan or stop. He had also shared the general outline of his childhood and his father's death with Al, and learned more about Al's career. Al must have been a good reporter to draw that much information from him. Not even Bates knew that much.

"Hot damn, can I put you on retainer?" Al handed him a towel, and then led him to the restroom at the back of the shop.

Scott washed his hands, splashing some of the cool water on his face, as the building wasn't air conditioned. He dried his hands and pulled out his business card. "You can give me a call if it seizes up again." He hung the towel back up. "Or if you hear any word in town about Delia's past."

Al cocked his head to the side. "You think people would tell a stranger anything?"

"They like you, I could tell from the restaurant." He tightened his tie. "And marrying a hometown girl makes you one of us. But one they have to explain everything to."

Chapter 15

Seated in the department car on the sand road that served as a street in front of Dean's house and working on the laptop, Scott found three promising addresses for Delia's former professors and grad students by the time he heard tires on the gravel of Dean's driveway. He glanced at the time on the computer. Three thirty-seven. Dean got off work at three, and the plant was only eight blocks from his house. It wasn't like he could have been caught in rush-hour traffic. Homedale only had rush-minute at its worst. Dean stepped from the four-wheel drive pickup with a "big gulp" cup in his hand. "Hey, Scott." He came abreast of the city car.

"Hey, Dean." Scott nodded at the cup. "You always go by the co-op on your way home?"

"When it's this hot, I do." He took a long pull from the straw. "Although sometimes on Fridays, I go to Buddy's instead." He tugged the International Harvester hat from his head and ran his fingers through his damp hair. His hairline was higher than in high school. "Come on inside where it's cooler."

"Sure." Scott followed him inside a nice manufactured home built, Scott suspected, at the plant in the city.

Hanging his hat on a peg, Dean crossed the living room to a well-worn recliner. Just before he dropped into it, he looked up at Scott. "Would you like something to drink?"

Scott shook his head and took a seat on the couch that matched the recliner. "Had a big glass of tea before I pulled in here."

"Okay." Dean settled into the recliner and leaned back. "Damn, I'm tired." He stretched. "Summer is the worst, no air-conditioning in the shop."

"I can imagine. I did six years in uniform, wearing a ballistics vest." It had only been last summer that he was still on patrol. "Like living inside a roasting pan in an oven."

Dean laughed. "Sounds miserable."

"Pretty much." He waited, and Dean filled the silence.

"So, have you got any leads on Margaret's murder?" Other than taking another long draw from the cup, Dean hadn't moved since leaning back in the recliner.

"Not really. I was hoping you could help me."

"What can I do?" He turned his head toward Scott, still resting it on the recliner. He truly looked as tired as he said he was.

"Do you remember who she used to hang with?"

Shaking his head, Dean looked up at the ceiling. "I'm ashamed to admit it, but I never paid her much attention. You know, captain of the football team is above the geeks and all that. Plus Janice pretty much took up all of my spare time and attention. And then some." He paused to smile as if he had dredged up a pleasant memory. "After the cheerleader incident, I noticed her if she crossed my path, and the fag, too, but otherwise, she was as memorable to me as the desks and lockers."

Scott believed him; he was pretty self-centered in high school. Had he been a better athlete or scholar, he probably would have been even more so. "Do you remember anything about the boy she was friends with?"

"Don't even remember his name. We always just called him 'the fag.'" He laced his fingers behind his head. "Another thing I'm not so proud of. I still don't like fags, but I got to be friends with a couple guys on the track team at K-State, before I found out they were gay. By the time I found out, we were too good of friends to stop. Once they came out to me, we had some talks, and I understood that poor kid had enough problems without me and my buddies making his life hell."

"His name was Kyle," Scott said softly. "Kyle Dane."

"He still here?"

"I heard his family moved away the year before he graduated."

"Hope he got treated better wherever he moved to."

"Me, too." Once he knew what was going on when the group of football players attacked the boy, he should have intervened before Delia did, but by that time, his habit of staying anonymous had become second nature. "You were on day shift Tuesday, right?"

"Yup, same as today. If I remember right, Tuesday was even hotter than today." He rubbed his eyes.

"What time did you get home?"

"About the same as today, though I stayed at the co-op a little longer and had some ice cream to cool off before I came on home." He glanced at the clock on the wall across from his chair. "Kids come home from the pool about four, so I can ramrod them to finish their chores and start supper before Jan gets home."

As if on cue, laughter and shrieks sounded just before the back door opened and a herd of children clattered into the living room. "Hey, Dad, can Shane and Michael stay for supper?"

Dean grinned, though his voice sounded stern. "You know the drill, kids. They have to call their folks and ask and then your mom or I have to confirm that they said yes."

The tallest boy, a childish version of his father, glanced at Scott, then turned his attention back to his father. "OK. Their parents aren't home till 5:30. Can they stay and then call and ask?" The rest of the children eyed Scott.

Dean sighed. "Sure. As long as you all go out and make sure the bucket calves and the dogs have water. And check the garden for ripe tomatoes and cucumbers."

"Sure." The whole herd traipsed back out the door through which they had entered.

Dean laughed and faced Scott. "I'll have to double check and send them back out at least three times before they get it done." He shrugged. "But what else do you do?"

"Sounds like a thankless job you love."

"It is." Dean looked down at his hands. "They are a lot of work, never a day off from parenting, but I wouldn't trade a minute of it." He laughed again. "Well, maybe I'd trade a long weekend of it for a weekend in Vegas, but you know what I mean."

Scott wondered if he'd ever get the chance to try the experience. "Yeah." He reminded himself of his reason for coming. "So the kids were here by four on Tuesday night?"

"Yeah," Dean answered and then stopped. "Wait, was it Tuesday or Wednesday? There was one day this week that they went out to Jan's sister's farm and 'helped' bale hay and played in the pond there." He stared off into space, mumbling as he tried to align his days. "Today's Friday, and yesterday, they were home by the time I got here, but Wednesday was peaceful, and I got a nap in before Jan got home, so it must have been Wednesday that they went to Sally's. Tuesday, that was the night we had a 4-H meeting, so they had to hustle with chores, we went to the meeting and then to Buster's for burgers. Monday was threatening rain and lightning, so they were home by the time I got here."

"Who did Jan's sister marry?" Jan's sisters, both older and younger, were all cheerleaders, and thus beyond his reach, so he hadn't paid much attention to them in high school.

"Dan Rayburn." Dean grinned. "I'll give you the number so you can check with her."

"I guess I'm not so subtle."

"Not as subtle as you used to be on the offensive line."

Chapter 16

Scott left Homedale with a sense of escape. Dean's sister-in-law confirmed that the kids had "helped" with the hay on Wednesday night. He had interviewed Dean's boss, learning that Dean's alibi was a good one; the boss worked beside him on the shift and could account for no more missing time than a few minutes in the bathroom. The only way Dean could have made it to the city, kidnapped and killed Delia, dumped her body and been back in two hours would have been if he had perfected time travel. And Dean's major at K-State had been ag science, not physics. His gut had told him that Dean wasn't guilty even before he rolled into Homedale, but he needed to be thorough.

One thing still puzzled him, though, and that was Kyle's life since Homedale. No one seemed to know where his family moved when they left, so that would take some legwork. He was mulling over how to begin the trace when his phone buzzed to alert him to an incoming text. He glanced up the highway; no visible oncoming traffic and no one in front of him. He risked grabbing the phone to glance at the message. From Rica, it simply asked, "When will you be home?"

That sounded innocent enough. He remembered the quick shop a couple miles ahead. He could use a bathroom break and another iced tea. He pulled into the parking lot and texted back. "4 or 5, can make earlier if needed." Slipping the phone back in his pocket, he entered the store and took care of his business. The phone buzzed again as he stepped outside.

"I'll have dinner ready at 5:30. OK?"

He let his breath out in relief. Hopefully, the recent winter of their relationship had given way to spring. "Wonderful. Need anything on the way home?" He could at least offer to be helpful.

"Not now. Let u know."

He began to whistle a tune he didn't even know as he pulled onto the highway. Back at the station, he turned in the car and jogged up the stairs to his office to write up a quick report on his interviews today and make some notes for follow-up on Saturday. He found a note from Bates on his desk: "Funeral tomorrow at eleven. Meet here at ten-thirty. We interview Moran at three."

Good, he had a hunch Moran would provide some interesting conversation. He finished the reports on today's interviews in record time. Then, because even he couldn't read his notes when they got cold, he typed up the miscellaneous notes he had made. They didn't seem to lead anywhere now, but might provide a start to a different direction on the investigation later. Then he jotted down some potential questions for Moran.

Finally, he plugged "Kyle Dane" into the national sexual predator database. Sometimes men with confused sexuality act out in inappropriate ways, and Kyle might have gone that direction, though Scott doubted it. The boy was too gentle in high school, but enough beatings like he got then could have changed him.

He opened another window on the computer; with

so many entries, the sexual predator database search would take a while to run. In this, he tried a white pages search for Kyle's name. Only two records came up, and further checking revealed that one was over sixty-five and the other was deceased. Finally, the sexual predator search flashed "finished." Kyle's name had not come up.

At four-thirty, he texted Rica. "Need me to pick up anything on the way home?" When there was no request from Rica by five, he left the office. On impulse, he swung into Dillon's on the way home to pick up a bouquet of pink roses. He hoped they kept her mood forgiving.

Scott opened the door to the scent of lasagna, his favorite of Rica's many culinary treats. "That smells good." He hung his cap and jacket on the peg by the door. He slipped his holster off his belt and laid it on the small console table under the coat rack. He crossed the living room, noting that Rica had completely cleaned and straightened the living room and lit candles. "Are we having company?"

"Don't we deserve to be treated like company sometimes?" She turned from the counter to greet him, her gaze falling on the roses he held. "My, these are pretty."

He leaned forward to kiss her lightly. "Pretty roses for a lady who is even prettier."

She returned his kiss, not so lightly. "Scott, I'm sorry. I was a little harsh with you after the party."

He ran his hands up her smooth back. "No, I should apologize. I was way out of line." He kissed her cheek, then continued down her neck. "I'm sorry. I knew better than to drink more than one."

She smiled. "I think you could have handled two." She stroked his cheek. "I didn't notice until later that someone was always putting another drink in front of you."

He laughed, relieved to see something besides anger in her eyes. "Probably someone with stock in a brewery." He slid his hands down to her hips. "I don't even know how many I had."

"Shall we just agree it was too many?"

"Agreed."

She moved toward the stove. "Still, we need to talk."

His stomach clenched. "Okay." He dropped his hands to his sides. "What about?"

She came back to hug him. "Just about us in general. Where we're going. How we're getting there."

He tried to relax in her arms. "About having kids?"

"That could be part of it." Once again, she stepped out of his arms. "We'll chat while we eat?"

He grinned, though he didn't feel it. "Then what can I do to help get dinner on the table. That smells too good to wait."

She smiled. "I knew you'd like it." She handed him a basket of breadsticks.

"Just don't expect a lot of talking until the first plate is empty."

At that, she laughed. "I didn't."

But they did make small talk during the first plate, chatting about the day's happenings for both of them. The conversation continued through the second helping. Rica stopped with seconds, but Scott reached for another serving. "I shouldn't have thirds after the meal I had for lunch." He spooned more lasagna and salad on his plate.

"What did you have?" Rica nibbled on a piece of lettuce.

He looked at her sheepishly. "Fried chicken."

She raised an eyebrow. "You'll need a good workout tonight."

"I was going to run—" He stopped as he realized what kind of workout she had in mind. "Don't think I'll need to run, then." He took her hand. "I love you, Rica." Except for the prospect of talking about "us," the evening so far was about as perfect as they had ever had.

She grasped his hand. "And I love you, too, Scott." She put her other hand over his. "So much that it hurts to see how we've changed."

"Changed?" He didn't think he'd changed that much. She had started to nag him occasionally, but he usually deserved it.

"Well, maybe we haven't so much changed our behavior as we have the way we look at it."

"What do you mean?" Now, three servings of lasagna didn't feel so good locked in a taut stomach.

"Scott, you are 'messy.' I knew that when I married you, thought it was kind of cute, but now it irritates me. Instead of cute, I guess I see it as irresponsible or lazy." She kept hold of his hands.

"But—"

She patted his hand. "I know you don't mean to be. It's just part of who you are. That's why you lose track of time and are late coming home from work or get sidetracked on a different task when you are trying to work on another." She paused. "You probably have attention deficit disorder."

"Maybe I do." He shook his head slowly. "But Rica, my being messy and forgetful is not intentional."

"I know, *mijo*, and I understand, I really do." She scooted her chair to face him more directly. "But, even when I understand, sometimes it irritates me."

"Well—"

"And I know I can be a real *cabrona* sometimes, when I nag you."

"Well, Rica, I know how ambitious you are, and how organized and disciplined, and that's part of what I love about you."

"And the fact that you aren't is what attracted me to you, Scott." She ducked her head. "Maybe somewhere deep inside, I thought I could change you, fix you."

He chuckled, though he didn't feel it. "A wise friend once told me that a man marries a woman hoping she'll never change, and a woman marries a man hoping to change him into the man he ought to be."

She smiled. "Your friend was indeed very wise."

His grip on her hands tightened. "So what are we going to do about it?"

She stared into his eyes for so long that he feared his heart would stop. "Keep working on it, *mijo*. Keep working on us."

He got up from his chair to take her in his arms. "I will do everything in my power to change my messy ways, Rica." She melted into him. "I love you, Rica. It took me so long to find you, I couldn't imagine living without you." Her non-verbal reply lasted a couple of hours and left the dishes to fend for themselves.

Later, when the dishes finally came to mind, they cleaned up the kitchen together, wearing only a pair of pajamas they shared between them. Scott rinsed and Rica loaded the dishwasher according to her own system.

"Rica," he began as he rubbed the plates with a soapy brush. "Do you ever think about your high school classmates?"

She stopped loading the dishwasher. "Of course I do. I work with Vanessa and four of my best friends go to church with us."

He rinsed another plate. "Oh, yeah. I forgot you grew up here." He handed it to her. "Do you think you'd stay in touch if you didn't live here?"

She put the plate in its place. "Probably not, except with Heather." She waited while he rinsed the glasses. "She's like a sister to me." She touched his shoulder. "Are you wanting to move away?" Glancing down at the beautiful face turned up to him, he thought he saw fear in her eyes.

"No, of course not." He gripped her hand to reassure her. "This is home now, and everything is going well for both of us on the job." A slight smile came to her delicious lips. "It's this case I'm working on. It's probably just a romantic notion from reading too many cop novels, but I can't seem to shake the feeling that the answer will come back to high school."

She stood on tiptoe to kiss his cheek. "You know, one advantage of being ADD is that you take in a tremendous amount of information without realizing it. The clue may be right in front of you."

"Well, if it is, it is well hidden." He rinsed the last casserole dish. "And Bates and I have to go to her funeral tomorrow and then interview her boss."

Rica closed the dishwasher and turned to face him.

"That's too bad."

"Yeah, I hate funerals, especially when I have to look at every one who goes as a suspect."

She grabbed his pajama pants. "I was thinking it was too bad we couldn't spend the morning in bed."

He placed a hand on either side of her. "I don't have to be at the office until ten-thirty." He leaned against her as her hands deftly untied the pajamas.

"We'll just have to make the most of the time we have then." Her lips met his as he lifted her to the counter.

Chapter 17

"I hate funerals," Bates muttered as he and Scott seated themselves in the back of the Methodist church. They were the first of the mourners to arrive, although the place was a bustle of activity as the funeral director and his staff arranged flowers, and the minister set out his Bible and a bottle of water. As soon as the family named a mortuary, the chief requested a photocopy of the funeral guest book. Scott knew that would provide hours of work winnowing through the names. Unless they could wring a confession out of Moran. Or someone else.

To engage himself until people began to arrive, Scott studied the architecture of the place. Classically appointed, with fluted columns and a two-story curved ceiling, the sanctuary boasted ornately carved wooden moldings around the altar, pulpit, and choir area. Technology intruded on the peaceful design with huge speakers hung from a massive iron rack bolted to the soaring ceiling. Viewing monitors for the choir were attached to one of the columns.

Beside him, Bates checked email on his cell phone, as few mourners had yet arrived. Though Scott tried to dodge the memories, they sneaked up on him, and he remembered his father's funeral. His dad would have considered it much dramatic foolishness taking time away from fields that needed planting.

Bates nudged his arm. "There's Shawna and Trish, and some of the other ladies from the office."

Scott looked up, glad to be distracted from his memories. "Bet Moran is happy the funeral is on a Saturday, so he doesn't have to close the office to avoid looking callous."

"Yeah, doubt he'd do that."

Mourner after mourner settled into the padded pews, occupying Scott's attention as he reviewed how the ones he recognized connected with Delia. He could identify less than half of them. Moran came out of the back of the church, probably having spoken to the family, and took a seat behind the family section.

Soon, the family, with Ellery Enfield carrying a cherubic, curly-haired toddler, filed into the reserved pews. A few more people entered the sanctuary, then the minister stepped to the lectern and the service began. Even from the back, they could hear Enfield's sobs over the minister's solemn voice.

Shawna went forward and spoke about the wonderful friend and co-worker Delia had been. Moran said a few words about her being a loyal employee with much potential. A woman introduced as a cousin of Enfield talked about her virtues as a mother. His shoulders shaking, Enfield held tight to the baby. Even if he had the gift for public speaking, he could not have made it to the podium, much less addressed the crowd. A woman whose quavering contralto made Scott wince sang "His Eye is on the Sparrow," and the minister concluded the service. He announced the cemetery where the graveside services would be held.

Bates and Scott scrambled out of their seats and stood discreetly to the side of the doors through which the mourners exited. Moran, Shawna, and the rest of the company entourage that they had interviewed glanced at them, but made no acknowledgement. It appeared all of the office staff had attended the funeral. Excluding the Moran staff and family, they had only a couple dozen mourners to track down. Ms. Frank nodded at Scott as she walked past, but said nothing. When everyone except the family had filed out, Bates and Scott headed to their car.

Though Bates had parked the sedan in the shade, 103 degrees made even shade hot. Bates started the car and rolled down the windows while they waited for the air conditioning to kick in. "In the movies, all they ever have is a graveside service, so we can be more discreet."

Scott fanned himself with the funeral program. "That's because the movies are always set in California." Finally, the air turned cool, and he rolled up the window. "They don't have our Midwestern sensibilities and ties to tradition. Or hundred degree summers."

"Right." Bates rolled up his window as well. "I forgot you're working on a Master's in psychology."

"Well, it made more sense than a Master's in physics." Scott adjusted his air vent for more flow. "Besides, I got a wife out of the deal."

Bates pulled into the end of the line. "By the way, did she forgive you yet?"

Scott yawned; there hadn't been much sleep last night. "Yeah, finally."

Bates glanced at him as they turned onto Main Street. "Hmmmm."

Not all of the Moran entourage accompanied Delia

to the cemetery. Just over a dozen people crowded into the shade of the tent as the minister said a few more words. Another half-dozen people hung back. The minister shook the hands of the family members. He paused to grip Enfield's shoulder, as the big man collapsed, sobbing, in the arms of an older woman. He patted the head of the baby and moved behind the family as most of the remaining mourners filed past. Some of the mourners drifted back to their cars rather than speak to the family. One slight young woman, wearing an old-fashioned hat with a veil, stood near a tree, watching the family, her shoulders shaking as if with sobs, before she turned and made her way to a small silver car. Chevy Cavalier, Scott noted, four-door. He couldn't see the plates.

Chapter 18

Charlotte Daniels twisted the key in the ignition with a hand that shook. She let go when the car started, adjusted the air vents, and turned on the air conditioner. She sat back in her seat, as the cooling air fanned the sweat on her brow and the tears on her cheeks. She pulled off her hat and dropped it in the passenger seat beside her purse.

The funeral, the simple oak casket even now being lowered into the ground—all of it still seemed surreal, like a bad horror movie she could walk out of into the light. She shuddered with sobs held deep inside her being. She couldn't collapse yet; she had seen the two men in cheap suits standing apart from the family and friends, much like she had, except that she would never wear anything as tacky as those suits. They had to be cops, and she didn't want to talk to them now. Or ever.

She put the car in gear and drove out of the cemetery. She threaded through traffic to a Sonic drive-in where she sat and ordered a raspberry tea. She glanced at the clock on the dashboard. She left the cemetery over twenty minutes ago. That should be enough time for everyone to have gone. She pulled away from the drive-in, and five minutes later parked her car in the same spot as before. She let it run and sipped her tea, as the cemetery workers took down the awning that covered Maggie's grave. They had already lowered the casket into the vault and sealed it. They put the awning and poles on a flatbed truck. Then, slowly, a backhoe crept up to the hole where Mags lay. The bucket grabbed a gulp of dirt, then drizzled it over the vault. Charlotte rolled down her window. Over the throaty rumble of the backhoe, she heard the clods of dirt hit the vault. Each ping shook her; each felt like a nail driving into her own coffin.

She put her hand on the passenger seat, then turned her gaze to it. A long, blonde hair clung to the headrest—Maggie's. She picked up the hair, wrapped it into a tiny coil, and placed it in her wallet in the same pocket that held the photo of her and Mags so many years ago.

The dam of reserve that held her tears back burst. So many years she had yearned to see her best friend again, kept apart by parents, distance, and her own fears. Then, by sheer chance, she had found her again, rediscovered their bond, and more. Now, after a few short weeks, it was gone for good. She let the tears flow for a few minutes, then realized that she no longer heard the backhoe. She looked up to see that the men had finished covering up Maggie's grave. Quickly, she wiped her eyes, for once not worried about running mascara, and left the cemetery before they could approach her.

Chapter 19

"Let's see, I had a meeting at the bank at ten, Rotary at lunch, then met a client at two, and was back at the office at four." Moran reconstructed the day Delia disappeared by referring to a detailed planner Scott recognized as an expensive status symbol. "What else do you need to know?" He clasped his hands on the table and gazed steadily at Bates.

"We'll need the name of who you met at the bank, some of the Rotarians who were at the lunch, and the client you met."

"Certainly." Moran turned to the back of the planner. Moran's suit easily cost more than Scott's entire wardrobe. Maybe Bates's, too. "I met with Warren Ochs at the bank, then we joined a meeting with Stanley Jones." He looked up at Bates. "The bank president."

"Yeah, I know," Bates said. "My wife's on the Chamber with him."

"Nice guy, isn't he?" Moran leaned back in the chair, relaxed.

"Ummm." Bates glanced at his notepad. "Ochs is head of the loan department, right?"

Moran sat forward. "Yes."

"Is your business in trouble, Mr. Moran?" It was Scott's turn to play "bad cop."

Moran studied him a second before responding.

"Every business needs capital to maintain cash flow." He looked toward Bates. "We're expanding, starting projects before we have others finished and paid for." He glanced back at Scott. "Business is good."

"What about the client you met with?" Bates pressed on.

"I'd rather not name the client." Moran looked down. "The client is not ready to go public with plans."

"Was that a female client, Mr. Moran?" Scott pressed on.

Moran shot Scott a look with daggers, but composed himself, and his voice was calm. "Yes, it was, Detective Aylward."

"We need to be able to verify that you were with her at the times you state, Mr. Moran."

Moran glanced at Bates, who nodded. "We do, Mr. Moran."

"Am I a suspect?"

"You are until we can verify your whereabouts between the time Delia left the office and we found her body."

A fine sheen of sweat broke out on Moran's upper lip.

"Where did you go after you left the office?" Scott took a different approach. Let him stew a little while.

Moran glanced at him. "I went to the gym, then went home." He looked down at the table. His shoulders sagged just enough to be noticeable. "My wife and I had a charity event at the country club. By the time I showered, it was time to leave, and we were there until eleven. Then we went home and to bed."

"Your wife can verify this?" Bates kept his eyes on his notepad. Scott knew they would also check with the gym.

Moran nodded. "You'll be talking to her, too?"

Scott shrugged. "Need to verify your story." He leaned forward so fast Moran's eyes widened. "Unless you have a confession to make?"

"N-no," Moran stammered. "You mean you really think I could have done that to Delia?" He shuddered. "Delia was a sweet gal, good worker. Why would I want to hurt her at all, much less brutally murder her?"

"You tell us." Bates looked up. "Maybe she wanted to stop her affair with you."

Moran's brow furrowed.

Scott spoke up. "Or maybe she threatened to tell your wife."

Moran looked down at his hands. "Look, my wife and I—" He took a deep breath and looked up at the ceiling. "My wife and I have an 'arrangement.'" He looked from Bates to Scott. "You know, the same old same old can get pretty boring for both of us. So we 'overlook' casual things." He paused as if he expected them both to agree.

"Not in my marriage," Bates stated.

"Maybe your wife isn't as bored as you think." Scott would never suggest such a thing to Rica. First of all, he loved her and wanted no other woman; second, she'd kill him.

Moran laughed. "She's the one suggested it. I know she's been sleeping with her golf instructor and the yard contractor and God knows how many others."

"What about you?"

"I find some entertainment." Moran folded his arms across his chest.

"With your employees who are recently divorced?"

Bates crossed his arms as well.

Moran glanced from Bates to Scott. "I've been known to try to cheer up a few of them."

"And if they don't like your form of moral support, they lose a job?" If moral fiber made the man, Sandy should treat Moran like she had treated Enfield.

Again, Moran looked from one to the other. "No, no. If they're not interested in 'extra-curricular,' I just let them know I care anyway."

"Are you this kind to the guys in your organization that get divorced?"

"I don't know." Moran leaned back. "Haven't had any of my department heads get divorced."

"So," Scott asked the question he had wanted to ask the moment Moran entered the room. "Was Delia interested or not?"

Moran sat up straight. "She was interested." He glanced again from Scott to Bates. "Took her a couple of weeks to decide to go through with it, but when she did—" He licked his lips. "When she did, wow. She wanted it a lot, whenever she didn't have her little girl. If she did, it was every time she went to make a bank deposit."

"Like she did the day she disappeared."

He blinked. "Yeah, I guess that's right."

"So why didn't you meet her that day?" Scott placed a hand on the table. "Or did you?"

"No, no, it's not like that." Moran's eyes were wide, his breathing fast. "She broke it off a couple of weeks ago, said she was a good girl, couldn't keep seeing a married man." He took a deep breath. "Then Tuesday, she asked me to meet her again when she made the bank deposit." He rolled his gaze toward the ceiling. "She was so aroused, almost frantic, but when we finished, she started crying and said it was wrong, it couldn't happen again." He sighed. "I told her it would be okay, I wouldn't pressure her, I'd try to stay out of her path, but she was pretty upset." He met Bates' eyes. "I made it a point not to go by her office on Wednesday, just to keep from upsetting her again. I accepted it was over."

"Or did you stay away from her office because you knew she wouldn't be there?" Scott fought to keep the anger from his voice.

Moran stared at him with a puzzled expression. "Knew she wouldn't be there? What do you mean, she wouldn't be there?" Sudden realization flashed through his eyes. "Oh, my God, she couldn't be there because she was already dead." His face turned pasty.

"Did you kill her, Mr. Moran?" Bates, stone-faced, pressured Moran.

"Of course not!" Moran's voice shook. "I may be an ass, but I'm not a killer." He glanced from Bates to Scott and back. "Look, when clients want to go hunting or fishing, I try to find an excuse to bail, because I can't stand to see living things suffer, but them knowing that would be bad for business."

"But maybe things got passionate, then she rejected you," Scott suggested.

"Or you were the one who wanted to meet and she refused you," Bates offered. "You really don't seem like the type to take rejection well."

Moran shook his head. "I've had lots of experience at it, but it's no big deal with women." Again, he looked from one man to the other. "I can always find another one, know what I mean?"

Bates and Scott looked at each other. In unison, they replied. "No."

Moran took a deep breath and ran his fingers through his immaculately trimmed hair.

"Will you give us a DNA sample?" Bates asked.

Moran licked his lips. "Well, I'm sure it will prove I had sex with her, so maybe I should refuse till I talk to my lawyer."

"We can get a warrant and get the sample that way. But it makes you look more guilty."

"Either way, all it proves is what I've just admitted."

Bates shrugged. "Maybe."

He sat in silence as Bates and Scott watched him. "Now is that enough? Can I go?"

"Just one more thing," Scott said. "The name of the client you saw last Tuesday."

He shifted in his seat. "Mrs. Warren Ochs."

Chapter 20

Whistling, Scott jogged up the stairs to their apartment. While they hadn't wrung a confession out of Moran, they hadn't completely eliminated him as a suspect, either. His wife might not be concerned about his affair with the banker's wife, but they had the fear of the banker finding out to pressure him for full compliance. They just might be able to get justice for Delia after all. He opened the door, excited at the prospect of having the rest of the weekend to spend with Rica.

"Scott, we need to talk." He froze before he even dropped his keys in the bowl. Those had to be the four words men feared most. They could lead to all kinds of outcomes, most of them bad. He stood with his keys in his hand.

"What—?" He decided to rephrase his response, make it less threatening. "Of course, Rica." He put his keys away and pulled his suit jacket off slowly, his eyes scanning the apartment to see if there was anything that might give him a clue to what he had or hadn't done. He walked to where she stood in the kitchen. He didn't approach her for a kiss; right now, she looked more like a mother about to administer a scolding than the wife eager to please that she had been last night.

"Scott, did you have breakfast before you went to that girl's funeral this morning?"

He blinked. "Yeah, I made some coffee and had a bowl of cereal. Why?"

She stepped aside from the counter. There stood a nearly full gallon of milk, the box of cereal, his coffee mug, and two spoons. "But you didn't remember to put anything away, did you?"

Faced with the incriminating evidence, he decided to confess. "Looks like I didn't." He hung his head. "I'm sorry, Rica." She was getting up as he walked out the door, he remembered. "I guess I thought you might want the milk for your breakfast."

"Scott." She gave him THAT look and used THAT tone of voice, the look and tone that said she was dealing with a very slow child. "When in the four years we've been married did I ever have milk with breakfast? You know I always just have coffee and fruit."

He started to shrug, but stopped himself. "I said I'm sorry, Rica." He stepped toward her, planning to put up the cereal and rinse the dishes to put in the dishwasher. "I can't go back and un-do leaving things out."

She grabbed the milk jug and shoved it into the trash can. "What is it going to take to get you to stop leaving them out?" Before he could reach the cereal, she snatched it up and slammed it in the cabinet. He had the dishwasher open before she could break the mug and bowl putting it in the sink. "Scott, how much money do we waste on things like this?"

"I dunno." He shrugged before he could stop himself. "Not a lot."

She faced him, leaning against the counter, in almost the same place as last night. "Any is too much."

Her eyes flashed at him, and she flung her hands in the air. "How can we ever afford a house, how can we hope to take care of it, if we can't take care of life in an apartment?"

"But, Rica—" He faced her, puzzled. "We have $20,000 in the bank, both cars are paid for, and we both make good money. We've taken the first-time homebuyer's class, so we qualify for the down payment grant." He dropped his hands to his sides. "I don't understand."

"That's just it, Scott." She glared at him. "You don't understand, you don't see how your messiness, your forgetfulness, your carelessness undermines your effectiveness. And our future!" She stalked past him, grabbed her purse from the spot it always occupied on the hook by the front closet, and opened the door. "I'm going to the movies with Heather." She looked at him. "I'll be back when I've cooled down." She paused before she stepped through the door. "You might look around to see what you can do to mitigate your messiness while I'm gone." The door slammed behind her, and Scott blinked. So much for spending the weekend cuddling together.

Chapter 21

Over the growl of the vacuum, Scott heard his cell phone. He flipped off the monster and grabbed the phone before checking to see if it was Rica. His eager, "Yeah?" changed to, "Oh, Del, it's you."

"Glad to be talking to you, too, buddy," Bates chuckled. "Expecting someone else?"

"Rica." Scott didn't want to explain.

Bates didn't ask. "I finally got hold of Mrs. Moran."

"Where was she?" Moran had told them she was out of town, but was vague about where.

"Minnesota. Fishing trip with some of her female friends."

"Sure." He sighed. How long before Rica started going places without him because she was angry? Then it hit him. She had already gone to the movies twice without him. "When's she get back?"

"She just landed at our local airport. Seems they had a private pilot fly them up there and back. And stay with them while they were there."

"Chauffeur slash bodyguard?"

"Something like that." Bates paused. "So she is available to speak with us between her shower and dinner at the Club."

"Wow." Scott marveled at the ego of some people. "Let me check my planner to see if I can spare fifteen minutes to see if she goes to jail or not."

"I'll pick you up in five."

****

Mrs. Moran was able to fit them into her busy schedule, but just barely. By the time Scott and Bates arrived at the Moran McMansion, she had run through a shower, and they interviewed her at her dressing table, situated in a closet bigger than Scott's entire bedroom. Bates wrinkled his nose at the scent of the polish she was brushing on her nails.

"So, Mrs. Moran, you were with your husband the entire evening last Tuesday?"

"Ummm." She focused on sweeping deep red polish on her thumbnail. "Tuesday was…umm, let me see—" Now her index finger. "Dinner and dance at the Country Club for—" She finished the left hand. "Something about children." She held her left hand under a nail dryer. "Orphans or cripples or something." She looked up at Bates. "We gave generously."

"I'm sure you did." He waited while she tested a nail to see if it was dry. "Were you together the whole time you were there?"

The left corner of her mouth flicked up for an instant. "More or less." She ran her eyes over Scott, who was standing at the other side of her table near a rack of shoes that took up more space than his bathroom. "I dashed outside and had…a couple of cigarettes."

"Where was Mr. Moran when you came back in?" Scott had her attention, so he asked the question.

"I didn't see him right away when I came back in, but he caught up with me within a couple of minutes." She took the nail brush in her left hand and began painting. "We stayed until it closed down." She looked up at Scott. "It's not often someplace around here has a decent band you can dance to."

"So, Mrs. Moran—"

"Call me Ronnie."

"Ronnie?" Scott thought she looked, with her privately-trained body, manicured feet and hands, expensively tailored hair, nothing like any "Ron" he'd ever known.

"Short for Veronica." She smiled and waved her now painted right hand in the air.

"Oh, I see." He and Rica had leafed through a book of baby names shortly after they were married; Veronica meant "faithful." Her mother probably wouldn't laugh at the irony of it. "So, where did you go after the Club?"

"We came home." She stood and turned to a bank of drawers behind her, drawing out something that looked like dental floss, but was probably her panties. She stepped into them and Scott caught Bates' gaze as they both turned away. When they glanced back to see her smoothing her robe down, the smile on her face said that she enjoyed putting them on the spot.

"Were you together then all night?" Bates buried his nose in his notebook.

She glanced at him as she started applying her makeup. "Of course. We spent some time in the hot tub." She smiled at Scott. "*Au natural*."

Scott took a deep breath. "Are you sure he was here all night?"

She tilted her head to the side. "If he left, I never noticed. After all that, and then some, I was out like a light." She stood again and patted the short robe down her thigh. "He was here when I woke up in the morning, but I didn't get up then." She pulled a piece of fabric that looked too small to be a dress from a hanger. "I need to get dressed now, fellows." She raised one eyebrow. "Keep asking questions if you want."

Scott looked at Bates. "No, I think we've covered everything we need to cover." He and Bates beat a hasty retreat as the robe dropped. The housekeeper met them in the hall to escort them to the door. They walked down the wide steps to their sedan, which looked as out of place on the patterned brick driveway as a battered old farm truck in a Mercedes showroom.

"Someone should explain rule six to her," Bates muttered as he slid behind the wheel.

"Rule six?" Scott stared at him. "Maybe somebody should explain it to me, too."

"Rule six," Bates began as the air started to cool. "Is 'you're not that damned important.'"

Scott laughed. "She'd never believe it."

Chapter 22

Writing up the interview with Mrs. Moran didn't take long. During the drive from the station, Scott created a "to do" list in his head: finish vacuuming, mop the kitchen and, oh, yeah, sort through the old magazines still in the box from the day he found Delia's body. He was mulling over other tasks he should start, hoping they would put him on Rica's good side, when he pulled into his apartment parking lot and saw Rica's car. She was home! They could talk out their differences, maybe go to dinner, or order in pizza and watch a movie. Optimism drummed through every fiber of his being as he danced up the stairs. The door swung inward as he reached for it.

"Scott!" The reproach in Rica's eyes echoed that in her voice.

He stepped inside the apartment. What had he done wrong now? "Rica?"

She moved aside and waved at the vacuum still sitting where it had been when he shut it off to take Bates' call. "You couldn't even put up the vacuum?"

"I got called out." He took a step toward it, ready to coil up the cord. "I was gonna finish when I got back."

"Two minutes!" She beat him to the machine, yanked the cord from the wall and wound it furiously. "You couldn't take two minutes to wrap up the cord

114

and put it in the closet?"

"Bates was on his way. We only had a short window of time to interview a suspect." He tried to take it from her to carry it to the closet, but she snatched it from his grasp. "I didn't know you'd be home by the time I got back."

She spun to face him. "Would it really have made that much difference, Scott?" She gestured at the magazines stacked on the table beside his chair. "We've had this argument over and over." Her gaze met his. "Do you even listen to me anymore, Scott?"

He studied her eyes, searching for the tiniest spark of mercy. "I listen, Rica, but I don't know what to DO."

"Do what you say you'll do!" she shouted. "When you say you'll clean up after yourself, do it! If you get it out, put it away!"

"Rica, I try!" His voice rose, though he willed himself to stay calm. Couldn't she see how much effort he made? He took a deep breath. "I'll try harder. I really will." He took another deep breath. "But when the job calls, I have to go. You know how it was when you were surgical on-call."

She glared at him. "Yes, but I managed to do what I could until the pager went off."

"And there were times when I had to finish what you started." He remembered many meals he kept warm for her, hoping she'd be home in time to eat with him. He made his voice soft. "Our jobs have placed a lot of strain on us sometimes."

Her brows, which had run together like two angry bulls, relaxed a little. "That they have, *mijo*."

At her endearment, hope began to seep back into his heart. "*Si, querida.*" She truly was his beloved, and he wanted her to realize that.

She placed her hands on her hips, and a different tone, more fear than anger, tempered her voice. "But what are we going to do about it, *mijo*?"

He looked at the floor, more shaken by her fear than by her anger. "Be a little more forgiving with each other?" He raised his face to her, prepared for her to run into his arms as she so often did after a spat like this.

She stayed rooted in her place. "I don't know if we can, *mijo*." She looked out the window. "I fear we're at an impasse."

His chest felt like an ice arrow had just lanced through it. "Do you want to try counseling?" He feared exposing himself to a stranger, but to save his marriage, he would do it.

She wrapped her arms around herself. "We could try, I guess." She dropped her hands to her sides, and her voice took on a sharper tone. "But I fear there are too many fundamental differences between us."

She's trying to find a reason for us to split, the investigator in him observed. The man in him denied it. "I thought that was what brought us together in the first place," he whispered.

This time, the look in her eyes approached panic. "It was." She took a step toward him, but he did not move. He was afraid he would spook her away if he did. "But maybe we didn't give it enough time to know what we were getting into."

"We were engaged over a year," he reminded her. After only three or four dates, Scott knew she was the woman he wanted to spend his life with, to bear his children, to grow old with, but she wanted more time, so he gave it to her. After two months, she wanted to date other men, so he agreed, staring vacantly at his schoolbooks in a vain attempt to do homework while he knew she was out with someone else. After three months, she told him she was certain. It was then he asked her to marry him, and she said yes. But she wanted to plan a wedding, so they waited another ten months, while she got every detail of the wedding the way she wanted. During those months, they spent most of their time together, and she learned how extensive his messiness was. He vowed to try to change, and she to help him. She said she needed to soften her control obsession. He thought they had meshed into a pretty good team over the past four years. But maybe he was wrong. That's why an investigator never worked a case involving people he knew, because he often overlooked the obvious in those he loved.

"True." She nodded. "Maybe I'm just PMS-ing."

"Shall I go back out for moose tracks ice cream?" He laughed, trying to lighten her mood. He saw the tears gathering in her eyes.

"You've always been very good at trying to get whatever I want, Scott." A tear ran down each cheek. "I don't know why I can't seem to see that, and your other good points, lately." *Maybe you compare me too much to the saintly Dr. Ambrose* ran through his mind before he could stop the thought.

He walked to her and held out his hands. She reached out and slipped her tiny ones in his. He squeezed. "Your hands are like ice." He pulled her close, nestling her head on his shoulder. "Maybe you need hot chocolate instead of ice cream." Her shoulders shuddered, as tears dampened his shirt.

"I don't know what I need, Scott." She sniffed and

117

looked up at him. "I don't know why I'm such a bitch anymore."

Again, he thought of the good doctor, but only squeezed Rica tighter. "Why don't we catch a movie?"

She stared into his eyes. "It has been ages since we've been out, just the two of us."

"I'll call dispatch and tell them that I'm off the grid for a few hours, unless at least half of the town is destroyed."

She smiled, as she wiped away tears with the heel of her hand. "Better make that three-fourths."

He let go of her as he flipped open his cell phone. "Do you want me to finish vacuuming before we go?" he asked, as the call rang through.

She shook her head. "Let's do it together tomorrow morning."

Chapter 23

The movie morphed into dinner at the new Italian restaurant in town that Rica claimed was supposed to be divine.

"Dr. Ambrose said he was here last week and the food was wonderful," Rica gushed. "He said the service was excellent, too." She sipped at the red wine that, Scott noted, cost more for the glass than she usually allowed them to spend on an entrée. *Oh, well, at least we are together and trying to relax.* Since he had only taken himself off call for four hours, he stuck to iced tea that, he had to admit, was some of the best he had ever tasted. When his glass was two-thirds empty, a waiter glided in to replace it with a fresh one. He did his best to ignore the references to Ambrose.

"It sure smells good." He wanted to be agreeable. "And the service has been great so far." Quicker than he expected for such an expensive restaurant, their meals appeared. Rica had ordered the shrimp scampi, while Scott opted for lasagna.

"You really should try something different once in a while," Rica said, as she tasted a shrimp. "Oh, this is heavenly."

I should take her on a date more often if it makes her this happy. He resolved to make this type of outing a weekly custom. "Glad it's good." He cut a piece of lasagna. "My test of an Italian place is always lasagna."

He savored the bite. "If they make good lasagna, they can usually handle anything else."

"That does make sense." Rica stopped eating to watch him. "How is it?"

He grinned and cut another piece. "It passes muster."

She laughed. "I'm glad we did this, Scott."

He reached across the table to take her right hand in his left. "Me, too." With his right hand, he cut another bite of lasagna.

That made her laugh again. "Glad to see you have your priorities, Scott. Hold my hand and eat at the same time."

He grinned. "I have mastered multi-tasking, my dear."

By the time they ordered tiramisu to share and Rica had a second glass of wine, he felt much better about the state of his marriage. He left a generous tip and paid for their dinner while Rica visited the ladies' room, then arm in arm, they walked to her car in the parking lot. She pulled him close as he reached to open her door. "Let's not go to a movie, Scott."

He nuzzled her neck. "What would you rather do?"

She spun away from him. "Let's go dancing." She twirled around the space next to the car.

"Dancing?" He dreaded it; he had two very clumsy left feet. But anything that would make her happy tonight, he was willing to try. Unless she suggested breaking into a bank or something. "Where would you like to go?"

"I hear the Thirsty Dragon has a good band tonight."

He opened her door and waited for her to dance

into her seat. "Thirsty Dragon it is, m'lady."

Occasionally reaching over to stroke his neck, she hummed while he drove. The Thirsty Dragon was the bar that Delia and her friends frequented. Would he run across any leads there? He could bump into her killer there. Would he know?

****

Charlotte Daniels kept the serene expression plastered on her face just as meticulously as the makeup she had applied. She thought of a huge tab and plenty of tips as she approached the happy couple at the table in the corner. Then, when he looked up at her to order a cosmopolitan for his wife and a Pepsi for himself, she caught a good look at his face. And that was the reason she scanned the room for Tessa as she chirped out the order to the bartender. Before Nate had the drinks drawn, Tessa clumped up to the bar.

"God, I'm tired." She put her hands on her back and stretched, then glanced at Charlotte. "Geez, girl, you look like you've seen a ghost."

Charlotte shook her head. "No, just a guy a little too handsy."

"Bastards."

"Sad thing is, I think he'll be a good tipper, but I don't want to have to beat him off to earn it."

"I don't care what I have to do, as long as they tip good." Tessa touched her fingertips to her lips. "Damn, I need a cigarette." She turned to look at the room. "Why'd they have to go and make this place 'smoke-free' anyway?"

"Make you a deal, Tessa." Charlotte leaned toward the girl. "You take Mr. Handsy over there, and I'll work your break and mine, so you can step outside for a cig."

"You have a deal, Charley-girl."

While Tessa made her way to the corner table, Charlotte carried a heavy tray of beer to a table of rowdy bikers. They pawed her, and the tall bald one pulled her onto his lap. With an effort, she struggled free, still smiling, and took orders from the table next to the bikers. Tessa returned to the bar with another order at the same time as Charlotte.

"I didn't have any trouble with Mr. Handsy," Tessa said. "In fact, he is probably the most polite guy in here tonight." She turned back to look at him. "And he has such a sweet smile."

"Give him time." She had two trays to carry for the next order. Her feet hurt, and her head ached from the noise of the band. Why did she do this? Her job as a graphics designer for an ad agency paid well enough for her to live comfortably on her own, and now Devlyn took care of all the bills. Was her self-esteem really that shaky that she needed a drunken groping to make her feel beautiful? "I'll bet by closing time, he'll be all over you." She didn't believe her prediction, but she had to have a plausible excuse to Tessa for avoiding that table. Not only did she recognize him from the cemetery, there was something familiar about his face that made her suspect she had known him from her old life. And that was just as frightening as today.

"I don't know." Tessa mopped at the sweat on her face with her apron. "He seems pretty much into the woman he's with." She stood still. "Just look at them dancing together out there. So sweet it almost makes you sick."

Charlotte turned to watch, and the ache knifed through her. The man and his woman moved together like matching wings on a butterfly, like they had danced together often, both this way and privately, away from prying eyes. He was tall, toned, with an air that was a mixture of confident hero and uncertain little boy, the kind that drew women like moths to a flame. The woman was luscious, ripe, gazing up at him with her lips parted. The woman licked her lips, and Charlotte did, too. Would she ever be the subject of such a scene? Would she ever have someone love her like that?

Mags had tried, in her own way, but the timing had never been right. When they were young, Charlotte's awkwardness in her own body got in the way, and then, with that past and Mags rediscovered, there was Devlyn. She sighed. "Time for you to take a break, Tessa."

While Tessa lingered over what Charlotte suspected must be at least three cigarettes, Charlotte worked both sides of the room. She cleared a table near the center, when she caught a motion from the corner table. The polite man was waving her over. Could she ignore him? She scanned the room desperately for Tessa, but the woman was still outside with her smokes. Reluctantly, she turned toward the corner table.

"Could we have Pepsis for both of us?" He gave her a slight smile.

"Right away," she said, trying to turn away quickly. He put out his hand with two twenties that would cover his tab and a hefty tip. She couldn't pretend she hadn't seen it, so she reached out for the money. Instinctively, she looked at his face, and their eyes locked. The polite smile froze, and his brows drew closer together. His eyes examined her face almost as thoroughly as a computer scanner. Her stomach flipped over with a thud. "I'll be right back." She ducked her head and headed for the bar as fast as her stilettos would carry her. By the time the Pepsis were drawn, Tessa returned.

Charlotte shoved the tray with the two drinks toward her. "Here, take this to Handsy." She stepped past Tessa before the girl could protest. "I need to use the can." She glanced back at the corner table as she opened the bathroom door. Though Tessa had arrived at their table with the drinks and the change she knew he would decline, Handsy was watching Charlotte. She fled into the cramped bathroom and shuddered against the walls. Suddenly, she hated this place, with its worn linoleum and leaky toilets. The only class in the joint was Charlotte.

****

Long after Rica breathed in a deep, satisfied sleep beside him, Scott lay awake staring at the ceiling fan. Something about the waitress tonight at the bar bothered him. He'd seen her somewhere before, maybe recently, maybe a long time ago, but he *had* seen her. Maybe he should go back and question her. If Delia and her friends were regulars at the place, maybe this woman had seen something. Or someone. He closed his eyes and willed his mind to shut off. He focused on the rhythmic sound of the ceiling fan. As he drifted out of consciousness, it began to chant to him. "Delia. Delia. Delia." He jerked out of the near-sleep and shook his head. He tried again. Once again, it began to hum. "Margaret. Margaret. Margaret." Soon, it whispered other names to him, but the sound moved farther and farther away with each revolution of the blades. At last, his mind and body let go. Thoughts crowded into his unconscious mind, and he hoped he would recall them in the morning.

Chapter 24

"We need to pay a visit to the Thirsty Dragon." Scott didn't even say good morning first when Bates walked into their office on Monday.

"Why?" Bates sipped at the coffee in his mug, grimaced, and set it down, then settled into his chair. "Has the day been that bad already?"

"No." Scott grinned. "My day's been pretty good, really." Rica had awakened him early to enjoy her day off and nearly made him late to work. "But Rica and I stopped in there last night, and my gut tells me we should talk to the staff, maybe see if Delia had any altercations with anyone there. Or if she met anyone else."

"We probably should check there, since we don't have enough to charge Moran." Bates rose, dumped his coffee into the peace lily by the coffee pot, and refilled his cup. "But I'll bet they're not open yet."

"Nope. Sign on the door said ten-thirty, for the lunch crowd."

"Maybe we should have lunch there." Bates stopped half-way to his chair.

"I hear they fry a good burger." Scott knew Bates would gladly combine work with lunch.

"Maybe we should go get some donuts so we can fit all the stereotypes today."

"They have some down at dispatch, and we already

have the coffee." Scott slid his chair back.

Bates turned. "Let's go." He clapped Scott on the shoulder as they left their office. "Maybe we can work on that burglary case while we wait for the Dragon to open."

Scott nodded. Right now, Delia's case absorbed him, but he knew that duty demanded they not forget the other cases assigned to them. Investigations took time, but time was a resource in limited supply.

****

Searching E-Bay and Craigslist for the items stolen in a string of burglaries worked up an appetite. Scott's stomach rumbled as they walked into the Thirsty Dragon at 11:10 a.m. At the bar, a young woman Scott judged to be in her early twenties looked up from arranging glasses. "Grill's not quite ready, gents, but I can take your order." Her eyes measured both of them. "Beer while you wait?"

Bates slipped onto a barstool. "Diet Pepsi for me."

Scott seated himself beside Bates. "Iced tea." Up close, the girl might be a little past twenty-five. And she was not either woman who had served him and Rica last night. "A Harvey burger, no cheese, grilled onions and fries."

She wrote briefly on a plain pad, then glanced up at Bates. "Cheeseburger and onion rings."

"Coming right up, soon's the grill's hot enough." She walked to the kitchen pass-through at the end of the bar, and clipped the order to a rotating steel ring. She leaned against the bar, two cold glasses in her hand. "Sure you won't have a beer?"

Bates shook his head, while Scott reached for his wallet. "We're on duty."

She straightened. "Duty?" She moved quickly to the soda machine. "You cops?"

Scott nodded and pulled out the picnic photo of Delia. "Wondered if you'd seen this woman in here in the last few weeks."

She placed their drinks in front of them, laid straws on the counter and wiped her hands on the apron wrapped around her waist. Glancing from Bates to Scott with veiled eyes, she took the photo as if it might bite her. "Don't think so." She started to hand it back to Scott.

He shook his head. "Can you take another look? We know she came in here from time to time."

Her chest moved with her rapid breathing. "Look, I only work the noon rush, guys."

"Take another look anyway," Bates urged, his voice gentle, fatherly.

She stared hard at Bates, and her breaths came slower. She took the photo to the kitchen entrance and studied it in the brighter light there. Skinny and nervous, she probably used speed or crack on occasion. She brought the photo back to them. "Naw, never seen her."

"How about your boss or the cook?" Bates asked as Scott laid the photo on the bar.

"Cook works both shifts sometimes, but hardly ever looks up from the grill. Boss works tables once in a while." She backed toward the kitchen.

"Could we talk to them?" Bates sipped at his Pepsi. "Just take a minute. They don't have to come out at the same time, one can stay and watch the grill."

"Sure." She disappeared into the kitchen. Minutes later, a big man with a beard appeared carrying their lunches on plates.

"What can I do for you fine officers?" He plopped his elbows on the bar and offered a huge hand. "Harvey Pennington, owner."

Bates shook his hand while Scott nudged the photo toward him, resisting the temptation to tear into his burger. He couldn't remember the last time he'd had one here. "You seen this girl in here?"

Wiping his hands on his apron, Pennington held the photo close, then, like the waitress, he took it to the light and studied it some more. While he studied, Scott and Bates dug into the burgers. Scott savored the first greasy, delicious bite.

Pennington returned to them. "Hard to say." He laid the photo down, but continued to look at it. "We get a lot of people in here, and as you can see—" He gestured around the empty room. "Light's not so good for seeing people too clear." He laughed. "It sells more liquor and makes people happier if they can't see what they're making a bargain for at 1:30 in the morning."

Scott nodded, remembering his single days. Tentative offers were made at midnight, and negotiations began in earnest at one, deals sealed by 1:45 before last call. Most made an exit with their chosen love-for-the-night before the lights came up. And didn't look too closely before breakfast. "She might have come in for lunch or early, right after work, sometimes. Maybe with a group of women."

Pennington stared at the photo a while. "Maybe come in with a tall brunette, a real looker? And a red-headed gal?"

Scott shrugged, halfway done with the burger. "Could have."

Pennington nodded. "Bunch of them, sometimes half a dozen or so, mostly on Fridays. Real rowdy at times, acted like man-haters, but they were on the prowl, for sure."

Bates finished his burger. "Any of them find what they were prowling for?"

Pennington looked Bates in the eye. "Oh, they danced and let fellows buy them drinks—they were good for my business—but they always left together without any guys in tow." He touched the photo. "Can't say they didn't meet somebody later, or exchange phone numbers, but they worked as a herd. Safety in numbers, don't you know?

Scott leaned forward. "Anybody ever cut one from the herd?"

Pennington straightened. "I can't see everything, cause I'm usually everywhere at once and nowhere very long. But I don't recall any of them making much time for anyone but each other." He looked at the photo again. "This the gal they found on the river bank?"

While the memory flashed before Scott's eyes and reached deep into his gut, Bates nodded.

"Too bad," Pennington said. "With the kid and all."

"What about your waitresses?" The reaction of the auburn-haired waitress from last night still bothered Scott. "Any chance they shared info with any of them?"

Pennington shrugged. "You could ask them."

"Will you give us a list of them?"

"Sure." He nodded toward their now-empty plates. "How were your burgers?"

"Great," Bates said. Scott nodded agreement.

"On the house, fellas." He turned toward the kitchen. "I'll get you a list of the gals."

"Thanks." Bates pulled out his wallet, while Scott opened his already lying on the bar. "But we can't accept freebies."

Pennington stopped at the kitchen door. "Suit yourselves. But do me a favor, will ya?"

Scott glanced at Bates. "What would that be?"

"Tell your buddies on the force how great the burgers are, okay?"

"That we can do," Scott agreed. Pennington grinned as customers began filling the place.

Chapter 25

With milkshakes to go in hand, Bates and Scott left the Dragon after a brief, uninformative chat with the cook, who saw nothing but the waitresses who brought him orders and raw meat searing all day or night.

Bates ran a quick copy of the list of ten waitresses. He started calling the top five, while Scott called the last half. With varying degrees of reluctance, all agreed to come to the station today or tomorrow for an interview. The last girl on Scott's list hadn't been hired until about six months ago. "Last one," he said to Bates. Bates merely grunted, dialing his last number as well.

Charlotte Daniels didn't answer her cell phone, so he left a message on voice mail. "This is Detective Scott Aylward of the Police Department." He hesitated, not wanting to stampede her into not calling back. "We need to ask you a few questions regarding an ongoing investigation." He left a message to call and set up an appointment. Then he hung up and faced Bates where he stood with an empty coffee carafe in his hand.

"We're out of coffee, so I think I'll make some before the first of the girls comes in." He glanced at the clock on the wall. "We have about twenty minutes." He headed toward the break room to fill the carafe with water. "Do you suppose they have any of those donuts left in dispatch?"

"Del!" Scott chided him, though coffee and a donut

did sound good now that Bates had mentioned it. "What about your girlish figure? Remember the milkshake. And that burger had to have 200 calories of fat alone."

"Yeah, but it was good, wasn't it?" He shook his head at Scott. "And I gave up on my girlish figure when Angie and I celebrated twenty years of marriage."

Scott's stomach clenched. Would he and Rica even make five? "More of you for her to love, I guess."

Bates grunted and went off on his mission. Which one of these girls had waited on him last night? And why was he so certain he had seen her before?

****

"You talk to the cops yet?" Tessa blurted the moment Charlotte Daniels entered the employee "lounge," a grim room with some folding chairs and coat hooks on the walls.

Charlotte swallowed hard and forced a casual, "No, why?" from her parched throat. Ever since the number flashed on her cell's caller ID, her heart had pounded. She wiped her hands on her jeans, trying to dry the sweat. Why hadn't she said she was busy when Harvey asked her on Friday to cover Danielle's shift tonight? It's not like he hadn't known for three months that the girl had tickets to the concert in Wichita tonight.

"They're trying to find out if any of us know anything about that girl that they found on the river dike." She faced Charlotte. "Didn't they call you?"

"I haven't checked my phone for messages since noon."

"You should check it." Tessa turned her back to Charlotte to slip on the lightweight Nikes she wore to race to customers. "They had us come to the station to talk to them." She stood and tied on a fresh apron.

"Handsy was one of them." She leaned close to Charlotte and lowered her voice. "I thought he was good-looking last night, but in the light, he's really cute." She headed for the main dining room. "I think he likes me."

"He's married," Charlotte called after her. She dropped into the uneven folding chair. It tipped with her as she rocked back and forth, hugging herself. Her instinct about the man had been right. Bumping into him was bad karma, now suddenly turning worse. What should she do? Leave town, set up somewhere new, far away from here? That would certainly arouse suspicion, probably cause them to come looking for her. But could she hold herself together enough to pull off the act of ignorance that would make them overlook her? She damned the compulsion that had driven her to mold herself into a woman who would attract attention.

Stuffing her cell phone from her purse into her pocket, she stuffed her feelings even deeper, in that place they were so accustomed to staying while she tried to function in a world that had never accepted her. Devlyn never offered acceptance, simply admiration of her physical body mixed with indifference to her psyche. Only Maggie had accepted her just as she was. She drew a jagged breath and stuffed the feelings further down. She checked her makeup and hair, dabbing at a mascara run with a tissue dampened by her tongue, then balanced on her red suede platforms and entered the dining room.

Chapter 26

"We're gonna have to make another trip to the Dragon to talk to that last girl." Scott reviewed his notes from the interviews with the nine others. It had taken till Wednesday to get the next to last one. A couple of them had not answered the original calls, but had returned the messages they had left. He had called Charlotte Daniels' number once Monday, once yesterday and twice today.

Bates reached for his coffee cup and took a sip. "Cold!" He stood up, cup in hand, and dumped his old coffee into the lily on the windowsill. Then he turned to the coffee pot on the shelf behind him. Fresh coffee in the cup, he leaned against the wall. "Yeah, looks kinda funny that she's not called back."

"Reckon she's out of town or something?" The other girls all remembered Delia's group in a peripheral way. The women weren't particularly good tippers—women usually aren't for female waitresses—but they had attracted men who were, and that is what the waitresses had remembered.

"I asked the last gal," Bates offered. "She said that Charlotte doesn't take much time off, works every Friday and Saturday night, fills in once in a while in between."

"Feel like burgers for dinner Friday night?"

"I was thinking about a chicken fry, myself."

****

Charlotte ignored the calls from the police station that came Monday, Tuesday, and Wednesday. When none came Thursday or Friday, her stomach began to unclench, and she was finally able to eat more than just tea and crackers. Not telling Devlyn about the calls hadn't been hard; they rarely talked about much anymore. No use upsetting a temporary calm.

Barely able to make her way through the crowded parking lot to her usual spot in the back by the old cottonwood tree, she tripped into the Dragon at her appointed five-thirty on Friday night. She really should quit this job.

"Hey, Charlotte," Harvey called from the kitchen as she headed for the lounge to put away her things. "Put on your racing high heels tonight." He passed her on his way to the freezer. "Looks like a big crowd here for the Little League tournament."

"They got wings on 'em, Harvey." Harvey's genuine appreciation of her skill with the customers kept her here. That and the way the other girls, not knowing her past, treated her like one of them. She quickly hung up her purse and tied on an apron.

"By the way, Charlotte." Harvey lumbered out of the freezer, a huge bag of frozen French fries on his shoulder. "The cops are here to ask you if you remember anything about that girl they found by the river last week."

"Cops?" She froze. Ignoring the calls may not have been the best tactic.

"Yeah," Harvey dropped the bag on the counter beside the grill. He looked up at her, and she guessed he read the look on her face. "Nothin' to be scared of, they

just want to know if you saw her with anyone unusual."
He ripped open the bag. "Real nice guys."

"Okay." She dampened dry lips with her tongue.
Maybe she could twist an ankle, throw up, fake a call
from Devlyn—anything to keep from going out into the
dining room to face the cops.

Harvey stepped behind her, propelling her with his
bulk toward the entrance to the dining room. "There
they are." He pointed. "Table by the corner." He turned
back to the kitchen. "Their dinners will be ready in a
few minutes."

"Maybe I should wait till then."

"Naw, talk to them first." He flipped a burger. "It
won't take long."

"Okay." Slowly, knees weak, she approached the
table near the corner booth where Handsy had brought
his woman Saturday night. Both men sat with their
backs to the booths, facing the room. The younger one
noticed her first and nodded a greeting. It was Handsy.
The other man, older, bulkier, turned his face toward
her. She forced her lips into the friendly, unconcerned
smile she had practiced all her life. "Hello, gentlemen,"
she greeted as she reached the table. Handsy was even
better looking in the brighter dinner lighting than he
had been in the dark booth.

He pushed out the chair around the table from him.
"Please, sit down, Charlotte." He nodded toward the
other man. "I'm Scott Aylward and this is Del Bates,
with PD."

She sat quickly, folding her hands in her lap to hide
their shaking. "Yes?"

"We'd like to ask you a few questions about a
customer who used to come in here occasionally."

"Okay." She glanced at Scott's face, then lowered her eyes to the condiment tray in the center of the table. He had big, smoky puppy dog eyes, the kind she always fell for.

Scott pushed the photo of Delia toward Charlotte. "Do you remember seeing this woman in here at any time?"

Charlotte let her eyes stray to the photo. A happy, glowing Maggie, just as she remembered her. "I think so." She flicked a glance at Bates. "She come in once in a while with a group?"

Bates nodded. "You ever notice her talking to anyone special, or leaving with someone?"

You mean, besides me? "No, no one special." She looked thoughtfully toward the crowded dining area. She was going to run her ass off tonight. But the tips would probably make it worthwhile. "From what I remember, that group was pretty careful and stuck together." She had to appear to have noticed a bit, but not much. Her heel tapped a rhythm on the floor and she consciously stopped it. "Look, we are real busy tonight. Is there anything else you need?"

Bates and Scott exchanged a look, just as Harvey appeared at the dining room entrance with meals in hand, headed toward them. "Just our dinners."

She started to rise from her chair, but Scott put a hand on her arm. A big hand, with long fingers she'd bet were gentle. In his other hand, he held a business card. "If you think of anyone who might have made a connection with her, anyone she might have refused to talk to, or dance with, give me a call." Though she tried to avoid looking at him, his eyes caught her gaze, and she couldn't look away. He pressed the business card into her hand. "I really want to find her killer."

She glanced toward Harvey, almost to the table. "I hope you do," she said softly. Harvey setting their plates on the table gave her a chance to escape. She walked to the ladies room as quickly as she could without running. She bent over to lean her forehead against the porcelain sink. She could almost hear her heartbeat echoing off the walls. What a joint this was. She should quit. But if she quit now, those cops might connect it with their questioning, and ask her more questions. She straightened up. Seconds. She had only seconds to compose herself before she would have to start working her side of the room. Thankfully, it was the side away from those cops. She pulled a lipstick from her pocket and applied it. *You look good.* She studied herself in the mirror. *Classy and cool, but hot, like hot fudge on a sundae. The tips should be big tonight.*

****

Scott stared after Charlotte as she fled their table. There was no other word for it. The girl was practically jumping out of her skin as she sat with them. And yet she didn't seem like the type to be covering up a drug habit or driving record, like the girl behind the bar the first time they came in here. He looked across the table at Bates. "You get a feeling about her?"

"MMM?" Bates was deep into his chicken fry. He finished chewing and tore off a paper towel from the roll in the center of the table. "Whaddya mean?"

"Didn't she seem a little nervous to you?"

He picked up a curly fry. "She struck me as the type that is afraid of her own shadow." He munched the fry. "Anything would make her nervous. Especially anything that might mess up all that makeup." He sliced off another bite of steak. "And she had the same general impression as the other girls." He skewered the bite on his fork. "I still think Moran is our guilty party."

"Oh, he's guilty as sin, all right, but not of killing Delia." Scott tapped a finger on the table. "I think I'll pull a background on Charlotte." He looked down at the sirloin with rosemary potatoes and steamed veggies that he had ordered. "Maybe the other girls, too." The aroma of the meal wafted to him. "But not till after dinner."

Chapter 27

Charlotte Daniels had something to hide; Scott was sure of it. But what? Drug use? Dealing? A record she didn't want her boss to find out about? Scott didn't even remember climbing the stairs to his apartment. Only when he heard voices just before he pushed open the door did his mind return to the here and now.

"Oh, Scott, I'm glad you're home." Rica smiled at him from the kitchen, and his heart tightened at how sexy she looked. She hadn't let herself go after marriage like some women. She watched what she ate and worked out three afternoons a week. His gaze took in her best friend Heather sitting at the kitchen table.

"Hi, Heather." He crossed the living room and took Rica in his arms, giving her a long, slow kiss. "That's hello to you from me," he murmured in her ear.

She returned the kiss, then pulled away from him. "Heather and John have asked us to join them and a few others at The Pub tonight."

He hesitated. "I'm sorry, Rica. I thought I texted you that Bates and I were having dinner at the Dragon while we interviewed a witness."

She waved off his apology. "I knew you were going to do that, so Heather and I grabbed a light supper after the gym." She looped her arm through his. "So we should just be able to go out and relax."

"Okay." Truthfully, the last thing he wanted right

now was to go out with a group. He met Rica's eyes, seeing an excitement there that mirrored his own. He resisted the urge to excuse himself to Heather and carry Rica to the bedroom for a couple of hours. Instead, he shrugged out of his jacket. "I should probably take a shower first." He loosened his tie. "Any suggestions on what you'd like me to wear, *mija*?"

Her lips curved upward. "I have a couple of suggestions." She took a step toward him, then half-turned to face Heather. "We'll only be a few minutes."

"Um-hum." Heather picked up her iced tea and walked into the living room. "I'll just watch TV till you come back in."

She followed him to the bedroom and closed the door. "That new blue shirt you got last week brings out the green in your eyes." She walked straight to his side of the closet and pulled out the shirt and a pair of jeans. "And these jeans make your ass look so nice."

He stepped out of his pants and boxers and slipped out of his shirt. "How does it look now?" He turned his back to her, watching her over his shoulder.

"Like it needs a shower." She grinned, walking over to him to slip her arms around his waist. "And I wish I had time to give it, too."

He turned to face her, moving tight against her. "We could make it a really fast shower." He nuzzled her ear.

"I think it will be a faster shower if you take it alone while you are thinking about what we can do all night when we get home." She leaned away, laughing. "Besides, it would be rude of me to leave Heather alone."

He pulled her back against him, and she kissed him

long and deep. "You and Heather have been friends since grade school." He kissed his way down the neckline of her top. "Don't tell me in all these years you never waited on each other to have a little time alone with a guy."

She stiffened in his arms. "Well, now we don't have to steal time with each other, Scott." She pushed his arms off her and took a step away. "We can spend all weekend alone together after we get home tonight." She reached out to stroke him. He groaned at her touch.

"Your wish is my command, *mi reyna.*" He would do anything to keep her, his queen, happy.

She smiled at him from the doorway. "Of course, it is." She paused before leaving the room. "Quick as you can, *mijo.*"

He nodded, already on the way to the bathroom. "I'll hurry, love." Thoughts wandered through his head as the water streamed over his body. Maybe she was more excited about just going out than she was about spending time with him. The "date night" they had last week had certainly been a positive experience. But his suggestion that she and Heather had covered for each other definitely cooled her off. Finished with his shower, he turned off the water. Maybe she wanted to make him more passionate by making him wait. He toweled his body roughly, trying to hurry. That had to be it. She was teasing him like she had when he was trying to get her to go out with him, as she did when they first started dating. Whatever her motive, he thought as he pulled on his jeans, she had him throbbing with anticipation.

****

Scott sipped at the iced tea. Maybe occupying

himself with drinking it would keep him from voicing the irritation that raised the hairs on the back of his neck. At the end of the table, next to Rica, sat Dr. Ambrose. At this moment, the good doctor was leaning toward Rica, telling her something in a voice so low that Scott, as close to Rica as he could get his chair, his own arm across the back of her chair, couldn't make out any words. Rica had curved toward the doctor, watching his face while his lips nearly brushed her ear. Scott took some of the ice from his glass and crunched it, wishing instead it was his hands crunching Dr. Ambrose's face.

Rica laughed then and leaned back against him. Her fingers stroked his face and then her hand dropped to his thigh. Ashamed of his earlier jealousy, he kissed the top of her ear. He saw her shoot a look at him, and she removed her hand and sat up straight away from him.

"Any progress on the murder?" Heather's husband John asked from his spot across the table. John and Scott represented the sole non-medical personnel at the table. John worked as an electrician; ICU nurse Greta was married to anesthesiologist Eric; physician's assistant Jane dated OR nurse Dan; Ellen and Sam worked in labor and delivery, while Jason was a lab tech. And then there was the delightful Dr. Ambrose, chin propped on his hand while he listened raptly to the story Heather was telling. Rica watched Dr. Ambrose instead of Heather. Maybe she had heard the story before.

"Not much progress," Scott admitted. "We've interviewed a lot of witnesses and are following leads."

"Not like it is on TV, eh, with the perp behind bars

in 40 minutes."

"Nothing like it is on TV." Scott laughed and shook his head. "It's mostly tedious and filled with paperwork."

Scott's pager beeped. Even as he reached for it, the rest of the people at the table looked for their own pagers to make sure the beeping wasn't for them. "Call dispatch immediately," the tiny screen said.

"Please excuse me." He slid back his chair, noting that only John's eyes followed him from the table. He walked to a quiet spot near the bar door before he pulled out his cell phone and dialed the station. "Aylward here. What's up?"

Melinda's usually pleasant voice carried a strain. "Double homicide at the Quick Shop on West Seventeenth." She drew in a breath. "Bates is already there."

Scott's stomach tightened. Two people dead, and investigating this case would take them away from working on Delia's. "I'll be on my way in two minutes or less." Snapping the phone shut, he turned to look at the table he had just left. No one seemed to be missing him.

Back at the table, he touched Rica's shoulder. She looked up at him, her eyes sparkling. "Yes, Scott?"

"I have to go to work." The conversation at the table paused for a moment, as if they were all waiting for gruesome details. "Do you want me to take you home first?"

"I can give you a ride home," Heather offered, her eyes on Rica.

Rica glanced at her friend, then looked back up at Scott. "Go on to work, Scott. I'll be fine here."

I'll bet you will be. Scott saw Dr. Ambrose watching Rica. Scott bent to give her a long, sensual kiss, hoping that kiss would remind her of the promise they had made to each other before they left the apartment. "I'll be home as soon as I can."

Chapter 28

As the chief addressed the media swarming around the ambulance, Scott ducked under the yellow "Crime Scene" tape and nodded to the officer dusting the door for fingerprints.

"Bates is with the bodies." The officer tipped his head toward the back of the store. "In the freezer."

"Thanks." Scott walked past another officer photographing goods dumped from the shelves to the floor. Through a grimy aluminum swinging door that only covered about two-thirds of the opening, he could hear voices. He stepped through the door, careful not to touch it. No blood on it, he noted. Just past the door stood a walk-in freezer, door ajar, Bates standing beside the door, listening to someone speak from inside the freezer.

"Hey, Scott." Bates looked toward Scott as he approached. "Doc is trying to determine exact time of death right now."

"Hell of a problem, Del." The voice of Dr. Reichmuller, a local family physician who also served as the County Coroner, sounded muffled from the freezer. "Cause of death is a no-brainer, both of them shot point-blank center chest. But them being in the freezer muddles up the body temp. I'll have to get them to the morgue for more tests."

Scott leaned forward to survey the scene inside the

freezer. Against the pizzas at the far end of the freezer, the bodies of two women, one wearing the red logo shirt of the chain, slumped on the floor. The blood that nearly matched the shirt had formed a pool around them before it froze. The expressions on their faces registered fear. It looked like the older woman had grasped the hand of the younger just before their lives ended.

"Regular customer came in about nine, found no one behind the counter and the store trashed. He backed out and called 911. Dispatch called the manager, who got here about two minutes behind the squad cars. When uniforms didn't find anyone in the store, they had the manager come in and open the freezer." Bates gestured toward the women. "This is what they found."

His stomach tight from the finality of the end for these women, Scott tore his gaze away from them. "ID's yet?"

Bates nodded, consulting his ever-present notebook. "Young one is Amy Erikson, came on duty at three, only her second shift by herself." Bates sniffed. "Damn freezer is making the whole place cold." He flipped the page. "From what we can tell by the tag on the Oldsmobile in the parking lot, the older woman is Helen Nice, a seventy-year-old widow who lived just a couple blocks away." He looked up at Scott. "Both their purses are missing. Most of the cash is gone from the drawer, but there wasn't much, because the manager left at four with a deposit." He took a deep breath. "And KBI is on the way."

"Great." Scott knew the Kansas Bureau of Investigation would come in and re-take most of the photographs, re-run much of the lab work, and re-question the witnesses with excruciating thoroughness.

"There should be plenty of evidence for them to collect."

Bates nodded. "And a major headache sorting out killers from customers."

Scott reran the trail he had followed from the door to the freezer. "Probably the best chance of identifiable prints belonging to the killer would come from the register or the freezer door."

"Probably—" A commotion at the front of the store interrupted.

The officer who had been photographing the store came to the swinging door. "KBI's here, Del."

"Good," Dr. Reichmuller came out of the freezer, shivering. "Now maybe I can get the bodies to the morgue and determine TOD."

Chapter 29

Scott stood at the swinging door and watched two KBI agents sweep into the Quick Shop, nodding cursory approval of the evidence being processed on their way to the freezer.

"Todd," Bates backed up to allow a tall man in his forties access to the freezer.

"Del, Dr. Reichmuller." The agent stepped past them and into the freezer, while Scott stood in uncomfortable silence staring at the younger woman in a gray pantsuit who followed Todd in.

Del nodded at the woman. "Del Bates, PD."

"Janice Fleming." The woman paused to look toward Scott.

"Scott Aylward," Scott offered.

She nodded her acknowledgement and stood beside Todd. Her lips went tight at what she saw, and Todd's brows wrinkled in a frown, but otherwise neither officer gave outward acknowledgement to the horror Scott had felt when he looked upon the bloody frozen death scene.

"Photographed and measured?" Todd asked Bates.

Bates nodded. "Completely. Ready to be packaged up for the morgue."

Todd turned away from the freezer. "Let's get them on the way then. Let EMS take them." He looked toward Scott. "Todd Horton."

Scott nodded. It seemed the way KBI communicated. "Scott Aylward." Bates spoke quietly into his microphone.

Horton walked past Scott to the center of the tiny storeroom. "Let's see if we can find some of the mistakes these bastards made," he said, more to himself than anyone in particular. No one responded.

Two EMT's, each pushing a gurney, rattled into the storeroom, followed by another EMT bearing body bags. The gaze of each of them darted quickly toward each of the people in the storeroom, before they parked the gurneys outside the freezer. Scott backed up against a wall of shelves bearing boxes of chips, hemmed in by the gurneys. After a second's hesitation, the EMT with the body bags moved into the freezer. The other two followed her.

"Have you looked at the surveillance tapes yet?" Looking to the right and then the left, Horton stepped into the store proper.

"Had the manager stop it, but we haven't viewed it yet," Bates said, following Horton, scanning high and low. "Wonder if these bastards trashed the store, or if some punks came in after and did it just for fun?"

Fleming followed Bates. Scott worked his way from behind the gurneys. He really didn't want to be in the storeroom anyway when those bags came out of the freezer.

"We might find out when we look at it." Horton stopped. "Where's the manager?"

Bates inclined his head toward the front of the store. "Out in the chief's unmarked." He glanced back toward Scott. "Didn't want her touching anything nor did I think she needed to be in there by the freezer any more than necessary." He moved past Horton to escort them to the door. "EMS had to use smelling salts to help her calm down, and her husband got here twenty minutes ago." He stepped carefully over the pool of melted ice cream where several boxes had been dumped on the floor. "What a waste," he murmured to no one in particular.

"Whole damn thing is a waste," Horton growled. "Those two women, the money, the mess. Damn punks."

Scott caught up to Fleming. Her gaze roved the store, and Scott looked where she looked at the bags of chips and snacks in the next aisle, thrown to the floor and trampled. "Looks like either the murderers or someone had a high old time being destructive."

"Yeah, they usually do on something like this." She, too, carefully avoided the melted ice cream.

Mint chocolate chip. One of the treats he brought home when he needed to soften Rica's attitude. Definitely a waste.

Horton reached the front door and the tech starting to lift prints. "Have you dusted the door of the freezer?"

The officer eyed Horton, then glanced at Bates. "Yes, sir, did that soon after Doc pronounced 'em dead." He faced Horton. "If they were smart, they would have had the clerk open the freezer and then bumped it shut with their shoulders." He glanced at the print he had just pulled from the door. "But I'm betting they weren't smart."

Horton grunted. "They usually aren't." He turned back to Bates. "Any indication they got into the manager's office?"

Bates shook his head. "She locked the office when

she left, and it was still locked when we called her back." He paused. "We dusted the door and door knob, just to be safe."

Horton studied the mirror above the door, angled to let the clerk see part of the store from behind the counter. "Well, then, let's get the manager in here and go over those tapes."

Chapter 30

Fifteen minutes later, Bates and Scott stood jammed into the manager's tiny office, viewing the video surveillance tapes over the shoulders of the KBI and the manager. The camera didn't run continuously; rather it swept the area by the cashier and the front door every other minute. The jerky video made Scott's stomach rock.

On the grainy screen, Scott saw two people wearing ball caps and hoodies come into the store. They looked toward the clerk, but not toward the camera, then shuffled out of camera range. He struggled to read the time stamp on the screen, but even his 20/10 vision couldn't make it out six feet away from a twelve-inch screen.

"That should be a cause for a clerk to be suspicious," Horton snorted. "What kind of idiot wears a hoodie in hundred-degree weather?"

"The kind that wants to be 'cool,' Todd." Fleming's voice carried a tone of authority. "Gang members and wanna-bes are so desperate to fit in, that they do stupid stuff like that." She leaned toward the screen. "Besides, it was 6:30 when they came in; it had cooled down to eighty-five or ninety by then."

Scott regarded her with more respect. It sounded like she knew about gangs. He wondered if the robbery/murder was an initiation. On the screen another person entered the store. Mrs. Nice stopped to greet Amy, chatting for a moment before she walked out of camera range. Less than five minutes later, Mrs. Nice returned to the checkout. The two people wearing hoodies moved into line behind her. She said something to them, evidently a cordial greeting, then shrugged when she got no response. She plopped her purse on the counter and drew out a wallet. Then, one of the people behind her pulled his hand from the hoodie pocket. In the hand was a semi-automatic, and the thug waved it between Amy and Mrs. Nice. The other person grabbed Mrs. Nice's arm and bent it behind her, pushing her toward the counter. Amy's face did not appear on the screen, but the video clearly showed her hands raised. The criminal with the gun waved it around some more, and then shoved it toward her face. Her hands shook as she pushed the buttons to open the register. She dropped several coins while she thrust two fists full of bills toward the robber. The accomplice grabbed Mrs. Nice's wallet, then punched the elderly woman in the stomach before shoving her toward the floor. She held onto the counter to keep from falling, and leaned her head on it. The robber with the gun looked briefly at the money before shoving it in his hoodie pocket. Then he waved the gun around more while his partner rifled through Mrs. Nice's wallet. He shoved cash from the wallet into his pocket, then smacked Mrs. Nice in the face with the wallet. At the edge of the screen, Amy's hands stretched out, as if she were pleading with the robbers. A few minutes later, she came into view, from behind the counter. The thug with the gun grabbed her shirt by the shoulder and propelled her toward the back of the store. The other one dragged Mrs. Nice to her feet and pushed her ahead of him. That one looked up momentarily toward the camera and Scott held his breath, trying to see details of his face.

"Amy's purse was in her locker in the storeroom." The manager's voice shook. "She might still be alive if we had a place to keep it up front." She dropped her head to her desk, shoulders shaking with muffled sobs. "Amy had two little kids, not even in kindergarten yet." More sobs. "And Mrs. Nice has been coming in here since before I started here ten years ago." Her hands gripped the edge of the cluttered desk. "Neither of them would have hurt a fly!" Bates reached around Fleming to squeeze her shoulder.

"We'll go back to that frame, see if the techs can enlarge and enhance it." Horton glanced down at the manager. The noisy clock on the wall ticked by the next few minutes. Everyone in the room knew that those moments of no action at the counter marked the last moments of life for Helen Nice and Amy Erikson.

Scott forced himself to focus on the details revealed on the screen. The only car visible through the front of the store was Nice's Olds. No one else moved past the windows. Suddenly the two hoodied criminals sauntered into camera view, one of them munching from a bag of chips. The other grabbed a handful of breath mints from the display in front of the counter and then moved behind the counter. He riffled through the still-open register, then tore off several strips of lottery tickets.

"It'll be a losing move for him if he turns in any of those as winners," Horton muttered. "And definite prints."

The manager raised her head to look at the screen.

"We have the serial numbers. We can put them out to all the stores in town."

"Nationwide." The ice in Horton's voice made the manager glance at him.

"Ok," she mumbled.

The crook with the chips dropped them to the floor, disappeared, then returned to view with a carton of ice cream and a spoon from the hot foods counter. He ate for a few seconds while his companion searched for anything of value behind the counter. Then he tossed the carton and spoon into the second aisle from the door.

"DNA for sure." Scott itched to get the results.

Fleming glanced at him. "If the lab ever has time or staff to get it processed." She turned back to the screen. "If he's even in the database."

Scott sucked in his breath. Budget woes had cut KBI lab staff, along with staff and equipment from nearly every state agency.

The man behind the counter came from behind it, and both men disappeared from the camera's view. Seconds later, both appeared on camera, carrying a carton of beer in each hand. They strolled from the store and the video.

"What about the cameras in the parking lot?" Horton barked.

"They're dummies." The manager clenched her hands before her. "We're just a local store, not part of a big conglomerate."

This time Horton's voice was arctic. "So for the ten bucks a month it costs to operate those cameras, we have no way of knowing how those killers got in here or which direction they went."

"Yes," the manager said softly. "For ten bucks a month." She dropped her head to her desk and began to sob again.

Fleming drew a deep breath and let it out. "Well, those guys didn't leave the store the mess it is now." She leaned forward around the manager to click fast forward. After screens that represented a half hour or so, a group of five tweenagers entered the store. Most scattered immediately toward the back of the store, but one lingered near the counter, studying what he could see. As soon as he moved to where he could see the open register, he turned and began to call to the others. Two came into view. One went behind the counter and went through the register.

"So much for the integrity of the prints," Bates muttered.

The one behind the counter, too, pulled off some lottery tickets, then grabbed a couple of cartons of cigarettes. The other disappeared into the store. Soon, kids appeared briefly, running from aisle to aisle, while the kid who noticed the register appeared to be arguing with them. He left the store, but the others stayed for what represented about twenty minutes. Then they left, each with bags of snacks and drinks. No one else opened the door to the store until the reporting party entered, stepped in a few feet, yelled a few times, then carefully backed out, cell phone in his hand.

Horton straightened from his hunched pose before the screen. "Let's get this video out and to our lab."

"Do you mind making us a copy of it first?" Bates stood solid, his arms crossed over his chest. "I'd like my guys to view it, see if any of them can recognize the perpetrators."

Horton hesitated, his eyes looking Bates up and down before he shrugged. "Sure, more eyes gives us more chance of catching them." He picked up the disk the manager handed him. "We'll email you the enlargements as soon as we get them done."

"Thanks," Bates grunted.

Scott stared at the now blank screen. He intended to study the video until he could recognize those thugs by the way they walked.

Chapter 31

Charlotte made sure her hips swayed as seductively as possible while she picked her way slowly to keep from twisting an ankle on the gravel parking lot. When she had to alter her course every few feet to avoid a pothole, she used the pause to glance back at the customers lingering at the back door. A couple of them had pressed scraps of paper with phone numbers into her hands along with their generous tips. The forty-ish assistant coach of one of the out of town teams had even been charismatic enough, with his easy, confident carriage and angular, tanned face, that she was almost tempted to keep his number, despite the wedding ring on his left hand. Ultimately, though, she followed her long-standing policy of hinting she'd call, then dumping the numbers in the trash as soon as she got back to the employee locker room.

Still, the approval and the tips buoyed her spirits. That, and the act of looking sexy, made her tiny black panties wet by the time she bent over to unlock her car door. With one last look back at the men watching as they slowly scattered to their cars, she swiveled her butt into the seat of the low-slung compact, and then drew one long leg at a time into the car. It was a hell of a well-practiced show that should bring many of them back tomorrow night.

She faced herself in the rear-view mirror as she

inserted the key in the ignition, and the image that surfaced in her mind was not the confident coach, but the earnest face of the young detective, as he touched her arm and met her eyes. She felt a warm surge run through her body, reliving the tender way he looked at his woman the first night she saw him, the intensity that radiated from his green eyes, the fullness of his lips, his warm hand on her arm. She shivered. That was the kind of man she was looking for: gentle but strong, protective but passionate, manly but boyish.

She sighed. Too bad this particular man could never be THAT man. Not only was he a cop, but his face looked familiar as well. She couldn't afford to get mixed up with cops or anyone from her past. Except Mags.

She closed her eyes, but a hot tear squeezed out past the mascara. Just when she had finally been able to let Mags know how important she was to her, it had all ended.

She sniffed back the tears and turned the key. The parking lot was now empty of all cars except Harvey's as she idled out. She had to do something to take the edge off this tension within her. Tonight, Devlyn would have to do. And Devlyn would never know that, when Charlotte closed her eyes tonight, it would be the young cop's touch and not Devlyn's she felt.

Chapter 32

Scott stood silent just inside his apartment door, keys still in his hand, trying desperately to pull his mind back from that freezer, that video, and into his own home. He and Bates had watched KBI interview the patron who called in the alarm on the store, combed the store for any potential evidence that could have been missed, written up reports and reviewed evidence with KBI and the street officers who had initially responded to the scene. Finally, at 1:30 a.m., there was nothing more that could be done until the most likely fingerprints were processed through IAFIS (Integrated Automated Fingerprint Identification System) and the DNA through CODIS, the FBI's Combined DNA Index System. And that would be tomorrow afternoon at best.

He took a step further into the room. The corner streetlamp threw enough cool mercury light through the mini blinds that he could see to walk around the coffee table and toward the kitchen without bumping into anything.

At the kitchen island, he hesitated. He knew, from the way his mind kept racing to potential methods to narrow the clues, to possible suspects, to what Amy's little kids would remember of their mom, that his tossing and turning to escape those images would simply wake Rica if he went to bed at this moment. And taking a shower to calm down would also wake her. Though waking her, and keeping her awake for a good long time, had been his intention when he left her at the bar, now he didn't want to deal with her, didn't want to confront the fact that the faces tumbling in his mind right now seemed more real than the hot flesh and blood woman sleeping in the next room. Try as she might—and she had tried—she couldn't understand how they called to him, begged him to win them justice, how hard he had to work to shut them out when he failed them. It was as if, when they lost their lives, they took over his. And now this case consumed him almost as much as Delia's, and in letting it consume him, he failed her, too. Again, her wide blue eyes met his just as they had on the banks of the river.

He stepped further into the kitchen and silently took a wine glass from the cabinet. He'd have a little more of the merlot they had left from their anniversary celebration. He opened the refrigerator and tried not to bump any condiment bottles together as he rummaged for the wine. He pulled the bottle from the refrigerator and held it up against the fridge light. Not much left, less than a third of the bottle. He set the glass back down on the counter. He'd just drink what was left in the bottle without dirtying a glass. He moved back into the living room with the bottle in his hand and sank into the recliner.

He shook his head and swallowed a long pull of the wine, trying to blur the faces and silence the begging. Rica, his marriage, and his future all deserved at least as much of his time and devotion as did the clamoring horde. He tried desperately to center on Rica, on the plans they had made, on the children they had talked about having from almost their first date. Yet the effort of staying focused on her felt as difficult as holding onto a life preserver in a choppy sea. If he let his guard down for even an instant, he lost his grip on the life preserver. If he let it get too far away, he might never be able to grasp it again.

Chapter 33

"Scott, what the hell are you doing?" The screech woke him, and for an instant, he couldn't understand where he was and who was yelling at him. He looked around, and the bright sunlight boring through the window made him squint against it. He put up a hand to block the sun.

"Rica?" Slowly, he realized she was beside him, kneeling on the floor, scrubbing at the carpet.

"You might have at least set the bottle on the table, instead of letting it tip over on the floor." She sprayed a dark red spot on the rug. "What did you do, drink the whole bottle?"

He lowered the footrest quietly. "There wasn't much in it." He stood and stretched. Maybe a shower would take out the kinks the chair had put in. "I thought I might as well save dirtying a glass."

She met his eyes. "Then why didn't you put the clean glass back in the cabinet?" She looked down at the carpet again. "Damn it, Scott, this isn't going to come out, and we won't get our deposit back when we move out."

"Try salt." He didn't know where that tidbit of information came from. Sometimes his mind catalogued the damnedest things.

"Oh, so now you are not only a lush, but you're an expert on cleaning up after yourself?" She stood up, her anger making her seem taller than she was. "You'd rather sit in here alone and drink yourself into a stupor than come to bed with me?"

He sighed, wishing he could explain to her what that one sigh conveyed. "Last night was pretty rough." He passed his hand over his eyes, the women holding hands in the freezer once again what he saw with more clarity than Rica's angry face. "It was one or two when I got in and—to tell you the truth, Rica." He hesitated, groping for words. "I didn't even want to be with myself when I got home, much less lie next to you with all that ugliness and violence sticking to me." He stood before her totally drained. If she slapped him or shot him or hugged him at that moment, he wasn't sure he could register an emotion.

"So you thought you could wash off the violence with wine?" Her eyes still flashed, but he could see a softening in them. Maybe she would try to understand.

"There wasn't much in the bottle, Rica, maybe not even a full glass." The observer in him came awake, seeing doubt in the slight droop to her shoulders. "I've read wine helps you sleep, though I didn't think I could." A question came to him. "Have you seen the news yet this morning?"

"No, Scott, I woke up and realized you weren't there and came in here and found you passed out."

He reached for the remote beside the chair, turned to the TV and flipped it on. He had to switch through a home improvement and a shopping channel to find the news, but then suddenly, there was the too-familiar Quick Shop, with side-bar photos of the two women he remembered so differently. His stomach clenched as he un-muted it to hear, "Brutally shot and left in the freezer for a robbery that officials say netted them less than $100 in cash." Then he saw the video he had imprinted on his memory, the hoodied thug glancing toward the camera, his face an invisible blob.

He turned back to Rica, reading shock on her face. "That's where I was till midnight or so, then we were at the station processing evidence and reports."

"Oh, Scott!" Her face softened into empathy, though she didn't reach for him. "How horrible!"

He didn't respond to her, his attention given to the TV screen. The announcer begged the audience to call the toll-free hotline if they had any information.

"Do you have any leads, Scott?"

"Leads?" Her voice brought him back from the scene. "Not much. Fingerprints, but a lot of people touch things in a convenience store in a given day. Nothing that stands out." He faced her and tried to voice his frustration. "Those ladies didn't do anything to anyone, didn't do anything different than millions of people do every day, but they just had the bad luck to be in the way when someone wanted to take." He looked down at the floor. The red spot was nearly gone as the carpet cleaner did its work. "And he not only took money that wasn't his, he took their lives and their futures. And took a mother away from two little girls."

"Scott." Rica's voice was soft, her eyes serious. "Do you ever think about changing jobs?"

He looked at her as if she had lost her mind. "What else would I do?" He honestly had never considered it once he decided to make law enforcement his life's work. "I'm good at it."

"But, Scott, the cost…"

He stared at her; he had failed to make her

understand what he tried to convey. "I'd better get showered and get back into the station."

She reached out to touch his arm. "Be careful out there, Scott." Finally, she stepped toward him to hug him. "I love you, Scott."

He started to kiss her, but she slipped out of his arms and bent over the carpet again. "And the gang wants to meet at the Club again next week." Her face turned toward him, but he had the feeling she didn't really see him. "That was fun, don't you think?"

"Yeah, fun," he mumbled as he headed to the shower. It had been a load of fun for Mrs. Nice and Amy Erikson.

Chapter 34

Sunday and Monday brought more hours sifting evidence and follow up talks with witnesses. Scott viewed that video at least twenty times. Street officers stepped up patrols of convenience stores, stopping by for historic quantities of coffee and donuts, in an effort to both thwart further robberies and in hopes of catching a glimpse of one of the killers. Finally, late Tuesday morning, one of the fingerprints on the freezer matched to an individual in IAFIS, last known address, 312 ½ East Avenue B. Street officers recalled him as a suspect in several purse snatchings and a few burglaries.

"Neighborhood sounds about right." Bates sipped at the coffee in his cup before pitching the remainder in the trash. As soon as the info came in, KBI and the PD Captains had put in for a warrant. When the unmarked unit spotted the suspect going into his apartment, they alerted the SWAT team and called in off-duty officers.

Scott double-checked his spare magazine as they headed to the conference room at 1:30. Horton stood at the front of the room. Fleming leaned against the wall, her arms folded. A mug shot of a surly youth with dirty blond hair in dreadlocks glared at them as they entered the room. Next, a photo of the suspect's apartment house loomed on the screen.

"He lives in this back basement apartment." Horton

moved the mouse to point to a stairway leading down a narrow cement cut toward a door with peeling paint. A railing made of welded pipe surrounded the stairway. A set of closed mini blinds, some of them broken, covered the only visible window. Scott knew the house; he had backed up detectives on more than a few drug busts and warrant arrests there during his years in uniform. Apartments in the house were cheap, rented by the week, and the landlord did no background check. And the stairways were always lousy for approach. "The unmarked on the street indicates he went inside an hour ago and hasn't come out." He glanced around the room. "Judge is issuing the warrant for the arrest and search now."

Captain Black moved, stepped to the other side of the projector screen, and began assigning positions for the take-down. Scott's mind visualized the routes others would take as he waited for his own path. Finally, "Aylward and Bates, you go in as back-up to KBI."

Scott and Bates locked eyes. That meant that they got none of the glory if it went down as planned and all the blame if it didn't. He shrugged. He didn't care either way, as long as they took murderers off the street.

"Let's roll," Black said. Horton shot him a look, and silently slipped into his ballistics vest, prominently marked "KBI" front and back.

None too eager to don the heavy vests in ninety degree temperatures, Scott and Bates carried their vests to their car, settling them on just before they got inside. Lights flashing, but silent, a caravan of vehicles descended on all sides of Avenue B. Officers moved into position, waiting for KBI to make the first move.

Horton and Fleming approached the stairway to

312 ½. Leaves from last fall still littered the concrete. Fleming pressed her back against the wall at the top of the stairs, Bates beside her, and Scott at the corner of the wall immediately above the door. Horton walked quietly to the door. The stairway was so narrow, the door so close to the window, that there was no place for him to position himself except for squarely in front of the door. Though his stance spoke confidence, Scott could see the sweat trickling from under the cap and down his back. With a final glance at Fleming, Horton rapped on the door. Peeling paint bounced off it, but there was no other response. Scott saw Horton's shoulders square with a deep breath. He rapped again. "Thomas James, this is the KBI. We have a warrant for your arrest."

Scott saw Fleming speak into the mic at her lapel. Then she nodded to Horton. "Unmarked confirms he's still in there," she said in a tone so low Scott could barely hear her.

Just as there was no room for backup behind him, there was also no room for a ram to break down the door. Horton braced himself and kicked the door near the lock. With his second kick, the lock gave way.

Scott lowered himself to a squat and drew his Glock. From his vantage point, he could see inside the apartment over Horton's shoulder. Horton drew his gun as well. "Thomas James, this is the KBI," he repeated. "We have a warrant for your arrest, and we are coming in."

Ducking as low as she could go to get under the window, Fleming moved down the stairs as Horton stepped into the apartment, Bates an arm's length behind her. Scott covered the doorway from his position. He lost sight of Horton, and then Fleming disappeared inside. Bates reached the bottom of the stairs.

Suddenly, a skinny kid in a wife-beater, baggy board shorts, and no shoes burst from the apartment. Bates went down as the kid caught him in the gut with a shoulder. Scott holstered his gun and yelled, "Stop, police!" Around him, he could see other officers aim their weapons.

The kid took the stairs in two steps, but Scott tackled him just as his foot touched the sidewalk at the top of the stairs. The kid's head bounced off the wall before he went down on the concrete. Scott pushed himself upright enough to jam a knee in the kid's shoulder blades. He pulled the kid's right arm back and slipped on the handcuffs. By the time he got hold of the left arm, Bates and Fleming stood beside him. "Thomas James," Scott gasped. "You are under arrest." Coach would have been proud of that tackle.

Scott stood up and grabbed the kid's right arm. Bates grasped his left, and together they stood the suspect up. "You have the right to remain silent," Scott began, while Bates patted the suspect down quickly. The wife beater and shorts left few places to hide weapons. A gun stuffed in the baggy shorts the kid belted down around his ass would have pulled them off. Scott had almost finished the rest of Miranda when the kid started to talk.

"My name's Aaron Anderson," the kid stated. "I didn't do nothin'."

Horton, missing his cap and rubbing his head, made it to the top of the stairs. "Son of a bitch hit me with a chair." Fleming appeared behind Horton. "And knocked Fleming down."

"There you go." Bates nodded. "You did, too, do something. Assault on three police officers."

"How was I to know who was bustin' in my door?" The kid's face twitched in a nervous imitation of a smile. Scott caught sight of rotten teeth, a good indicator the kid used meth on a regular basis.

Horton stood in front of the kid, studying him. "Because we identified ourselves as KBI officers."

"I was takin' a nap." The kid could hardly hold still, fidgeting even with the handcuffs on. "And my name ain't James."

"You got ID that proves it?" Scott glanced down to see nothing in the pockets to indicate the bulge of a wallet.

The kid nodded. "Wallet on the table by the door."

"I'll get it." Fleming practically flew down the stairs and returned moments later with the wallet in her left hand and a driver's license in the other. She looked hard at the DL and even harder at the kid. "He's not James."

Horton folded his arms, as though thinking. Scott suppressed a smile. He knew that the judge would probably throw out the charges, but he hoped Anderson didn't know that. If they leaned on him a bit, made him think he could do life for accessory to murder, he'd probably tell them anything he knew. Or thought they wanted to hear. "Yes, but now we've got him on assault."

"Yeah," Bates inserted. "Three officers. Maybe four." He glanced at Scott. "He hit you, Scott?"

Scott nodded. "He hit my knee with his back, when he failed to obey the lawful order of a police officer."

The kid danced around like a racehorse anxious for the post. "How was I to know you was cops?" He looked at Bates. "I was sleepin' real good, hard, when all of a sudden my door busts open, and big guys with guns is runnin' into my house." He tried to hold still. "You'd 've run, too."

"I wouldn't be giving 'big guys with guns' reason to bust down my door." Bates moved into the kid's space, his face inches from the kid's. "And one of those 'guys' was a lady."

The kid glanced at Fleming. "Sorry, ma'am." The kid looked down at the ground. His mouth opened and closed, and for a moment, Scott thought he was going to cry. Then he shivered. "What'd this James guy do?"

Horton moved even closer to the kid than Bates. "You know him?"

The kid squinted up at Horton and tried to step back, but Scott's body behind him kept him in place. "Might, but maybe not by name." He glanced at Bates, then back at Horton's chin. "Know a lot of dudes by sight."

"Hmmm." Horton turned away from the kid and looked at Fleming. "Well, we have a warrant to search the apartment, doesn't matter that James wasn't there."

"Warrant?" The kid practically swallowed his tongue. "Whatcha need a warrant for? Whatcha lookin' for?"

Horton swung back toward the kid. "Evidence in a murder."

"M-m-murder?" Eyes wide, the kid tried to turn toward Scott. "I don't know nothin' 'bout no murder, man."

Horton leaned in just a little. "Of course, if we find

evidence of any crime, it's admissible under the search warrant. And if you do know James and don't tell us where he is, that would make you accessory to murder." He leaned still closer. "Don't suppose you know this, but any crime committed where a death occurs leaves anyone a party to that crime open to the death penalty."

"D-d-death?" Scott wanted to move away from the kid, because he had the uneasy feeling that the kid would soon lose the contents of either stomach, bladder, or bowels. He didn't want to be in range.

Horton nodded, waiting.

"James the guy used to live in this dump?" The kid jerked his head toward his apartment. Horton nodded again.

The kid wobbled toward Horton. "I ain't never actually talked to the dude, but when I was lookin' for a place a few days ago, friend of a friend pointed him out at a party, said he was fixin' to move, 'cause of the heat."

Scott gripped his arm tighter. "Heat?"

The kid looked sideways at Scott. "From the cops, man. They was tryin' to pin some shake-downs on him. He was movin' in with some chick, so my friend talked to some people, and I just moved in. He left a lotta stuff there, clothes and such." He squinted at Horton again. "That help me out any?"

Horton shrugged. "It might, especially if you know the chick." He started walking away. "But you'll have to come downtown with us anyway, while officers search this place."

The kid turned even paler than the pasty white he already was under the tattoos. "You still gonna search it?"

"Oh, yeah." Horton marched off toward his car, Fleming at his heels, while Scott guided the kid toward a black and white.

Chapter 35

Charlotte clumped into the employee locker room to refresh her lipstick. She hated working weeknights, especially Tuesdays, because the place was all but dead. And the few customers who came in were families with kids, or old people looking for the half-price specials. Her wages and tips wouldn't even cover the cost of getting ready and coming to work. "Talk about a waste of makeup," she murmured, even as she admired her full, now rosy, lips in the mirror. "I say again, girl, you are too good for this dive."

She sat in the hard plastic chair to rub her feet. Four-inch heels with half-inch platforms weren't exactly her mother's sensible shoes, especially with the amount of standing she'd had to do tonight. She stretched her legs out before her. Non-sensible or not, those hot pink heels made her calves look fabulous and gave her ankles just the right curve. She sighed and looked at the door. Too bad nothing hotter than a thirteen-year-old or an eighty-year-old would notice tonight.

As she sat there, her mind wandered back to a Friday night, about six months ago, when a group of classy women had taken a table in Charlotte's section. She had recognized a few of them—the brunette with the chestnut highlights and the red-head with the brassy dye job. But this time, they brought a new girl, a blonde with enormous blue eyes and a sad set to her lips. Charlotte kept sneaking glances at the blonde while the others ordered. The woman seemed detached from the group, studying the menu, tapping her fingers on the table, gazing out at the room as if she really were somewhere else.

"What'll you have, sweetie?" Charlotte had given her the brightest smile she had. Most customers couldn't resist smiling back.

This woman simply looked at her, held her gaze for a moment, then mumbled, "Margarita."

In the moment their eyes stayed locked, Charlotte felt a shock run all the way down to the tips of her heels. She knew this woman.

Chapter 36

Scott and Bates merely watched while Horton questioned Aaron Anderson six ways to Sunday about James, his whereabouts and associates. If Anderson knew anything, he didn't comprehend it. By the time Horton stood up to walk out of the interrogation room, the kid had squirmed enough to have almost worn the finish off the chair, and Horton acted like he could snap a pencil in half just by looking at it. "I'll leave you alone a few minutes to gather your thoughts," Horton said to him as he paused at the door, then joined Fleming, Bates, and Scott in the observation room. Apparently unaware he was being taped, Anderson scratched himself and shook.

Scott watched him fidget. "He couldn't gather his thoughts if you gave him a sheepdog to gather them with."

"Meth'll do that to you," Horton observed. "This friend of the friend who might know the chick James is shacked up with is the only halfway decent lead he provided." He turned to Bates. "Lab guys turn up anything yet?"

"A few prints that could be James', another that looks like it could be a match for one at the scene. Few ounces of pot and some hash, couple rocks of meth. Enough to file charges, not enough to get any serious jail time." Bates shook his head. "What a waste of potential."

"Yeah, and a waste of our time if we don't find anything that leads us to James or his accomplice." Horton stretched and ran his fingers through his hair.

"You get any leads from the forensics on the Delia Enfield case?" Even absorbed as he was by this case, Delia's was never far from Scott's mind.

"Enfield?" Horton turned a blank face to Scott.

"Found nude by the river, throat slashed," Fleming supplied. "It's a priority as a capital murder case, but lab is down three techs." She looked at Scott. "They are trying to ID the DNA to see if it matches your suspect."

"He's already admitted to having sex with her that day," Bates offered. "And I really don't think he had a window of opportunity."

"What would help is if you can ID someone else's DNA from her." Delia's memory nagged at him not to let her down.

"Lab has all the swabs taken from her body, plus the fibers the coroner got out of her hair and her skin." Fleming glanced at Scott. "There's just not a lot there to work with."

"I know. Not much in the way of leads connected with this case." Scott focused on the kid in the interrogation room, who had begun to scratch his forearms hard enough to make them bleed. "Shouldn't we stop him?" He reached for the door, but Horton was already opening it.

"Looks like he's goin' to detox," Horton muttered.

Chapter 37

Sauntering through the Dragon's parking lot, dust puffing from each mincing step, Charlotte left the August night, still ninety-five degrees at ten-thirty, and went back to that April evening, when even the air was pregnant with expectation. It had been a Friday, a convention in town, so the tips should be great. Charlotte had donned a classy but short black pencil skirt, low-cut red satin blouse, her hardest-working push-up bra, and her pointiest stilettos. The memory of Devlyn's harsh words had faded rapidly away; the best tips and most appreciation should come her way tonight.

Then the group of women had come in, their rosy faces and animated conversation suggesting that they had had a few drinks with dinner prior to arriving at the Dragon. When Charlotte brought their drinks back to the table, she served the blonde last.

"Here you go, sweetie," she said in her gentlest voice as she set the margarita at the woman's fingertips.

"Thanks." The woman's hand grazed hers as she reached for the drink and brought it to full lips that quivered slightly, as if holding back a sob. The blue eyes looked as enormous and sad as a Hummel figurine's.

"Should I bring you another on my next pass this way?" Charlotte stood close to this woman, oblivious to the rest of the raucous crowd at the table, entranced by the melancholy emanating from her. Even in the low light, Charlotte could see the heart shape of the woman's face, the full breasts sheathed in the business-like blouse, the long, slim legs peeping from under the table. This woman dressed to hide her sensuality, not enhance it like Charlotte did.

The woman looked up at her and their eyes locked again. Charlotte studied the color of those blue eyes, the line of her nose, the curve of her lips. "No, well, maybe." The woman shrugged and swung toward her, tight gray skirt sliding up to mid-thigh. "Oh, sure, why not."

Charlotte stood frozen for a moment, stunned by a familiar note in the carefully-modulated voice. She recovered. "I'll have one here the moment you finish this one."

The blonde's lips curved in the hint of a smile, while Charlotte tried to hide her shock. "That may not be very long." She lifted the glass to her mouth, tipping back her head to expose a soft, elegant neck. Charlotte forced herself to pay attention to the other women clamoring for refills, though her gaze remained on the blonde. The woman flashed Charlotte a smile and squared her shoulders as if the alcohol had started to flush away the sadness.

Chapter 38

"Yes, I remember, honey." Scott stifled the sound of frustration he felt creeping into his voice. "I'll be on my way by five o'clock and ten seconds."

"Just don't be late." Rica didn't even try to keep the snap out of her voice. "The gang will be waiting on us at six."

Scott flipped shut his cell phone without responding. He knew she would hear the sarcasm if he said, "Yes, dear."

"Marching orders from the boss?" Bates made his way past Scott's desk with still another Styrofoam cup.

"She's got this damned coffee klatch at the Pub with her co-workers she wants to subject me to tonight." He scanned his report for errors. "Same place we were when the murders went down. Getting to be an every Friday night thing."

Bates took a sip from the cup and frowned. "Doesn't sound like it bodes well for an enjoyable evening."

"Nope." Scott watched as Bates poured the contents of the cup on the thriving peace lily beside his desk. "All but one of the 'gang' works together at the hospital. One of the husbands and me are the two non-medicals." He turned back to the screen. "And that damned Dr. Ambrose…"

"What?" Bates froze in the act of sitting in his

chair.

Scott shook his head. "Nothing, just talking to myself."

"Okay." Bates sat. "What do you think—"

"Bates, Aylward!" Captain Black stuck his head in the door. "Uniforms just picked up the main suspect in the Quick Shop murders." He turned to head to interrogation. "Should be here in about five minutes."

"Hot damn!" Scott rolled his chair back so fast it bounced off the wall behind him and nearly took out his knees as he trotted out the door. "I want a piece of this interrogation."

****

Twenty minutes later, Scott texted Rica. "Not going to make it tonight. Questioning a suspect." There. By texting, he didn't have to listen to her either threaten or cajole. And staying to question James kept him away from the ugly meeting at the Pub. He felt sorry for Heather's husband John. He didn't wait to see if he got a text in response.

****

Scott flinched as Horton slammed his pen to the interrogation table. Thomas James merely tipped back his head and stared at the KBI agent walking toward the mirror that afforded Bates, Fleming, and Captain Black a view of the interrogation room. "What can I say, man? I didn't do nothin'. Was home with my peeps playin' HALO all afternoon and evenin' the day that went down." The exaggerated nonchalance said James had denied culpability before. Though having to leave his many body-piercing pieces of jewelry and the hat he usually wore cocked to the side with the jailer left him looking a bit less confident. And Scott could see sweat glistening below the thin mustache on James' upper lip, even though the temperature in the room should have had him in goose bumps wearing nothing but a dirty wife-beater and baggy shorts.

Horton studied his own face in the mirror. He snorted and whirled to face James again. "Hell of a productive way for a thirty-five-year-old adult to be spending an entire day."

James shrugged. "Relaxes me, man."

Horton placed his hands on the table and leaned within six inches of James' face. "So if you were home playing video games, how did your fingerprints get on the freezer the bodies were found in?"

"Dunno, man." James looked directly into Horton's eyes. "Maybe I helped a dude deliver some frozen pizzas there once."

"Oh, really." Horton leaned closer. "What delivery company?"

"Dunno, man. I just rides with my buds when they wants some company."

"So you are not actually an employee of this delivery company?"

"Nope."

"And I suppose your buds wouldn't admit they were taking riders along against company policy, would they?"

"I wouldn't 'spect them to."

Horton stood up. "Well, Mr. James, unless one of these 'buds' comes forward to corroborate your story, you'll be sitting in jail charged with first-degree robbery, kidnapping, and murder."

"I'm innocent."

"That's what they all say." Horton perched on the

edge of the table. "Say, just for fun, that your alibi can't be confirmed, so the only way you might get out of this is to let us know who else was with you, who might have actually pulled the trigger." He leaned a little toward James. "Would you really want to fry—you know Kansas still has the electric chair—and let the real killer walk free when all you had to do was roll on him?"

"I'd sure as hell roll if I knew somethin'." James nodded earnestly. "But I was home all afternoon." He leaned back in his chair. "'Sides, Kansas does lethal injection now."

Horton stood up. "Sit here and think about your buds for a while." He took a step for the door, and Scott rose from his seat. "Think about them playing HALO while you sit in a cold gray cell."

They left James in the room. Horton's shoulders sagged as soon as he closed the door to the interrogation room. "That's one cold son of a bitch." He ran his hand over his face.

Scott nodded. "In and out of local jail and state prison since he was fourteen. Robbery, assault, car theft, burglary, receiving stolen goods, meth. Like he has no conscience."

Horton looked at Scott. "Jail was college to him." He rolled his shoulders. "Just taught him how to take whatever he wanted easier."

"Let's just hope that the apartment and car search turn up something." Scott looked up at Horton. "Like maybe one of those lottery tickets."

Horton nodded and opened the door to the observation room. Fleming turned toward them. "Tough one," she said. "Lab radioed they were bringing in some hoodies and shoes. And some scratched off lottery tickets."

"If they're the right tickets, they'll be losing tickets for James."

Horton shot him a look. "If we can prove someone else didn't give them to him."

"I don't understand why he doesn't give up his accomplice, lay the blame on him."

Horton's shoulders sagged. "Because even if we find the right lottery tickets in his apartment, or blood spatter on his shoes, or the murder weapon, it's no proof he was there or pulled the trigger. If we don't find the accomplice, he can lay any blame on him. It's too far out from the murder to find gunpowder residue." He looked through the window at James, still cool and calm. "And if we do find the accomplice, it devolves into a game of blaming each other. Convictions might be hard to come by without a shadow of a doubt on this one, and that's what it takes."

"Aylward," Fleming called to him. "Lab got DNA results from the samples on your Enfield case."

Scott snapped James' file shut. "What did they find?"

"Some DNA matched the suspect you said admitted having sex with her. Then there was female DNA on the body, but it didn't match anyone in the system. And another DNA sample with some anomalies. They'll get back to studying that one when they have more time."

Time. That was what everyone wanted, but no one could buy.

Chapter 39

At nine o'clock, Scott pulled his cell phone from his pocket as he trotted across the parking lot. Rica answered on the fourth ring, just before it rolled to voice mail. "Hello, Scott." Her voice, or what he could hear above the background din, sounded flat.

"Hey, honey." He tried to hold on to the jubilation he felt that James was behind bars and evidence that could link him to the murder would be processed in the morning. "We finished with the suspect."

"That's great, Scott." She offered no more comment, though he could hear lively conversation going on behind her words.

"Do you want me to join you after I shower?" He had reached his truck.

"Don't bother, Scott." He heard her take a drink of something. "We won't be here much longer, and I'm sure you're tired from your long day."

He stopped with the key in his hand. "Okay, honey." His fingers tightened on the keys. "Whatever you want." He opened the door and sat in the truck with the door open, broiling with the temperature still in the nineties. What *did* she want? What would it take to put her in a good mood. He started the truck, flipping the air on max. A clean house? All his stuff picked up and put away? That was it. He'd rush home and finally sort through the magazines he'd left by the bed the day he

188

found Delia's body. And maybe when that was done, he'd organize the videos scattered around the entertainment center. And shower and have a drink waiting for her when she got home. She'd finally be proud of him.

****

"Scott!" Rica hissed the moment she stepped through the apartment door. "What on earth are you doing?"

He pulled his attention from the true-life mystery on the screen. "Huh?" Gradually, his mind came back from the crime that appeared about to be solved to his life. "I'm sorting through those papers you wanted me to sort."

"I wanted you to sort them three weeks ago." She jammed her keys back in her purse. "No, actually, I wanted you to sort them as you brought them into the house." She took a step into the room. "But why do you have to scatter them all over the living room to sort them?"

He stopped to study his system. "That's stuff I need to read before I pitch it, that pile is for recycling, that pile is to be shredded…"

"Never mind." She threw up her hands. "It's a good thing I told the gang I'd come up and see if you were asleep before I invited them in." She turned toward the door. "It's obvious I can't bring them to a house looking like this."

"I can put everything back in the box—"

"And then have you make this mess all over again? No, thank you." She opened the door. "I'll just tell them you were already in bed, and we'll go to Heather and John's." At the threshold, she stopped. "And don't wait

189

up. I'll just stay there tonight."

"But—" Before he could protest, apologize or say good night, she was gone. He looked around the room. It really did look a mess, even though he knew there was a method to it. The mystery show ended, crime solved, and he had missed it. He reached for the remote, flipped the channel to the news, and grabbed the soda he'd been drinking. The first sip told him it had gone warm and flat. He glanced toward the kitchen. If he remembered correctly, there was some wheat beer in there with a smooth and soothing taste. He grabbed the papers meant for recycling, dumped them into a paper bag and wandered into the bedroom for the shredder. It made more sense to shred as he went along than to make a pile he could get confused with the other piles. He set up the shredder by the couch, and then went into the kitchen for the beer. He didn't have to report to work tomorrow; he could work all night on organizing things, and then maybe Rica would forgive him. He opened the beer and swallowed a long pull. It went down easy.

Chapter 40

"Isn't that right, Aylward?" Bates' voice jerked him out of wondering how Rica would treat him when he got home tonight. Horton, Fleming and Bates watched him as he blinked to jog his memory to what the conversation had concerned before his mind wandered off alone.

"Sure, Del. You're the supervisor." He grinned, hoping to pass the incident off.

Horton laughed, shaking his head, while Fleming just stared with her calculating gray eyes. Bates slapped his shoulder as he stood to walk past him. "I knew you'd agree that Marvin's was the best place for lunch."

"Always." Scott stood, glancing at the time on his computer. Eleven-fifty. The last time he realized the time, it was eleven-thirty. He stretched, and Bates hung back, as Horton and Fleming disappeared through the door.

"Somethin' goin' on, boy?" With twelve years on Scott, Bates assumed the father role when it suited him.

Scott shrugged and shook his head. "Rica—"

"Rica is being a passionate, hot-blooded Latina, eh?" Bates smiled. "The best thing about a fight is the making up."

Scott studied the worn floor tiles as he made his way to the door. "Not sure there'll be making up this time."

"Give it some time, boy. There will be making up."

"I sure hope so." He followed Bates down the hall, into the elevator, and out the front door in silence. His mind ran free again as they joined Horton and Fleming to walk the three blocks to the barbeque restaurant. Rica hadn't come home Saturday morning or Sunday morning. Only his morning run Sunday along the north end of the river allowed him to hold it together. Not until eight o'clock Sunday evening did she walk through their door. Then he tried to show her the organized videos, the clean kitchen and neatly hung laundry, but she just shook her head.

"I don't want to talk now, Scott." She had gone into the bathroom to shower, then went into their bedroom and firmly closed the door. He slept on the couch, fitfully, until he awoke to the slamming door of her leaving for work. He had the uneasy feeling that this fight would not be fixed by flowers or dinner. This would take digging in and pushing her to talk. He might not like what he heard.

He nearly ran into his partner as Bates stopped before the door to Marvin's. Horton opened the door, and Fleming stepped through. Bates turned to face him. "It'll be okay, Scott," he murmured. "Stop worrying."

He stared at Bates. He hoped he was right.

****

"I tell you," Horton waved a finger around the table to make his point. "The most horrifying crime scene I ever worked was—"

A buzz from Fleming's left hip stopped the conversation as the diners in the next booth fled. She snatched her phone. "Fleming," she answered crisply.

The men paused, taking bites of their ribs or pulled

192

pork, hoping the call came from the lab. "Yes. Yes. I see. Thank you." Fleming's side of the exchange was brief, as she listened for several minutes. When she pressed the red button and laid the phone on the table, the men all watched her in silence.

She took a bite of her sandwich and chewed slowly, as her lips turned up slightly on the right. "So, fellas, how about going back to the jail to talk to Mr. James after lunch?"

Horton grabbed a curly fry. "Lab?"

She nodded, then glanced around to see who might be close enough to hear their conversation. "There was blood splatter on the boots from James' apartment. It had been wiped off, but there was enough left to make a DNA match for both women."

"Son of a bitch!" Horton slapped the table lightly. "And the print work?"

"They are still running prints from the apartment, but they have a couple that could be matches for the ones on the freezer door."

"That would certainly make someone seem like a possible accomplice to be with James at the crime scene and his apartment." Bates started to smile.

"Now if that person just has some of the other lottery tickets, we might have a good case." If they could bring the killers to justice, maybe Amy and Mrs. Nice would give Scott some peace so he could sleep.

Chapter 41

Charlotte dropped into the chair in the employee lounge. Two more hours and she could slip off these shoes in her car on the way home. Right now, if she took them off, she might not get them on again. The other girls wore sneakers, but Charlotte enjoyed the looks she got from both men and women in her short skirts and high heels. She leaned her head against the wall. The pain in her feet was worth it, just as the other pain had been worth it.

She closed her eyes and remembered. The group of predatory women had come in nearly every Friday for a couple of months, always sitting in her section. The blonde with them had begun to shake off her unhappiness, smiling more frequently. Charlotte always made a point to pay special attention to her, and the woman treated her with kindness and respect. The hair might be blonde now instead of brown, but the eyes and the attitude hadn't changed in a decade. She was slimmer and contacts had replaced the glasses, but Charlotte was sure of her identity—almost.

This particular Friday—she couldn't believe it was only four months ago—the blonde wore a fitted blue silk sheath cut low in front and back. She cut a striking figure walking into the place, and many men stopped talking to stare. Charlotte zipped right up to their table, pad in hand to take their drink orders, though she had learned what most of them usually ordered. She saved the blonde for last, and the woman waited patiently, flashing her big smile.

"And for you, sweetie?" Charlotte gave her biggest smile in return.

"It's Delia, hon." Delia leaned on the table, looking up at Charlotte. "What do you recommend? I'm in the mood to try something new tonight."

Charlotte tensed inside, though no one could have told. "Sangria's always good, refreshing on a hot night like tonight." She folded her arms below her breasts, the action drawing attention to the deep vee of the purple shirt. "Or tequila sunrise can be good."

Delia tilted her head, a smile dimpling her cheeks. "What's your personal favorite?"

Charlotte grinned. "Personally, I like Sex on the Beach."

Delia laughed, throwing back her head in a way that accented the long line of skin from throat to the neckline of the dress. "By golly, that does sound good. Bring me one, and be ready for another one."

"That I can do." She struggled with the name. "Delia."

It was a busy night at the Dragon, and Charlotte hustled for the next hour, bringing one more drink to Delia and her friends. Finally, she escaped to the lounge during a short lull. There she struggled with the memories, and the memories of the feelings, that she had kept hidden for more than ten years. Those ten years had wrought more changes, both physically and emotionally, in her than in Delia, but beyond a doubt, both of them had changed drastically. She could tell by the tenor of the background noise that the lull had ended, and she rose to resume her work.

Charlotte had taken two steps out of the lounge when the door of the adjacent ladies room opened, and Delia lurched out to bump into her. Charlotte put her hands on Delia's shoulders to steady both of them. Charlotte held on a few seconds after they regained their balance.

"Do you recognize me?" She stared intently into Delia's eyes.

"Recognize you?" Confused, Delia shook her head politely, but stopped when it threw her off balance again. "I don't. The first time I ever met you was when we started coming in here a few weeks ago."

"Go back a long time." With effort, Charlotte forced her voice to resume the pitch she had worked for the past eight years to lose. "The last time we saw each other was the week after our junior year in high school, Mags."

Mouth open in shock, Delia stared at her for a full minute. Then tears began to well from those enormous eyes. "Oh, my God!" She leaned forward to fold Charlotte in a hug.

****

Charlotte opened her tired eyes and sighed. The lull was over; time to go back to work. She glanced at the ladies room door as she passed it. She smiled, even as a tear tried to work its way out of her left eye. No fateful collision tonight; never again. She breathed deeply to compose herself. Two more hours, and then she would be on her way home to Devlyn. Her freedom to be herself had ended with Delia's death.

Chapter 42

Seeing Rica's SUV in their apartment parking lot as he pulled in made Scott feel better than he had in days. Maybe they could spend some time together. He bounded up the stairs and flung open the door. "Rica, honey." He greeted her from the threshold where she stood in the kitchen. "I'm so glad you're home." He hurried across the room, talking as he walked. "We caught one of the Quick Shop killers, got enough evidence to charge him with murder, and—"

"That's wonderful, Scott." Her flat tone negated the words.

He stopped before he reached her. His mind stumbled over words he wanted to tell her, but fear held his tongue silent. She simply stood there, the counter between them, studying him with one eyebrow raised. Finally, with a deep breath, he took the bull by the horns. "What's wrong, Rica?"

"Oh, Scott!" Both eyebrows drew together. "It's us. We're wrong." A tear slid down her cheek, but she batted it away. "We're just always on a different schedule, a different frequency, all the time anymore."

"But, honey, we caught the killer." He took a half-step toward her, his palms out in supplication. "Things will slow down now."

"There'll be another killer. Or maybe it will be a string of burglaries." She stepped forward to grip the countertop with her fingers, those long, sensitive fingers, with finely shaped nails, that could drive him wild with just one touch. "There will always be something that pulls you away when I need you."

"Need me?" He tipped his head to the left. "But I was late for a couple of get-togethers with your friends. It wasn't like you broke a leg, and I left you at the hospital before you went to surgery."

Her eyes flashed then, and the brows lowered. "See? You didn't even realize how important it was to me that you be there."

"How can I realize if you don't tell me?"

"I shouldn't *have* to tell you!" She slammed a hand on the counter. "You should know that when I ask you, it is important to me."

"Rica, I'm sorry. If I'd have known—"

"If you'd known, you'd still have stayed on the case till it was solved." Her face and voice softened for a moment. "That's just you, Scott, and it's not fair for me to expect you to change." She looked down at the counter and traced a circle with her finger. "That's why I'm moving out, moving in with Heather and John for a while."

His heart stopped; his lungs forgot how to breathe. "But—"

"I don't know that it will be permanent, Scott." She looked up at him again. "I just need to think some things over."

"But, Rica…" She didn't stop him, but he didn't know what to say. He forced air into his lungs. "How long?"

She moved from behind the counter, taking a half-step toward him, as if she wanted him to hold her. "I don't know."

He looked into her eyes, frightened by the determination he saw behind the tears that had yet to fall. Then he turned toward the bedroom. There, he saw three bags, packed and ready to go. She had evidently spent quite some time here today, getting ready for this. "Will you call me sometimes?" He faced her again. "Or can I call you?"

"Wait for me to call you." She sniffled. "I won't wait long before I call, I promise." She took a step toward him, her hand out to take his. "I don't want to hurt you, Scott, and I know you don't intend to hurt me."

His fingers tightened around hers. "I never want to hurt you, Rica."

"I know, Scott." She swayed toward him for a moment, and then she dropped his hand. "But we do hurt each other, and we need to stop it." Turning, she walked past him into the bedroom to gather her bags.

He stood where she left him as if his feet had no will to move. Then he saw her struggling with the biggest bag, and he took it, and the next largest, from her. "I'll get these for you." His throat was so tight, the words barely came out.

She touched his cheek. "Thank you, Scott." She gathered the smallest bag, rolling it behind her while Scott followed. "I know this is hard for you."

"I think it's hard for you, too," he said to her back. *At least I hope it is.*

She paused at the door. "It is, Scott, it's very hard."

At the stairway, he stopped her. "Leave the bag, Rica. Go on down and get the car open." He blinked. "I'll bring the bags to you."

She stared at him. "Okay." She trotted down the stairs, and he carried the two smallest bags down, then went back for the big one. Then he rolled all three at once toward her car and loaded them in the cargo area. She slammed the hatch, and they stood there, awkward.

She stepped to the side to go around him to the driver's door. He turned to be out of her way, then walked her to the driver's door. "I hope you call me soon, Rica."

She reached out to stroke his cheek. "It won't be long, Scott." Then she slid into her seat. He gently closed the door for her. She smiled at him, a smile he could tell she forced and didn't feel. Then she turned the key, snapped her seatbelt, checked her mirror and backed out of her space. He stood in the parking lot watching through the shimmering heat waves as she pulled out onto the street, turned left, and disappeared from his life. Despite her words and the hope in his heart, his gut knew she was done working on them.

When the heat began to make him dizzy, he thought about the beer still in the fridge. It would feel good after the heat, might start to numb the loss knifing through his heart. He glanced toward the apartment building, already feeling the cool liquid soothing his throat. Then he looked to the right, toward the park and the tall cottonwoods that shaded the path that led to the trail along the river. The other salve to his pain would be to go for a run by the river. He wavered for a moment, then decided he would go for a run. There would always be the beer after the run, if he still needed it.

Chapter 43

Charlotte put down her cell phone and picked up a colored pencil to finish the sketch she'd been working on when Devlyn called. But her hand trembled so much that she knew she would ruin the sketch if she worked on it now. With a deadline of tomorrow, she couldn't afford to start over. Harvey had her on the schedule tonight at the Dragon, so she would not be able to stay late at work to re-do the drawing. And Devlyn had ordered her straight home after the Dragon. She dared not disobey.

She got up to stretch and walked to her window. Floor to ceiling, third floor view, corner office, freedom to design the artwork to meet the customers' desires. This was a dream job, and she knew it. For the thousandth time, she wondered why she had ever accepted Harvey's offer of the job at the Dragon. She didn't need the money or the tips. The owners and other designers here respected her work and herself as the person as she was now, not judging her for her past.

If only she had declined Harvey's offer. Then she would never have met Devlyn, would still have her own cozy apartment to go home to in peace and privacy. But then again, she would not have run into Margaret again, to pick up that old friendship where it had been cut off so many years before.

She closed her eyes and started to tremble again. If

she hadn't met Devlyn and run into Margaret, Mags might still be alive.

Chapter 44

Scott's head nearly bumped the screen as he dozed off momentarily. "That's it." He swiveled his chair around to face Bates' desk. "I can't look at another set of silverware on E-Bay."

Bates grinned. "Shopping for stolen goods not your favorite pastime, boy?"

Scott shrugged. He hadn't heard from Rica in the forty-two hours and thirty minutes since she left. He ached with missing her presence. "Never was."

The smile dimmed from Bates' face. "Something bothering you, Scott?"

Scott trusted Bates with his life and knew the older man would have plenty of advice to give. But before he gave advice, Bates would give sympathy. Scott couldn't handle that at the moment. "No, just tired of sitting in the office."

"You could check the pawn shops."

"Did that yesterday." Though he couldn't remember a solitary thing he'd seen. All he had seen was Rica's face, scenes of their lives together, scenes he had hoped to see in the future.

"Get me some coffee?" Bates held out his cup.

"I can do that." Scott took it and wandered to reception. They brewed better coffee, and they made it more often than Bates did. None of the women there even looked up when they heard the carafe clank against Bates' cup. In moments, Scott was back and set the steaming cup on his partner's desk. "I think I'll run over to Homedale and see if I can dig up any more leads on the Delia Enfield case."

Bates studied him over the rim of the mug. "That one still eatin' at ya?"

Scott shrugged. "I guess so. Maybe it's that hometown connection."

"Could be." Bates sipped the coffee and made a face. "Theirs is too strong!" He sipped again. "Want some company?"

"Naw." Scott grinned at him. "You look too comfortable browsing Craigslist for antique settees." Two months ago, thieves had stolen every stick of furniture from several unoccupied farm homes.

Bates smiled. "Well, the thieves have to sell them somewhere, don't they?"

Scott shook his head and headed to the garage to see if they had any unmarked cars available. If he turned the radio up loud enough, maybe he couldn't hear himself think on the hour-long drive. He had tunes going before he even pulled out of the parking lot. Yet every song that came on his favorite station reminded him of Rica—somewhere they went, something they had done, some memory of her. He punched the presets, finally landing on a classical station. But that one was playing selections from *Romeo and Juliet*. He flipped some more buttons. There, a Christian station. On that one, the preacher thundered vehemently about the sins of divorce, of forgiving and taking back an errant spouse. Scott gritted his teeth. There had to be something to listen to that wouldn't make him think of Rica. Finally, he settled on NPR. Water wells in Africa.

Nothing there to remind him of his marriage. Yet, the calm, modulated voices grated on his ears instead of soothing as they were designed to do. With expletives muttered under his breath, he punched the "off" button.

Who did Rica think she was, anyway, demanding that he be the only one who needed to change. He bet the only change that would make her happy would be if he changed into Dr. Ambrose. By then, he was only fifteen miles from Homedale, about to cross the river.

He slowed as he approached the bridge. Something about the river called to him. Since Rica pulled out of the driveway, he had become fanatical about his morning runs along the river, as the running seemed to pound her memory out of his brain for the duration of the run. Here the river flowed more like he'd known it in childhood. He was only eight when he found a dusty old canoe in the garage rafters and dragged it to the river as it ran past the farm. On summer days when neither his mother nor father needed him for chores, he'd often made a couple of sandwiches, grabbed an apple and a can of soda, and pushed off from the willow tree at the bend behind the bean field. He'd float all afternoon, and his dad would meet him with the pickup about six to help him load the canoe and come home for supper. The river had taught him much on those floats—what types of pools the herons preferred over what appealed to the dowitchers; how vulnerable were the nests the terns made on the bare sand; how the subtle changes in the colors of the prairie grasses told the coming changes of the seasons; how like ghosts the bare white limbs of the cottonwoods appeared in winter, especially when the entire waterway was rimed with frost; how deceptively treacherous the deep pools could be.

Now, he pulled the car to a stop a hundred feet west of the bridge and edged it well onto the grassy shoulder, hoping the hot muffler wouldn't set fire to the grass, still dangerously dry even though it had rained last week. Glancing up and down the highway, he saw no traffic from either direction, so he crossed the roadway and picked his way through the stubbly grass to the river bank. There, on the south side of the bridge, the current swirled around the bridge pillar, allowing the sediment to settle from the water there, forming a sand bar that would have made a good launch point. In fact, he could see the impression where a canoe or kayak had rested on the sand. He walked until he got close enough to the water to sink a half-inch into the sand, then he stopped.

The August rains had greened the grass, but not affected the river much. A dam in Colorado, built long before he was born, had tamed the river, so that it no longer roared as winter snowmelt swelled it. Now the reservoir caught the snowmelt, parceling it out throughout the year to keep flows steady and prevent flooding. Irrigation had sucked much of the water out of the aquifer that underlay the river since Scott was a boy, so that here in Kansas, steady meant barely flowing. At low flows, the sand dropped to the river bottom. To canoe the river near the bridge would mean frequent portages over water barely six inches deep. The river had changed since he was a boy, and life had changed as well.

Mosquitoes swarmed around him, and after he smashed the tenth one, he decided he'd had enough nostalgia. He returned to the car, now an oven after sitting in the bright sun for just a few minutes. The air conditioner had barely kicked in before he drove into Homedale.

Chapter 45

Since it was nearly noon, he headed for the café. His regular runs had trimmed his waist, so he ordered the three-piece chicken dinner. Besides, what was the point of taking care of yourself if no one was there to notice? He took a deep breath and tried to steady his attitude.

Today it was a different waitress than the one who had served him the last time. He didn't even try to strike up a conversation with her. He had to get his mind in a better place first. He swirled his glass and studied the ice as it spun.

"Hey, Scott."

Pulled from his thoughts, he looked up to see Al standing by his booth, with filled coffee cup in hand. "Hey, Al." He hoped the man moved on to have lunch with someone else.

Al dropped to the bench on the opposite side of Scott. The waitress brought Scott's lunch and a carafe of coffee to refill Al's. "What'll ya have, Al?" She didn't even pull her pad from her pocket.

"Special, Becky."

"You got it, Al." Less than a minute later, she was back with a plate of meatloaf and a pitcher to refill Scott's tea.

"I didn't think you liked the meatloaf." Scott dug into his chicken, but after the first bite, decided he really wasn't hungry.

Al shrugged. "Never said I didn't like it, just that it's not like Sarah's." He took a bite, chewing thoughtfully. "Sometimes I just get hungry for meatloaf."

Scott took another bite of his chicken; it did taste good. "Guess food can be a memory trigger."

"Amen to that." Al picked up his coffee cup. "It's a proven fact that taste and smell trigger the deepest memories."

"Deep, eh?" Scott started on his second piece of chicken. "I think I like fried chicken because, well, I just like it." He paused. "Though no one can make it like my mama could—can." He doubted his mom cooked much anymore, living with his oldest brother the way she did. And he didn't go to see her like he should; Ohio was a long way from Kansas.

"See." Al ate his meatloaf slowly, as if he were evaluating it, measuring it against Sarah's. "Brought back a strong memory, didn't it?"

"Looks like the food is doing the same thing for you."

Al nodded. "Yes. This meatloaf is good—very good—but not the same as Sarah's." He closed his eyes. "Still, tasting it makes me remember how Sarah made hers, gathering all the ingredients and the pans together before she started, so she wouldn't have to get anything else once she buried her hands in the meat." His smile turned beatific, as if the memory transported him somewhere else. "She took her rings off first, and put them in her empty coffee cup, then dumped everything in, and went to work." Al's hands moved, as he acted out the scene in his memory. "She usually hummed while she mixed. Squeeze and turn, squeeze and turn, until it was completely mixed. And then she would divide it in half and form two perfect loaves in the nine by thirteen glass dish, shaping and smoothing till they were just the way she wanted them." He opened his eyes. "She put a lot of love and a little bit of herself in every meatloaf she ever made." He picked up his cup and cradled it before his face. "If I had every meatloaf she ever made, maybe I'd have just a fraction of her." He focused on Scott again. "So that is why I sometimes order the meatloaf."

"Wow," Scott muttered. "All I remember is that mom's chicken was good."

"Your mother wasn't the love of your life, at least after you learned to walk."

The roll that had tasted so good to Scott suddenly seemed dry and about to choke him. He gulped his tea. "Right." Al studied Scott's face for a moment. Al had to sense a story there. "So, have you heard any gossip about the Enfield case?"

Al's sharp gaze stayed on him even as he spoke. "As a matter of fact, I have. Just this morning, at coffee."

So much for Al's promise to call him with info. "And?"

"Well, people thought pretty well of Margaret's— Delia's family around here, except that they took in foster kids, and all the misfits seemed to end up at their house. Some people were conjecturing that someone from the past had a grudge."

Scott sat there with his eyebrows raised. If he left a silence, Al might be compelled to fill it, and might provide helpful information instead of stuff he already knew.

"But all the foster girls either went back with their families, or moved on in the system, at least when they left here." Exactly what Scott had found.

Al plowed on. "Anyway, one of the misfits was a gay boy named Kyle."

Ah, yes, the now non-existent Kyle Dane.

"Seems some people in town were a bit ashamed of how they treated the boy." A hint of a smile crinkled the corners of Al's mouth. He evidently understood why Scott stayed silent; of course, he used the same tactic to interview sources. "So some of them have done some checking into what happened to him, too." Al sipped his coffee. He could play the game, too.

"And what did they find?"

"Not much. He moved away end of his junior year. Rumor has it they moved to Vegas or there about."

"Any idea why Vegas?"

Al smiled. "If I were a guessing man—and after all, guessing is just trying to make the connections between the facts—I would guess that the boy might be more accepted there. Or more anonymous."

"Any info on them after that?"

Al shook his head and sipped coffee. "Nada."

"Anyone mention what Kyle's mom did when they lived here?"

"Mac said she was an accountant. Did taxes and bookkeeping for some businesses. Barely kept a roof over their heads."

"So your anonymous source is Mac?"

Al grinned. "Who knows more than Mac about everything around here?" He finished his meal. "He sure figured out who you were real quick. That means the guy has an eye for faces and details as well as a good memory." He dropped his napkin in the plate. "He's what we refer to in the news business as a reliable source."

"That's what we call 'em in law enforcement, too." Scott found the strength within himself to polish off the last piece of chicken. Once he started eating, he found it hard to stop. Just like with the beer the last couple of nights. One beer to cool down after his run sent him back to the fridge for another and then another. And last night, it had taken four to lull him to sleep.

Al cocked his head to the side, as Sandy refilled his coffee cup and Scott's iced tea. Then she moved on to the next table. "Funny how we use the same techniques."

"But different outcomes." Scott never trusted the media, had had his words twisted more than once.

"Depends on the reporter. A good reporter is after the same thing as a good cop." He sipped. "The truth."

"And the bad ones are after—?" Scott paused.

"The ones with less integrity are out to find the facts to fit the story they already have written." Al ran his finger around the rim of the cup. "The good ones follow the facts to the story that needs to be told."

Scott took a gulp of his tea and studied Al around the glass. The old editor was watching him, wondering maybe which kind of cop he was. "I'll bet you've followed a few trails in your day."

"That I have, Scott." Al smiled. "That I have." He raised his cup. "I've always been curious about what motivates people, makes them do the things they do."

"That's a lifetime of study."

"Yes, it is. Some do things out of love, some from

fear, some to get away from pain." He sighed. "It's never simple." He glanced at the silk daisies in the bud vase next to the menus and napkin holders. "Take flowers, for instance. You walk into a house and there are flowers in a vase. You can get a story about motivation from what kind of flowers they are, who brought them in, and why he or she brought them in."

Scott simply nodded, waiting to see where this lead would take them.

"If they are carnations, and the wife brought them in, maybe they are having a party. Or maybe she was down and wanted a lift. If they are roses and the husband brought them, maybe he's hoping to get her in the mood for a little lovin'. Or maybe he's trying to tell her he appreciates her, so he can get a little. Or maybe he's trying to apologize for something he shouldn't have been doing in the first place." He paused to watch a couple walk into the restaurant and seat themselves at a table near the register. "Those two, for instance. They don't look upset with each other, but they look a little stressed. They are sitting where a quiet relaxing lunch is not likely, but fast service is. They are not sitting next to each other, but across the table. My guess is that they are focused on working on something, and they need to get back to task quickly." He continued watching, as Sandy waited on them. Seconds after she appeared at their table, she left for the kitchen. "They are talking to one another, but no hand holding or slamming fists on the table. This is a working lunch." He glanced back at Scott. "Also, not likely to be flowers on their table tonight."

"Looks like Mac's not the only one who has an eye for details." He took another sip of tea. "So when were you going to call me with this information?"

Al shrugged. "Not till I had a bit more. What I dug up is probably available in official sources or on the internet." He glanced back at the couple, already digging into their meal. "Not until I had something you couldn't find out otherwise. Or until I check it out further. You can't call something a fact unless you can verify it somewhere else."

"So how were you going to verify it?"

Al picked up his cup and drained the last of his coffee. "Well, I thought I'd head to the high school and talk to teachers that might have remembered Margaret. As I understand it, that's what she was called when she was a kid." He pushed his plate back from the edge of the table. "And maybe talk to old neighbors, the librarian, and so forth. Follow each lead till it hit a dead end." He stood. "Care to go with?"

"Thought you'd never ask." Scott gulped the last of his tea before he stood up. "But what makes you think they'll talk to you instead of me? I'm the hometown boy."

Al looked up at him. "Hey, you may be the native, but you're also a cop. I'm just 'Sarah's husband.'"

They reached the door to the restaurant. "And what happens when all your leads turn to dead ends?"

Al grinned as Scott opened the door. "Then I get off the road and start digging past the dead end signs."

Chapter 46

The corridor to the high school office seemed shorter than it had when Scott attended school there. The lockers looked smaller, too. And the "All Visitors Must Check in at the Office" sign was new. He stopped before the door that said "Office" on the glass, still feeling a little dread, even though he had done nothing wrong. Taking a deep breath, he opened the door and stood, once again, before Ms. Hefferman.

"May I help you?" she said, looking at him over her glasses as she always had. She looked past him. "Hello, Al."

"Hey, Pauline."

"Yes, ma'am," Scott answered reflexively. Then he remembered his task. "I'm Scott Aylward with City PD." He paused to show her his badge; it didn't impress her. "I'm investigating the murder of Delia Enfield, who attended school here as Margaret Stillman." She still simply stared at him. "I wondered if I could talk to anyone who may have been here when she was in school, like yourself, for instance. And if I could get last known address information on some of her classmates."

She did glance at his badge then, and read his ID carefully. "Well, Mr. Aylward, I do remember you, but that doesn't mean anything when it comes to access to student records. You will have to have a subpoena."

"That's prudent," Scott responded, slipping his badge back into his pocket. "Could you tell me which teachers or staff are still here that were here when she was in school?"

She pulled out a pad. "Let's see, Ms. Frank still teaches math, Mr. Smith history, Ms. Nelson is still here as counselor, but no longer gym teacher." She wrote a few more names. "Lillian Helms still cooks. And Mr. Potter is still janitor." She added one more name. "Judith Vendace is now librarian here; she was a classmate of Margaret's." She looked up at Scott with empathy in her eyes. "It really was a tragedy, her ending that way. She was such a nice girl and had so much potential."

"Yes, ma'am." He looked up as a teenaged girl in ripped jeans and multiple shirts entered the office. "That's why I'm determined to bring her killer to justice."

"Hi, Ms. Hefferman." The girl slipped around the counter and picked up a stack of papers. She moved to the north wall of the office and started distributing the papers into the cubbyholes on the wall.

"Mr. Aylward, I hope you are able to do that." She handed him the list of faculty and staff she had jotted down. "We can't let you interrupt any classes to talk to the faculty, but school will be out in a couple of hours. And you could talk to Ms. Vendace and the other non-teaching staff." Tapping a sheet of paper on the counter, she reached under the counter and pulled out two plastic clip-on ID badges marked "Visitor." "If you'll sign in, I'll hand you your ID badges, and you can start talking to them."

"Thanks, Ms. Hefferman." Scott signed his name,

then clipped the badge to his shirt. "You were always so helpful when I was in school here."

"You always managed to stay out of the office as much as possible when you were in school here, Mr. Aylward." She must have been in the prime of her life when he attended Homedale High, but at the time he considered her ancient.

"See you around, Al," she said as Al clipped on his badge.

"You, too, Pauline. Tell Ed I'll drop those iris bulbs by in a couple of weeks." Al followed Scott through the door. They turned left toward the stairway that would lead them to the second story library. "Pauline and Sarah were classmates."

Scott shook his head. "You do have a leg up on me."

"And a few more years experience."

Scott pulled out his cell phone and dialed Bates' desk. "Hey, Del, I need a favor." Quickly he outlined the years of attendance records he needed to view from the school. "Thanks, Del." He smiled at Al. "Should have the subpoena soon, maybe even before we leave."

"That's good," Al said, as they turned into the library.

A slender woman with auburn hair looked up at them from a stack of books she was cataloguing at the counter. Her gaze flicked to the "Visitor" badges. "Hello, Al. May I help you?"

Once again, Scott pulled out his ID. "Are you Judith Vendace?"

She nodded, glancing at Al.

"I'm investigating the Delia Enfield murder."

Judith looked down. "Poor Margaret."

"Yes," Scott agreed. "That's why I'm still trying to piece together the story to see if I can find her killer." He paused. "And get justice for her."

A sudden fire passed through Vendace's eyes. "She certainly deserves it."

Scott could see Al watching as intently as a brown bear poised at a trout stream. "How so?"

Wariness replaced the fire in Vendace's gaze. "Margaret was always so—so *fair* to everyone." She slid the books to the side and leaned her elbows on the counter. "She always stood up for the underdog, like those foster girls her mother took in, and that boy, Caden or something."

Al moved closer. "Sounds like you knew her well."

"I wish." Vendace ducked her head. When neither Al nor Scott said anything, she went on. "I wasn't the 'librarian' type in high school." She propped her hands on her elbows. "I was with the 'in' crowd then, and I did my share of making fun of Margaret for being such the hero. And I wasn't the only one."

"Who else was involved?" Scott's pen hovered over his notepad.

Vendace met his eyes for a second. "I wouldn't say people were 'involved' in making fun of Margaret and other kids as much as they were just being a part of a crowd." She shrugged. "A stupid, teen-aged crowd. Not as mean as I see today, but mean enough."

"Any of them mean enough to want to hurt Margaret?"

She shook her head. "I can't imagine anyone that I knew hurting anyone more than maybe keying a car." She studied her nails. "And they were much meaner to some of those foster girls and that boy than they were to

Margaret."

Al spoke up again. "What about those girls and the boy? Any idea where they ended up? Or how they felt about Margaret?"

"Oh, the boy and Margaret were best friends. You could see that he worshipped the ground she walked on." She stared at the desk for a moment. "Those girls? Well, some of them came from some pretty rough backgrounds, but I think most of them made the best of their time in Margaret's house."

Scott would run down each and every girl who had lived in Margaret's family home. Interviewing her mother was out of the question. The woman was succumbing to Alzheimer's, not able to put together a coherent sentence. She might remember the girls, but would never be able to communicate anything she remembered. It was a blessing that she would never understand how her daughter had died. He pulled out a business card. "In case you think of anything else that might help find anyone who had a grudge against Margaret, please let me know."

Vendace took the card and fingered the edge. "I will. But what if there's no connection, no reason? What if she just happened to be in the wrong place when someone snapped?"

Scott stared at her and felt Al's eyes upon him. His stomach tightened at the possibility. "There still has to be a way of finding him."

****

Fred the janitor had more information. "All them cheerleaders had it in for Margaret," he said, as he ran an oily rag over the boiler in the maintenance shop. "Probably because they knew deep down that she stood for the right thing, but they was afraid of the others making fun of them, too." He stopped to take a sip from a plastic bottle of Diet Coke. "But Margaret wasn't the pure angel they are makin' her out to be neither."

"Oh," Al leaned against the boiler. "How so?"

"Well," Fred paused to take another sip. "Once I come around the corner into the shop, and caught her and that Kyle boy makin' out." He waited while the air conditioner squealed as it kicked on, then settled down to a mild roar. "Another time, I almost caught her and some of the foster girls smokin' pot down by the stream."

"Pot?" Scott would have to check these girls out in detail. Maybe one of them had stayed in touch with Margaret. Maybe there was a dark side to the hero.

"I think it was pot." Fred shrugged. "Coulda just been a cigarette."

"We'll check it out." He flipped the notebook shut. "Anything else you can tell us?"

"Naw, not that I can think of now."

Chapter 47

As the last student filed out of her classroom, Ms. Frank looked up from her desk even as she tapped a sheaf of papers into a neatly aligned stack. "Hello, Mr. Aylward. Hello, Al."

"Hello, Ms. Frank." He greeted her with less trepidation now than the last time he had faced her. "Did you think of any other leads I should check out in Delia's case?"

"No, Mr. Aylward." She tapped the stack again, then laid it down at the front of her desk. "Nothing more than the leads I already gave you." She tipped her head toward him. "Did you follow any of those?"

"Yes, ma'am." He nodded. "Found most of them on Facebook."

"It's the basis for 60% of all divorce evidence these days."

He suppressed a shudder as the thought hit him that he should check Rica's Facebook page. What would he find there? "Yes, it is. I guess some folks don't realize how many people actually read their pages." His mind wandered to Rica, but he forced it back to work. "But I did find them, one way or the other. Dr. Athens died three years after he moved to Montana. Mr. Denton moved to Illinois after he graduated and was laid up in the hospital with shoulder surgery the day Delia died. Robert James is in Virginia, teaching at a private school. He did admit that he stayed in touch by phone and email for a few months after Delia left school, but—" He flipped back through his notes. "He was judging a science fair that day."

Ms. Frank looked skeptical. "Still, it could have been someone they introduced her to, someone from those days."

Al spoke up. "But it could also be someone who never laid eyes on her until that day."

Ms. Frank stared at him. "Statistically, that's unlikely. Most murder victims are killed by someone they know."

"That's true, Ms. Frank." Scott suddenly wanted to go home to his computer and check out his own life online. "And that's why I'm trying to find out more." He closed his notebook. "And I think I'm going to head home soon and track some of those new leads."

"Good luck, Mr. Aylward."

****

"Well, Al, what do you think?" Scott waited for the car's air conditioning to start cooling before he pulled away from the curb.

Al waved at school staff he knew as they drove through the school parking lot. "I think that I may find out more at the co-op with a cup of coffee before you get the subpoena to look at old student records."

Waiting for a traffic jam of five cars at the bottleneck that served as the only entrance and exit to the faculty parking lot, Scott glanced at Al. "Ye of so little faith."

"I just know how long it takes to get legal paperwork, unless someone is in immediate danger." Al leaned back in the seat. "The victim here is already dead, so I'm sure the judge won't be in a big hurry. Plus, the Quick Shop case is the news now, and you have the killer in custody."

"Except that it's an election year, so the judge wants to be seen as hard on crime, so he keeps his seat."

"Maybe," Al agreed. "Plus, I'm not so sure that you will find out much by tracking down fellow students. Maybe the foster girls, but it sounds like there was no horrible rivalry between Delia and anyone."

Scott shrugged. "Looks can be deceiving."

****

Scott sauntered into the station at 4:55, ready to type up his notes. "Aylward," the dispatcher said as he started past her desk. "Chief wants to see you." She glanced at the clock above Scott's head. "He might still be here."

"Sure." Scott turned the other way down the hallway from his own office to approach the chief's.

"Aylward."

"Yes, sir."

"What the hell do you think you are doing taking an afternoon to hang out in your hometown, when we still have a suspect outstanding in the Quick Shop murders?"

"I don't know, sir, except that I wanted to work on the Enfield case because we had reached a dead end in the Quick Shop murders until more of the tests come back from KBI lab."

The chief stared at him. "Well, okay, Aylward, just don't make it a habit to spend inordinate amounts of time in ways that are not likely to produce results." He ran a hand over his balding head. "We are now 'performance based,' you know."

"I know, sir, and I believe that my investigation will produce results."

"You'd better hope it does, Aylward. Go on back to your desk."

"Thank you, sir." Scott spun and headed toward his desk. Why had he just thanked a man for chewing his ass? No matter; he *would* find Delia's killer. He kicked his chair out from under his desk and settled in front of the computer. He began typing his notes, but after a half-page, he clicked open another window and logged into Facebook. In seconds, he had pulled up Rica's page. No posts there more recent than a month. Evidently she wasn't airing their private laundry in public. For that he was grateful. He studied her photos. Those full lips of hers parted in a near-constant smile had attracted him in the first place. He hadn't seen a smile on them in a long time. Not since their night at the Thirsty Dragon. He closed the window and resumed typing his notes. By 6:30, he finished and headed to his truck. Since he had left his windows down a quarter inch, some of the heat had escaped. The truck was almost cool by the time he made it home to his apartment and trudged up the stairs. Funny, it didn't feel like home any more.

The silence overwhelmed him as he pushed open the door. Though he had told himself he needed to go for a run, right now he couldn't summon the strength. Finally, he walked to the refrigerator and pulled out a beer. A beer and a little rest should rejuvenate him enough to go for a run. Besides, the asphalt path would still be hot; waiting an hour or so for it to cool down a bit was smart. He flipped on the news channel and settled in his chair.

A loud commercial startled him awake. He checked his watch. Two hours he'd been asleep. He thought for a moment as he let the rest of his body come awake. Too late now to fix dinner or go anywhere. He rubbed his eyes. He didn't feel much like eating anyway.

He rose from the chair, stretched, and headed for the bedroom to change for a run. Rica would have had my ass for not making the bed, he thought as he sat on the bed to lace his shoes. But Rica wasn't here to yell at him, or to make him even want to sleep in the bed. Since she left, now fifty-four hours ago, he'd done most of his sleeping on the couch or in his chair. He clipped his house key to his running shorts and headed out the door. He walked the four blocks to the trail. At the trailhead, where the sidewalk that ran past his apartment building joined the trail, he stretched, and turned south.

Before, he had just as often turned north and followed the path around the new developments in that end of town, or veered east and circled the medical center. But lately, he found himself always heading south. Some days, he followed the trail to where it ran out of asphalt, just sand on the top of the dike bordering the river. Usually, he stopped on the north side of the K-61 bridge, but today, he ventured under the bridge. Just past the bridge, he stopped. Another quarter-mile would take him past where he found Delia's body. Was he ready for that?

He looked up in the sky, saw the geese heading in to spend the night at the ponds in the nearby park, and decided it would be best to do the same thing himself. He turned his back on the river, and jogged toward his apartment. He might eat a bowl of cereal for dinner and maybe have another beer. He picked up his pace.

Chapter 48

Charlotte stood with her hand on her car door. Work had been easy today, enjoyable, and she didn't have to work at the Dragon tonight. Devlyn was working the evening shift at the plant, so she had nowhere she had to be, no one to answer to. And no one to be with, either. She opened the car door, and the memories flooded over her.

She went back to the night she revealed her old identity to Mags. "Is it really you?" Mags had gushed; three drinks had made her a bit tipsy.

"It's me, Mags, like I always wanted."

Mags hugged her again. "Can you come sit with us and catch up?"

The caution honed of painful experience returned. "I can't, Mags. I'm working." She pasted on the smile that had become her uniform. "Besides, it's best others don't know, so I'd appreciate it if you didn't tell the rest of your group."

Mags blinked. "Of course, I won't. Haven't I always kept your secrets?" She looked around to see who might be watching and hugged her again. "You look so great!" She stepped back to give Charlotte a once-over. "Better than I ever imagined."

Charlotte basked in Margaret's approval. "It cost plenty, but was worth every penny."

Mags reached out for her hand. "When can we

catch up?"

Charlotte shrugged, knowing how jealously Devlyn guarded her time. "I can leave work early some time that I don't have to work here. What time do you get off?"

Margaret pondered a moment. "I make a bank deposit on Tuesdays. I can be done by three-thirty or four."

Charlotte beamed. "Great. My other job is at Delco and Sims Graphics." She heard the din of the room growing louder; her boss would come looking for her any second. "It's by the Taco Shop on Fourth Street. You know where that is?" Mags nodded. "Park in the Taco Shop lot, because D&S doesn't have much parking." And that would keep Devlyn from making any connections. "We'll go have a soda and catch up."

That afternoon had led to many such afternoons of cherry limeades and early movies, giving each other pedicures on a blanket at the park, talking about men. For the first time in her life, Charlotte had felt nearly complete.

And now she felt so empty. She sagged against the car.

Chapter 49

The subpoena for the school records still hadn't come through by Friday afternoon. And neither had an identification from the DNA or fingerprint from James' apartment. Though James languished in custody, charged with capital murder, conviction beyond a doubt might prove impossible unless they found the accomplice. Unwilling to face another trip to Homedale or the chief's wrath, Scott searched Facebook and Twitter for information on Delia's case, the Quick Shop homicides, and the home burglaries. Unlike on TV, computer screens did not automatically open multiple windows with all the answers. Real detective work involved tedious following of leads that often proved to be dead ends. Though sometimes it was helped along by a little luck. So Scott read tweets.

His cell phone buzzing at his side startled him. A text from Rica. He grabbed it and read. "Let's meet for dinner tonight." His heart leaped. She was ready to talk, maybe even come home.

"Where and when?" he responded. If she wanted, he would cook. Or he'd take her to the finest restaurant in town. Or even out of town. Heck, he'd take the weekend off, whisk her away to a romantic bed and breakfast.

"Delmonico's at seven?" She had named the finest. So be it.

"Want me to pick you up?" He would meet her with red roses, dressed in his best suit. Or the jeans and blue shirt she liked.

"No, let's meet there." Maybe she was afraid he was mad and would strand her there. She should know him better than that.

"OK." He ended the text and sat with the phone in his hand for a moment. "Del, I'm taking off early tonight."

Bates looked up from his searches of E-Bay and Craigslist for the stolen items. "Hot date?"

"Hope so." Without waiting for Bates to question him, he took off. He needed to make the bed—maybe he should wash the sheets, in case she was ready to come home. And vacuum. And pick up a bit. And maybe take out the beer bottles from the past week.

****

Scott arrived at Delmonico's at 7:01, early for him, but Rica had beat him there, already seated and tapping her fingers on the table. He had decided on a suit and tie. She looked up at him as he arrived at the table, as nervous as he had been on their first date. "You look nice, Scott,"

"Thanks." He pulled out the chair around the corner from her. She wore a dark blue sundress, one he didn't recognize. It accented her caramel skin and made her eyes sparkle. God, how he loved her. He wanted to jump out of his seat and crush her to him. Or get down on one knee and propose all over again. "You look wonderful."

"Thank you, Scott." She paused to take a sip of the water from the glass before her. "You've always been so complimentary of me."

"Why not?" He leaned toward her to stroke a loose strand of hair. She had put it up somehow, something he always found exciting, especially trying to figure out how to get it down again. "You are wonderful." He pulled his hand back when she didn't respond and studied his fingers. "You are wonderful in every area that I'm lacking."

"Don't say that, Scott." She reached out to put her hand over his. "You have so many wonderful qualities as well." She paused. "That's why I fell in love with you."

He felt like his heart started to beat again, instead of being frozen in cold storage like it had been since she said she was leaving. He turned his hand up to grip hers, but she pulled it away and tucked it under the table on her lap.

The waiter arrived at the table to take their orders. "I'll have the California salad."

His focus on Rica, Scott never even looked at the menu. "Me, too." He had no clue what that would be, but he didn't care about food anyway. He took a deep breath. "How have you been, Rica?"

"I've been doing a lot of thinking, Scott." Her gaze met his and then she looked away. "But let's just chat for a while." She unfolded her napkin. "How's the case going?"

"Quick Shop or Enfield?"

"Either one."

"No new progress on either one." She didn't sound really interested anyway. What could he ask her? How was Dr. Ambrose? Nope, didn't think he'd go there. "How's work been for you?"

"Busy." She smoothed the napkin on her lap. "We

had to reattach a couple of fingers from a farming accident yesterday."

He took a drink of his water. "Bet that was stressful. How did it go?"

"Too soon to know. They should be able to tell if he'll be able to keep the fingers by the end of the week."

"Hope he can." Their salads arrived at that moment, and their conversation died as they ate. Scott picked at his. It tasted like cardboard to him. Rica didn't eat much either. Finally, Rica pushed her plate aside.

"Scott, I want a divorce."

The words hit his ears like cymbals smashing into either side of his head. He put down his fork. "What?" He wasn't sure the word even came out of his dry throat.

"It's just not working any more, Scott." She leaned her elbows on the table, left hand placed over the right.

"Can we try counseling?" His hands trembled.

"I don't think it would do any good, Scott." She looked past him. "There are just too many differences between us. In the first blush of lust, we thought we could work them out, but the gap is just too big."

"But what about a separation?" Anything to hold on to her until he could change her mind.

"They almost always lead to divorce anyway, might as well save the money."

"Have you already talked to a lawyer?" Where else would she get that information?

She flashed him a look that said she was angry with him for thinking that. "No, but I've been doing some reading."

"But, Rica—" He reached out to put his hand on hers. She pulled her hands out from under his and slipped them under the table. "Can't we try something besides this?"

"Scott—" She looked away from his eyes. "I'm done trying, Scott." She glanced back at him, then looked away again. "We've been 'trying' for the past three years, as soon as the honeymoon wore off."

"I'll try harder. I'll get the counseling, I'll hire a maid—"

Rica put a gentle hand on his forearm. "Scott, don't beg." She rubbed his arm tenderly. "It makes me feel like I'm doing this just to hurt you."

"Well, it does hurt me." He put his free hand over hers. "I love you, Rica. I'll do anything to make our marriage work."

She pulled her hand from his arm. "That's just it, Scott." She took a sip of water. "It's too much work, and one person alone cannot make a marriage."

Scott felt the blood pounding in his ears. She had already given up, already talked herself into moving on. "Are you seeing someone else, Rica?" His breathing grew quicker. "Is that it?" He should stop; he was making a fool of himself. But he'd throw himself under a bus to keep her. "Have you found someone better and want to trade up?"

Her chin rose. "That's enough, Scott." Her eyes went dark and her brows drew together.

Heedless of the signs, Scott plunged on, his voice rising. "Are you already sleeping with Ambrose?"

Eyes glittering, she rose from her chair. "I will see you again in court, Scott." With that, she dropped her napkin in her salad bowl, turned and walked away from the table.

Struck dumb, Scott watched her march out of the dining room and his life. He sat staring at the last place he saw her. The diners around him tried not to look while still watching his reaction to the drama they had just observed. He lowered his gaze to his shaking hands, working hard to slow his racing heart and ragged breathing, to bring his life back into focus. He failed at all of it, just like he failed at being a husband. Dimly, he saw their waitress walking past the table. He caught her eye. "Could I have the check, please?" he croaked.

"Oh, sir, the dinner's already paid for." She nodded toward Rica's empty chair. "By the lady."

"Okay." It was all he could say. When the woman moved on, he pulled a ten from his wallet, stuck it under his plate and managed to stand. Trying to avoid the stares of those around him, he followed Rica's path out of the restaurant.

His gaze roamed the parking lot, hopeful he would find her waiting in her car, but two sweeps of the lot showed her gone. Pulling his keys from his pocket, he stumbled toward his pickup, stepping right into the path of an Envoy. The SUV rocked as the driver slammed on the brakes to avoid hitting Scott. He nodded at the driver and ambled on. If he couldn't pull his act together, he'd make Rica a widow before they could get to court.

Without further mishap, he got to his pickup. He shrugged out of his jacket and tossed it on the passenger seat before he slid behind the wheel. He didn't start the truck, but tugged at the tie until he got it loose enough to get out of it. Then he unbuttoned his collar and cuffs. He rolled up his sleeves and then placed his hands on the steering wheel. He leaned his head on the wheel between them. There, on the back row of Dominique's parking lot, where he hoped to God no one could see him, he could no longer hold back the sobs that now shook him. He let the tears fall—had no power to stop them anyway—until he felt as dry as corn stalks in winter.

Finally, when there wasn't enough moisture left in his eyes to let him blink, when his throat was so dry he couldn't swallow, he sat up and stared out the windshield. If anyone saw him, he didn't notice. Rubbing his hands over his face, he started the truck. He remembered putting it in gear, but when he pulled into his parking space at the apartment, he honestly could not recall what route he had taken to get there.

Like a robot, he shut off and locked his truck, then trudged up the stairs to their—his—apartment. He dropped the keys on the table by the door, then felt tears start again, from a well deeper than he imagined he could hold. He fell onto the couch and waited until the well ran dry again. Then he chugged a glass of water and changed into running shorts. Maybe the endorphins from runner's euphoria would make him feel better— feel anything—again.

Chapter 50

Charlotte bent forward, wrapping her hands around her calves to hold the stretch.

"Nice ass." The guy she thought of as "Blond Abs" offered the compliment as he jogged past her at the entrance to the trail that followed the drainage ditch to the park.

"Nice abs." They had been passing each other on the trail for nearly a year now, usually with the same greeting. Smiling, she straightened then reached upward into a yoga sun salute. She bent again to touch her toes, aware of the admiring glances of the two men jogging north past her. No jogging for her; had to keep her breasts firm, didn't want them bouncing. She wanted to protect her investment. After a couple of side stretches, she walked briskly south.

She used to walk the southern end that started near the trailer park where Devlyn had lived. In fact, hers and Devlyn's paths first crossed on the trail, but they didn't realize it until months later, just before she moved in with Devlyn. But no more, not since—since Delia's death. Now she stayed on the north end of the path. It was closer to home and work, she would tell anyone who asked.

She picked up her pace and swung her two-pound hand weights with each stride. She felt the blood coursing through her veins.

"Hey, cutie." She looked up to see a new guy she'd never seen before jogging toward her, almost even with her now. She swung her head around to watch him run past her. He had a nice ass. Great hair, too. He looked back at her and smiled, as he trotted on.

A couple of women she encountered often on the trail approached, power walking and swinging weights. "Howdy."

She nodded to them. Right now, on the trail, life was good. No worries beyond keeping her stride smooth, her arms pumping. The people who regularly walked the trail formed a community of sorts, one where she was accepted. No one dug deep; they simply nodded and smiled. And by not walking the south end of the trail, she could avoid any sights that might trigger the memories that forced their way to the surface if she got too close to the spot where Delia's body was found.

With the rhythm of her stride automatic, she allowed her mind to wander through memories, both near and distant.

High school had been torture for her. Only Mags—Delia—had accepted her just as she was, despite her awkwardness. The rest either shunned her out of fear or made fun of her, probably also from fear. For two years, she had leaned on Mags to protect her, to listen, to entertain. Other girls had sleepovers, but Charlotte was never allowed to stay. Still, she and Mags spent hours in Mags' room or down by the stream, talking about the future they'd have once they escaped Homedale.

She remembered one hot September afternoon in their freshman year, after school, in Mags' bedroom. Charlotte, dropping her shoes on the fluffy rug beside the bed, settled on the bed, her legs pulled up before her. "I just can't take it anymore, Mags." She dropped her head to her knees, and let the hot tears fall.

Maggie slipped onto the bed beside her and wrapped her arms around her. "Sure you can." She hugged Charlotte, her ripening breasts pressed tight against Charlotte's back. "If we stick together, watch each other's backs, in three years we can blow this taco stand."

Charlotte stopped crying and let herself absorb the love she felt in Maggie's arms and voice. "Yeah, I know." She sighed a ragged breath. "On to the university, where our brilliance will be appreciated." She stroked Maggie's hair. "Then after graduation, I'll be a famous artist and you'll be a Nobel prize-winning psychologist."

"We will be!" The fervor of her belief in herself made Maggie radiate her passion. "I know they don't understand us here—it's like they want to keep us in a cage to protect us from them and them from us, but there's a bigger world out there that isn't so stifled."

"But Mags, sometimes I feel like a moth trying to break out of its chrysalis, and if I don't get free and have the chance to spread my wings, they'll be forever stunted and deformed."

"Not a moth, dear, a butterfly." Maggie ran her hands up Charlotte's back. "And you'll fly free one day."

Charlotte studied Maggie's glowing face. Even behind the huge glasses, Maggie's blue eyes sparkled like sapphires, her full lips moved in an impassioned speech. Charlotte didn't hear the words, but the sound of that musical voice and the sight of those lips were enough to soothe her anguish and dry her tears until the next time.

But then, Charlotte had indeed escaped her cocoon and flown free, while Maggie lost her dream somewhere. Their meeting again had seemed to bring peace to both of them for a few precious weeks. And then—

A man approaching her from the south on the trail brought her out of the past. In this heat, he was running far too fast to keep up the pace for long. Sweat had soaked almost all of the gray T-shirt he wore, and dripped from his face. Damn fool was working up a heat stroke. Though he was cute enough that mouth-to-mouth would be fun if he needed it. Or stripping off his shirt to cool him down. At his pace, he was almost abreast of her before she took a good look at his face.

The cop. Handsy. Aylward, was that the name on the business card he gave her? She had thrown it away, lest Devlyn find it. The cop swept past her, not looking at her or anyone else he passed.

She stopped walking to watch him travel on. He looked like he was running from a ghost. If he collapsed on the trail, someone else would have to take care of him, no matter how good-looking he was. She couldn't afford the questions.

She focused on the trail ahead of her. She had almost reached the spot where she turned around. She shivered despite the heat. Turning around now threatened her grasp on peace. Going forward would force her into memories she wanted to forget; going back to the trailhead might cross her path with Handsy and force her into questions she didn't want to answer. Trembling, she stepped off the path to sit on a stone bench in the shade of a cedar tree. She pulled her legs up before her, dropped her head to her knees and let the tears come.

Chapter 51

Scott crept into the office six minutes past eight, an extra-large Sonic coffee in his hand. Bates raised his head from studying his computer. "You look like hell, Scott," he boomed. "Happy Monday morning."

The greeting reverberated inside Scott's skull. "Happy fuckin' Monday to you, too." With his hearing impaired from years of shooting without ear protection, Bates couldn't hear him.

"Huh?" Bates stood, coffee cup in hand.

"I said happy Monday to you, too."

Bates took a sip of coffee, frowned, and dumped the contents of the cup in the peace lily. "I thought it was something like that." He turned to the coffee pot behind him and poured another cup.

The phone on Scott's desk rang. He grabbed the receiver before it could clang again, as much to silence it as to find out who was on the other end. "Aylward."

"This is Debbie from Judge Morton's office," a brisk voice responded. "We have the subpoena you requested for records from Homedale High School."

Thanks." Scott sipped from the coffee. The caffeine began to soothe the pounding in his head. "I'll be right down there."

Bates looked up from his computer, eyebrows asking questions.

"Subpoena for Homedale High School came

through." He gathered his notebook from the desk. "I'm on my way to get it."

"Want some company?"

That was the last thing Scott wanted, someone to make small talk on the hour drive to a town he once considered next door to hell. "No, thanks. Because I know the families around there, it won't take me as long to go through the records as it would to explain what to look for." Especially since he didn't really know himself what he hoped to find.

Bates opened his mouth as if to ask a question. Then he pointed to his computer screen. "Well, I think I found one of the stolen plates on E-Bay, so I'll just keep following up on that." He glanced back at the screen. "Maybe by the time you finish up at Homedale, I'll have enough for a warrant here."

"Sounds good." Scott hustled out of the office before Bates could ask further questions. He'd grab the paperwork, then check out a car and maybe be back before the chief could get bent out of shape.

Scott hadn't realized until he and Rica hit the rough patch just how many songs on the radio were love songs. Or love gone wrong songs. He couldn't handle how close so many of them came to his own life, didn't want to let classical music soothe him enough to doze off while driving, and was not in a mood to listen to NPR or a preacher. So he punched off the radio and listened instead to the hum of the tires against the pavement. He had never noticed what different sounds they made depending on the type of pavement. Such information might be useful if he were ever kidnapped and blindfolded. "We drove 3.2 miles on aggregate surface, then 2.1 on concrete and 5.7 on new asphalt," he could hear himself saying as the FBI questioned him. A smile tugged at his lips, the first one in days. Even "Saturday Night Live" had left him mirthless. What circumstance could possibly lead to him needing to identify a road surface by sound?

His mind turned instead to what he hoped to find in the school records. Forwarding addresses for Kyle Dane and the foster girls. He had a feeling all of them knew Margaret better than any of the other students or the teachers. Maybe he could find if any of the other students attended the same college as Margaret, in the same degree program. He could track down to see if any had lived in the same dorm or apartment. He glanced out the window at the fields sliding by. Most of the wheat stubble had been plowed under, and the milo was growing slowly in the drought.

He neared the river bridge, but did not stop, though he could see that the water was as low here as in the city. Rain had not come much this summer. Most of the state was caught in a drought cycle, had been for the past five years. Here, the mighty river trickled in narrow individual streams less than a foot deep in most places. Except for the occasional treacherous pool or the constantly shifting sand, it could be waded easily.

His phone vibrated. He grabbed it; it could be Rica, ready to change her mind. "Hello."

"Scott, it's Al."

"Oh, hi, Al." He hoped Al couldn't read the disappointment in his voice.

"I was wondering if you had that subpoena yet."

"Just got it this morning, Al. I'm on my way to Homedale to look at the records." Al couldn't accompany him to see them.

"Why don't we meet for lunch at the Diner? I've turned up a little background that might mean more to you than it does to me."

He hadn't wanted to stay in Homedale that long. "Okay. I'll call you if I get done with the records before lunchtime."

"Deal."

Scott slowed as he neared Homedale. It looked like the Brown farmstead had been abandoned. He studied the boarded up house. He and his brothers had spent many afternoons at that house playing with the boys and their sister, while his dad and Mr. Brown worked fields or repaired equipment together, and his mother and Mrs. Brown canned the bounty of their gardens. He wondered if the boys had sold the place or just rented out the fields.

And then he was in Homedale, driving down the main street that might as well be named Memory Lane. In fact, one of the streets in the "subdivision" carried that name. He reached for his coffee, but it was nearly gone and now cold. He drove to the west end of town to the Co-op Quick Shop. He needed a tea or something to drink to get through the records. He parked the patrol car and strolled from the bright sunlight into the cool interior of the convenience store. From the mechanic's bay that shared a wall with the store, he heard the buzz of a torque wrench. The co-op had always done a brisk business in tires.

"Hello, Scott." Ed McBeal leaned against the checkout counter with a donut in one hand and coffee in the other. He put down the coffee as Scott approached and thrust out his hand.

"Hey, Mac." Scott took the hand.

"Saw you on the news bringin' in the Quick Shop killer." He grinned. "Our local boy is a hero."

Scott moved toward the soda fountain. "Just doin' my job, Mac."

"Well, doin' it right well, as far as we're concerned." He finished the donut and groomed his goatee with a napkin. "Any progress on finding the killer of the Stillman girl?"

Scott had filled a cup with iced tea. "Workin' on it now, Mac."

Mac studied him a moment while he paid for the tea. "Well, I won't get between a man and his work." He moved away from the counter and toward his office at the back of the complex. "Unless it's me and my work. See ya around, Scott."

Scott nodded and headed back out to the car. He had downed nearly half the iced tea before he pulled up in front of the high school.

"Good day, Mr. Aylward." Ms. Hefferman greeted him with familiarity as he walked into the office.

"Morning, Ms. Hefferman." He stopped before her counter. "Got the subpoena to look at the records." He pulled the papers from his pocket.

"Good." She studied them. "I hope it brings some answers in poor Margaret's death." She pulled the clipboard from under the counter. "If you'll just sign in, I'll take you into the records room and help you find what you need."

"Thanks." He signed in and clipped on the "Visitor" badge she gave him.

"What specifically are you looking for?" She led him behind the counter down a narrow corridor to an office far from the door. With no window and rows of water pipes in the ceiling, it looked like it had been the office no one wanted, now converted into storage for student files. Outfitted with just one small table and a chair, the room contained racks and racks of files. The district had had a high school since 1910.

"Last known addresses of Kyle Dane and the foster girls Margaret's mother had in her home." He stared at the volumes of information. "And anyone who might have gone to the same university Margaret did."

Ms. Hefferman smiled. "A daunting task, Mr. Aylward." She pulled a file from the second shelf on the row nearest the outside wall. "Here's the file on Kyle Dane." She turned to leave the room. "I'll be back in a few minutes with the names of the foster girls and anyone I remember who may have gone to KU from Margaret's class."

"Thanks, Ms. Hefferman." Scott loosened his tie and sat at the table, opening the file that he hoped would give him answers about what had happened to Kyle Dane. The photo in the file revealed the slight, sad boy Scott remembered. Numerous notes from doctors excusing him from PE. Transcript of grades, mostly B's and C's, except for A's in art and literature. A records transfer request from a high school in Nevada. Scott wrote down the name and address. Precious little else to describe the hell this boy's life had been at Homedale High. He swallowed the guilt that he hadn't done more to stop it when it was happening.

The foster girls' files provided more interesting reading. Four girls had spent time in Margaret's home from the time Margaret was in middle school through high school. The records of one girl indicated that she was in the home for a year after Margaret graduated.

Each girl had records of several transfers and requests for transcripts both before and after leaving Homedale High. He dutifully took down all the names and details, so he could follow up to see if any of them could provide leads. Ms. Hefferman came back to the office a couple of times with names of students who went to KU at the same time Margaret did.

Finally, he closed the last of the records. The subpoena was not specific, so he could come back to look through more if any of his follow up indicated a need. He looked at his watch. Two hours he had been prisoner in the tiny cell of a room. He stood and stretched to get blood flowing to his muscles again.

As Ms. Hefferman had instructed, he left the files in a tidy stack on the table. He wound his way through the corridor to the front counter. Ms. Hefferman looked up at him.

"Did you find what you were looking for, Mr. Aylward?"

"I found some information that may lead to more info." He shrugged. "That's all I can ask for." Yet, somehow he knew that the morning's work had provided vital information, if he could just ask the right questions, follow the right trail, and recognize the information when it presented itself.

"Well, I hope it leads to a killer's conviction."

"Me, too." He laid the visitor's badge on the counter. "Thank you for your help, Ms. Hefferman."

"You're welcome, Mr. Aylward."

He walked out of the office, turning left down the corridor toward the exit door. He was still rolling his shoulders to loosen up his muscles when he opened the door. Immediately, the scent hit him—that rusty, wet bird smell that meant rain had fallen nearby. Then he heard the low rumble that could be thunder, could be a train, and could be almost anything, so quiet and unthreatening. For an instant, he was a boy back in his alcove of the upstairs bedroom in his parents' house, awakened first by the smell of coming rain and then the comforting grumble of clouds about to give it up, all rolling in through the open window. Except for harvest and haying, a farmer always welcomed rain. There was still a lot of farm boy in him yet. His older brothers, on bunk beds at the other side of the room, never stirred at the storm, tired from long school days and helping their dad with the manual labor. He shrugged and stretched, then hurried to the car parked at the edge of the school parking lot.

Chapter 52

The car's air conditioner hadn't even caught up with the outdoor temperature by the time he pulled up in front of Debbie's Diner for his lunch meeting with Al. He hurried into the cool sanctuary of the Diner at 11:20. Debbie greeted him as he laid his briefcase on the seat in the window booth furthest from the door. "What'll ya have to drink, Scott?"

He looked up, surprised that she already remembered his name. "Iced tea, please." He hesitated only a moment before he left his briefcase there and went into the restroom. When he returned, not only was his briefcase still there, untouched, but a glass of iced tea set sweating on a napkin. He settled into the seat facing the door and downed a third of the tea in one gulp. Debbie refilled it before he could get his laptop out of its case. He flipped open his cell phone to call Al while his laptop booted up, when the diner door opened and Al strolled to the seat facing him. Scott turned the phone toward Al to show him the cursor on his number.

"I guess great minds think alike," Al said. "Lunch is always a priority."

"Has been since I was born. What info do you have?"

"Well—" Al hesitated while Debbie placed a glass of water and a cup of coffee in front of him. "I'll have a hamburger with fried onions and fries, Debbie."

249

"Me, too." Scott nodded at her. "Sounded good."

"It is good, trust me." Al leaned toward him as Debbie left their table. "I found out that one of those foster girls you were trying to track down moved back to Homedale."

"Really?" That surprised Scott. All of the girls had been from urban areas, mostly Wichita. Provincial Homedale should have been the last place any of them would want to live. Outside, the blinding sunlight had dimmed. Gray clouds roiled overhead.

"Yep." Al pulled a reporter's notebook, nearly identical to the police one Scott used, from his back pocket. He flipped back a couple of pages. "Brandi Smith back then." He looked up at Scott. "Brandi Obermann now. Seems that Homedale itself didn't change her much, but a certain football player named Brad Obermann did. After she left here, she got back with her mom, cleaned up her act, stayed in touch with Brad, went to the same college he did, married him, and now helps him run the family farm."

"I'm impressed." Scott leaned back. "How did you come by this tidbit of information?"

Al grinned. "Well, a good newsman never reveals his source, but you'd be surprised what you hear when you spend a couple hours a day eating donuts at the local co-op."

"The sacrifices you make for your craft." Al shrugged. Not only was this useful information, he felt very comfortable with the retired reporter. In fact, he was more content at this moment than any time since Rica walked out. Until Debbie set his burger in front of him, done just the way he liked it, a thin patty cooked till it was just crispy at the edges, bun toasted on the grill, onions soft and brown. The fries were cut from a real potato with the skin on, thick and liberally sprinkled with salt and just a dash of seasoning. Neither he nor Al spoke again until Scott's plate was empty.

Scott crumpled his napkin and pushed his plate toward the edge of the table, where Debbie could pick it up more easily. "So what about young Brad turned our girl Brandi around?"

Al finished his last bite of burger and dipped the remaining two fries in ketchup. "Dunno. Could have been his good looks, or the full ride scholarship he had, or the successful corporate family farm." He savored his fries. "Could have been time in Margaret's house, as all I've been hearing tells me she was the quiet, unassuming, lead-by-example type. But whatever it was, Miss Brandi pulled her grades up and stopped causing trouble the rest of her school year here."

Scott looked down at his notebook. He hadn't thought to look at grades beyond Kyle's, only forwarding addresses. "And would she be available to talk to me?"

"Yup." Al tore a half sheet out of his notebook and pushed it toward Scott. "Don't call her between three and four, because that's when she picks up her kids from pre-school."

"Wow." Scott stared at the paper. "And all this cost you was some donuts?"

"Actually, all it cost me was some time and calories. I asked a couple questions of Mac while I was pouring the coffee, and he comped the coffee and had the donuts in his office." Al tapped the notebook. "It's all about relationships, Scott."

Yeah, relationships. I'm not so good at those.

251

"Most detectives would say it's about facts and evidence."

"In the long run, yes, but the relationships are what get you access to the facts."

"That and a good warrant."

Al laughed. "Well, if you can get people to voluntarily give you the info without a warrant, isn't that better and faster?"

"Yeah, I see your point." He looked around the diner, filled with people he didn't know. "But I don't have relationships here anymore. You do."

"You're the homeboy. You have more relationships here than you think."

Scott stared out the window. Thunder rolled again, and the clouds opened to dump rain in buckets on the street outside. People ducked and ran for their cars or storefronts, but otherwise paid it no mind. The thunder and rain matched his emotions.

"Something's bothering you, isn't it, Scott?" Al picked up his coffee cup. "Something more than this case?"

Scott glanced into Al's blue eyes. Beyond the sharpness of the reporter, not missing a detail, those eyes bespoke understanding. He looked down at his notebook and began to doodle around the spirals. "My wife—" Al simply nodded, and Scott found himself going on. "She wants a divorce."

"How long have you been married?"

"Four years. Met in college. She's four years younger than me. A nurse—surgical nurse. Ambitious." Scott stopped. Random facts just seemed to tumble out of his mouth.

Al tipped his head to the side and sipped more

coffee. "And she doesn't think you're moving up the ladder fast enough?"

He studied the notebook, while his thoughts yelled at the back of his mind. "Or she decided to hop to a ladder already at the top rung."

Scott didn't realize until he heard Al's quiet, "I see," that he had actually said the words.

Al set down his cup. "I have a small print job to get done by five this evening." He stood up. "Why don't you come to the print shop with me to make sure I can get that old press to cooperate."

Scott hesitated, "I really should call Brandi—"

"You can call her from my shop." Something about the way Al said the words and the kind look in his eyes said that he wanted Scott to be free to talk without fear of anyone overhearing their conversation.

"I guess there would be a lot of background noise if I called her from here." The place was practically packed now, filled with the sounds of diners conversing, silverware clanking against plates, tables being cleared. "I'll take you up on the offer."

Chapter 53

"Sure, I'll be there at 3:45." Scott flipped his cell phone shut. "Guess I'm yours for two hours, Al." He moved closer to the press. "Her littlest kid is down for a nap, and I can't come till after she picks up the older two at school."

"So your wife—" Al turned the rollers on the old press to pre-load the ink. "What is her name, Scott?"

"Rica." Scott chewed on the straw in the "to-go" tea he had purchased with lunch. "She's half-Mexican. Her grandmother was illegal, but her mother was born in Oklahoma. Met her in a psychology class while we were both taking courses for our Masters."

"Smart girl, then."

"So smart." He looked out the window, where the downpour had settled into a slow soaking rain. "She figures things out so much faster than I can. She'd have figured out how to put something together while I was still studying the parts." He closed his eyes, realizing just how big a gap she would leave in his life. Though he had lived on his own for a long time before he met Rica, he didn't think he'd make it now. "So neat, so organized, so together."

Al looked up from his alignments. "And she complained that you were always just a dreamer?"

Scott nodded. "How'd you know?"

Al flipped on the press. "Seen it many times." The

machine groaned, but then lumbered into action. Slowly paper fed into the press, and then printed pages fluttered into a tray at the other end. "People are attracted to those who have the qualities they think they lack. Then sometimes the very habits that attracted them become the ones they can't stand." He stepped toward Scott with some of the finished pages in his hand. "I was married, and then divorced, before I met Sarah."

"Oh."

"And I've covered some nasty divorce stories." Al paused in front of the window, to hold the pages up to the light. "And some nasty murders as well." He studied the print job for a long time, and finally turned back toward Scott. "Some of which were a direct result of the divorces."

"Yeah, me, too." Scott shivered, hoping he and Rica wouldn't get to the point where they were hateful to each other. Then he remembered the words they'd shot at each other in the restaurant. Maybe they were already there.

Al paused to put his hand on Scott's shoulder. "Scott, I've learned over the years that people change. Hopefully, they grow. And if they are wise enough, and love each other enough, they stay connected to each other and grow together." He stepped forward to shut off the press. "And they can help each other grow in the process."

"Do they ever change their minds?" Scott's voice came out as small as when he was a preschooler asking his mom if monsters were real.

Al looked into Scott's face for several minutes. "Sometimes, Scott. But often it takes years or a crisis." He looked down. "Usually they don't."

Scott swallowed hard. He had come to Homedale to lose himself in the case, to forget about Rica, and suddenly, she was all he could think about. Al walked past him and started up the press again. Scott just stood there, a man with a jagged hole in his chest. Above the rhythmic whoosh and clack and grind of the press, he heard Al step close to him again. "Scott, you'll survive."

He looked up at Al, knowing that his implacable cop's mask had melted. He just stared.

"Scott, since Sarah died—well, not right away, but after I came out of some of the numbness—I started interviewing people for a book about those who survived loss. All kinds of loss, from the death of a spouse, to abuse victims, to amputees, to those who survived when others died." Al looked at Scott so hard that Scott had to focus on those intense blue eyes. "Even divorce, Scott." Scott held onto Al's gaze, his lifeline for the moment. "I found that survivors overcome. They learn that they can't change the circumstance that brought about the loss, but they can change themselves and how they view the loss."

The press lost its rhythm, and Al jumped toward it. He stopped it and cleared a paper jam. When it was clear and he had it running again, he stepped back toward Scott. "You'll get through this, Scott. You may not want to for a while, but you will." The press ran out of paper, and Al shut it off. "If you are honest with yourself and work at it, you'll come out of this a better person."

"That would be a blessing," Scott mumbled. "I've been a fucking mess."

"I doubt that. You wouldn't have been promoted to

detective, wouldn't have pursued this case so far, if you were a total screw-up." Al patted Scott's shoulder. "Don't be so hard on yourself."

Chapter 54

The fresh-faced, smiling woman who answered the door on the first knock didn't track with the angry girl in dark Goth makeup and clothes that Scott had seen in the school photos. He didn't remember her personally at all. "Come on in," she invited, opening the door to a room that ran the width of the house. She nodded toward a burly man on the couch with a tow-headed little girl on either side of him, and a baby dressed in blue on his lap. "The rain drove Brad out of the field, so he's volunteered to read to the kids while we talk."

Scott nodded toward the man that he thought he remembered from football. "Brad, that's nice of you." Brad would have been a sophomore the year Scott was a senior.

"It's okay, Scott." Brad ruffled the hair of the little girl on his right. She appeared to be about four, the other girl maybe three. "I'm so busy in the summer that I don't get to do this very much."

Brandi picked up a glass of iced tea from the table that dominated the east end of the room. She carried it to her husband and handed it to him, pausing to kiss him briefly. Scott shoved down the envy of their easy relationship. She returned to the kitchen end of the room where Scott stood. "Iced tea?"

"I believe I'll take you up on that, Mrs. Obermann." Though dust had already begun to swirl in the roadways, the fields soaked the rain up like sponges, and it had driven the humidity up to the intolerable range.

"Call me Brandi, please, Scott. Everyone does." She ran ice from the refrigerator dispenser and then poured sun tea over it. "Let's go to the sun room to talk."

The name "sun room" filled him with dread; in this heat, the last thing he wanted was to sit in a room being cooked like a bug under a magnifying glass. However, he followed her through the kitchen to a shaded former porch now enclosed with tempered glass. An air conditioner vent poured a liberal flow of cool air into the room.

Brandi seated herself in a white-painted rocker, leaving the choice of another rocker or a straight chair for Scott. He grabbed the straight chair. Brandi took a slow sip of her tea before setting it on the small table beside her. "I know the girls were gone all afternoon and the baby was napping, but—" She leaned back and rocked. "It sure is quiet and peaceful out here knowing that their dad is taking care of them, and I can relax for a minute." Then she focused on Scott. "But I don't suppose it's very relaxing to be investigating the murder of someone you know—knew."

Scott shrugged. "If you investigate long enough, you get to know them all." He swallowed a drink of tea. "But it does make me really, really want to find her killer."

"How can I help?"

"What turned you around from where you were headed in high school?"

She smiled, a dimple showing in her cheek.

"Brad."

"What was it about Brad that turned you around?"

"He wouldn't go out with me the way I was, or just for sex." She stared out the window-walls into a grove of cottonwoods. "He said he could tell there was a very nice girl hiding under all that makeup and rage. I wanted him so bad, I cleaned up my looks. He started talking to me, but still said he just wanted to be friends. That's when I started cleaning up my act." She looked back at Scott. "The better I acted, the more I found I wanted to BE that way. I finally realized it had to be genuine for Brad to accept me, and whether he ever did or not, I wanted it for myself. I brought my grades up and earned the right to move back in with my mom. I kept writing to Brad, enrolled at the same college, and we got to be friends." She grinned. "And then more than friends."

"And did Margaret help at all in this process."

Brandi swirled the ice in her half-finished tea and watched it until it stopped. Scott waited. "I don't want to speak ill of the dead." She looked up, but avoided his eyes. "I mean, she was a great person in school, and I'm sure she was a wonderful adult and mom and all that, but—"

Scott forced himself to remain slouched on the chair, his hand relaxed on his notepad, but inside he quivered like a dog on point. It was always what they didn't think they should tell you that was exactly what you needed to know.

"Margaret had a bit of dark, wild side that most people never saw." She ran her fingers around the rim of her glass. "I guess most of us do, really." She flicked a glance at Scott. "I really hate bringing this up. It seems so cruel after the way she died." She sat as if waging a silent war within herself over whether to reveal the secret. Scott waited, knowing that if he gave her enough time, she would. Otherwise, the thought would not have come up.

Brandi glanced toward the main room of the house, as if to check for anyone who could overhear. "Margaret came to my room one night in the spring." She watched the ceiling fan as if it would help her remember dates. "Let's see, that was my junior year, so would have been her senior." She glanced into the other room again and leaned forward toward Scott. "She wanted me to set her up with a guy to lose her virginity, said she'd waited long enough. She had tried everything she knew to get Kyle to do it with her, but I could have told her that boy would never have been able to go through with it."

"Why's that?"

She stared at him for a moment. "Do you remember Kyle? That boy was so gay he could have burst into flames at any moment." She started rocking again. "But maybe he hadn't come to terms with that yet."

"Any idea where he is now?"

She shook her head. "I didn't stay in touch with anyone but Brad after I left Homedale."

"Well, did you get her set up?"

Brandi pressed her lips together into a thin line. "I knew many of the boys in a way that I could figure out which ones would make it good for her." She took a deep, ragged breath. "I came up with three I thought she might like, and she chose one. For a while, she went a little crazy, sneaking out every night, often with a different boy every night." She shivered slightly, even though outside the sun baked the grass. "That used to be me, then I was lecturing her, and staying in." She cupped her glass in her hands. "I'm glad that's not me anymore." She looked around the room, her gaze taking in the yard, and then nodded toward the family in the main room. "This is so much better than that."

Scott held his tongue for a while, but her story had evidently ended. "Were you close to any of the other girls?"

She shrugged. "Mostly just competitors to see who could get which boy, or get in the most trouble, at first." She leaned forward. "But then I saw the error of that way, and I tried to stay away from them when they were where they could get in trouble. At first they made fun of me, but then, toward the end of the school year, when I learned I could go home to Mom, I saw envy in their eyes." She shook her head. "They never said anything, never let up on me, but you could see they all wanted that, too, just didn't know how to change."

Scott glanced down at his notes. He hadn't taken many, but the story was burned in his memory. Gay Kyle, wild Margaret, all those hurting girls. He looked up at Brandi again, saw her studying an iris bed beside the porch. "Need to mow those things down soon," she murmured. Then she focused on him. "Did anything I say help?"

"Who knows?" He folded up his notebook. "Maybe she still had a little wild side and got mixed up with someone a little too wild. Maybe it was nothing like that." He stood. "You certainly put more dimension to Margaret, and maybe it will lead somewhere." Brandi stood, too, and took his glass. "Thank you so much, Mrs. Obermann, for your tea."

She stepped past him into the main room. On the couch, her husband sat with his head against the back of the couch, eyes closed, both girls slumped against him asleep, the baby snuggled close against his chest. Brandi smiled and walked Scott to the door. "I'll start supper without waking them," she whispered as she let him out.

He stood on the stoop for a moment, as the heat and humidity claimed every spot of his body that had been cool and comfortable. Would he ever have the opportunity to be that man on the couch, with a woman as devoted as Brandi Obermann? Could he earn that privilege by finding Delia/Margaret's killer?

He turned toward the patrol car he had parked in the shade of a sixty-foot tall cottonwood that had to be over a half-century old. Earning privilege or not, he *would* find the killer. He owed it to Delia.

He opened the car door. Even though he had rolled the windows down an inch or so and parked it in the shade, the interior was a sauna when he slid behind the wheel. He put the windows all the way down, seeking a breeze until the air coming from the vents turned cool. Only then did he belt in, put the car in gear, and head toward home. He glanced at the clock. Four-thirty. No way he would get back before the chief left for the day. That would put off his ass-chewing until at least tomorrow morning.

When he got to the station, he turned in the car and went straight to his truck. The rain had avoided the city, and the thermometer in his mirror read one hundred nine. It was too hot for a run yet, but not too hot for the cold beers in the fridge.

Chapter 55

Charlotte put off her walk as long as she dared. Devlyn would be home by 11:15 or so, and she needed time to shower and make herself presentable before then. Still, it was so un-Godly hot out. The "If you want to know what hell feels like, visit Kansas in August" jokes were wearing thin, but they felt true. Finally, at 9:30, with the thermometer still registering a hundred degrees, she parked her car in one of the long shadows by her usual entrance to the walking path. Stretching as she made her way to the hot black asphalt, she kept a wary lookout for Handsy. The last thing she needed was for him to recognize her and strike up a conversation.

As she walked, she nodded and exchanged greetings with the regulars she often encountered. Then, a half-mile from her turnaround, she saw him. Again, he was running too hard for this heat, pushing himself, running like a man possessed. Sweat soaked his shirt and dripped from his face as he pounded closer to her. She scanned for a distraction and spotted a family of mallards on the water. She left the path to get closer to them, so her back would be to Handsy. She heard his labored breathing as he blew past and turned to watch his back. What the hell was he running from?

****

Scott knew he should slow his pace. He'd had a couple of beers when he got home from the station,

264

then fallen asleep watching the early news. Then, when he woke up, he forced himself to eat a TV dinner that had looked good in the store, but tasted like cardboard with sauce. He ended up throwing half of it out and had another beer instead. He kept an eye on the outside temp and finally decided at nine that it wasn't going to get cool enough to run. So he changed his clothes and headed for the running path along the river anyway.

He tried to go slow and take it easy in the heat, but somehow, it seemed the faster he ran, the quieter his mind got. He could no longer hear the voices that told him that Rica would still be with him if he was just neater. That she would not have left if he'd taken her out more often. That it was because they had to watch their pennies on his salary that Ambrose looked so much better than he did. That it was all the baggage from work he carried in his head that made her leave. That he didn't love her well enough or often enough. When he reached a certain speed, all he could hear was his lungs laboring to pull in enough air to keep his arms and legs and heart pumping. All he could feel was the blood surging through his veins and the sweat pouring out of him, like it could wash out all his faults.

By the time he reached the parking area where he usually circled around to head back home, the endorphins had kicked in and he no longer heeded the voices in his head. It was then that his policeman's instincts took over, and he began to catalog the people he encountered. The mother with the jogging stroller ahead of him. The auburn-haired woman at the river's edge watching the ducks. The man with the Weimaraner trotting south. He circled through the parking lot and noted the cars there. Three SUV's, a pickup with a topper, a Toyota Camry, and a Chevy Cavalier.

He headed back toward his apartment. As the sun dropped, a slight breeze picked up, cooling him as he ran at a more sensible pace toward the home that no longer felt like home. The voices began again, and he sped up.

****

The mallard hen stood on the shore near Charlotte, quacking and shaking her head. "I don't have any bread," Charlotte whispered. "I didn't plan to visit with you this evening." She heard pounding footfalls on the path and waited until the runner was well past her before she looked up to confirm it was Handsy headed south. "Later, duckies." Charlotte climbed the river bank to the path and hurried back to her car. She'd skip her walk tonight. And find another place to walk from now on. She couldn't risk starting a conversation with that cop.

****

Scott tried to force his mind onto police work as he ran, hoping it would drown out the self-accusations he kept hearing. He didn't recall any of the vehicles in the parking lot being on any stolen or watch lists. Still, something he had seen there nagged at him. There was something he needed to remember from that parking lot. He shook his head. Maybe the beers had been too much. He needed to watch that they didn't become a habit.

Chapter 56

A month later, on a September day that promised to be a scorcher, Scott hustled to his desk at 8:07, Sonic Drive-Thru coffee cup still hot against his hand.

"Oversleep again, rookie?" Bates looked up from his computer monitor. He, too, had a fast food cup on his desk—Dunkin' Donuts. He reached for it and made a face. "Stuff tastes like crap when it gets cold."

Scott set down the cup with a little more force than he intended. "Not exactly." He flipped the switch on his computer. "Put on a load of laundry after I got up, and then it got unbalanced, so I had to move stuff around and turn it off before I left." He grinned at Bates. "It'll be okay sitting all day, but I sure hope we don't get called out on something that keeps us all night."

"Well, Rica could always finish it when she gets home."

With Bates watching him, Scott knew he needed to confess, but just shrugged. "We get any of the warrants for that stuff from the break-ins?"

"Not yet. Chief thought it might be later today."

"Good." Scott sat and faced his monitor, his back to Bates.

Just then, a uniformed deputy strode through the door to their office. "Hey, Roger," Bates called out. "Those our warrants for the theft ring?"

Scott looked up, the coffee suddenly acid burning

in his stomach. "No, Del." The deputy stopped before Scott's desk. "Sorry, Scott, but I have to do this." He handed the folded paper to Scott. "You know what it is, don't you?"

Scott nodded, his throat too dry to speak. He glanced at the paper to confirm what he already knew: Rica had served him with divorce papers. She hadn't even had the kindness to allow them to be served by mail, had forced a fellow officer to embarrass them both. "Thanks, Rog."

"Sorry, man." The deputy shot a look at Bates, then turned and left the room.

Scott sat staring down at the papers, reading the words that told him his hopes that Rica would cool down and come back were gone. He felt Bates' hand on his shoulder. He sat, silent, wishing he could turn to stone, then he wouldn't hurt anymore, wouldn't have to face Bates' questions, wouldn't have to go through the court hearings, the settlement process.

"Let's go get a cup of coffee, Scott."

Numb, Scott got up and followed Bates without question, without a word being spoken until they had two hot cups in their hands from the McDonald's six blocks from the station. Bates drove to the park at the south end of town, pulled into the shade, and parked. "Ok, Scott. Are you ready to talk?"

Scott sipped his coffee. All he tasted was heat. Outside, in the park, a few yellow leaves dropped from the elm tree above them, victim of too little water this summer and an early turn of cool fall nights just a week after Labor Day. "Not really."

"Officially, you have to, you know."

Scott shrugged. "I know." He ran his thumb around

the lid of the cup, pressed the flap a little more firmly in its slot. "I just kept thinking she would get over it and come home."

"How long has she been gone?"

Scott mentally added the last forty-eight hours to the tally he had kept since she walked out. "Six weeks, five days and—" He checked the dash clock. "Ten hours." He looked out the window again. "More or less."

"Damn, Scott." Bates took a long swallow of coffee. "I knew you guys had had some ups and downs lately, but I never suspected it was that bad." Scott could feel his partner watching him, but he couldn't look away from the squirrel frantically burying a nut thirty feet from where they were parked. "I should have figured something was bothering you when I noticed you were losing some weight, but I just thought it was the Enfield case." He paused. "I'm sorry, Scott."

The squirrel dashed off to find another nut to bury. Scott remained silent; having told Bates, he had now done half his duty. All that remained was telling the chief and then sitting through the required counseling sessions with a Department-paid shrink. "Maybe when I'm done with the shrink, they'll leave me alone to focus on the job." It was all he had left.

"Don't focus so much on the job that you don't do the work it takes to get over this."

Scott shook his head. "There's no getting over this." He sighed. "I never dated much before I met Rica. Once I met her, I knew she was the one."

"Scott," Bates began, then hesitated. "I know it feels like the end of life as you know it right now. And it is the end of life as it was for you, but it isn't the end of everything." He shifted in his seat. "Ellen and I have served as marriage mentors in our church for years. We've counseled with couples that ended their marriages and others who worked it out, and still others who were working hard on making a second marriage work. Believe me when I tell you that you will survive this, and when you have another relationship—"

"I don't think—"

"Just hear me out, Scott. I said when, not if, you have another relationship, it can be stronger and healthier than what you had with Rica."

Scott stayed silent. Rica was all he ever wanted. Rica and children with her.

"Or, if the divorce takes long enough and you both do some counseling, you could end up back together, much better than before."

"You really think so? I could win her back?" Bates' words represented the first tangible hope Scott had felt in a long time.

Bates stared at him a long time. "I don't want to raise any false hopes, Scott, because it doesn't happen often. You would both have a lot of changing to do." He waited. "Wasn't she a little…temperamental?"

Scott shrugged. "Only when I was stupid, like I forgot an important occasion or was late."

"That happens with our line of work, Scott. A mate has to be a bit forgiving."

"Rica was forgiving." Scott looked out the window again. The squirrel was back, and down the curve of parkway, Scott could see another one, also digging furiously. He'd bet this was gonna be a rough winter.

"Don't be too hard on yourself, Scott. It takes two giving 110% each to make a marriage work. One person can't hold it together alone."

"We were both trying. We did counseling, I tried hard to change, to be neater, to be better at letting her know when I wouldn't be home on time."

Bates' voice grew gentle. "What was Rica trying to change?"

Scott stared at Bates. Finally, a light began to come on. "Me?"

"That's what it sounds like from where I sit," Bates said. "There is always another side to the story, but it seems like she wanted you to do all the changing."

Scott shrugged again. "Maybe I just didn't see it very clearly."

"Or maybe you did." Bates sighed. "Man, I am so sorry you have to be going through this."

Silence fell as they sipped their coffee. Scott finished his first. "Guess we'd better get back to the station so I can tell the chief and only get half my ass chewed off for not telling him before the papers came."

Bates put the car in reverse. "You'll be lucky if that's all you get."

****

"You knew the regulations, Aylward," the chief thundered in his best Clint Eastwood-style whisper. "I'm giving you administrative suspension for the rest of the week, and you had damn well better arrange your first visit with our contracted counselor before this week is over."

"But, sir, it's hard to get in to the counselor—" Scott began.

"I don't care if it's impossible, Aylward. Just do it."

Scott took a deep breath. Even though it was

Tuesday, it sure felt like a Monday. "Yes, sir." Scott retreated from the chief's office and went to his desk to pick up his notes on the Delia Enfield case. He might be suspended, but that didn't mean he couldn't work on his own.

Bates looked up as he sat down at his desk. "How did it go?"

Scott picked up his notebook. "Suspended till next Monday."

"Geez." Bates hit a key on the computer and leaned back. "I didn't expect him to be that mad."

"Well, he was." Scott found the file on his computer and printed out the two pages of notes he had entered.

"You want to come over for supper tonight?" Bates got up from his desk. "Meatloaf, I think, but it'll be good."

Scott looked at his partner. Bates was trying to be helpful, as always. "Not yet, Del, but thanks for the offer." He folded the pages of notes and stuck them in his notebook.

"Don't wait too long, rookie. Looks like you're starving to death on your own cooking."

Scott shook his head. "Just been running more to try to stop thinking." And not even bothering to eat most of the time.

Bates nodded toward the notebook. "Don't spend all of your suspension working. Get some rest and eat."

"I will." Scott turned toward the door. "Thanks, Del."

Chapter 57

At his apartment, Scott opened the notebook on the kitchen table and unfolded the two pages of notes he had printed, trying to flatten them out again. He scanned the notes quickly, then suddenly turned toward the bedroom to grab his old high school annual. Returning to the kitchen, he opened the fridge to see what it might offer up for lunch. Moldy bread, a wizened apple, sour milk, a third of a bag of baby carrots, a jar of mayonnaise, one dill pickle spear remaining in a jar of juice, and a half-empty twelve-pack of Bud Light. He knew the cabinet beside the sink contained a few cans of soup. Maybe he'd heat a can of soup later. Right now, he grabbed the baby carrots and a Bud, twisting off the lid. He put the bottle to his lips and took a long pull.

Swinging his leg over his chair, he opened the annual and looked at the faces now involved in this case. Delia—Margaret then—so serious and studious, at least most of the world. Brandi, Goth then, now the all-American girl. Kyle, such a slender, delicate boy. The photos didn't reveal much detail, but now he did remember that Kyle had unusual colored eyes. What would a police sketch artist call them? Pale hazel? The girls had always giggled about how unfair it was that a boy had such pretty eyes. And long eyelashes. Scott picked up the bottle again.

He looked at his notes. There was a phone number from the school in Nevada that had requested Kyle's transcript. Setting down the beer, he dialed the number.

"Mustang High School," came the crisp answer.

"Hello, I'm a detective from Kansas, Scott Aylward with City Police Department. I'm trying to find a student who may have attended your school twelve to fourteen years ago."

He heard a hesitation in the voice. "Just a moment, please. I'll connect you with the principal."

A voice much softer than he expected came on the line next. "Helen Quinn, Principal. May I help you?"

He repeated his request.

"And how do you think we can help in your search?"

"His records at Homedale High, in Kansas, indicated that your school had requested a transcript. I'm trying to find out if he actually transferred there."

"I'm sorry, Detective, but I'm afraid you would need a warrant for us to release that information."

"Thank you for speaking with me, Principal Quinn. I'll see if I can get the paperwork." He hung up and sat there with the phone in his hand. As long as it took to get the subpoena for Homedale High, there was no way in hell he'd get a warrant for a school in Nevada, unless he turned up some connection. By all accounts, Kyle and Delia had been best friends. Unlikely he would bear a grudge against her and materialize out of nowhere to kill her. The slight boy he had been, he wouldn't have had the strength to make the slash that had killed Delia. Unless the boy had turned around and become a championship body builder. Yet this loose end nagged at him. His gaze fell on the business card for the city-contracted shrink. He supposed he could call and make his appointment while he still held the phone. Or not.

But he wasn't under house arrest. He could leave the apartment. He could go to Debbie's Diner for lunch; their chicken was the best he'd ever tasted. Or close. Abruptly, he stood, set the beer in the sink and headed for the door.

Debbie met him at his usual booth by the window at the far end. "Iced tea?" When he nodded, she spun toward the kitchen and returned before he had time to finish reading the menu.

"Special today?" he asked.

"Old fashioned hot roast beef sandwich and mixed veggies." She smiled at him. "Just like I'll bet your momma used to make."

A flicker of guilt told Scott he should probably call his mom; hadn't talked to her in a couple of months, maybe more. "She did make good ones. I'll have that."

Minutes later, Scott saw Al walk through the door. He waited, hoping Al would see him and join him. Al scanned the room as he walked toward the first row of tables. He smiled when he saw Scott.

"What brings you to Homedale today, Scott?" Al slipped into the booth without asking permission.

"Day off." Al's presence across the table from him comforted him.

Al sat watching him, as Debbie set a cup of coffee and a glass of water in front of him. "Coming here for lunch was the best way you could think of to spend a day off?"

Scott looked down at his tea and shrugged. "Food's good."

Al studied Scott for a long minute. "That it is." He

looked up at Debbie. "I'll have the French dip, please, Debbie."

"Coming right up, Al."

"So, no new leads?" Al folded his napkin in half, then in half again.

"Nope." Scott watched Al folding. "Everything has run into a dead end."

"Now what?"

"Case gets shoved to the back burner, and no more active investigation unless something new turns up."

"By 'no more active investigation,' I'm guessing you mean that you will continue to watch for clues?"

Scott nodded. "Can't let this one just go." He lined up his silverware. "I guess it's the hometown connection, or because I'm the one who found her." He sighed. "We got the second suspect in the Quick Shop murders, but neither will implicate the other one in pulling the trigger, so that case will drag on for a long time." He spotted lunch coming their way. "So that means it's back to hunting down stolen bric-a-brac on Craigslist."

Al smiled as Debbie set a plate in front of him. "I take it you don't like bric-a-brac hunting."

"I don't even like bric-a-brac." Scott took his first bite. "But I do like this." He tried to remember if he had eaten dinner last night, but failed. All he remembered was falling asleep in his chair when he got home from work, waking up to go for a run, then falling asleep in front of late night talk-show hosts when he returned. Dinner wasn't part of that memory.

Al, too, stayed silent as they ate the first few bites. "So," he said finally. "What really brings you to Homedale on your day off with no new leads to pursue?"

Scott stopped eating for a moment. "I don't know." He shrugged. "Maybe I think being here will bring back something I need to know."

Al dipped his sandwich. "About the case or about yourself?"

With three-fourths of his meal gone, Scott lost his appetite. He reached for his tea. "The case." He drank the tea and looked down at his hands. "Maybe both."

"And why do you have today off?"

Scott looked out the window at the cars parked here and there along Main Street. Two more cars pulled up in front of the Diner and one parked at the antique store across the street, which was only open from eleven to two on Tuesdays and Thursdays. "I got suspended for the rest of the week."

Al continued to eat his dinner. His silence pushed Scott into going on. "It's department policy to let your supervisors know as soon as there is a major change in the household." He looked down at his plate. "Like your wife moving out."

"And you hadn't mentioned that to your supervisor?"

Scott shook his head. "I kept thinking she'd change her mind. She's pretty volatile sometimes."

"Then how did they find out?"

"I got served divorce papers at work."

"Oh."

"And then I have to see a shrink before I can come back to work."

Al finished his sandwich. "And you don't want to see a shrink?"

"None of the guys ever do." Scott shook his head.

"It's against 'the code.'"

Al crumpled his napkin onto his plate. "Yet you have a degree in psychology."

"That's just so I can understand the bad guys." Scott smiled. Even though he had already told Al more than he had planned to tell him, it seemed right to do so.

"I see." Al leaned back in the booth, as Debbie swooped in to refill his coffee and take away the plates. "Nothing about understanding some things about yourself that may have been puzzling you?"

Scott focused. "Like what?"

"Like why you can't focus on doing chores around the house, but neither can you pull yourself out of focusing on every aspect of any case you are on." Al took a sip of coffee. "Any case that doesn't involve bric-a-brac, that is."

"Well, you know, that doesn't really make sense, does it?"

"It does if you know how your brain is wired."

"Backwards?"

Al leaned forward. "Our youngest son was the same way. Couldn't remember where his shoes were or whether he did his homework. Took him forever to clean his room, because we'd come in to find that he was rearranging his bookshelf instead of just putting things away to vacuum. When we finally started seeing doctors, they told us he experienced attention deficit disorder."

Scott nodded. The story sounded like his autobiography.

"They wanted to medicate him, but Sarah resisted. She knew how intelligent and creative he was. So she did a lot of research into behavior modification and learned that we could teach him to live *with* the disorder instead of constantly fighting against it. We helped him set up routines and schedules to keep him on track."

"Did it work?"

"He'll get his M.D. in two more years. On the Honor Roll, involved in half the clubs on campus." Al met Scott's eyes. "I see a lot of Sam in you, Scott."

Scott sat silent. Al had hit the nail squarely on the head. But what to do about it?

"So what are you so scared of seeing the therapist about, Scott? They don't make you feel like a horrible person, in fact, most of what they do is to help you feel better about yourself."

"I don't know." Scott looked down at his hands. "Maybe there's some things about myself I just don't want to face."

"Scott." Al's voice made him look up. "Fears are like noises in a closet on a dark night. In the dark, it sounds like there's a bear in the closet. But if you get up, decide to face your fear, and turn a light on it, it's nothing more than a mouse, if it's that big. And it's easy to defeat then." The skin around Al's eyes began to crinkle. "Unless you have a phobia about mice."

Scott chuckled, something he hadn't done much lately. "Not mice. Spiders."

"So 'Itsy, Bitsy Spider' wasn't your favorite nursery rhyme as a child?"

Scott shook his head. "Not so much."

Al laughed. "You know, I have it on good authority that they got in some fresh-baked pies this morning. How does coconut cream sound?"

Scott turned over his coffee cup. "Lemon meringue sounds better."

Chapter 58

Scott took his time on the drive back from Homedale. Overhead the brassy blue sky contrasted sharply with the molten gold of the cottonwoods lining the riverbank. Most people liked the bright reds of fall maple leaves, but Scott preferred the twinkling yellow of the cottonwoods, the plains version of the aspen. As the shorter days and cooling temperatures caused the chlorophyll to draw out of the leaves into the branches, all that was left was the color of the sunlight the leaves had captured over the summer.

The couple of rains they'd had since Labor Day had been the slow, soaking kind. And now, thanks to that rain, the winter wheat carpeted most of the fields he passed with bright green. He paused at the bridge over the river. The rain had rescued it as well, though there was still more sand than water between the banks. He pulled his truck to a stop and parked. Walking down to the riverbed, he pulled off his shoes and socks and let his feet sink a half inch into the sun-warmed sand. A gnarled bit of gray tree trunk presented itself a yard away, so he sat down with his back against it and watched brown and yellow leaves float slowly past him. "What do you know, river?" He tossed a twig into a channel where it joined the leaves. "What secrets are you hiding from me?" He continued to sit and watch as he waited for the answer. The quiet lulled him to sleep, until a grain truck thundered over the bridge and startled him. He blinked a few times and checked his watch. He'd slept nearly a half hour. Time to get moving again. He stood and stretched.

By the time he got back to his apartment, he'd be ready for a run. And he just might call that shrink before he left the house.

Chapter 59

Scott strolled into his office five minutes before eight on Monday morning. Bates looked up from his desk. "I take this to mean you saw the shrink."

Scott plopped into his chair, then rolled it toward Bates. "Yeah, I saw her and she saw me."

"And?" Bates took a sip of his coffee, then dumped it in the plant on the windowsill.

"She wants to see me every other Friday for a while."

"That's not so bad." Bates poured another cup of coffee, then set it on his desk to cool.

Scott shrugged. "I guess it could be worse."

"Yeah." Bates tried his coffee, still too hot to drink. "She could have made you turn in your gun and pull desk duty till after the divorce hearing."

"Glad she didn't do that, but I still don't like it."

"Just go until she gets tired of you and then you're free." Bates turned back to his computer. "Who knows, you might get something good out of it."

Scott rolled back to his own desk. "Yeah, callouses on my ass from sitting in her chair."

"What?" Firearms training had done Del's hearing no good.

"Nothing, I just agreed with you."

The phone on Del's desk jangled. "Bates."

He followed his terse answer with three "uh-huhs"

and a "yeah" before he hung up. "Let's go, rookie."

"Oh, yeah?" Scott rose and slipped into the jacket he had just shed. "Where?"

Bates pitched his coffee cup in the trash. "Ten miles west of town." He reached the door to their office.

"Isn't that a little out of our jurisdiction?" Scott continued to sip from his McDonald's coffee.

Bates grinned as he headed down the stairs to the garage. "Yeah, but SO just got called to a burglary that is the same MO as our unsolved ones." He paused a moment at the door to the garage to catch his breath. "They thought we might stand a better chance of catching them if we worked together and compared notes."

"Imagine that." *More bric-a-brac theft.* "You know, maybe the thieves are doing the homeowners a favor."

"How so?" Bates pressed the clicker on the key fob in his hand, and the Crown Vic they usually used gave them a friendly wave with its headlights from the other end of the garage.

"Well, if thieves stole all the bric-a-brac there is, worldwide, think how much less dusting would have to be done."

Bates opened the driver's door; keyholder had the call to drive or ride. "I see your point, rookie, but what would that do to the furniture industry?" He slipped behind the wheel. "What about all those poor workers overseas who build the china cabinets they put this stuff in?" He looked at Scott as he slid into the passenger seat. "What about their families?"

"As usual, oh wise one, you are right." He set his

coffee cup in the holder. "If we can solve this crime and continue the collection of bric-a-brac, we can save families, whole villages even, from losing their way of life."

"Amen." Bates started the car and pulled from the garage. "Truth, justice, and the American way."

Scott nodded. "We are making the world safe for capitalism, so that Americans can collect more stuff for others to covet." He picked up his coffee again. "God, it really is Monday, isn't it."

Bates sighed. "Yup. I'd much rather wrestle a sweaty drunk to the ground than investigate something like these have been."

"Yeah, it's like these thieves are in there as much to destroy someone's memories as they are to find anything to sell."

"It would sure break my mom's heart if anyone stole the stuff I used to hate to help her clean."

"My mom, too." Scott closed his eyes, realizing how much of his mother's bric-a-brac had been boxed up and placed in storage near his brother's house, while the influence she had wielded over the style and substance of an entire farmstead was now reduced to one small bedroom and a chair in the family room. Never again would he grumble as he washed china lambs and shepherdesses while she told him the history of how each one had come into the family and then into her hands. To be fair, she should have had one daughter who could have appreciated the stories wrapped up in each figurine or knick-knack, instead of boys who simply wanted to be done with them and run outside. Of her daughters-in-law, only Rica, with her solid sense of family heritage, could have appreciated the sacrifices made to build lives on the prairie each piece represented. But he had never taken the time to help Rica get to know his mother. Not until his mother lay recuperating from a broken hip, and Rica made it a point to stop in to visit her at the end of her shift every day, had the two women begun to bond, and then his mother moved to a rehabilitation hospital near his brother, and from there into his home, and Scott lost one more opportunity to build family that he would never regain. He really needed to go visit his mom.

They turned off the highway and followed a sand road between irrigated cornfields, now dry and brown awaiting troops of upland bird hunters in another two months. Bates slowed as the car wallowed in the sand.

Two more miles, and he turned back east a half mile to a farmhouse that had once been surrounded by a windbreak of mixed evergreens and deciduous trees with barns and granaries. Now, leaves blown south by the wind, the trees that had escaped tornadoes and ice storms stood as a battle-scarred army around the house. One of the barns was settling back into the ground, like a mortally wounded elephant sinking slowly to its knees and then leaning over on its side. Inch by inch and year by year, the barn yielded to time. Near the barn, a combine that had been state of the art right after World War II sat rusting, a redbud tree growing through its header. Another barn had been converted to a shop and then the effort abandoned. A door swung in the wind. The house itself needed paint and the yard some tender care, though scattered and bent rose bushes and beds of dried flowers provided evidence that the yard had once been loved.

Bates pulled into the circular driveway behind the

Sheriff's Office Blazer. Deputy Lyle Nash stepped out of the Blazer. "Mornin' Del, Scott," he said as he strolled to their car.

"Hey, Lyle." Scott hopped out of the car, camera in hand. "How bad is it?"

"I think it's worse than the ones you had in town."

"Wow." Bates stood beside Nash while Scott snapped pictures of the house. The back door stood ajar, framed photographs littering the steps and keeping the door from closing. Items of clothing, left as if the thieves had no concern about what they dropped, trailed to a spot where a large vehicle had been parked near the door. The thieves had driven over and shattered a crystal plate in their haste to leave.

"Any prints?" Bates had drawn out his notebook, pen poised.

"I already lifted a few from the door, but it'll be hard to sort through. The little old lady that lives here had a stroke three weeks ago, and her family stayed here a week. Her oldest boy has been out a few times since to check on the irrigation pump, but not been inside the house. Hard to say when this happened. He found it when he came out to check on the pump today."

"Did you get to talk to him much?"

"A bit. He had to get to town to help move his mom to a rehab unit. He was gonna go get her insurance policy to see if anything is listed." Nash sighed. "So we may never know what items were stolen to be able to identify them if they turn up anywhere." He glanced at Bates and then at Scott. "You ready to see the inside?"

"Not really," Bates responded. "But I guess we

need to."

Together they followed Nash through the back door into a utility room that had once been a back porch later enclosed. There a large upright freezer stood open, with packages of meat rotting on the floor beside cartons of what looked like homemade stew and garden bounty. Both sides of the door showed dark smudges where Nash had dusted it with fingerprint powder. The prints Scott could see were indistinct and smeared.

They stepped through a doorway into a kitchen that looked like a meal had exploded inside. Dishes and canned goods littered the floor, mixed with cereal, flour, and broken jars. Beyond the kitchen, the dining room stood nearly empty. Imprints on the area rug showed where a massive dining table and eight chairs had once been. On the far wall, a light shadow on the paint indicated a china hutch had been removed. Papers dumped from a drawer littered the floor.

As they made their way through the first survey of the house, they saw continued evidence of the same lack of regard. The thieves had prepared some of the food from the kitchen, carried it with them through the house, and then dropped what they didn't want wherever they stood. In the first bedroom, which apparently had been used by the occupant, they found pieces of a fragile lace wedding dress, a chili footprint ground into it.

Scott shivered. "Good thing she was in the hospital when this happened."

"Yeah, but that seems to be the MO, just like yours in town. They find out when no one will be home for a while, then clean out what they want." Nash shook his head.

"And how long before their intel fails them and they crash into a house with someone's grandma asleep in her bed?" Bates gritted his teeth. "Then we might be investigating a homicide."

"Exactly," said Nash. "So let's see if we can get them this time."

Scott shivered again and raised the department camera.

Chapter 60

At 5:30 p.m., Scott moved toward his recliner, weary mentally and physically. Working up the burglary had taken all day. The complete ravaging of a family's history bothered him. Had his mother not sold most of her possessions before she moved in with his brother, it could have been their house. He flipped open his phone and scrolled through his contacts until his found his brother's home number. Alicia picked up the phone on the third ring.

"Hi, Scott." Her voice, though cheery as always, sounded out of breath. "How's my favorite brother-in-law?"

"Tired, Alicia. Is Mom around?"

"Of course, she is, Scott. If we're here, she's here."

"Yeah, I guess that makes sense."

"It's not that bad, Scott. She's making friends at church. She's gone to lunch with a couple of the ladies while we were at work."

Scott swallowed hard. "That's good. Is she getting around okay now?"

"She takes her time, especially on stairs or slopes, but she's doing very well, Scott." He heard Alicia's heels clicking on their hardwood floor. "But why don't you ask her yourself."

"Scott?" The excitement he heard in his mother's voice lifted his spirits at the same time as it bathed him in guilt. "How have you been, son? It's been ages since we talked."

"I know, Mom. I've worked a lot of long days lately on some cases. It was late when I got off, and I didn't want to wake the house." His excuses sounded lame even to himself.

"Well, it's good to hear your voice now." She paused. "Will you and Rica be up for Thanksgiving?" Her excitement seemed to rise with the prospect.

He swallowed hard. She had no idea that things between them had been tough since long before she fell. "Probably not, Mom. You know how her extended family makes a big deal of every holiday."

"Well, you wouldn't have to come Thanksgiving weekend. You have some vacation time, don't you?"

"Yeah, and maybe some other weekend would be easier to get away, not as many shifts to cover." He really needed to go up to see her. No way he could tell her over the phone that his marriage had failed.

"Oh, boy." She covered the mouthpiece with her hand, but he could still hear her call to Alicia. "Scott and Rica may be up around Thanksgiving."

"Can I talk to Rica?" He heard his niece Vanessa in the background. Twelve-year-old Nessa wanted to be a nurse and loved talking shop with Rica.

"I don't know, honey, I'll ask." His mother spoke directly to Scott. "Is Rica home?"

"She's—she's working a double shift tonight." His throat almost closed with the lie. He didn't know what shift she was working, or even if she was working anywhere. He knew nothing about Rica and her life now. "Mom, I gotta go now, need to get a run in before it gets dark."

"Okay, son." He heard the life go out of her voice, like the air from a balloon when no one holds the end closed. "Call again as soon as you know when you can come up." Her voice grew soft and tender. "I love you, Scott." As her baby, he had always held a special place in her heart; she had told him so many times after his brothers grew up and left home. And more after his father died.

"I will, Mom. I love you, too." He flipped shut his phone and hung his head. The guilt at not being more useful to his mother weighed so heavily on him, that he almost felt he should be pressed into the floor. Trying to shake it off, he stood and went to the bedroom to change for a run.

He walked the six blocks to the running path, through the tunnel of shade made by the big trees that graced the yards of the old houses lining the sidewalks. Though the days were still warm in this Indian summer first week of October, the nights had begun to chill. He needed to put in for the time off if he wanted to go to Ohio for Thanksgiving, now just six weeks away.

He reached the path and stretched well. Now he faced a choice: run north as usual, or turn south toward the spot where the path ended and he found Delia. With one last stretch, he started south. At first, he ran slowly, just a jog until he could feel the blood coursing through his entire body. Then he picked up the pace, to where he could feel his hair ruffling a bit from the speed. Often, a run helped him flee from thinking about his problems. Today it worked, and he got relief from worry about Rica, his job, and life in general.

A mile from the end of the path, he looked to the west. The clouds that brought the heavy dew, which lately had turned to frost, spread low against the horizon. They absorbed the colors of the waning sun and spilled them into the sky as splashes of wine and honey.

He watched the sunset display as he ran. Before he realized it, he had to make a choice at the end of the path: hop the two-foot high barrier and proceed in the dark to where he found Delia, or turn back the way he had come. He shook his head, not ready to face that yet, and turned back to the north.

Chapter 61

Charlotte put down her pencil when she heard the tone of a new email delivered. Life had settled into an uneasy routine of smiling her way through designing the ad campaigns at work, dodging customers at the Dragon, and tiptoeing her way around Devlyn's wrath at home. After so many years of practice, functioning as if nothing troubled her was an act she could pull off with little effort.

She glanced at her computer. The email was a birthday reminder.

"Charlotte?" Her supervisor popped into Charlotte's office.

Charlotte turned to face her. "Almost got the preliminary sketch done, Erin." She held up the pad for Erin to see.

"That looks great, honey." Erin picked up the pad and turned it so the light from the window illuminated it. "I like the art-deco feel of it. Will be super in full-color." She set down the pad. "Is something wrong, honey?"

Charlotte brushed away the tear that had crept down her cheek. "No, but today would have been my mother's sixty-fifth birthday."

Erin came around the desk to hug her. "Oh, sweetie, I'm so sorry."

Charlotte leaned into Erin's comforting shoulder,

glad of the warmth but wary of the desire to let down her defenses and bask in it. "It's okay, Erin. She's been gone five years, but sometimes…"

Erin leaned back, her hand still on Charlotte's arm. "I know, sweetie, you wish you could still call them."

Charlotte nodded. "For so many years, it was just Mom and me." She dabbed at her eyes and nose with a tissue. "But her last months were so difficult, with the chemo and radiation and all. Then finally, they said there was no need to do anything more. She just wasted away."

"Take the day off, if you want, honey." Erin stepped back to the other side of the desk. "I can show the client the concept with what you have here."

Charlotte shook her head. "If I go home, I'll just think too much." She ran her hand over the drawing. "This campaign is intriguing me, helps take my mind off it."

Erin turned to leave. "Okay, sweetie, but if you change your mind, just give me a jingle."

"I will." Charlotte looked down at the drawing and picked up her pencil again, only to put it down as Erin's heels clicked down the hallway. Her mother's last months had been agony for the both of them. Mom had feared how Charlotte would navigate without her there as a beacon, while Charlotte had just wanted to ease her suffering in any way she could. And yet, even in death, her mother had cared for her. Charlotte hadn't known how large an insurance policy that her mother had maintained payments on throughout her last days. In death, Mom gave her the gift of transformation.

Chapter 62

Eight o-clock Friday morning found Scott in the waiting room of the psychologist, nursing the coffee he had made at home. For once, instead of running out of time to make it in the morning, he had set it up to brew the night before. Dr. Warren appeared in the open door of her office, leaning against the door frame.

"Well, Scott, what's new?"

He looked up. "Not much, doc."

She studied him for a few seconds. "Ready for your appointment?"

He stood. "Ready as I'll ever be." He followed her into the room, as she moved behind her desk and he took a chair facing her.

She consulted the file on her desk. "How was the past week for you?"

"Better, I think." He shrugged. "Kind of in limbo."

"How so?"

"Waiting on more paperwork from Rica about the divorce."

"How long has it been since she told you she wanted a divorce?"

"Five weeks ago today." He knew how many hours less it was, but didn't want to share that information.

"Anything else happen?"

"We helped SO work a farmhouse burglary."

Her body appeared relaxed, but Scott noticed that

the focus in the doctor's eyes appeared to sharpen. "Was this different than the usual procedure?"

Now cautious, he leaned back in the chair. "Well, they called us in because the MO was similar to the ones we'd worked in town—isolated house, no one living in the home at the moment. Plus there was a lot of evidence to document." He smiled. "Truthfully, it was better than searching Twitter for clues."

"You like to be moving about, don't you, Scott?"

"I guess. My dad always said idle hands were the devil's playground."

"You looked up to your dad?"

Scott hesitated. "Yeah, I guess every kid does. When I was little, I thought my dad was the biggest guy in the world, and he could fix anything."

"And when you were not so little?" she asked softly.

"Well, my dad died when I was fifteen." In truth, how he had let down his dad by losing his marriage was never far from his mind.

"That must have been hard." She let the silence lie there for a moment. "Was it sudden?"

Scott nodded. "I found him. In the field, on his tractor."

The day his childhood ended, he had come home from school and noticed his dad's tractor nudged up against the trees at the end of the soybean field. He ran into the house. "Mom, how long has Dad been in the soybean field?"

Her hands in dishwater, she looked toward the field through the window. She couldn't see the field because of the row of trees between the house and the field. "I don't know, two or three hours, I guess."

"I'll go give him a hand to finish." Once he was out of sight of his mother behind the trees that separated the house from the field, he had run for all he was worth toward the tractor a half-mile away. As he got closer, he could see that it was idling. Though he yelled for his dad, he got no response, and when he climbed up to the cab, he found his dad resting on the steering wheel, his left arm dangling almost to the floor of the tractor cab. Scott had shaken his shoulder, calling for him, and then checked the cold wrist for the pulse he knew wasn't there. Mindful from birth not to be wasteful, Scott turned off the tractor. Then he sat on the floor of the cab next to his father and wept.

"They said it was a heart attack." He had dried his eyes on his shirt and run back to the house to break the news to his mother and call for an ambulance to make it official.

"And you had to tell your mother?"

He nodded. "And call the ambulance and my brothers." He drove his mother to the hospital behind the ambulance. By the time they made it back to the house after the paperwork was done, friends and neighbors had arrived to help. Scott slipped out of the house, jogged back to the tractor, and finished planting the field by the tractor headlights. He knew there wouldn't be time to finish it tomorrow, and it needed to be done for the beans to come up in good time.

It was just the first of many farm management decisions he made alone for the next three years, until he began applying to colleges, and his brothers convinced his mother to lease out the fields to another farmer. Then he went to college and took the job at the city, and his mother grew frailer without him noticing.

"How often do you see your mother, Scott?"

He looked at the doctor and then at the floor. "Not often enough." When the silence grew, he went on. "She moved in with my brother Dennis in Ohio after she broke a hip a couple years ago." He looked down at his hands. "Haven't seen her in nearly a year."

"Does she know that Rica has left?"

Still staring at his hands, he shook his head. "It's something I wanted to tell her in person, that I let her, let the family, down. Divorce is not something we do." He looked up. "I'm planning to go up around Thanksgiving."

"Do that, Scott." The look Dr. Warren gave him reminded him somehow of his mother. "I'll bet your family is more supportive than you expect."

He sat silent, watching her, his mind far away. He had imagined telling his family of his impending divorce now for weeks. He could hear his brother's tone, as he affirmed he had always expected it. He could see Alicia's sympathetic gaze, see Vanessa storm from the room, watch his mother's lips quiver in disappointment. "I don't know why they would be. I've let them down."

"Scott." Dr. Warren stopped and then started again. "Even if a family sides with an in-law in the beginning, 99% of the time, blood turns out to be thicker than water. They almost always come around to agree with their relative."

Scott stared. "I hope so."

"Give them a chance, Scott." She glanced at her watch. "Next Friday, same time?"

He stood. "Works for me." Relieved, he walked from her office, only to be hit in the face with a blast of cold air and a handful of sleet pellets. The cool front he remembered hearing about on the weather last night had evidently moved in. He shivered, having only tossed on a light jacket. He supposed winter would come early this year. He remembered a Halloween with a foot of snow. And another one when the high was nearly ninety. He hurried to his truck, turned on the heater and defroster, and headed for the station. He paused long enough at the McDonald's halfway there to pick up two cups of coffee.

He set one cup on Bates' desk as soon as he made it through the door to their office. Bates looked up. "Thanks, rookie."

"Don't mention it." Scott dropped into his chair and sat holding the cup to warm up his hands before he turned on his computer. "I just get tired of those faces you make when you drink the coffee you brew."

"Hey, I just don't like it cold."

"Two words." Scott hit the power button on his computer. "Insulated cup."

"Rookie," Bates muttered. "How are things going with the shrink?"

"I continue to see her, and she continues to see me." He punched in his password. "At least by now, I guess we've ruled out being figments of each other's imaginations."

"We got some hits on Craigslist on items taken from the last farmhouse burglary."

"That's good. I just *love* shopping on Craigslist. Can we get warrants to pick anyone up?"

"Nope. But we could get to go undercover to go buy stuff. Though all that's turned up so far is dishes, so they were going to send Marlene."

"Dang." He popped into Facebook, clicked on Rica's page. "Couldn't we pose as guys trying to collect dishes to make our wives happy?"

Bates snapped his fingers. "I never thought of that." He reached for the phone to make his pitch to the chief.

While Bates was busy, Scott scanned Rica's posts. Good day in surgery. She was happy. Evening at the dinner theatre. Trip to Wichita to the symphony. Stuff he had tried to take her to because he knew she would like it, but she turned him down so they could save money for a house. No mention of with whom she had attended these festivities. He heard Bates hang up the phone. He clicked back to the Facebook page of the girlfriend of the first suspect in custody for the Quick Shop murders.

It appeared the girl was engaged in a running feud with another woman, complete with name calling. Suddenly it jumped out at him. She mentioned having a winning lottery ticket, and plans for how to spend the money (hair extensions, new tattoos), but they had to wait for things to "chill" before they could turn it in. "Hey, Del."

"No, we don't get to go buy dishes. At least not this time."

"Forget that." He motioned Bates to his screen. "Take a look at this."

Bates slipped on the trifocals he used for computer work and leaned over Scott's shoulder. "Well, I'll be damned. Looks like our girl has a winning ticket." He dropped the glasses into his pocket. "Let's go have a chat with her."

Chapter 63

"Man, I told you I ain't got no winnin' lottery ticket!" Felipa White twisted the ring made from a spoon that encircled her thumb. Each finger wore a ring of some sort. "And if I did have one, you cops'd pro'lly steal it anyhow."

Bates leaned back in his chair. "Then why were you bragging about it to Tina?"

"Oh, that." She played with an earring. "I just get tired of her braggin' all the time about the stuff her man gets her. Wanted to let her know my guy gets me stuff, too."

"Like he brings you a whole roll of lottery scratch-off tickets?"

Her eyelids flickered. "Naw, he just brings me a few when he gets a little cash." She took a deep breath. "We can't afford to go to them fancy new casinos, but for five bucks we can pretend we gonna win for a little while." She paused to study a chip in her acrylic nails. "And this one time, one time we got a $100 ticket." She closed her eyes and savored the memory. "We lived it up on that one." She opened her eyes and faced them again. "Never have won that big again."

"Oh, but it's worth trying, isn't it?" Scott drummed his fingers on the table. "Just think about the odds. The more tickets you have, the more chances one of them would be a winner." He looked at Bates. "What would you say the odds would be, Del, if you had a hundred tickets at the same time, that one of them would be a big one?"

Bates shrugged. "I'll bet it would be at least twenty to one. Maybe better odds. Or maybe you'd get ten twenty-dollar winners. Or twenty ten-dollar ones. It would sure boost the odds."

Scott could see the woman working numbers in her head. Even if they couldn't get a search warrant for the woman's apartment on evidence as flimsy as her Facebook post, maybe greed would drive her to risk redeeming one. "You been to visit Tommie lately?"

She looked at Scott, then down at her hands. "Well, ya know, he ain't bringin' in no rent money settin' in jail."

Scott nodded. "So you've been working extra shifts to cover your bills?"

She rolled her eyes until she noticed him watching. "Somethin' like that."

Bates raised his eyebrows. "Got a new sugar daddy?" He shook his head. "Tommie's not gonna like that."

"Hey, girl's gotta do what a girl's gotta do, ya know?"

"Oh, we understand, we do." Scott shook his head. "But we're not the ones who would be pissed off and looking to get even if we got out. It's Tommie." He leaned across the table and lowered his voice to barely more than a whisper. "And if he did what we charged him with, well, I'd say he has one nasty temper."

Felipa's eyes widened.

Bates nodded. "And if we can't find more evidence soon, he'll be out sooner or later." He doodled in his notebook. "He doesn't seem like the forgiving type to me."

Scott spoke louder. "But now if someone were to give us some evidence that could convict him of the shootings, he'd never see the light of day again and couldn't hurt you."

Scott noticed that her hands trembled a bit as she continued to play with her rings. "What kinda evidence would it take?"

Scott shrugged. "Breaking his alibi that he was with his friends. Knowing where some of the things missing from the Quick Shop are."

"What kinda things?"

"Lottery tickets." He watched as her face changed expression as she mulled possibilities in her mind. "But now, if someone were to cash in one of those lottery tickets, that would make that person an accessory to murder. That person could get the death penalty same as the trigger man. On the other hand, I think there's a reward out for information, isn't there, Del?"

"Yeah, I think Quick Shop put it up. Ten grand for information leading to conviction." He paused. "That's sure a lot more than a scratch off ticket could get you."

"And the person that turned in the information wouldn't go to jail?" Her hands trembled openly now.

"No guarantees, but the DA wants to make this case airtight, so I suspect there would be no jail time." Bates sat back in silence, and Scott did the same.

Perspiration beaded Felipa's forehead, and she licked her lips and twirled her rings. "Aw'ight, it's like this, ya see." She leaned forward. "Tommie didn't say how he got 'em, but he told me that he got a bunch of lottery tickets, but we couldn't scratch 'em or turn 'em in just yet." She looked down at her hands. "I didn't know he had anything to do with the murders."

"Did he tell you where they are?" Scott glanced at Bates.

"Him and a buddy share a locker sometimes at the gym. Said he put 'em in the bag with his boxin' gloves."

"Which gym?" Scott heard excitement in the higher pitch of Bates' voice.

"Gold Ring. Caters to boxers and fighters."

"Buddy have a name?"

"All's I know is 'fonse."

Bates stood up. "Thank you, Felipa, you've been most helpful."

She focused on him. "What about my reward?"

"We'll see about that when we find those tickets." Scott stood up. "You wait here till we get back."

Chapter 64

In the two hours it took to get the warrant and head for the gym, the sleet had piled up into drifts. They drove south from the LEC into a manufacturing district that had thrived during the years after World War II. Sometime between Korea and Iraq, manufacturing began the migration overseas. The Crown Vic bumped over several tracks of railroad sidings that once brought raw materials in and manufactured goods out of the buildings that dominated the area.

"Inspiring place," Bates remarked as he parked close to the door of a former machine shop. A vinyl banner, with a graphic of an ornate championship-style ring in bright yellow, laced tight above the battered entry door, proclaimed the place to be the "Gold Ring." High in the walls of the building, multi-paned windows allowed natural sunlight into the building. Two overhead doors tall enough to accommodate semi-trucks flanked the entryway. Stained cardboard substituted for several missing windowpanes.

"I dunno." Scott scanned the half-dozen cars parked close to the building. Two fancy, low-rider pickups, a sports car, a minivan, and a couple of beaters. "Kinda makes me feel like beating on someone."

Shaking his head, Bates opened the door, looking relaxed, but in reality as on edge as Scott. "PD," he announced. "Who's in charge here?"

"That would be me." A muscular Hispanic man, maybe in his twenties, with long black hair tied back in a ponytail, stepped away from the punching bag he was bracing for a fighter. The two men sparring in the ring dropped their hands and turned to face them, and their trainers stepped out from behind the ring. The young woman working on a speed bag stopped her workout. "What can I do for you fine officers today?" He walked toward them without swagger, but with confidence in the walk.

"We have a warrant to search the gym locker of Tommie James and Alfonse Ribiero."

With an appraising glance at Scott, the young man stopped in front of Bates. "Can I see the warrant, please?"

Bates handed it over. Scott noted that the others in the gym remained silently watchful, bordering on hostile.

The young man handed the warrant back to Bates. "I can show you which locker is the one they use, but I don't have a key to their lock."

Scott spun for the door. "I'll go get the bolt-cutters out of the car." He hustled to get the tool from the trunk of the Vic, concerned about leaving Bates alone in the building with a half-dozen toughs. Even the girl looked like she could take either him or Bates down without trouble. In a minute, he returned.

The trainers had begun rubbing the shoulders of their fighters, but all kept a close eye on him and Bates. Scott suspected that only the influence of the manager kept them from turning antagonistic.

The manager turned and led the way to a row of

ancient Army surplus lockers against the wall of what was probably once the plant offices. He walked about a third of the way down the row and stopped. "This one is theirs, number 33." A bicycle padlock secured the latch. Only three other lockers sported locks. "Most folks don't leave their stuff here," the manager explained. "Rough part of town."

Scott handed the cutters to Bates. It took a couple of tries, but finally the cutters severed the lock. When the door opened, they waited a minute for the smell of stale sweat to vacate the locker. Evidently, Alfonse had not opened the locker since Tommie had been in custody. Slipping on a pair of rubber gloves, the kind that were supposed to protect against needle pricks, Bates reached in and pulled out a faded red Nike duffel bag. He used his pen to move items around inside the duffel. Scott glimpsed athletic tape, sweatbands, and what looked like tank tops before Bates pulled out a scuffed pair of boxing gloves. One hung limp, as if it had fought its last fight, but the other stretched out like the fingers inside wore splints. The glint in Bates's eye as he glanced at Scott said, "Aha!"

Bates turned the cuff of the stiff glove toward him. "Well, well, what have we here?" Scott could see a huge stack of lottery scratch-off tickets stuffed into the glove until it would hold no more. Bates removed the stack of tickets. Scott unfolded the list that contained the bar code numbers of the stolen tickets.

"Read me the first number," he said.

Bates had to turn the tickets toward a window and squint to see the numbers. "Four five seven three three seven six eight."

"Bingo!" Scott felt the excitement rise. "That

number is on the list."

"We got him." Bates placed the glove back in the Nike bag. "Thank you very much, Mr.—"

"Rodriguez," the gym manager supplied. "I always want to cooperate with the police, officer." He glanced at Scott. "You wanna work out sometime, you come on down. We give discounts for city employees."

"Thanks," Scott mumbled. For now, all he could think of was verifying the rest of the numbers on those tickets. Circumstantial evidence, yes, but it was one more in a growing list of evidence.

****

Tommie James sat quietly in the interrogation room, facing Bates, who, wearing rubber gloves, looked through the stack of tickets. In the darkened hallway beside the interrogation room, Scott watched through the small window. Bates paused to look at a ticket. "Oh, look here, Tommie, this one's worth a hundred dollars." Bates laid the ticket down and faced James. "I'll bet it was tough to let that one sit."

"How would I know?" James shrugged. "Them ain't my tickets." He looked at the stack, and his right index finger twitched ever so slightly. "I never seen 'em before."

"Right, someone else put your fingerprints on them."

"Must've." A sheen of sweat appeared on James' forehead.

"Or just maybe, after you killed Amy Erikson and Helen Nice, you helped yourself to most of the scratch-off tickets at the store."

"I never killed nobody."

"But you did steal the tickets."

"I never said that."

Bates leaned toward James, his voice kind. "Look, Tommie. If you don't finger your accomplice, you'll be the one that will go down for both murders and the burglary." Bates sat back in his chair. "But if you let us know who else was with you in this, it would go a lot easier for you."

"And if I don't say nothin', you gotta let me go."

"No, Tommie, we don't. With these tickets, we have enough to hold and charge you with the murders and burglary." Bates slid back the chair. "Why don't you sit there and think about it a while." Bates walked out of the room.

"You think he'll roll?" Scott continued to watch James, who now sat with his hand over his mouth as if deep in thought.

Bates sighed. "I would if it was me. I'd blame the other guy as the trigger man, cut every deal I could." He glanced back through the window. "But this is a cool one. And unless one of them blames the other one for the murders, the case is kinda flimsy." He headed for the hallway. "Keep an eye on him, rookie, while I go get some coffee. We'll let him cool his heels for thirty minutes or so and then try again." He turned at the doorway. "Did you know that there were about twenty scratch off tickets in that stack that were winners? Worth about a grand, total."

Scott shrugged. "Who says crime doesn't pay?"

Chapter 65

They let James think for nearly an hour, but he still maintained his innocence, and they finally returned him to his cell. By the time Scott bounced through the front door of his apartment, the wind was blowing a gale and going for a run was out of the question. He foraged through the nearly bare cupboards and finally turned up a can of chili he had purchased since Rica left. She almost always cooked from scratch, and would have been horrified at his choice of dinner. But Rica wasn't there, so he could eat what he chose. No matter how horrible it might be.

His phone rang. He glanced at the ID before answering. "Hey, Al, what's up?"

"Nothing much." Scott pulled the bowl of chili from the microwave and tossed in a handful of grated cheese as Al went on. "I just have to come to the city tomorrow on some business and wondered if you'd like to do dinner somewhere that is not Debbie's Diner."

"Sure." Scott stirred the chili; he'd almost burned it. Leave it to him to fuck up a microwave dinner. "Not eating my own cooking improves my chances of survival."

"I hear ya there, Scott. I hadn't cooked much in thirty years until Sarah got sick. After she died, I didn't care if I ate or not. But now I can follow the instructions on a box as well as any college student."

"How about Enrique's?"

"Always a good choice. Six-thirty?"

"Sure, I should be off work by then."

They hung up and Scott turned his attention to dinner. Though it tasted like chunks of cardboard, it was warm, and he ate enough to chase away the chill of the wind that still howled outside. It would probably warm up to the fifties or sixties tomorrow—he could watch the weather or be surprised—but for now, Mother Nature gave warning of how brutal Kansas winters could be, at least for a few days at a time.

Finally, with the chili sitting like a smoldering ember in his stomach, Scott pulled his laptop toward him. While Rica still lived here, he kept the computer on the desk set up in the second bedroom. With her gone, though, he had fallen to leaving it on the kitchen table or beside his chair. He spent some time each evening reading her Facebook page, but so far she had not changed her status from married nor mentioned him in her posts. All she posted were notes about the weather and her outings. And notes praising Dr. Ambrose for brilliant surgery. He opened a search window, but then he wasn't sure what to search for. He had found everyone but Kyle Dane, and had hit a dead end in that search.

But Kyle had a mother. He looked at his notes again and typed in "Irene Dane." In an effort to narrow the search, he typed a comma, and added "Nevada." Surprisingly, several references popped up. The first was an obituary:

"Irene Karina Dane, 60, of Reno, Nevada, passed away after a long illness in Trinidad, Colorado, on January 13, 2008. She is survived by one daughter,

Charlotte, of Trinidad and a sister, Lucinda Hayes, of Greenville, South Carolina." The obit went on to list Dane's birthplace as somewhere in Tennessee, with a marriage to a Ken Dane, from whom she was divorced after only five years of marriage. He went on to read the rest of the entries. None of them proved fruitful or appeared to have any connection to the woman who had borne the boy he remembered.

He played a few games of solitaire on the computer, trying to calm his mind. He knew he should put on a batch of laundry or load the dishwasher, but he could always do that later. Right now, he focused on trying to get his percentage won back up to 48%. Maybe solitaire proved the anti-gambler's theory that the house always wins in the long run. At long last, he gave up the game, checked the weather (yup, 60's tomorrow, but a freeze over the weekend) and headed for bed.

The next day crawled by, spent in checking Craigslist, Facebook, E-Bay, and other public sites for stolen items offered for sale. They wasted one of the last nice days of fall indoors, instead of finding some excuse to be outdoors. Finally, at five, he hurried home to change for a short run, before showering to meet Al. He went north, away from the spot where he found Delia, and tried to keep his mind calm.

But when he faced Al over a steaming plate of Burritos Monterey, Al's conversation brought him back into the search. "Status on the hometown case?"

He shook his head. "Officially, it's been moved to cold-case, no active investigation status, but we never close a case. Some theorize that she's a victim of the serial killer that committed suicide by cop in Florida last month."

"But you're still working on it on your own, right?"

Scott nodded, mouth too full to respond.

"It bugs you, doesn't it?"

He nodded. "I guess I feel like I owe Delia more, since I knew her."

"A lot of debts to people have to be paid forward, because we can't repay them to the ones we owe." Al busied himself with Enchiladas Rancheros. "I heard you got more evidence in the Quick Shop case."

Scott shrugged. "Conviction might be iffy, though."

"That's too bad." Al paused to watch the diners around them.

"You miss reporting the news that bad?"

Al grinned. "Am I that transparent?"

Scott laughed. "Only to a highly-skilled detective."

"So what have you found on the Enfield homicide? Unofficially."

"Nothing, really." He gulped his iced tea to put out a jalapeño fire. "I've found everyone connected with Delia except the boy she befriended, Kyle Dane. So I started looking for his mother. Found nothing except for an obituary that doesn't even appear to be hers, except that it lists her residence as Reno, Nevada. That's the school that requested his high school transcript. And she didn't even die there."

Al focused. "Where did she die?"

"Trinidad, Colorado. Said after a long illness. But it only listed a daughter, no son. Usually if they have kids that died, they say 'preceded in death by.' It's like Kyle Dane dropped off the face of the earth."

Al picked up his coffee cup, sipping, his elbows propped on the table. "Maybe Kyle Dane did drop off the face of the earth."

"Where else is there to go?" Scott guzzled another half glass of tea. "We haven't begun colonizing the moon yet."

"No, but—" Al set down his cup. "Did you know that Trinidad is, or at least was a few years ago, the 'Sex Change Capital of the US?'"

"What?" Scott dropped his fork.

"Hear me out, I'm just speculating here." Al paused to sip more coffee. "If Kyle's mother moved him near Vegas to find a place that would be more accepting of him as an effeminate or gay man, maybe Kyle had enough struggles within himself that he would have felt more comfortable as a woman."

"Do many people really do that?" Scott thought about the surgery required and shuddered.

"More than you would think." Al shivered himself. "I don't remember the numbers but our paper did a story on it about ten years ago, and it was surprisingly high." He looked around the room, as if the details of the old article could be found on the walls of the restaurant. "Some start the process, with hormone therapy and never completely transition, but still live as the opposite sex. I think the doctors require a person to live as the other sex for a year or so, maybe longer, before they will even do the surgery."

"Wow." Scott sat with his mind churning, meal forgotten. Something about what Al had said, though, made sense, especially as he reviewed what little he remembered about Kyle. The boy was small and delicate, with those unusual pale hazel eyes. He would have made a very pretty girl. "That has certainly given me food for thought." He scooped up rice and beans with a chip and chewed slowly. "Maybe I'll do a search for Charlotte Dane."

"I could be all wrong, of course, but there are enough coincidences to make it worthwhile to consider." Al picked up the dessert menu. "Flan?"

"What?" Scott was still considering how a man could want to make the sacrifices necessary to give up manhood to become a woman. Much as Scott loved women, he would never want to be one. He enjoyed being a man and all that went with it: doing the heavy lifting, getting the car in the rain while a woman waited indoors, not worrying about his wardrobe, killing bugs, shaving only his face, being the protector. Yet he hadn't done a good enough job of protecting Rica to make her want to stay with him.

"Dessert, would you like dessert?"

"Oh, sure. I never turn down dessert." The conversation steered him into another memory. "I sure do miss Rica's *dulce de leche* bars. Though she wouldn't make them very often, said they were too many calories for us." He broke a chip in half, then the piece in half again. "And the desserts her mother made." He swirled the chips into his beans. "I wonder what Mama Hernandez-Duncan thinks of her *guero* son-in-law now." He broke another chip. "She never was too keen on me, but she kinda warmed up after I painted her house and roofed the porch."

"You need flan." Al signaled the server and ordered two. "How is the counseling going?"

Scott shrugged. "Going. I don't think we are getting anywhere, but I guess she'll keep me coming until the number of visits the city will pay for runs out."

"My, aren't we cynical today."

"Well, it's against 'the code.'" Scott toyed with his napkin, now that the waitress had taken his plate. "I'm gonna go see my mom after Thanksgiving." Until he said it, more to himself than to Al, he hadn't really made up his mind.

Al studied him for a long few seconds. "I think that is an excellent idea, Scott." He looked up as their dessert approached. "Almost as good an idea as flan."

Chapter 66

Scott sat with his cell phone in his hand for ten minutes, watching commercials and a sitcom he didn't even like, before he finally hit the speed dial for his brother's house. His niece answered on the second ring. "Hey, Uncle Scott," she chirped. "Z'up?"

"Not much, Vanessa. Z'up with you?"

"Made the cheerleading squad for next semester. And may be going to state in debate."

"That's great, sweetheart. You always did like to argue."

"Not fair, Uncle Scott. You want to talk to Grandma?"

"Well, it's always a trip talking to you, Nessa, but moms like to think they are the reason their kids call."

"I totally get that." He could hear her moving around. "Here, Grandma. It's Uncle Scott."

"Son, how are you?" Somehow, his mother sounded even smaller than the last time he talked to her.

"I'm okay, Mom." Fine sure didn't seem like an honest answer. His life was in shambles; okay was the best he could do. "Would you guys like company for the weekend after Thanksgiving?"

"Sure!" New life came into her voice. "Alicia, Scott and Rica are coming up for Thanksgiving. Well, I mean the week after, but still—they're coming!" He heard Alicia say something, but she must have been in the kitchen. He could also hear the TV in the background. He didn't hear his brother's voice; probably still at work.

"Let me know what you need me to bring, Mom."

"Oh, honey, just yourselves is all we want to see."

"Okay, Mom. I haven't officially put in for the time off, wanted to clear it with you guys, but I'm sure it'll be approved."

"Oh, son, I can hardly wait to get my arms around you."

"And I can hardly wait to get there." *And let you know what a total failure your baby is.* "I'm gonna go right now and send an email to the chief putting in for the leave time."

"Okay, son. Call again before you start this way."

"I will, Mom. Love you. Bye."

****

"Of course, you can have the time off, Aylward. You are covering Thanksgiving, and you gave up sixteen hours of vacation last year that you didn't use." The chief hesitated, then went on, in a softer tone. "You know, Scott, maybe—" He stopped, then plowed ahead. "Maybe it would have been better for your marriage if you had taken more time off."

Scott stared at the gruff old man, not sure whether to be hurt or touched by the comment. "Thanks for the advice, Chief." He stood up to leave the office. "And thanks for the time off."

"I didn't say it to be mean, boy." The chief leaned back in the old leather chair, and stared at the line of photos on his wall, officers from the Department's past. "Just makin' an observation from seein' too much around here."

318

Scott looked down at the floor. "Well, thanks, Chief."

"Quit goofing off and get back to work, Aylward, before I change my mind."

"Yes, sir." Scott spun and left the room, more comfortable with the whispering dragon chief than the gentle one. He knew Chief had his back, but he really didn't want to feel like a son to him. He had had a wonderful dad, and now he had none.

Bates looked up as Scott came into their office. "So, you goin' to see your momma for Thanksgiving?"

"Not till the week after." He settled in front of his computer again.

"Yeah, that's what I meant." Bates rolled his chair closer to Scott. "So that means you are coming to our house for Thanksgiving dinner?"

"I'm working a street shift seven to three."

"Trust me, we'll either still be eating or will be eating again."

Scott logged in to Facebook. The last thing he wanted was to be trapped in the circus that was the Bates family home on a holiday. Kids and in-laws and cousins and neighbors—it was raucous and far too happy to suit Scott this year. Sadly, he reflected, had he just found Rica sooner, convinced her to have children earlier, that circus could have been his house. "I'll see. Depends on if I get off in time."

"We'll have food for at least a week, rookie." Bates rolled back to his desk. "If you don't come by the house, I'll be forced to bring the food to you." He picked up his coffee cup, sipped, and poured it on the plant. "No partner of mine is going to make me eat pumpkin pie and stuffing and candied yams without sharing in the pain."

****

Scott solved the dinner dilemma by stopping by for a few minutes at two while he was on patrol. He only had thirty minutes for lunch, then protested that he had to get to the station to file reports for the next shift. That allowed him just enough time to accept a small plate of leftovers and a huge piece of pie. He insisted the kids had grown a foot each, and that Bates's wife was the second best cook in the world (the first being his mother) before escaping into the quiet of the patrol car. Except for a minor bumper scrape where someone misjudged distance in backing out of a driveway full of dinner guests, the day was quiet and peaceful.

As he drove home end of shift, he thought about calling Al to see if he wanted to do dinner, but then remembered he had flown back to New York to be with his sons. On impulse, he pulled into a convenience store and picked up an overdone burrito and a salad. He settled into his recliner with his sad dinner and clicked on the TV, then glanced at the laptop on the end table beside him. Kyle had been a lonely boy with no one to turn to for companionship except Delia. Not so very different than Scott at this moment. Maybe he and Kyle were more alike than he wanted to think. He bit into his burrito and decided the salad was the better choice.

Chapter 67

Charlotte checked the oven one more time. The turkey breast was still the pasty beige that said it wasn't done, instead of the crisp golden brown that Devlyn liked. The yams and mashed potatoes were done, but would have to be heated in the microwave without Devlyn finding out. The green bean casserole would be overdone by the time the turkey browned, and she couldn't start the crescent rolls until the turkey came out of the oven. Devlyn's mother must have been one hell of a cook, Charlotte reflected, to make Devlyn such a stickler for perfection on those special meals.

And yet, such a procrastinator on her own projects. As Charlotte studied the old window that looked out on the tired back yard, she remembered the first time Devlyn had brought her to the house on the river, just a scramble over the dike to the meandering waterway. The house set on a dead end road south of the city in a forgotten part of the county. No Jehovah's Witnesses called here, no traveling salesmen stuck flyers in the door. The mail carrier didn't even deliver; Devlyn had a post office box in town.

"And I wanna put French doors here, and build a deck to a flagstone patio," Devlyn had said, waving an arm grandly around the room before dropping it comfortably around Charlotte's shoulder. "My momma left me this house."

Charlotte took in the faded sixties wallpaper, the sun-bleached gold satin drapes that covered the tall windows. "It has a lot of potential." Gutting it, and ripping out everything that represented a memory to Devlyn, was all it would take, and that, Charlotte later learned, would never happen.

"Momma never changed a thing in the house after daddy died." The arm snuggled Charlotte closer. "Daddy came from Louisiana bayou country, never liked living far from a river, but the oil job was here. They got this place when I was just little, ten or twelve or so." The arm relaxed. "Daddy and I went fishin' every night we could, kept a trotline out most nights. He had some friends that let us hunt on their land along the river, so we had deer and turkey, pheasant and quail and rabbit a lot."

"Sounds like a Waltons kind of existence."

"Not always." The arm tightened. "Daddy could be…harsh when he'd been drinkin' and things didn't go his way." A heavy sigh shuddered through Devlyn. "Momma never wanted a man around after Daddy. Said they was good to have and good to be rid of." They paused before a china hutch full of carnival glass reproductions from a seventies fad. "She got her a job at a restaurant, cookin', and worked there till life and the cigarettes wore her down."

Charlotte felt something, premonition perhaps, shiver down her spine. For a moment, she had the urge to fake a stomach upset and ask Devlyn to take her home. In retrospect, that would have been best. Instead, desperate to feel protected, she had ignored the whispers in the back of her mind and become entangled deeper and deeper into Devlyn's world.

"And then I quit school and got the job at the airplane factory in Wichita. Made as good a money as my daddy did, kept momma and me right comfortable." Devlyn's face scrunched up in what Charlotte learned to recognize as deep thought. "But it don't seem to go as far anymore, so I haven't been able to make my improvements." Improvements, Charlotte also learned, was Devlyn-code for dreams that would never come true, in fact never even be attempted.

Charlotte wondered once again why she had ever been attracted to rough, uneducated Devlyn with whom she had so little in common. Maybe it was because Devlyn made her feel like the adored little woman, more woman than she had ever felt. But even before Mags re-entered her life, she had begun to tire of the play she was acting, and probably would have already left by then had she not given up her apartment so they could save money for the "improvements." She dropped into one of the old chrome kitchen chairs and went back, for the hundredth, or maybe thousandth, time over the "if-onlys" that might have kept Mags alive.

One more time, she looked through the oven door instead of opening it and making the cooking take longer. For two cents, or maybe even less, she would pack her things and be gone before Devlyn came home from work. Pack her bags and leave, run to another town and start over once again. Except that she had nowhere to go, no one to turn to, no refuge where Devlyn could not find her. And because of what she knew, Devlyn *would* find her.

Chapter 68

"Hey, bro." Scott's brother greeted him at airport baggage claim with a quick bear hug. Then he let Scott loose and looked around. "You leaving Rica to pick up the bags?"

Scott cleared his throat. "She didn't come."

When his brother looked at him sharply, he went on. "She asked for a divorce, Denny." He looked down at the single carry-on that was all the luggage he had brought. "We go to court second week in December."

Dennis put a hand on his shoulder. "Damn, Scott, I'm sorry."

Scott took a deep breath. "That's why I asked you to pick me up by yourself."

"I understand."

"I couldn't tell Mom over the phone." They started walking to the parking lot. "How do you think she'll take it that I'm a failure at marriage?"

Dennis stopped abruptly. "It takes two people to make a marriage, and it takes two people to break one, Scott." He started walking again. "She might not take it as hard as you think."

Scott scurried to catch up. "What do you mean?"

Dennis stopped again. "It's just that we always thought Rica was a bit too, well, demanding of you." He put his hand on Scott's shoulder again. "And you tried everything to please her."

"Really?" Scott had thought the world adored Rica as he did. "You guys didn't like her?"

"I didn't say that, Scott. It's just that Alicia and I could see warning signs of potential for friction. Not to say that we expected you to split, but that we could see how there could be some strife there."

"And Mom?"

"She never said much, but we could see the worry in her face when Rica would get on you. Don't get me wrong, Mom—all of us—appreciated how much Rica went out of her way to help when Mom was in the hospital and rehab, but we were always afraid that the two of you were just too different in temperament."

"That I guess we were." With much to think about, Scott fell silent.

Dennis stopped when they reached the car. "You'll get past this, Scott."

Scott stared at his brother over the top of the Camry. "That seems to be popular opinion."

"I'm serious, Scott. It will hurt like hell, but gradually, it will hurt less and less, and then one day, you'll realize you don't hurt anymore."

"You sound like you've been through it."

Dennis shook his head. "My best friend at work did, about four years ago. He shared a lot of what he got out of counseling with me. After I picked him up at the bar a couple of times." He opened his door. "But now, Vanessa, you may have to take her for ice cream to make it up to her."

Scott tossed his bag in the back seat. "I know she idolized Rica." The guilt weighed on him again.

"Not as much as she idolizes Uncle Scott." He started the car. "And ice cream."

Chapter 69

When they pulled up in front of his brother's house, Scott sat waiting, staring at the windows that cast golden pools of light in the deepening gray outside. Dennis reached out to squeeze Scott's shoulder. "The only way past it is through it, Scott." He opened his door. "Just remember we love you here."

With a sigh from the depths of his pain, Scott unfolded from the car and followed his brother up the sidewalk, across the porch and through the door. He caught Dennis and Alicia sharing a look, and then Alicia crossed the room to wrap her arms around him. "Scotty, how good to see you."

By then his mother had reached him, slowed by the pins in her hip. She simply put her arms around him and rested her head against his chest. He held her gently, alarmed by how frail she seemed, afraid he'd break her if he hugged her as hard as he wanted to. Her hair was grayer and thinner, as was she, since he had last seen her.

Vanessa bounded into the room. "Hey, Uncle Scott." She gave him a big grin, because with his mother and her mother hanging on to him, there was no room for her. "Where's Aunt Rica?"

Both Alicia and his mother stiffened in Scott's arms, and he saw his brother shoot a look at Alicia. "Scott came alone this time, Nessa," Dennis explained.

"Why?" Only a twelve-year-old could be that direct.

Scott disentangled himself from Alicia and his mother. "Because we're getting a divorce, Nessa." He took a step toward Vanessa. "She wanted it, and I don't have much choice but to agree."

Vanessa spun and ran toward her room. He heard a door slam down the hallway and felt Alicia's hand on his shoulder. "Talk to her later, Scott, when she's had time to process." She moved toward the couch. "Talk to us now." His mother reached up to stroke his face before she allowed Alicia to help her to her chair, a recliner especially made to make it easier for her to get to her feet.

Dennis settled into his chair, and all turned expectant faces toward Scott. He paced the length of the braided rag rug to the piano bench and then turned. "We'd been having some issues for a while, and then I was late for a party her work people had, and then one thing led to another, and she went to stay with her friend Heather a couple of nights. Then—" He took a deep breath. "Then she told me she wanted a divorce."

Alicia spoke first. "Scott, if she wants out of it, there is nothing you can do."

"I know." He looked down at the piano. Nessa must be taking lessons. None of the rest of them played. "I've been in counseling."

"Good, then you know that."

Finally, his mother spoke up. "Scotty, I never said anything at the time, but when she would get upset with you about this or that, I often wanted to tell her to shut up and appreciate the good things about you." She pressed her lips together. "But she was your wife and you loved her, so I tried my best to love her, too, to see the good in her."

Scott stared at his mother, shocked at the anger in this mild-mannered woman who never said an ill word about anyone. "Wow, Mom, I never knew you felt that way."

"I was trying to be supportive of you, dear." She folded her hands in her lap. "And Rica was so sweet in so many ways, but I just felt she was too hard on my baby."

He sighed. No way around it, he would forever be his mother's baby. He might as well accept that as inevitable, just as divorce from Rica was.

"See, Scott." Dennis spoke from his chair. "I told you we'd stand by you."

Scott faced them all. "I don't know what to say." He looked down at the floor. "I've been so afraid to tell you, so ashamed."

"Scotty, there is nothing to be ashamed of." Alicia stood up and put her hand on his shoulder. "We haven't been around you a lot, but Denny and I could see you were trying hard, and we thought Rica was far too critical. If you both wanted to work on it, I'm sure you could have worked it out, but it takes two giving two hundred percent each to do that." She squeezed his arm. "One person cannot hold a marriage together alone."

"I guess you're right. The shrink and my partner, even the chief, keep telling me that."

Dennis flipped down the footrest on his chair. "It's that hard-headed Midwestern do-it-alone mentality we grew up with, Scott." He stood. "The same work ethic that kept Dad in the fields when he didn't feel good." He glanced at their mother, whose eyes had filled with tears. "Sorry, Mom, but we've talked about this before. Same thing that kept Mom trying to mow the yard after you went to college."

"I wanted to help, but I couldn't be there enough." Even now, Scott felt the guilt, torn between needing to be at college and needing to work the farm.

"I know, Scott. None of us could. That's why we convinced Mom to rent the farm out, and finally sell it." He looked back at their mother. "Sometimes you need to go it alone, push yourself, prove you can do it. But wisdom is in knowing when the smarter, more efficient, healthier thing to do is ask for help."

Scott swallowed hard, trying to take in all his brother had said in such a short speech. "How'd you get so smart when you were so dumb all those years?"

Smiling, Dennis cuffed his ear. "I could still take you down, Pee Wee."

"Right." Scott jabbed him softly in the belly. "I'm two inches taller, ten years younger, and I train in self-defense every week."

Dennis laughed. "Yeah, but I'm still the smart, good-looking one." He turned to his wife. "Alicia, is dinner ready?"

"I never saw the day you Aylward boys weren't hungry." Alicia stood. "I think we can find something in the kitchen." She nodded at Scott. "Why don't you go see if you can get Vanessa to come to the table."

"Are you sure she'll even speak to me?" Scott started down the hall.

"God is the only one who knows the mind of a teenaged girl," Dennis responded. "And I think even He throws up his hands sometimes."

"Sure, toss me to the lions." Scott rapped gently on

Vanessa's door. "Vanessa, can I come in?"

"Okay," came the muffled response.

He pushed open the door and entered the glittery, neon world of a teenaged girl. Posters of pubescent male heartthrobs with emphasis on hair circled the walls. Bottles of nail polish in as many hues as the big box of crayons littered her dresser, her desk, and her nightstand. He shook his head at the alien-ness of it all; he had only brothers, and Rica always kept her toiletries neatly put away. Vanessa lay sprawled face down across her half-made bed.

"Hey, Nessa." When she rolled sideways to face him but didn't speak, he continued. "Can we talk?"

"Yeah." She looked down at the floor and propped her chin on her fists. "About Aunt Rica?" She rolled over again. "Except I guess she won't be my Aunt Rica much longer, eh?"

Scott perched on the corner of the bed; clothing covered the desk chair and beanbag. "Not officially, but I'm sure she'd be happy to talk to you anytime. You still have her number, don't you?"

"Mom does." She met his eyes. "I called my friend Janie to talk about it, and she told me what it was like last year, before I knew her, when her parents split up. They fought a lot, and neither one was happy, and they never had time to spend with her because they were so miserable." She pushed her hair back out of her face. "She said life was a lot calmer now, even though it is more effort to see her dad. She said her mom told her that sometimes people just grow apart." Her lower lip trembled. "Is that what happened with you guys, Uncle Scott?"

He smiled and stroked her hair, remembering when

she was a tiny baby with only fuzz for hair and had hung on to his finger to walk across the room. Where had the time gone? "Kinda, Nessa. We never fought that much, but there was tension." He sighed. "Rica said it was too much work." He smoothed the corner of her bedspread. "Maybe we didn't know each other as well as we should have before we got married. Maybe we were just too different."

"I know one thing." Vanessa sat up. "It wasn't because you weren't nice to her."

"Oh, yeah?" Her comment surprised him.

"Yeah." She turned to sit beside him, her bare feet, with green painted toenails, on the floor. "When we would see you guys, you were always trying to do nice things for her and for grandma and Mom. And Dad and Uncle Ian and Aunt Marsha and Jerry and John and Jason."

He laughed. "You make me sound like Mr. Rogers."

"Well, you are, kinda." She giggled. "But Aunt Rica was always trying to get you to do this instead of that. I just thought that it was because nurses were bossy."

"She was that, wasn't she?" A month ago, he would have bridled at any criticism of Rica, but now he had begun to see her in a different way.

"A little." Vanessa threw her arms around him. "I may call her about being a nurse." She jumped up from the bed and crossed the room to an electric guitar in the corner. "But I don't think I want to be a nurse any more." She strummed a chord, sort of, that made him wince. "I think I'm going to work on writing songs and performing." She sang a short ditty about breaking up and vandalizing lockers and finding someone new. Maybe the kid had a better grasp on life than he did.

Somehow, he heard Alicia's voice over the screeching of the guitar. "Your mom's calling. Dinner's ready."

She switched off the guitar. "Okay." She linked her arm through his as they left the room. "But will you take me for ice cream after dinner?"

He pinched her nose. "That I will, sweetheart." Walking down the hall with her skipping beside him, he wondered what her career goal would be by next year. Physicist? Professional wrestler? Maybe he wasn't ready to have kids of his own yet. He sighed. Life had many surprises ahead of him.

Chapter 70

December came, and Scott could not force himself to put up a Christmas tree. Though he promised his family he would be there to share Christmas-in-January as had become their custom in the past few years, he fell just short of "bah-humbug" every time he saw Christmas lights. He scrupulously avoided every showing of "It's a Wonderful Life." Then he found himself face to face with Rica in a courtroom, listening to their past and their future dissolve through a series of questions establishing uncontested "irreconcilable differences." And then his lawyer and he, a single man instead of a married one, walked out of the courtroom.

"You know, Scott, you can't marry again for thirty days," his attorney said.

"That won't be a problem." Pausing to listen to his lawyer put him at the courtroom door as Rica came through with her attorney. She stopped, facing him, tears in her eyes.

She extended her hand to him. "I'm sorry, Scott."

Automatically he took it, surprised that the electricity that used to flow between them was gone. He could only nod, and let go of her hand. He struggled to sort out words, to make the right ones roll off his tongue. "Me, too." He blinked back his own tears. "If you ever need anything, call me."

"Ah, Scott." She put out her hand to caress his

cheek. "You are like a knight of the round table, always willing to help a damsel in distress." And then she walked down the stairs and out of his life forever.

His attorney finally cleared his throat. "I know this isn't the outcome you wanted, but when there are no kids involved and one party wants out, there isn't much the other can do."

Scott forced his gaze from the last place he had beheld Rica. "I know, Evan. Thanks for being so straight with me."

"You may not thank me when you get the bill." Evan gripped Scott's shoulder. They had crossed paths many times in Scott's line of work; he just never expected to need an attorney for anything like this.

"Then I guess I'd better get back to work to pay it off."

"Consider taking the rest of the day off, Scott. Give yourself time to process." Evan closed up his briefcase and started down the stairs. "Merry Christmas."

"Yeah."

****

"What are you doin' here?" Bates greeted him as he entered his office.

"Working off my attorney's fees."

"No way." Bates rose, tossed his coffee cup in the trash without even tasting, and crossed the room to sit on Scott's desk. "You'll be useless today—"

"Gee, thanks." Scott looked up at his partner. "Why more so today than any other day?"

"Because you have a lot to think about—"

"Yeah, paying off the damned attorney."

"I'm serious, Scott. Don't make me drag the chief down here." He put a hand on Scott's shoulder. "Go home, go for a run, call your mom, do something for yourself."

So, on one of those warm Kansas December days that make it seem impossible for Christmas to be right around the corner, Scott found himself dressed in his running clothes, barely needing the sweatshirt he had thrown over the T-shirt, and turning south along the river. To divert his mind from thinking about Rica, he turned his thoughts to Delia and her unsolved murder.

He reached the official end of the path, just on the north side of the bridge that carried Highway 50 across the Arkansas south of the city. A couple hundred yards to the south of the bridge, he had found Delia's body. He hopped the barrier and continued south along the unofficial path. Worn graffiti decorated the underside of the bridge. He walked on, scanning the east side of the dike for the old cottonwood tree that marked the spot. When he found it, he forced himself to walk on past it, another few yards south.

Officers had scoured this entire area for evidence, cutting the grass with scissors around where her body had been found, finding nothing conclusive. Several indistinct footprints, bicycle and ATV tracks, just like could be found all along the dike area. Nothing that could be tied to Delia's killer. Finally, where the river made a slight bend to the east, he stopped and lowered himself to the sand.

He sat by the river, possibly on the exact spot where she died, certainly within a hundred yards of where he had first stumbled over her body, and thought about her life, and how it was now somehow inextricably bound up with his. The breeze that ran its fingers lightly over the little bluestem around him was not cold, almost balmy, and the sunlight that beat down on him warmed him, making him drowsy. The words in the state song, "And the skies are not cloudy all day," rang true most of the time, with brassy blue skies the norm.

Perhaps it was the end of his marriage or the warmth of the sun that made him introspective. Maybe it was the whisper of the wind in the dry russet stalks of the bluestem. He raised his gaze from the buffalo grass under his crossed knees to the bare-limbed cottonwoods across the river. He missed the twinkling leaves of summer. In the fall, they turned the color of sunshine, and then scattered with the first north wind.

The river barely flowed through this area. Little more than scattered shallow pools in a wide bed of sand, connected by trickling rivulets, it was what ecologists termed a braided river, whose streambed fluctuated, running bank to bank at high water, changing its path through the cut with every flow event. A hundred miles west, he knew, it ran only under the surface of the sand.

A little further east, the river deepened into a channel that could properly be called a river. At the confluence of the Big and Little Arkansas, within the city of Wichita, stood a famous statue by Kiowa artist Blackbear Bosin, "Keeper of the Plains." Raising its hands to the sky, the statue, many believed, gave thanks for the river and the life it represented. Yet, here, for him at least, the river represented death. Delia's death. And the death of his dreams.

He pulled a few stems of the buffalo grass and let the breeze blow it from his palm. He identified with this river. Like the river, he had started his public life roaring with power and purpose, cutting a swath through school, social life, and profession much like the Arkansas cut the Royal Gorge. Later, like the river, he moderated and matured, still full of power, but more restrained, useable, like the Ark was for irrigation. And now he sat, like the river, meandering, not making noticeable progress, sometimes nearly disappearing in his lack of direction, other times creeping along. Like the river, his life contained deceptively deep, dangerous pools, and quicksand that could pull him under if he let his attention wander. Would he, like the river, regain his purpose and power? Or would he end here, like Delia?

The sun began to drop in the sky, and with it the temperature. A glance at his watch confirmed it was about four. Time to finish his run and shower. And, he decided, rather than a frozen pizza, he would treat himself to a nice dinner tonight. He had the rest of the run and shower time to pick out where.

Chapter 71

Charlotte paused to look out her west office window at the waning sun. Almost time to change for her shift at the Dragon. These past few months, she had been working nearly every shift Harvey asked for, saving her money, though she had no idea what for. Devlyn would never do the major remodel they talked about. Charlotte would never pack her bags and run. Or would she?

For the thousandth, or maybe ten thousandth time, she relived that last day with Mags. As had become their custom on Tuesdays, she had left her office at four, walking around the block to the parking lot shared by the Taco Casa and a convenience store. Mags always parked nearer the Taco Casa, where her car couldn't be seen from either store, then they walked together to either their destination (sometimes a malt shop, sometimes a nail salon) or to Charlotte's car. Then, if Devlyn was working the late shift and Mags didn't have custody of her baby this week, they would have dinner together and just enjoy making up for lost time. But this particular day, Mags jumped out of her car, leaving the door open, to meet Charlotte. She had been crying.

"Why do I do it, Ky?" Mascara softened by her tears smudged her huge eyes, making them even more vulnerable. Her hands shook.

Charlotte glanced around to check who could see

them, before she slipped her arms around her. "Do what, Mags?"

Mags shuddered with a sob. "Continue to meet up with *him*."

"Oh, *that*." Charlotte let go a dry laugh. "Oldest reason in the book, honey." She patted Mags' hair. "Sometimes you just need a man, no matter how little he cares, no matter how cheap, no matter how married, you just need to get laid to feel alive."

"Am I really that desperate?" She had taken a few steps away from the car, to the shade of an old elm. Charlotte bumped the car door with her hip to close it.

"We all are at one point or another." Desperation had driven her to Devlyn and now kept her there. But maybe… "C'mon, hon. Let's blow this Taco Casa." She put her arm over Margaret's shoulder to direct her between the stores toward the lot where Charlotte's car was parked.

Mags half giggled, half choked on Charlotte's feeble attempt at a joke. When they reached Charlotte's car, she seated Mags in the passenger seat, handing her a box of tissues she always kept under the seat. And then, because Devlyn had called about working a double shift and would not be home until the wee hours, Charlotte took Mags to what she had come to think of as her home for the time being.

"Wow, this place would be impossible to find without a map," Mags commented as they pulled up the long, cottonwood-lined driveway. Cedars guarded the yard to the north, serving as a break against the wind that sometimes whistled down from Canada in the winter with little to stop it except the stalwart trees. To the west and south, cottonwoods and elms, mixed with some historic Osage orange trees, fenced the yard. To the east lay the dike and, beyond it, the river.

"Took me weeks to learn the way." Charlotte whipped her car into the old lean-to against the even-older barn that served as the garage for her car. "I had to have Devlyn meet me and lead me out."

By the time Charlotte turned off the car, Mags was sobbing again. Charlotte stroked the shaking shoulders, trying to convey sympathy, understanding, comfort—and more. "C'mon, Mags." She gathered her purse. "I'll make you some lemon tea. Maybe with a shot of tequila in it."

Nodding, Margaret opened her door and picked her way around the rusted disc and flat-tired planter that represented the failure of Devlyn's father's attempts at farming. They entered the house through the back porch, which had once served as the washroom. An old, pink wringer washer still sat in the corner next to a water spigot.

"Wow, what an antique!" The washer took Margaret's mind off her troubles, so Charlotte let her examine it.

"I understand it was here when Devlyn's parents bought the place, and the mother kept it because she was never sure the new washer was dependable." She opened the door into the kitchen. "I'd love to restore it and use it as, well, a plant stand or something."

"How fun would that be!" Mags wandered around the kitchen and dining room, exclaiming over items that brought back memories from her grandmother's house, while Charlotte brewed some strong black oolong. She added a generous dollop of honey and a thin twist of lemon to each cup, and carried them into the dining room. She set the cups down on the old oak table covered with a hand-crocheted tablecloth made by Devlyn's grandmother.

"Here you go, Mags." Charlotte stood beside her chair. "See if this will calm your nerves." If she washed the dishes and took Margaret home in good time, Devlyn need never know that a guest had been in the house.

Margaret seated herself in the other chair. Her hands trembled as she picked up the rose-patterned china cup. "I don't know why I give in, Ky." She sipped. "I told him again it was over, but he asked me to meet him at his fishing lease, just to talk, he said." She set down the cup, running her slender fingertips around the rim. "But then he took my hand, and then he started rubbing my arm, and then my neck, and I—" She dropped her head to her hands and started sobbing again. "I just melted. Caved. I actually ached to have him make love to me right then and there." She laid her head on the table. "And when it was over, he got up, thanked me, and I felt like a two-dollar whore." She raised her head. "That's when I hurried to be able to meet you."

Charlotte felt a rush of emotion. In high school, it had been Mags who had comforted and protected her. It felt good to be the one doing the nurturing. "It's okay, Mags. As sins go, his is bigger than yours because he's married and you're not."

"And then there's that." Mags wiped her eyes with the edge of her left hand. "I wanted to be married forever, thought El was the one, never wanted my baby to grow up like I did, bouncing back and forth between mom and dad." She gulped the tea, which had

341

thankfully cooled enough it didn't burn her throat.

And such a lovely throat. Mags had been stocky in high school, but had grown taller after Charlotte moved away. Now the strain of the divorce had made her almost waiflike. Charlotte covered Margaret's hand with her own. "And that's why you were so vulnerable." When Mags looked at her, Charlotte wanted to fold her in her arms and make the world leave her alone. "And he knew it."

Margaret nodded, sipping again. "He made a hobby of preying on newly divorced women." She set down the cup. "Who worked for him."

"He should be slapped with a sexual harassment suit." Charlotte wanted to punish him, somehow, for making Margaret cry.

"He will be someday." She stroked the delicate handle of the cup. "But most women are ashamed to admit they were such easy prey, fell for his line." She met Charlotte's eyes. "I mean, we had the option to say no. I wouldn't have lost my job." She looked down again. "Or my self-esteem." She shivered. "I just feel so cheap. And dirty."

Charlotte stood. "Well, honey, we can fix that." She took Margaret's hand, gently forcing her to stand. "You just go take a nice, long, relaxing shower, and I'll whip you up a meal that no prince could afford." She hugged Margaret. "You'll be clean and rich."

Margaret hugged her back, crying afresh. "How did we ever lose each other, Ky?"

"We never will again, Mags." She stroked the silky blonde hair. "Never again."

Chapter 72

Scott ran the list of restaurants through his mind while his feet ran over the path. Italian wasn't his favorite, so that was out. He wasn't hungry enough for Chinese buffet. They had Mexican at work yesterday. Seafood sounded good, but yet, he wasn't in the mood. Last night for dinner he had had…nothing, now that he thought about it. Breakfast—and lunch—had been a single protein bar. Well, at least I don't have to worry about finding a restaurant to satisfy Rica, he thought as he jogged up the stairs. And with that, he decided on steak. There was a new steakhouse in town, pricey, but, aside from his lawyer, he had no bills. True, he only had half his savings now, but no one else would decide how to spend his money. Now that his hope of Rica changing her mind and them rebuilding their relationship had been dashed against the sharp rocks of the courts, he felt lighter. He no longer had to waste his time waiting before a door that had now been slammed in his face and locked. He could try other doors.

He hit the shower and shaved, then wandered, sans towel (oh, how Rica would have protested. "Scott," she said so many times. "How many showers have you taken in your life? Don't you always need clean clothes after? Why not take them into the bathroom with you?") into his (not their) bedroom to choose his clothing. He slipped on a pair of jeans, ironically, the ones Rica had said made his ass look good. She was probably right, he reflected, as she always had good taste in clothes. So, if he followed her choice of jeans, he might as well pair it with the shirt she said made his eyes look—what was it, more green? He thought he had nondescript gray eyes, but if she thought they were green, that was okay.

He began to hurry a bit to get ready. Acknowledging his lack of meals made him realize he was hungry. He threw on a healthy splash of cologne and his jacket and headed out the door. The sun set completely while he cleaned up, and a chill descended with the darkness. He waited a moment for his truck to warm up before starting for the new restaurant on Thirtieth Street. If the TV ads were to be believed, they served aged Angus steaks cooked over hickory or mesquite coals, baked potatoes as big as a man's hand, and bought their homemade pies from Amish bakers. His stomach started to growl, just thinking about it.

Must be good, if the parking lot was this full at six o'clock on a Thursday night. He swung into a spot near the back of the parking lot. Hopping out of the truck, he tossed his keys in the air and caught them as he walked past two rows of parked cars toward the restaurant's entrance on the west side of the building. He had expected to be down in the dumps today; he didn't really understand why he felt this relieved, but he was glad of it. As he neared the building, he saw a group exiting, laughing, and heard snippets of conversation. "Best steak in a long time." "Cooked just right." His stomach growled louder.

Suddenly his ears caught laughter from the west row of parked cars. He knew the voice, had heard it earlier today. He stopped in the shadow of a topiary tree and watched as Rica and Ambrose strolled their way toward the entrance. Ambrose said something to her in a quiet voice. She tipped her head back, and laughter bubbled from that throat he had kissed his way along so often.

Relieved to be over the ordeal of the divorce or not, he hadn't reached the point where he felt nothing upon seeing her. His heart thumped a flamenco in his chest, and he could barely draw a breath. His stomach fell silent, and his mouth went dry. Every time they had ever made love ran through his mind like a movie on eight-times fast motion. Part of him felt numb, but the other part felt like he was standing on the sidewalk bleeding from a gaping hole in his chest. He turned and walked back to his truck, knowing he needed to be anywhere except where she was.

How could she bounce back that fast? He knew, from reading her facebook page, that Ambrose now played a significant role in her life, but she had been discreet in her posts, no hint that they were dating. But a woman didn't curve toward a man like that on a first date. They looked comfortable together, like they spent a lot of time that way. His heart squeezed. If there's a breakup, and you hurt and the other doesn't, it seems like the other one never cared.

He wasn't hungry anymore, but he needed to be somewhere else, as far from this restaurant as he could get, somewhere dark, with noisy people and alcohol. He started the car and headed out of the parking lot.

Chapter 73

Charlotte applied her makeup with care tonight. Thursdays weren't the best night for tips, but with JV games going on, they weren't bad, either. Eyes still pink from the crying she had done in the shower, Charlotte elected to skip the colored contacts she wore sometimes to turn her eyes turquoise or amethyst or emerald. She would just go with her natural color tonight.

While she painted her face with the care DaVinci had stroked color on the canvas the world knew as the *Mona Lisa*, she tried hard not to continue the memories that had haunted her at work and failed.

That night, she had prepared her masterpiece—baked chicken breasts with savory rice and artichoke hearts, with a spinach and raspberry salad. She had bragged about it to Mags often, but this was her first chance to prepare it for her. By the time Devlyn got home at seven in the morning, she would have all the dishes done and a leftover breast with trimmings for Devlyn as an offering.

She had lit candles in the bathroom, laid out her softest towels and a robe, and let Mags shower until the chicken was about twenty minutes from done, then she tapped lightly on the bathroom door. She heard nothing but the shower continuing to run. Alarmed, she opened the door, afraid of what she might find. Margaret hadn't heard her come in, but stood there under the stream of water, clearly visible through the glass shower door, illuminated only by the soft lights in the shower stall, as the flickering candlelight played over her body. Charlotte stifled her gasp and listened as Margaret talked to herself.

"Damned fool, that's what you are," Mags hissed at herself. "Two-bit whore. Floozy. Slut." She rapped her knuckled fists against her wet skull.

Charlotte stepped to the shower door, opening it an inch. "Margaret Stillman, stop that." She ducked out of her apron.

Margaret looked at her, startled. "It's true, Ky." She took a ragged breath, tears mingled with the shower water. "I'm a mess."

Charlotte shrugged out of her dress and stepped into the shower with Margaret. "You are not," she said as she took Margaret's arms firmly. "You are a very good woman in a bad situation preyed on by a wolf in man's clothing." She drew Margaret close, nestling her friend's head on her shoulder. "You just need what we all need." She stroked the wet hair. "Love and caring."

"I don't deserve it," Maggie sobbed, though her arms went around Charlotte as a drowning person grabs a rescuer, threatening to sink them both.

"Yes, you do. Everyone does." *Even you, Charlotte*. More than just a relationship of convenience. She reached for the silky pouf she used to bathe herself and poured on a generous dollop of the stress-relieving body wash she used so often. She paused to strip off her own now soaked bra and panties, and ran the pouf lightly over Maggie's back and shoulders.

Margaret turned and stretched her arms up the

shower wall, leaning against it with her back to Charlotte and water streaming over her. Charlotte tried to focus on stroking the stress from her muscles, on helping her friend achieve a more positive frame of mind, but she couldn't stop thinking about how much she had longed to touch Margaret like this when they were sixteen. She finished Margaret's back and began stroking the slender abdomen, and then suddenly, she *was* touching her like she had always dreamed.

Margaret turned to face her, fear in her eyes at first.

Charlotte cupped Margaret's face in her hands. "I would never do anything to hurt you, Maggie." She leaned closer. "You mean more to me than any person on earth."

Margaret relaxed and let go of the fear.

Chapter 74

Scott drove the streets of the city, searching for a place that beckoned him. The places on Thirtieth were too close. So he turned south on Main and kept driving, until he found himself crossing the river. Nothing there. He drove the three blocks back west to the river bridge and crossed the river again. Off the freeway, he followed the river west a few blocks. "Always the river," he murmured. At last, he whipped into the gravel parking lot and slowly walked into the Thirsty Dragon. He stood in the doorway a moment, allowing his eyes to adjust to the darkness and his senses to test the feel. Yes, this would do. It was dark and noisy with families eating out, due to the Thursday night special advertised on the flashing sign outside: Kids under 12 eat free on Thursdays with paid adult meal. He could drink until he felt better, and not be noticed.

Glancing at the booth he had shared with Rica—maybe this wasn't the best choice—he made his way to the opposite side of the restaurant to a booth in the corner, a few tables away from a family of six. A waitress approached with a glass of water and a menu. He studied her face a moment. No, not one they had interviewed about Delia; this was a new one.

"Bud light," he ordered. And then, as another waitress carried a tray of burgers and chicken fries to the family table, he added, "cheeseburger and fries."

"Coming right up." She spun on her running shoe heel and left him alone. Seconds later, she was back with his Bud. With a long pull on the beer, ingrained habit made him study the customers. Couple of single ladies at the bar, both in their sixties, he would guess. Four guys that looked like oil roughnecks at a booth on the other side. A group of college students near the door. He watched families drift in and out of the restaurant. His waitress served the college students, and he caught her eye by raising his now-empty bottle.

A minute later, a different waitress arrived at his table with his burger and another beer. She leaned low over the table, probably to afford him a look down her low-cut blouse, and smiled at him as her face came into the light of the lamp hanging over the table. He recognized her as one of the women they had interviewed about Delia. Charlotte Daniels her name was. Her smile trembled a bit as she evidently recognized him as well. She blinked her long lashes slowly, and he stared into her pale hazel eyes.

She stood up quickly, while chills ran up and down his spine. "Will there be anything else, sir?" She had already turned toward the kitchen, poised to flee on her stilettos.

"Maybe," he said, trying to keep her there. Could it be that what he had been searching for was in front of him all along? "Charlotte, right."

She nodded, licking her lips. "You're one of the officers that asked us questions about that girl that was killed?" Her voice caught on "that girl." If Charlotte was who he suspected, "that girl" had once been her best friend.

He nodded. "Do you remember anything more

about her?"

She shook her head and took a step toward the kitchen. "No, we get lots of customers in here."

He let her go without further conversation, and took a long pull of the beer. Suddenly, Rica going on with her life without him didn't seem to matter so much. He glanced around the room, spotting Charlotte working a table near the door, and picked up his burger. He might be a failure as a husband, but he was a damned good detective. And a hungry one. The burger and fries went down quickly.

Chapter 75

Charlotte concentrated on working tables on the opposite side of the room from Handsy. Sneaking a glance at him as she cleared a table and pocketed the tip, she wondered why she still thought of him by that ridiculous description. He had never acted like anything other than a perfect gentleman, albeit one very passionate about finding Delia's killer. And that passion was what made him so dangerous.

She slipped into the locker room for a quick break. Hands shaking, she wished she smoked to have something to occupy them. She peeked into the mirror and rubbed her cheeks to bring back some color. Automatically, she reached for the ever-present makeup bag in her purse and touched up her blush, so no one would notice how pale she had turned. Dare she try to throw up and convince Harvey she was sick, so she could leave, before she had to take another beer to Handsy? No, Bethany and Andrea had already bailed on him, leaving her and Rachel as the only waitresses. She faced herself in the mirror and lifted her chin. She would just try to stay on the other side of the room. She paused, studying her face. She didn't know why she wore the colored contacts so often. Her eyes were striking.

She smoothed her blouse over her breasts and minced back into the dining room.

****

When Scott finished his second beer, he caught Charlotte's eye and signaled he wanted another. The other waitress delivered it. So he had to finish it, and watch until the other waitress was busy with a large family at a table. He raised his bottle as Charlotte left a table with an order. She nodded, and he waited several minutes, noting that the other waitress was still taking orders, before Charlotte glided up and set the bottle on his table, moving to glide away just as quickly. But he was ready and caught her hand.

"Daniels is your last name, right?"

She nodded and stood passively before him, waiting for him to let go. He dropped her hand gently. "Are you from around here?"

"No," she said, taking a step away.

"I just got back from visiting my family for Thanksgiving." He watched her face closely. "Did you visit yours?"

"No." She took another step away.

"Not even your mom?"

She turned then. He couldn't see her face, but he heard the tremor in her voice. "My mom…passed, several years ago." She started for another table.

"I'm sorry. My dad died when I was fifteen." When she was a few more steps away, he added softly, "Kyle." He thought he saw her shoulders tense, but she kept going as if she didn't hear him. He nursed the beer slowly, knowing he'd had enough, thinking he should switch to soda or tea if he had to stay longer. He waited, as the dinner rush slowed close to children's bedtimes. Another type of customer began to filter in—the regulars, those who went to the bar every night, because there was nowhere else they belonged.

The other waitress disappeared, maybe taking a break, and Scott raised his water glass so Charlotte could see it. He thought her lips tightened a moment, but minutes later, she appeared with a pitcher of water. Good, it would take her a few seconds to fill it. While she focused on pouring, he spoke. "Did you ever know a boy named Kyle Dane?"

A drop of water sloshed onto the tabletop, but she presented him a composed face. "No." She finished filling his glass and turned to leave. "Is he a suspect?"

Scott shook his head, watching her face. "He's missing."

"Good luck with finding him."

He noticed that the hand she slipped quickly into her apron pocket shook just a little. "Thanks. Could you bring me a Coke?"

Chapter 76

Charlotte dashed into the locker room. In a moment, she wouldn't have to fake throwing up. Handsy was on to her, had found her out. Once again, it was time to run. Only this time she couldn't. At least not right away. She would have to make an excuse to quit her job, find another, start over again. She picked up her cell phone to call Devlyn before she realized that Dev was still at work and couldn't receive a call. For now, she was on her own to handle this.

Her gaze fell on her purse. She had just refilled her prescription for sleeping pills; the full bottle was still in the sack in her purse. If it took one to make her drowsy, two to give her a good night's sleep, how many would it take to make a man Handsy's size pass out? He was tall, but not heavy. What would he weigh? 180? 200? Would it take three? Four?

She tore a corner off the sack and opened five capsules into it, then folded the corner securely closed. She'd dump it in his Coke, then Harvey would have to call him a cab. She'd phone in with her resignation to Harvey tomorrow, then stay home sick from work for a week while she hunted for a new city and a new job, with insurance. She knew Handsy would look her up, but maybe it would take him a little while, because she had not bothered to change her address at work from her apartment to Devlyn's house. And by then she would be gone. At least the money she had put back to do improvements on Devlyn's house would keep her going for a while, buy the meds she had to have, until the new insurance kicked in.

But what about Devlyn? Would she be begged to stay? Would she be allowed to go? Could she resolve the problem with Handsy? She stepped to the soda fountain and, with a smooth glance around to be sure no one was watching, poured the contents of the sleeping pills into a cup. She ran a generous spray of soda into the bottom of the cup before adding ice and filling it to the brim. Eyeing the cup, she was glad Harvey used cheap, textured red plastic glasses; they hid anything that hadn't dissolved yet. Without fanfare, she delivered the cup to Handsy's table.

"Thank you," he said as she handed him a straw. "You know, I went to school with Kyle, but I barely remember him. He was a freshman when I was a junior."

"Oh." She forced disinterest into her voice. "What school was that?"

"Homedale High."

The name turned her stomach into quaking Jell-O. "Sounds quaint."

He laughed, a gentle laugh. "Kinda what we thought at the time we graduated."

She smiled. "Don't most teenagers?" She walked off to fill water glasses at another table, risking a look back at Handsy as she returned to the kitchen. He sat swirling his cola with the straw, but had yet to take a sip of it. She glanced at her watch. Two hours to close. She hoped he drank some of that soda by then.

She wandered by his table again as she carried an

order to a couple two booths down. He smiled and nodded as she came back by, then turned himself so his feet were in her path. "Where did you go to school?"

She glanced down at him, noting that he no longer wore a wedding ring. She looked up again into his face. Such a handsome face! "All over. My family moved a lot." She dodged around him and headed back to the kitchen for the next order.

Was this some joke fate was playing on her? Finally, she found a man who fit all the requirements she had laid out long ago, and he was The-Cop-Who-Knew-Too-Much. Maybe he was just flirting with her, maybe wanted to take her home. She stopped her run into fantasy land. If he was just flirting with her, he would not have said that name.

Chapter 77

Scott downed half his water and just sipped on his soda. The beer, coupled with the fact that the burger was practically the only food he'd had in over twenty-four hours, had given him a bit of a buzz. He wanted to rehydrate before he used caffeine to overcome the buzz.

He watched the dinner crowd evaporate. All those remaining now were there to drink. A few ordered appetizers, but as he remembered from the menu, the kitchen closed at ten. He checked his watch. Nine-thirty. He supposed he could go home now; he was certain that Charlotte Daniels had once been Kyle Dane, but what reason was there to bring her in for questioning? Completely changing one's identity was not a crime. But had she reconnected with Delia?

He drank his soda as he reviewed the facts of the case. Moran had admitted meeting Delia for a round of sex after she made the bank deposit. That could account for there being no signs of struggle in her car, but why leave it unlocked? The Casa Taco bordered a neighborhood of cheap apartments that meth and coke addicts could afford for a while. PD worked a lot of cases of purses stolen from locked and unlocked cars at the businesses there, as the addicts worked to finance the next fix. Unless she never intended to go with him and planned to hop right back in her car.

But the coroner had placed Delia's time of death at

around midnight. Moran could account for his time from about four-forty-five (Delia had been a quickie) until the next morning. Unless he and his wife slept in separate rooms. But she had testified that they had been in the hot tub until eleven, and then made love until the wee hours. Apparently, for them, infidelity spiced up their sex life. She didn't seem the type to lie about her conquests, and the fact that her husband stayed with her despite the many affairs they both had seemed to say she had completely conquered him.

Delia's husband wasn't even a suspect, in Scott's mind. The man loved Delia too much, was too devoted to the baby. He would never have left the sleeping child alone to go murder her mother. He—Scott lost the thought he was pursuing. The beer must have hit him more than usual. He took another sip of the cola to try to clear his head.

Who else would have had motive to kill Delia? Charlotte swayed seductively on her stilettos across the room to wait on a table of mid-thirties men already two sheets to the wind and working on their third. Could Delia have recognized Charlotte as her teenaged friend and threatened to out her? A pretty waitress who used to be a man wouldn't get nearly the tips as simply a pretty waitress. He watched as Charlotte minced back to the kitchen. He still didn't think that small, slender Charlotte, even as a man, would have the strength to gash a throat as thoroughly as Delia's had been slashed. He tried to recall the details of the autopsy report. It had said—he shook his head to try to bring his memory into focus, and took another sip of the cola.

Chapter 78

Charlotte checked her watch. Thirty minutes to close. Harvey had already announced last call and the six regulars at the bar all had two drinks sitting before them. Handsy, though, continued to guzzle water and sip at his soda. At last he rose from his booth, but instead of heading for the door, he turned toward the men's room. He lurched as he made his way around the first table, but steadied and walked slowly to the restroom.

Harvey, alert from long experience, noticed. "How many's he had?"

"Three that I know of," Charlotte answered.

Harvey glanced toward Rachel, who simply shrugged. "Keep an eye on him, then. If he stumbles again, we can't let him drive out of here."

"Okay." Charlotte would make sure she reported a stumble to Harvey, whether Handsy did trip or not. She popped into the employee lounge one last time to check her makeup. Her cell phone vibrated as she was dropping her lip gloss back into her purse. She grabbed it. Devlyn, on "lunch" break for the eleven to seven shift, Dev's second of the day. "Devlyn," Charlotte whispered. "Hold on a second." She slipped out the back door to have a private conversation. "We have a problem."

"What is it?" She could hear Devlyn's bag of chips

rattling in the background.

She decided to be careful what she said, just in case. She had never allowed Mags to call her on the cell, in case Devlyn checked the call log. Now there was even more reason to be cautious. "That cop that interviewed me about…that girl that was killed came to the restaurant tonight."

"And?" She heard Devlyn take a swig of soda.

"He recognized…who I used to be."

She heard Devlyn sit up straight. "Make a connection?"

"Maybe."

"Can't have that." There was a pause. "He drinkin'?"

"Some."

"Make sure he drinks too much to drive, then offer him a ride. You know where."

"Yeah. But I think I could just send him home, and he would forget."

"Can't take that chance, can we? See you when I get off." Devlyn ended the call, and Charlotte clicked off hers. Frightening, it was, that she had begun to think like this. She closed her eyes for a moment, wishing there was some way she could go back and rebuff Devlyn. Then she would never have moved in, would have been free to explore options with Mags. And Mags would—she didn't dare think that way. The past couldn't be changed, and it had set her future in stone as well.

Chapter 79

She went up the concrete stoop and into the back door of the Dragon. Handsy stepped out of the bathroom just as she closed the door behind her. He stood staring at her. His eyes appeared a bit glazed, and as he shook his head as if to clear it, he tipped into the wall. He caught himself, but Charlotte moved quickly beside him.

"Looks like you may have had a little too much tonight, sir." She slipped her arm around his waist (my, no love handles there), and he automatically draped an arm around her shoulder. She caught Harvey's eye when she and Handsy waltzed out of the restroom alcove. She smiled at Handsy and tightened her arm around his waist.

With surprise in his eyes, he paused and looked down into her face, but she knew Harvey would read the gesture differently. Glancing toward the bar, she saw Harvey shake his head with a knowing smile. Good. Harvey might think she wanted to hook up with Handsy and not protest when she offered to drive him home. No one at the advertising firm or here knew about Devlyn.

She stopped in front of Handsy's booth and let go of him. "Here you go, sir." He stood there as if confused, and she smiled at him, making sure the generous dimples that framed her full lips showed.

"What was your name again, Officer?"

"Scott," he said with flash of nice white teeth. "Scott Aylward."

"Well, Officer Scott." She shifted her weight to show off the curve of her hip and breasts. "Should we call you someone to give you a ride?"

He grinned. "I guess you understand that I know better than to drive home like this." He dropped to the seat and rubbed his face. She heard his hand rasping over the bit of stubble that simply gave depth to the sexy creases in his cheeks. "I didn't think I'd had that much, but I have to admit, I'm not up to par."

"Would you like me to bring you some coffee?" She knew Harvey always made a pot fifteen minutes before close. He said he figured if no one needed it to drive home, the help could drink it while they were closing up.

"No, thanks," he said, looking at his water glass. "That just makes a wide-awake drunk." He took a sip of water. "But maybe a water refill when you have a chance." He pulled out his wallet and peeled off a couple of bills. "This should take care of my tab and something for you." She took the cash, her fingers grazing his as she did so. "No change for me."

"Thank you." She looked into his face for a second before turning toward the kitchen. "Be right back with your water." Definitely a handsome face. She glanced down at the bills in her hand. A good tipper, too. None of the other customers needed attention; Rachel had already begun turning the chairs upside down on the tables. Charlotte was free to devote her time to Handsy. She returned with his water refill, noting as she filled his glass that he had only downed about a third of the

Coke. Doing quick calculations, she figured that meant he had only downed at most, two or two and a half sleeping pills. Probably not enough to do more than make him a little drowsy.

"Thank you," he said again.

"You're welcome." She set the carafe of water on his table. "Scott." She said his name softly, as seductively as she could, hoping he was at least still awake enough to pick up on it. Although, if he knew who she once was, he might be turned off. She began turning up the chairs on her side of the room.

"Here, let me help you with that." He rose to his feet and took a step toward her, but as he did, he walked as if the floor was moving under him.

"Why don't you just sit down a bit longer." She put her hand lightly on his chest, feeling the fine muscle definition beneath her fingers as she did so, and directed him to the booth beside her. She grabbed the cola from his table and handed it to him. "Now how about someone driving you home?"

He ran his fingers through his short dark hair. "I guess I'll have to call a cab," he said, with a wan smile. "I don't want to wake any of my friends at this hour."

"We'll get someone on the way for you," she promised, moving to the next table. As she flipped chairs on three more tables, she watched him sip at the soda. Then he stood, steadying himself with the back of that booth, and returned to his own table, without the soda, to finish the glass of water. She glided back past him on her way to the kitchen, snagging the nearly empty soda glass on her way. He smiled at her, and she gave him her sweetest one. Behind the bar, she dumped the remaining contents of the cup down the sink, and dropped the cup into the dishwasher. Within another half hour, all evidence of the sleeping pills would be gone. Along with her fingerprints.

Chapter 80

"Anybody else need a cab, Harvey?" Charlotte asked the question standing next to the phone while her boss wiped down tables. Three regulars at the bar sipped at their final drinks. She sneaked a look toward Scott. He sat on the edge of the booth, elbows on his thighs, head down.

"Nope," Harvey said. "These guys have someone picking them up."

"Okay, I'll call one for our customer over there." She picked up the phone, knowing no one was close enough to see her holding down the switch hook, and faked a call to the cab company. Seconds later, she walked up to Harvey finishing the last table. "Cabs are all busy for nearly an hour, Harv." She took a look at Scott. "But he lives close to my apartment. I can drive him home."

Harvey straightened and gave her a long look. He glanced at Scott and back to Charlotte. "Are you sure you know what you're getting into?"

"He can barely walk, Harv. I can handle him."

"Oh, I know you can." He tossed the cleaning rag over his shoulder. "Head out now, then. But be careful."

"You know me, Harvey. Careful is my middle name."

"Umm." He flipped off the lights to the sign

outside and flashed the interior lights. "Call me when you get him dropped off and get safely to your house."

"Okay, Harvey." She untied her apron and headed for the employee room. Grabbing her purse, she walked back into the dining room to where Scott sat. He was practically asleep now; he posed no threat to her.

He raised his head as she approached. "Is the cab on its way?"

She stopped in front of him. "Well, there's good news and bad news." He looked up at her, trying hard to focus. "Cabs are all tied up, but your apartment is on the way to mine, so I'm giving you a ride home."

He frowned. "But how do you know where I live?"

She hesitated. She really didn't know. "Your business card."

He stood. "My home address isn't on my business card."

Now she frowned. "Maybe you told me. I don't remember the exact street address, but I remember thinking it was almost on my way home." He swayed, and she moved close enough to put her arm around his waist. "Let's quit haggling over details and get you home before you pass out."

He rubbed his eyes. "Yeah, I guess you're right." He followed her lead toward the back door. "I've never had beer affect me like this."

"Maybe you were tired or something." They made it through the back door. He felt steadier as he walked with her to her car.

"Could be. Got divorced today."

She tightened her arm around his waist. "Well, one girl's loss will be another girl's gain."

She stopped beside the passenger door and Scott

folded himself into her little car. "Nice car," he said as he struggled to fit himself into the passenger seat.

"I think the seat adjusts." Charlotte belted in and started the car.

"It's okay." He leaned toward the door to give himself more room. "My truck is pretty small, too." He yawned. "I don't know why I'm so sleepy."

Charlotte pulled from the parking lot onto the street that would take them to the main drag. "Maybe, knowing your divorce hearing was coming up, you haven't been sleeping well, and now that it's over, your body is letting go."

"Could be." He yawned again. "Better give you my address before I can't remember it myself."

"Okay."

"It's 525 Park Lane. Apartment 5 B, but I can get into the house if you just get me close."

"Fair enough." She glanced at him, his head leaning against the door, his eyes already closed. "Why don't you see if getting some sleep will help."

"Mmmmm." He was out, and didn't appear to notice when she turned south on the main drag instead of north toward his apartment. She looked at him occasionally as she drove. Sensuous lips, long eyelashes, curly hair it would be a pleasure to run her fingers through. Why did it have to be him? Why could he not let his job go and give up on the case like all the rest?

Twenty minutes later, she pulled up to the back door of Devlyn's house. Quietly, she slipped from the car and opened the door to the house. Making her call to Harvey to tell him she had safely delivered Scott to his apartment, she hurried inside and made sure the bed was ready for him. Then she went back to the car and opened his door. He practically fell into her arms and she worried that she would not be able to get him inside. But the cold air outside roused him enough he could get his feet under him, even though he couldn't seem to keep his eyes open. That way, she didn't have to explain where she had taken him instead of his house. With her arm around his waist, his over her shoulder and him leaning on her, she guided him into the bedroom and eased him onto the bed. As he lay there, beginning to snore, she hesitated, almost tempted to drag him back out to the car and take him somewhere—anywhere—else.

She glanced at the clock. At least six hours until Devlyn got home. Maybe she'd have time for one last fantasy.

Chapter 81

Scott struggled his way out of sleep. He couldn't seem to break the hold it had on him, and he repeatedly came to consciousness and then drifted back into a deep sleep. Finally, he rose enough out of slumber to realize that his arms felt heavy. He tried to move them, maybe they had fallen asleep with the rest of him, and felt resistance. Fighting to raise his arms, he forced his eyes open. At first, he couldn't make sense of what he saw. Strange surroundings, himself naked in a strange bed. Turning his head to confirm what he felt, he saw that his wrists were tied to the posts of a bed he had never seen before. Sleep tried to pull him back into its depths, but a rapidly rising surge of adrenaline blocked the pull. He forced himself to lie still, to backtrack to the last steps he could remember.

The Thirsty Dragon, because Rica had claimed the steak restaurant with her new love. Too much beer, because his feelings had been in turmoil, and he needed to quiet them. Realizing that one of the Dragon waitresses that they had interviewed about Delia's death had once been Kyle Dane. Too much beer to drive home. Charlotte—Kyle—offering him a ride.

He felt movement beside him and looked toward it. Charlotte, curled up beside him with her back to him, shifted in her sleep. At least she was dressed. Choking back fear, he scanned the room for information. High ceilings and imperfect plaster walls suggested it was an old house. Tall, narrow windows covered in drapes at least twenty years old occupied the centers of two walls. No light filtered through, meaning it was still dark. A table lamp on a dresser across the room from the bed provided the only light.

He lifted his head slightly to see more of the room, hoping to find his clothes. If Charlotte had undressed him, she had found his off-duty piece tucked in his right boot. His movement made her stir again, and he froze, hoping she would stay asleep until he figured a way out.

With his eyes alone, he studied the ties that bound him to the bedposts. Scarves, twisted and knotted around his wrists, just tight enough that he couldn't slip them off, holding his arms far enough from his body that he couldn't gain leverage to move any direction. He felt Charlotte move again, and she snuggled against him with her head on his shoulder and her hand on his ribs.

She smiled at him. "Are you feeling better now?"

He forced a smile. "Like I got kicked in the head by a whole team of Budweiser Clydesdales." He shifted his weight. "And I have to piss like one of them, too." Even half-drunk, he thought he could overpower Charlotte and retrieve his gun. And he really did have to go.

"Sorry, sweetie." She reached up to stroke his cheek. He forced himself not to react. "No can do." She ran her fingers down the center of his chest.

He kept his voice calm. "So am I now your personal sex slave?" God, he hoped that was all she had in mind. He had thought he was vulnerable when Rica stomped his heart. Now he knew what true vulnerability felt like. A foreboding clutched his lungs. "I can do lots better when I'm comfortable."

She stroked his chest. "I'm sure you can." She snuggled closer, and, against his will, he began to respond to her.

"I have a question." He worked hard on trying to stay awake and focused.

She nuzzled his neck. "What's your question?"

"Why?"

"Why what?"

"Why tie me up?" As he fought to stay awake, another realization hit him. It wasn't the beer that had made him so shaky. She must have drugged him. "Why drug me? I might've gone home with you without it."

"Really?" She smiled. "Even knowing who I…used to be?"

Studying her face, he knew she had lived with the secret for so long, she surely heard such lines before. "I'll have to admit, I'd probably have hesitated."

She turned her face away. "So many wanted to just because they were…curious."

"It can't have been easy for you all these years."

Her shoulders shook as she took a deep breath. "You can't imagine."

"I know what it's like to be misunderstood, to be doing the best you can, but it's not good enough."

She turned to face him again. "What have you ever screwed up that you had to hide who you were, what you were?"

"My marriage."

"If you ask me, it's your wife who screwed up."

He looked toward the ceiling. "No, it was me.

Never around when she needed me, never neat enough, never focused enough."

"But you can start over, with someone new."

"You already did, you started your life over."

"Yeah, some start over." She rested her hand on her forehead.

"It looks to me like it worked." He hesitated. "I could tell by watching you tonight that you are one of the most valuable waitresses in the restaurant."

"That's not even my day job." She laughed. "I'm an artist. I design the artwork for ad campaigns. Make good money." She took a deep breath. "I don't even know why I took the job at the Dragon." She lowered her voice. "And so many times, I've been sorry I took it."

"Why?"

"If I hadn't taken it, I wouldn't have met—"

"Who?" He tried hard to look at her face, but from this angle, all he could see was the top of her head. "Delia?"

"No. Yes." Her voice was so soft, he could barely hear her.

He felt tears on his chest. "You didn't kill her, did you?"

She shook her head.

"But you know who did?" Jealous boyfriend? That didn't bode well for his current situation.

"I tried to stop her." Charlotte's voice sounded like a small child's.

"Stop who? Delia?"

"No." She shuddered. "Devlyn."

"Devlyn, your boyfriend?"

"No." She turned to face him. "My *girl*friend."

"Your *girlfriend*?" His mind reeled in a new direction. "Tried to stop her from what?"

"From killing her."

"Killing Delia?"

"Yes." She crawled out of the bed to sit on the end of it, hugging herself, tears running down her face. "Killing Maggie, the only true friend I ever had." She put her hands to her face. "The only one I ever loved." She turned toward Scott. "She came home and found us." Her tears flowed freely. "And then she made me help her take Maggie to that awful place and leave her there, alone." Her shoulders shook. "It was so horrible."

The facts swirled around Scott as he tried to make sense of them. He had solved the case, but little good it did him trussed up like a Christmas goose. And likely to be Devlyn's next victim, unless he could convince Charlotte to let him loose. "You must be very afraid of Devlyn."

"You have no idea."

"That's true, but I know it must be bad if it's better to stay with her than to leave."

"I want to leave." Her hands trembled.

"You could."

"How?"

"Let me loose, and we'll go down to PD and make the report, file charges. Provide you protection until we bring Devlyn in and the trial is over. With your testimony, I'm sure she'd be convicted."

"You could do that?" The tears stopped, and the face she turned toward him looked like that of a five-year-old promised a trip to the ice cream store.

"We could keep you safe till she's in custody."

"But what happens when she gets out?"

"Charlotte, she committed murder." He tried to keep his voice calm, because winning Charlotte to his side represented the only chance he had. "She won't get out."

"Not even on bail?"

"Not likely, but if she does, we'll keep you under protection." He gritted his teeth. "I'll do it myself if I have to."

"You'd do that?" She leaned toward him. "For me?"

"I'd do it for anyone who needed protection." He hoped the real conviction of his words held the sincerity she needed to hear. "Please? Turn me loose and we'll go together."

She shook her head. "I don't know. Devlyn said—"

"Do you want to believe what Devlyn said, after she killed your best friend?"

"Well…she said if I ever told anyone, she'd…"

"She said she'd hurt you, didn't she." He almost had her convinced. "Did she threaten to kill you like she did Delia?"

"No. Worse." Tears came again. "She said I'd go to jail as an accessory, that they wouldn't give me my hormones there, that I'd become…a freak!"

"Haven't you heard of the battered woman defense?"

"Yeah." Her lips trembled. "Would it work for me?"

"It could." His life depended on his being convincing. "I'm no lawyer, but it would give you a better chance than staying with Devlyn." When she just stared at him, he went on. "Think about it, Charlotte. Right now, you and I are the only ones who know she killed Delia. If she goes through with what I think is her plan, soon you'll be the only one alive that knows, and you will then be accessory to murder of a police officer. And then one day, Devlyn will tire of you and think you are just too dangerous a loose end to have dangling." She began to shake. "And, *voila*, you end up same as Delia."

She buried her face in her hands. "I have made such a mess of my life."

"You can still make it right, Charlotte." He noticed a clock on the dresser across the room. Nearly seven a.m. He had been here almost five hours. How much longer would he have before the killer came through the door? If Devlyn worked the eleven to seven shift, the sand was running out. "Let me go, give me my clothes and my gun, and we'll get out of here before Devlyn gets home."

"I don't know." She stood up. "Devlyn promised."

"You want to trust someone who killed your best friend, or someone who's sworn an oath to protect you?"

"Would you give your life to protect me?"

"I would." He tested the ties again. "It wouldn't be my first choice of ways to protect you, but if I had to, I would." His gaze caught hers and held. "Please, Charlotte."

She moved toward the bedpost. "All—all right." Her hands shook so much, she fumbled with the tie.

He watched her in frustration, as the clock ticked their lives away. "Why don't you give me my gun first, just in case, and then get some scissors."

"But, it's a Ralph Lauren—Oh, right, never mind." Almost in shock, she fumbled around a chair in the room, until she came toward him with his gun, still in the ankle holster.

"OK, now, Charlotte, go get some scissors or a knife or something." He glanced toward the clock again. Six-fifty. "I think we may be running out of time here."

She wandered out of the room, and he lay there with his gun six inches away and no way to use it if he had to. This Devlyn sounded like a force to be reckoned with, if she had struck the blow that nearly decapitated Delia. He didn't want to face her unarmed.

Charlotte returned to the room with a pair of dainty scissors. He wanted to yell at her to get something bigger, but she went to work with determination and soon had one layer of the scarf around his left hand severed. Suddenly, he heard the sound of gravel under tires. "Charlotte, cut that side and then unholster my gun."

She faced him with wide eyes and froze. "Devlyn!"

"Keep cutting, Charlotte, and it will be okay."

One more snip and his left hand was free. Before he could stop her, Charlotte dropped the scissors and ran from the room. With his left hand and teeth, he unsnapped his holster and worked his gun out. He grabbed the scissors and began to saw at the scarf holding his right hand.

Chapter 82

"Devlyn." He heard Charlotte greet the person who threw open a door that sounded like it was two rooms away from him.

"Where is the bastard?" a rough voice rasped, then coughed. "Is he still out?"

"Yes, Devlyn, he's still out like a light, so there's no hurry."

"No hurry, my ass. We gotta get this done before it gets any lighter out. Don't want no one to see us."

He heard heavy boots on the floor, coming closer. He dropped the scissors and picked up his gun with his left hand. Thank God for the training with the off hand. He had never thought he'd need it.

"What the—" A tall, rawboned woman in a flannel shirt and worn jeans, holding what looked like a hunting knife in her left hand, stepped through the door, and then turned to swat Charlotte with her right hand as a giant swats a fly. "You were gonna let him go, you little bitch." Charlotte crumpled into the other room, and Devlyn faced Scott. "So it ain't gonna be easy, Barney, but it'll still be." She advanced on him, and he brought up the gun.

"Stop right there. You are under arrest for the murder of Delia Enfield."

Devlyn laughed. "Gotta hit me first, Barney." She crouched low and lunged toward the bed. He fired one shot, then she hit the bed, slashing with the knife. He brought his feet up to push her away, firing again, but her knife found his thigh, even as his foot landed in her gut.

He thrust her back and she stumbled, but regained her footing and launched herself toward him again. He tried to aim, but missed again. He twisted on the bed, but her knife slashed his ribs. At least she was slashing, not jabbing. She punched him, a powerful blow to the side of his head that nearly knocked him out, and he lost his grip on the gun.

He pulled against the tie for all he was worth, and the scarf holding his right hand tore, freeing his hand. He punched her back, and then grabbed her hair to try to control her head, but she snatched his arm, and they flipped off the bed. She dropped the knife as they landed, and he kicked it as far under the bed as he could. She gave his left leg a savage twist, but he kicked her hard in the face with his right foot. He jumped to his feet, but she kicked them out from under him before he could get to his gun on the far side of the bed. She reached for it, and he kicked her in the gut.

She went down, but immediately threw herself on him, her elbow in his ribs. He wrapped an arm around her throat, but she bent back his thumbs until he let go to keep her from breaking them. Again, she jabbed him in the ribs. He caught her chin and tried to twist her head, but she pulled free, reaching under the bed as she did. She stood, with the knife in her hand.

"Stop, Devlyn!" Charlotte stood facing them, Scott's gun in her hand, gun and girl shaking. Scott scrambled to his feet. Even if she meant to help him, Charlotte armed was as much a danger to him as to

Devlyn, who laughed. He didn't like the sound of that laugh.

"Gotta hit me first, you bitch." She swung the knife toward Scott, as he hopped onto the bed toward Charlotte and the gun.

Charlotte squeezed the trigger and the shot shattered the window between Scott and Devlyn. Devlyn lunged at him as he landed on the floor and seized the gun from Charlotte. He spun and squeezed the trigger just as Devlyn's knife raked down his ribs and hip. The bullet found her thigh, but she didn't stop. She slashed at Charlotte as she passed her, and Scott saw blood on Charlotte's blouse as she dropped to the floor against a dresser.

He backed up a step, and Devlyn charged again. His second shot caught her in the shoulder and spun her around. She turned back toward him. "Daddy didn't raise no quitter," she hissed. She raised the knife for a downward plunge and took a step forward, balancing on her good leg.

He steadied himself. "Drop the knife," he ordered. "I won't miss this time." He could hear Charlotte sobbing, which meant she was still alive.

Breathing heavily, Devlyn laughed again and then coughed. "Maybe I'll take out this worthless bitch first." She turned, and her knife arm started to drop. Scott fired. With her at an angle to him, his center mass shot entered her side low and at an angle. She collapsed, knife still in her hand, next to Charlotte.

With his gun at the ready, Scott pried the knife from her fingers. She looked at him, but put up no further fight. "Charlotte," he said in a voice much calmer than he felt. "Can you get up?"

She stared wide-eyed at Devlyn, whose glare would have killed if it could. "I-I think so." Shaking, she struggled to her feet.

"How bad are you cut?" He didn't dare take his eyes off Devlyn.

She looked down at herself. "It hurts, and there's a lot of blood."

"Can you step away from Devlyn, into the other room?" She nodded and did as he said. "Do you know where my cell phone is?"

"Yeah. It's still in your jeans, on the chair there."

Still eyeing Devlyn, who was conscious and watching him, her hand over her side wound, he fished his phone from his pocket.

"If you're calling 911, I already did that," she smiled at him. "When Devlyn hit me. They said they were coming."

"Okay." He didn't know where they were, what the response time might be. "Call them again, and ask for an ambulance. Tell them Officer Seventy-Three has the suspect in custody and the situation is under control, but there are three injured parties."

"Okay." She paused before she opened her phone. "You know, I could just leave now, run away and not have to face this."

"You could." He noticed that Devlyn's eyes had closed, but she still breathed shallowly. "But then you'd always be wondering when you'd be found out. You have to stop running someday." He pulled the top sheet from the bed. Laying his gun down on top of the dresser behind him, he tucked the sheet around Devlyn's side wound the best he could to try to stop the bleeding. While he ministered to Devlyn, Charlotte made her call and returned with two towels. She tossed him one and touched her wound with the other. "Ouch."

Scott dabbed at his cuts and thought about slipping his clothes on, because he felt, well, naked. "You could put your clothes on now," Charlotte suggested.

"And have the paramedics cut up my best jeans and shirt? No thanks." He wrapped the towel around himself. He heard a siren, and then another. He stood and picked up his gun again.

"I guess if I was going to run, I've waited too long," Charlotte said.

"Yup. Today's as good a day as any to make stand." He sat down on the edge of the bed. "I'll put in a good word for you, because you did try to save me." The blood loss, aftereffects of whatever she had slipped him, and the ebb of adrenaline began to take hold.

"But I'm still in trouble, right."

"I won't lie to you, yes, you are." He rubbed his face to stay alert. "You witnessed a crime and didn't report it. You helped to conceal a felony, and that is serious business. And then you kidnapped a police officer and collaborated to murder me." He watched her stand there bleeding and dry-eyed. "But you also saved my life just now, and you committed your crimes in fear of your life. I'll do my best to get them to take that into consideration."

At that moment, officers arrived at the back door. In the whirlwind of explanations and examinations, Scott lost track of Charlotte, until the first ambulance left with Devlyn and an officer, and he and Charlotte stepped into the second. She wore handcuffs, and an officer sat beside her.

"Thank you for saving my life," Scott said as the

big rig swayed its way out of the driveway.

"Thank you for saving mine." Charlotte smiled. "In more ways than one."

Chapter 83

Scott told his story at least four times to three different officers, including Bates, as well as a doctor. Finally, after they stitched up the worst of the cuts Devlyn had bestowed, they insisted he spend the night in the hospital.

Exhausted from his ordeal, still drugged from what Charlotte had confessed was five sleeping pills, and sore as the local anesthetic wore off, Scott didn't even react when Rica walked into his room and grasped his hand.

"Scott, I'm so proud of you." She brought his hand to her cheek and kissed it.

"Thanks," he said in a leaden voice. "I'm tired."

"I know you are." She laid his hand down gently and patted it. She stepped closer to him, and folded her hands behind her back. "I just wanted to say I'm sorry."

"It's okay, Rica." He felt his eyes trying to close. "What's done is done."

"But it could be undone." Her voice was soft and musical.

His eyes flew open. "What do you mean?"

"I mean—maybe I rushed things, maybe I made a mistake in wanting to be away from you."

A month ago, those words would have made his heart sing. Now they just made his head hurt. "No, really, Rica. It's probably for the best."

"But, Scott—"

"Neither of us was really happy, Rica." He was surprised to hear the words coming from his mouth; maybe it was the sleeping pills. No, he had realized as he lay there trussed and helpless, with death coming through the door at any minute, that he wanted to live for himself, not for Rica or anyone else. "It's better that it's over. You can move on." He managed to focus for a moment. "In fact, you have."

"Ambrose?" Her eyes flashed for a moment, before the tears gathered. "Turns out I was just flavor of the month. Once I was free to be with him, he wanted to be with someone else. And head surgical nurse went to Bonnie."

"I'm sorry to hear that, Rica." His eyes closed, hard as he tried to keep them open. "But he was just the catalyst to get you to make the move you needed to make for a long time."

"But, Scott, I—"

"I have some things I need to work on about myself, but you do, too." He shook his head, trying to clear it. "When we're done working on them, then we'll be ready to connect with someone. Not before."

"Then we really are done?"

He tried to nod, though he wasn't sure which direction his head actually went. "Never say never, Rica, but I'm certainly not ready to try again, with you or with anyone." He yawned. "I'm not saying we can't be on cordial terms. There was a lot of good between us." He opened his arms to her, and she rushed to him to lay her head gingerly on his chest. "Just not enough to overcome the differences."

"Oh, Scott, I was such a fool." Tears soaked

through the thin hospital gown. He patted her shoulder.

"We both were." He yawned again. "I'm sorry, Rica, but I can hardly keep my eyes open." She pushed off his chest and stood beside him again. "Maybe if I'm still here when you come on shift again, we can talk some more."

"I don't work again till Tuesday, Scott."

He shrugged, forgetting the stitches, and wished he hadn't. "Another time, then." He yawned once more and his eyelids drooped. "You still have my number." He didn't even hear her leave.

Epilogue

His mother, brothers, and their families all came down for the ceremony awarding Scott the Department's Distinguished Service Medal. He had protested that it was no big deal, but they insisted that it was simply an excuse to celebrate an early Christmas. As Scott sat on the dais, he saw his family, Al, Bates, his other colleagues, Ms. Frank, so many people who meant so much to him. Far in the back of the room, near the door where she could slip out, he saw Rica. And felt—nothing.

Bates beamed when Scott went forward for the chief to pin the medal on him. He beamed even more when Scott's speech was simply, "I was just doing my job like any other officer would do."

When the Mayor's much longer speech was over, many officers shook Scott's hand or clapped him on the shoulder, accompanying their gestures with comments like, "Gettin' a medal for bein' beat up by a *girl*!" Yet they were glad he had made it through the ordeal.

He invited Al to join his family and the Bateses for lunch. They hung back as the rest of the crowd trooped into the restaurant. "Well, Scott, you kept at it till you solved the case." Al held the door open for Scott. "Did you learn anything along the way?"

Scott looked up into the bright December sky. "You know, Al, if I get tired of this line of work, I just might finish my degree and hang up my shingle as a counselor." He met Al's eyes. "There are a lot of messed up people out there, but they are still people. If they can get help, maybe they won't mess up someone else."

"Scott, I think you learned something that most people never figure out." Al smiled. "Now, let's eat."

A word from the author…

I vividly remember when I first considered writing. I was less than five years old, galloping about our yard at the farm, probably pretending to lead a cavalry charge or round up a stampede. On one of the few smooth limestone slabs that made up our sidewalk, I paused and turned to face the east, where the yard sloped down into a grove of evergreens that led to our garden and the highway. I focused on something far beyond the highway, even past the hay meadow and the locust-forested pasture. "Maybe I should write books," I thought. "Someone has to." I pondered this momentous choice for a while. Then I decided that it would be more logical for people who could read to write books, and galloped off again.

Like many people, I began writing in my teens. Unlike others, though, the stories within would not allow me to stop. Ideas clamor "Pick me, pick me!" to be let out of the files and into a completed story.

A thirty-year career in state government has afforded me insight into the layers of motivation that keep the world turning—and authors writing about it.

http://katherinepritchett.com/